The Collected Short Fiction of John R Little

Volume 1: Little by Little

Cover by Luke Spooner, © 2019 LVP Publications
Interior illustrations by Luke Spooner, © 2019 LVP Publications
All stories © John R Little

The Collected Short Fiction of John R Little, Volume 1: Little by Little
© 2019 LVP Publications

All rights reserved. No part of this book may be reproduced in any form, including in print, electronic form or by mechanical means, without written permission from the publisher, author or individual copyright holder except for in the case of a book reviewer, who may quote brief passages embedded in and as part of an article or review.

This is a work of fiction. Names, characters, businesses, places, events and incidents are either the products of the author's imagination or used in a fictitious manner. Any resemblance to actual persons, living or dead, or actual events is purely coincidental.

Lycan Valley Press Publications
1625 E 72nd St STE 700 PMB 132
Tacoma, Washington 98404 United States of America

Printed in the United States of America

LVP Publications Illustrated Edition

ISBN-13: 978-1-64562-953-5

For Fatima, always and forever.
Where you go I will go, and where you stay I will stay.

CONTENTS

Welcome! I'm pleased that you found this edition of *Little by Little*, or as it's now properly titled, *The Collected Short Fiction of John R. Little*. I'm thrilled to be able to share this collection with you.

So, let's start with the original title. The first edition of *Little by Little* was published in 2014 by Bad Moon Books. It contained 10 short stories and novellas and enjoyed really nice reviews. It was a finalist for the Bram Stoker Award for best collection in 2015, which I was thrilled to see. The original cover contained cover art by an artist I wasn't familiar with at the time, Luke Spooner. I loved that cover!

As happens, *Little by Little* went out of print. My publisher, Roy Robbins take a decidedly unusual career change and is now a Pastor in a church in southern California.

I hated seeing the book out of print, along with its companion volume, *Little Things*. And then in late 2017, in a rather surprising twist, I received an offer from Lycan Valley (LVP Publications) to reprint both volumes of my short work (plus two new volumes).

Well, then. You may not know how unusual that is, to bring back to print older titles, when there are so many good new books being published every day. I was thrilled to email with MJ Sydney, the publisher at LVP Publications and find that she wanted to publish not only a trade paperback version, but also a hardcover edition.

I'd had various limited editions before, but never for a previously published book.

On top of that, MJ wanted to have every story illustrated in full color, by none other than Luke Spooner.

Additionally, we wanted something additional to be added to each book so that my loyal readers who had already picked up the original editions would have something new to bite into. You'll find a new story in this volume that I'm particularly proud of.

There are new introductions for each story, longer, more intimate than the original book. You'll find them all in front of each story. Rather than just the pure publishing history, I wanted to show how each story fit into my life.

Most of all, and perhaps a little bit arrogant of me, I wanted these editions to be definitive...and to continue past the two existing volumes. This should be the best and most permanent record of all my short work that's been published.

Whether you're a new reader of my work or a seasoned veteran, I want to thank you for joining me in this journey. I hope you pick up all the volumes. For now, I'll leave you with the titles of the volumes in this series:

The Collected Short Fiction of John R. Little:
Volume 1: Little by Little
Volume 2: Little Things
Volume 3: A Little Bit More
Volume 4: Lost Little Tales

John R Little
April 2019

Dreams in
Black and White

I wrote the first draft of the story when I was living in a suburb of Vancouver in 2005. I had been writing and publishing short stories since my first big sale in 1982, so more than 20 years. But, the one thing I couldn't do? Write anything longer than a short story that anybody wanted to read.

Flash forward to 2009. By then, my writing had taken a 360 degree turn. The Memory Tree had been published, as had "Placeholders," "Miranda," and "The Gray Zone." My work was getting great reviews, and I remembered the old manuscript I'd shoved away in a drawer. I pulled it out and re-read it, and I realized I really liked it. I remembered thinking about "The Monkey's Paw" by W.W. Jacobs and Pet Sematary by Stephen King as I wrote it.

Mostly, though, I remembered the damned 4:42 thing.

For years, I'd woken up several nights each week in the middle of the night. I'd glance at the clock, and it seemed like every freaking time I did, it was 4:42 a.m. I kid you not, I was doing this so often, and I could never come up with even the vaguest resemblance of a rationale. How the hell could it always be 4:42?

Well, it was.

I needed that to be part of a story. In fact, it's slipped into many other stories as well. If any character has reason to look at a watch or a clock in my work, chances are it's going to be 4:42. If you ever want to impress me, you can hunt them all down.

For this story, though, I couldn't have been happier when it was published by Bloodletting Press as a limited edition hardcover short novel.

Chapter 1

CHARLIE PARKINSON WOKE sometime in the middle of the night. He knew the fancy alarm clock Selina had given him last Christmas would be shouting the time in bright red numerals, but he didn't open his eyes.

He didn't have to. He knew it would be 4:42 a.m.

The house was dead silent.

Groping in the dark, he felt Selina's silky night shirt as she slept beside him. Sometimes he wished she snored, just to break the tedious silence when he woke up while the rest of Long Island slept.

He felt cold and carefully tugged at the covers, not wanting to pull them off his wife. Charlie had lots of practice taking covers back. In the fifteen years they had been married, Charlie had never once slept through the entire night.

The slightest noise would wake Charlie up, to his constant frustration: a car driving anywhere in the neighborhood; a cat's lonely meow down the block; the furnace kicking in; even Charlie's own quiet breathing would sometimes be enough to wake himself up.

His toes were cold, so he carefully wrapped the blanket around his feet. He still refused to open his eyes. He didn't want to see 4:42 staring back at him from the clock. He'd wait until 4:43. Or 4:44.

Every morning, when Charlie finally gave up on sleep, he'd crawl out of bed, deathly tired, stumble down the hallway to the kitchen to put a large pot of coffee on, stand under a steaming hot shower while it brewed, and finally pry his eyes open completely after two cups.

Selina would usually join him by the time he was finishing his third or fourth cup. She would be bright-eyed and wellrested. He was insanely jealous of her ability to sleep eight hours without so much as moving an inch.

For years, he'd been bewildered and sometimes even angered at their differences. Selina was only two years younger than him, thirty-eight to his forty, but she looked as if she hadn't yet reached thirty. When *he* glanced in the mirror, he looked ten years older than he really was.

"Tell me your dreams," he would ask her every morning. He could only dream vicariously through her. He hadn't dreamed himself since he was a teenager. "Every detail."

Usually, Selina remembered her dreams clearly enough to tell him bits and pieces, but they were always scattered images.

A week ago, at his request, she thought for a moment and said, "We were in Paris. I think it was summer. I remember the Eiffel Tower and eating snails." He smiled as she scrunched up her nose when she said this. "I think we were there for "

"For what?"

She shook her head. "I can't remember. I had it for a minute, but it's gone now."

He nodded in frustration. He missed her dreams: it was especially bad when Selina would start to sip on her coffee and just smile, shaking her head, not remembering any dreams at all from the previous night.

All of that changed three days earlier, on December 1. *December 2, actually*, Charlie thought, since it had been 4:42 a.m. in the morning.

Last Sunday night, Monday morning.

Charlie fell asleep sometime around eleven o'clock and didn't wake until 4:42 a.m. He woke up and couldn't believe the time on the clock, couldn't believe it possible.

I slept for more than five hours.

He jumped from his bed and picked the clock up, staring at the time, mentally checking to be sure he had his facts straight.

"Unfuckingbelievable," he said. He glanced over at Selina, but she slept on, not woken by his words. Her hair was splayed out like a halo on her pillow, and he was struck by how beautiful she was, and how lucky *he* was.

She breathed quietly, her golden skin showing her Latino heritage. He wanted to wake her and tell her about his sleeping, but he knew that was selfish. Still, he wanted to.

He drummed his fingers on the bureau, continuing to stare at the clock, as the last digit flipped over silently to move him a minute further along his life.

"Five and a half hours," he whispered. "No fucking way."

He sat back down on the edge of the bed, feeling the cold hardwood floors on his feet. In the far distance, he could hear a whirling sound, like a police siren, but a siren whirling under water, gurgling its way out to him.

"No," he said, "I *dreamed* that."

This realization startled him even more than sleeping for so long.

A dream.

He felt tense, thought back to the dream. A police car chasing somebody. "Chasing *me*," he whispered. He was driving his Mazda down a country road, the cop hot on his tail. He raced around a curve in the road just as the cop was catching up to him. The officer who was driving didn't realize the curve was coming, and he smashed through the flimsy barrier separating the road from Long Island Sound. In his rearview mirror, Charlie could see the car barreling down the hill. He pulled a Uturn and drove back, just in time to see the flashing lights of the car disappear into the inky darkness of the clear cold water.

And then he woke.

He didn't go back to sleep that night.

By the time Selina joined him in the morning, he had already drained two pots of Starbucks Italian Roast coffee. He was wide awake, having had a good night's sleep for the first time in longer than he could remember.

Selina instantly knew something was up. Charlie looked relaxed and smiled at her. "You'll never guess what happened last night," he said.

The next night, Monday night, Charlie was still wellrested when Selina started yawning at midnight. They went to bed and made love, temporarily erasing any thoughts of sleep from Selina's mind.

I wonder how long it's been since we've done that. Charlie didn't want to think about it, knowing he was always so tired that lovemaking almost seemed like a lost art.

That night, he again slept through, and again he dreamed. The same dream. This time he remembered more details. The police weren't really chasing him; they were after a different car. Charlie was following the other car as well, but he didn't know why. He clearly remembered one of his cameras was on the passenger seat beside him. The cop car went off the road and sank without a trace at exactly the same place.

The dream was in black and white.

That didn't particularly surprise Charlie, since he had no expectations of any kind. He had nothing to compare the dreams to.

When he looked at the clock that night, he was surprised to see it read 4:42 a.m. "What're the chances of that?" he laughed.

He wasn't laughing the following night when he snapped his eyes open and saw the familiar time staring back at him.

The dream was clearer this time. He could see the flashing light bar of the cop car, could see the two police officers inside, could see the one in the passenger seat reaching up to the window in terror as they crashed over the bank. There was actually a small cliff the car broached; he knew the Long Island Sound was unusually deep at this point. The car bounced a bit on the water, then quickly sank like a drowned rat. The two cops were stuck in the front, never having a chance to escape.

This time, he heard their screams for just a second as they went down. He could see the lights flashing as the car sunk farther and farther out of sight.

He watched with the camera in his hand, taking pictures.

Now it was the fourth night of dreams, the fourth night of wonderfully relaxing sleep. He kept his eyes shut as he thought of the faces of the cops staring back, their eyes wide open, yelling. There was a sign near the highway he could now see, saying this part of the Sound was more than a hundred feet deep. There was nothing he could do to help. So, he snapped pictures.

This time, he dreamed the date. December 5. *Today*, he knew. And he dreamed the exact location. Twenty miles west of his home, right there on Long Island.

He waited a good five minutes, then five more. Finally he blinked his eyes open and reluctantly looked up at the bright scarlet time on the clock. It was 4:42 a.m.

Chapter 2

SELINA PARKINSON YAWNED as she slowly dressed. Charlie would have been up for a couple of hours already, she knew. He was always awake before her. Even now that he seemed to be sleeping more at night, he was always up and well-coffeed before she moved her first muscle.

She stared at herself in the mirror. "Another December," she said quietly. "Another birthday coming up, another Christmas."

It was the birthday part that bugged her. December 23, only a couple of weeks away. She'd be thirty-nine. Although she didn't feel as bad as she would a year from now, thirty-nine was still sounding pretty old.

Her face still looked slim in the mirror, though, and there were only a few almost invisible wrinkles pulling out of her eyes. She brushed the scattered knots from her long brown hair, not seeing any gray today. She had pulled out a couple of strands last week.

As always, she started to make a mental inventory of what she needed to focus on.

Christmas was number one. It always was in December. Becky had written up her wish list almost a month ago and was more excited than in any of her previous years. "I probably was when I was nine, too," Selina said.

Becky was still asleep, would be until somebody roused her. *That somebody would be me*, she thought. *It's always me.*

"I guess it's going to be one of those days," she said to her reflection.

"One of those days" meant a day that she resented Charlie. Resented how he never seemed to notice his home and family. Never noticed little things like the need to buy Christmas presents for their daughter, never noticed housework doesn't happen by itself, never noticed Becky's teacher had sent yet another note home about her behavior in class, never noticed... well, Selina herself.

She shook her head, trying to clear the negative thoughts. All those negatives normally actually added up to a positive. The reason she fell in love with Charlie all those years ago was his freespiritedness, his artistic nature, the way he could see things with his camera that nobody else knew existed. His focus.

Can't have it both ways.

"Christmas. First, make a shopping list," she said as she ticked off one finger. Then the next, "Call Becky's teacher to make an appointment to see her."

It was Friday, but Selina worked from home as a graphic artist, and that gave her the freedom to pick her own work days. Today wasn't going to be one of them.

"Three, make dinner reservations for my birthday."

She ticked off the fourth finger, not saying out loud what the chore was. It was the worst part of this Christmas, the secret she couldn't share yet, even with Charlie.

Maybe I'll never have to, she hoped.

Her thumb was the catchall. Housework. Cooking dinner. Cleaning the toilet. Whatever needed to be done, she'd do. As she always did.

With her mind organized for the day, she walked downstairs and into the kitchen, and poured herself a cup of coffee she knew had been sitting for a long time. The aroma wasn't close to being fresh.

Charlie was staring out the back window and didn't hear her come into the kitchen.

"Hon," she said. She went to him and hugged him from the back. He jumped a bit at her touch, then turned around.

No smile today. She looked up into his face and gave him a kiss on the cheek. "Everything okay?" she asked.

"Yeah. Just that dream again."

She nodded and patted both his cheeks. His short gray beard matched the color of his hair. He'd been gray since they first met, and she loved it. Very distinguished, handsome even. His hair was longer than most men wore theirs, tied in a bundle in the back, not long enough to be a real pony tail, but he always stood out in a crowd. Just the way he liked it.

"What happened?"

He pulled back from her. "Same old, same old. Just a bit more detail. It happens today. I knew the date this time."

"Maybe that means you won't dream it again tonight."

"And I know where it is."

"Where?"

"Just down by Harver's Cove. You know that switchback there?"

Selina tried to think of the place, but nothing came to her. She didn't drive much, preferring to stay at home or to go east, into the small towns scattered along the northern shore of Long Island. Charlie often drove to Manhattan on business and knew the western part of the Island much better than she did.

"Anyhow," he said when he realized Selina didn't recognize the place. "I think I'm supposed to go there today."

Selina just stared at him for a moment. "What do you mean you're *supposed* to go there? This is a dream we're talking about."

"Yeah, I know." He looked back out the window. Frost was covering their yard. At the back of their property, he could see the Sound in the distance.

"So..."

His voice was quiet, almost shaking. "So, I just think I need to go there."

"Charlie, this doesn't sound like you. You don't believe in things like this."

"I've never had dreams like this before. You know that."

She laughed. "I've had convincing dreams before,

but that doesn't make them prophecies."

"Yeah. But I've got to go."

She turned back to the cupboards, pulling down a box of Rice Krispies. "Can you wake up Becky?" she asked.

He didn't reply at first, but then slowly turned around to her. "What if it's true?"

"What if it's not?" she replied.

"In the dreams, I'm taking black and white pictures."

"You said your whole dream was black and white."

"I've only shot color for so long, I hope I can still capture the mood."

This got a chuckle and a smile from her. "You're such a worrier about your work. You're the best photographer in the state and you still worry about every shot. Go! Get your stuff and go down to Harver's Cove or wherever you need to go."

"Yeah. I'd better get ready."

"Don't forget Christmas is coming."

He nodded.

She got the milk from the fridge and then went to wake Becky.

Chapter 3

CHARLIE SPENT AN HOUR searching out the perfect spot to watch the Sound. He found a pullout not far from the switchback he'd dreamed about, a wide gravel shoulder that wouldn't interfere with the accident.

"It was just a dream," he kept cautioning himself. "Nothing's going to happen in the real world." He wasn't convincing himself.

Charlie walked over to the white metal sign warning of the steep slope down to the Sound. It was identical to the sign in his dream. He could even remember the bent lower right corner.

As he climbed over the rail, he turned back, knelt, and took a quick snapshot of the road he'd come from. A bit of frost twinkled in the sun. If nothing else, that one photo would hold promise. The reflected light seemed to cascade off the flakes, and captured in black and white, the result should be striking.

It was after threethirty in the afternoon, not long till

dusk.

Charlie climbed down between a clumping of trees and found where the ground suddenly took a steep slope downward. His feet slipped, and he grabbed a nearby branch. In front of him was nothing but another twenty feet of sloping ground and then a dropoff, a cliff hovering fifty feet above the Sound. He hadn't realized there were any cliffs this tall nearby, and his mind wandered, composing shots.

He smelled the ocean breeze and felt the wind whip against his cheeks. He could taste the salt when he licked his lips. The wind bit into him like teenage kids snapping towels at each other in gym class.

Immediately, Charlie's professional side took control. It just clicked in, and he found himself a willing prisoner of his experience.

Selina never really understood how taking pictures was art.

"It's just being in the right place at the right time," she would say.

"Sure," he answered the first time she said that. "Getting the right place is the easy part. At least part of it's easy."

"You just drive around until you see it," she insisted.

"That's like saying Leonardo da Vinci just painted until the Mona Lisa happened to show up."

She laughed at him. "Comparing yourself to da Vinci now?" she teased.

"No, no, I mean, any kind of art takes creativity, skill, and experience. Photography isn't any different. Sure, sometimes I trip across a scene to shoot, but most people can walk by the same place and not recognize that it would make a great picture."

She didn't look convinced. He continued, "And even if they did, they wouldn't think of the different view points, the different backgrounds, and most of all the timing. Some shots need to be taken right at sunset, others at noon. You need to consider where the shadows will be, what the reflections will look like, what weather will best show it off. It's putting together a jigsaw puzzle, and you have to have the pieces exactly right to make a great picture."

He would never convince her.

Doesn't matter, he thought. *All I can do is my best.*

The rock was off to one side and jutted up out of the ground, but its backside had a slope he could climb. He sat crosslegged on a small brown mat he had brought along just for this purpose and waited.

Earlier he considered which camera to bring with him. He owned four he considered topnotch, and each had a special feeling he meshed with. His Pentax IQ was perfect for group shots, like sporting events or weddings. He had two Nikons, each with great resolutions at low levels of light.

All the other photographers he knew had long-ago made the switch to digital, but Charlie liked film, liked developing his work slowly in his dark room. Fossil be damned, he didn't know a megapixel from a megaphone, and the day he had to learn would be the day he retired.

In his hands now, though, was his personal favorite, his Canon Rebel, a strong Americanbuilt 35mm SLR. It was the camera that always gave him the highest confidence level, and he almost always picked it for his most important shots.

"Like this one," he said. "Nobody else is gonna catch that car going over the cliff."

He sat on his mat for almost an hour, watching the sunlight fade, making mental adjustments of apertures and shutter speeds to compensate as the lighting slowly changed. Each level of lighting has its own advantages and disadvantages. Being watchful was the key.

He wore wool gloves that had the fingertips snipped out, so he could feel the smooth metal of the camera. His back was to the Long Island Sound, and the harsh wind pressed against him harder and harder the longer he sat. For a short time a light snow started to fall, which he cursed, knowing it might interfere with the shot, but it stopped soon after it started.

After sixtyfive minutes, his ears perked up. He could hear the sound of an engine. He flexed his fingers and readied his camera.

Something's wrong, he decided. *It's the wrong direction.*

He spun around towards the water. Coming in from his right, he could see a small twinengine plane sailing down from the sky. His eye for detail showed him instantly that one of the engines was dead; the left propeller wasn't moving.

Without thinking, Charlie pulled up the camera and snapped a picture, easily centering the falling plane in the view finder.

The plane was tilting left and right, as the one remaining engine tried to compensate for the missing one. The pilot kept pushing down on the throttle, trying to stop the plane from barrelrolling. As he did, the plane dived closer and closer to the Sound.

Charlie was a machine. He snapped picture after picture, keeping his vision wide, aware of every background image the plane was going to fly in front of. More importantly, he was mentally calculating exactly when the plane would hit the water.

When it did, he snapped the perfect photo.

Chapter 4

SELINA WAS SITTING at the kitchen table with Becky when Charlie came in after his photo-shoot. She smiled and stood to give him a hug, feeling as always a small sense of relief that he was back home safely.

She felt him hold her much tighter than he normally did, stroking her hair. "I love you," he whispered to her.

She pulled back from him. "I love you, too." She looked at him and could see the unease in his eyes. "What happened?"

He glanced at Becky, who was ignoring them. "I got the shot. It was " He slowly took off his jacket. " I'm not sure how to describe it."

"Do you want me to put some coffee on?" She glanced at the clock. A bit after eight. Probably too late for coffee.

"Beer would be better," he said. She watched as he gave Becky a kiss on the cheek. The nineyearold grinned and jumped at him.

"Becky, time to go to your room," Selina said.

"Ahh, Mom..."

"Ahh nothing. Mom and Dad have things to talk about."

Becky flipped her braids over her shoulders and packed up the book she'd been reading at the table.

"Night, kiddo," Charlie said.

"Night." She showed the stunning smile she had inherited from Selina, the smile that always grabbed Charlie and shook him senseless.

Selina brought back two bottles of Coors Light and a glass for herself, just in time to pat Becky's shoulder as she marched to her room. Selina popped the caps and handed one to Charlie. As she poured her own beer, she said, "Tell me about it."

"It wasn't like the dream, not exactly. It was a plane that crashed, not a car."

"You saw a plane crash? Oh my God. Did you call somebody?"

"Yeah, called the cops. They're still out there. That's what took me so long."

"Was anybody hurt?"

"Killed. I'm pretty sure. I know there was a pilot. Not sure if anybody else was on board. When I develop the pictures, I might be able to tell."

Selina sat, waiting for him to tell her more. She knew he always had to take his time with his stories, couldn't ever just spill it like she would have.

He rubbed his beard and seemed to concentrate on something in the distance. "When it was happening, all I could think about was getting the shot. But, when it was over, it hit me that a guy had died right there. And I just watched."

"What else could you do?"

He shook his head. "I don't know. Nothing."

Selina didn't know what to say, so she just gave him another hug. "Must have been awful," she finally added.

"The dream was right," Charlie said. "That's the worst part about all this. The dream told me where to go, what to do, even to shoot it in black and white. That was the right thing to do. The contrasts should turn out great."

"Dreams can't predict the future."

He just shook his head and got two more bottles of beer from the fridge. "It was too weird."

He took a long drink from the bottle. "What's even weirder..."

"Yeah?"

"After the plane went down, I looked at my watch. Thought the cops would want to know." She heard his voice crack a bit. "It was 4:42."

Chapter 5

A WEEK LATER, Selina got the call she was dreading.

She was watching TV with Becky, halfway through *The Price is Right*. Somehow, Becky always knew the prices of everything much better than Selina did. It didn't matter if it was peanut butter or a new car.

"And what is your bid for this new Maytag refrigerator?" asked Drew Carey of the contestants.

"Seven hundred ninety-nine dollars," said the first woman, a middle-aged, spinny housekeeper from Boston. Becky laughed and pointed at the television. "What a moron!" Her braids bounced when she laughed.

Selina didn't hear the other bids. She turned to Becky and asked, "How much is it?"

"It'd be closer to fifteen hundred. Look at all the features it's got! Top of the line Maytag? Who'd think you could get all that for less than a thousand?"

Well, Selina thought, *I might*. She smiled at her

ignorance, knowing Becky would be right. She was always right.

The phone rang before she found out for sure. The call display showed it was her doctor, Jamie McKay. Four rings went by before she could force herself to answer.

"Hello?"

"Hey, Lina. It's me."

After Selina got off the phone, she went upstairs and locked herself in the bathroom. Becky would be glued to the rest of the show and wouldn't miss her.

She closed the toilet lid and sat, her head in her hands. She didn't cry, though, and actually giggled at one point.

But mostly she felt sad. This would be her last Christmas.

Charlie still didn't know she was sick. He would never notice something like that unless she fell down in pain right in front of him. It wasn't like that. She did feel pain, but it wasn't catastrophic, more an annoying irritation. Well, sometimes. At others, it was worse—a diffuse burning that ran through her abdomen. And there were sharper pains, like her bones were being snipped with wirecutters.

She almost didn't go to see Jamie, but she remembered berating her mother when she had waited too long to have *her* cancer diagnosed. She could have been treated if it had been caught earlier.

Now, Selina was in the same boat.

Jamie hadn't wanted to tell her over the phone, but

they'd known each other for so long, Selina made him promise. In return, she promised not to break down if it was bad news.

The cancer started in her kidneys. That was the pain she felt around the edges of her back. But, it had already spread like wildfire. Her lymph nodes were dripping with the stuff, her liver, pancreas, even her lungs.

Jamie had spoken softly on the phone. "You've had this for a while, Lina. I don't understand why you didn't have symptoms earlier."

She shrugged that off. No point dwelling on the pain. "What do we do now?"

"Chemo."

She had to ask. "Is it too late?"

After a long pause, he said, "It's never too late to try, but I won't lie to you. The chance of winning this war now is very slight."

Very slight. She kept hearing those two words over and over in her mind as she sat on the toilet. *Very slight*. The words sounded so innocuous. Three little syllables were changing her future.

What future might that be? she asked herself sadly.

Jamie talked to her for a few more minutes on the phone and promised to call back after arranging her chemo treatment. Selina barely heard anything he said. All the words just seemed like static to her brain, not quite decipherable. Her mind was too busy with the two little words. *Very slight.*

When there was a long pause in the conversation, she asked the one other question she needed the answer to. "How long do I have?"

"It's so hard to say, really..."

"How fucking long do I have, Jamie?"

"Maybe a few months. Four, five, six, something like that. But with the chemo "

"No. No chemo. I'll deal with this."

"Lina "

She cut him off again. "I watched my mother go through chemo when it was too late. I'm not doing that." He was still talking when she hung up the phone.

She leaned back on the toilet seat. It crumpled a bit beneath her.

Involuntarily, her fingers spread out. She needed to start a new list.

A will. She didn't know if she really needed one. Wouldn't Charlie just inherit whatever assets she had? Most things were in joint names anyway. Best to check, though.

Her second finger clicked out. *Hospital bills.* She didn't know how much their insurance would cover.

Third finger. *Becky.* How could Selina tell Becky her mother was dying? She needed to think of a communications plan. She snickered, as she realized she was switching to her graphic arts mindset, using terminology she would never normally use in her own life. *But all of a sudden, we're not in normal times,* she knew.

Fourth finger. *Charlie.* Same problem. How to tell him? Right when his career is going through the roof, she was going to bring him down to Earth, sinking him like a rock. Or maybe not. How would he react? How long would he mourn her? She felt an attack of selfpity as she realized she had no idea what he would say or do or feel. She shook it off.

There was a more important issue with Charlie. If he couldn't even notice how sick she was, how would he ever be able to care properly for Becky?

Thoughts for another day.

Christmas. The fifth finger. She decided right then that her secret would stay hidden until the new year. No way she would ruin it for them with only a couple of weeks left until Christmas. She vowed to make this the best holiday season ever.

January would come soon enough.

She moved over and started to run a bath. A *very slight* bath. She giggled again.

Selina quietly picked up her housecoat from their bedroom and could hear Drew Carey yelling from downstairs, the live studio audience cheering him on.

She lowered herself into the nice hot water, lay back, and covered herself with bubbles. Her eyes were closed, and she reached her foot out to shut off the water when it neared the top of the tub.

Below the water, she used her hands to feel her body, her hips, her tummy, her breasts. Maybe her body wasn't that of a youngster anymore, but she had taken care of herself, and it bothered her that her body had betrayed her like this. She could feel nothing unusual.

"Not fair," she said.

Chapter 6

THE DIVE TEAM didn't find the pilot for a week after Charlie snapped his picture. Bits of the small Cessna eventually floated onto shore. It was an old hobby plane, flown by a retired farmer. He had a heart attack in flight. There was no black box, and if it wasn't for Charlie being in the right place at the right time, nobody would have ever known where to look for his body.

Time and *Newsweek* both bought his photo for their covers the following week, each paying ten thousand dollars for the right to use the photo once. They both wanted complete ownership, but Charlie wasn't selling.

The photo haunted everybody who saw it. A black and white picture, reeking of oldfashioned values, seeming to bring the viewer back to a simpler time. The picture captured the left wing snapping and ripping off the fuselage. The waves of the Sound were frozen in time, but the viewer was haunted by the old farmer, his eyes screaming as much as his mouth. His face was perfectly framed, the face of a man who would be dead a second later and who knew it.

People could stare at the picture for an hour and still find new details they hadn't noticed yet.

One instant, one snap of the finger, the steadiest his hands had ever been, earned Charlie Parkinson almost as much money as he'd ever earned for a year's worth of photos, let alone one.

In early January, Charlie was summoned to The Kensington Gallery of Art. Janis Kensington herself had called him, asking him to meet her to discuss a business opportunity she had been thinking about. A showing.

The Gallery was located on Fifth Avenue near 72nd Street, just east of Central Park. Charlie knew the area, having spent countless hours in the park, looking for new ways of photographing the same old thing everybody's seen a million times before. He still hadn't found anything that suited him, and he always thought of the park as his Holy Grail. *One day*, he knew, *the right shot will call to me.*

"Charlie, come on in." Janis Kensington found him daydreaming as he stared at a couple of pieces of neoexpressionism hanging in the nearly empty show room. None of it had really appealed to him, but he readily admitted he wasn't much of a judge of painted artwork. He loved photography, and although he could appreciate the work involved in other kinds of art, it didn't sing to him.

He was dressed in his best clothes: a dark brown pair of cords and a tan dress shirt. Not dressy by anybody else's standards, just the best he had. And sneakers, he reminded himself. *Bet that doesn't happen much here.*

Charlie had done a quick check on Janis over the Internet before meeting her. He knew The Kensington Gallery of Art was only ten years old, opened up by Janis Kensington with some money a rich dead uncle had left her. Now, everybody just called it The Gallery, as if it were the only one in Manhattan. In a sense, it was. It was *the* place to have your work shown. Charlie was vague on the details of how that had happened in such a short time period, but he knew it was true.

The Gallery only opened when there was a show that Janis wanted to present. In the previous two years, The Gallery had opened for six shows, each show lasting exactly ten days each. sixty days out of seven hundred and thirty. The other days, The Gallery's doors remained locked. They only opened when there was a truly unique reason to do so.

And now Janis had called to discuss a show for him.

"I've never done a photography exhibit," she said bluntly when they got settled in her office. "Frankly, photographs mostly bore me."

Charlie asked in a puzzled voice, "Then why did you ask me here?"

He looked at her as she smiled back at him. She didn't look more than thirty, but he knew that was misleading. She had looked exactly the same when The Gallery had opened. He hadn't been prepared for how short she was, less than five feet, he had judged, compared to his sixone.

Her shining smile, long platinum hair, and piercing blue eyes took all attention away from her height, though, and her clear, commanding voice made him realize that she played second fiddle to nobody. In a meeting of any ten people, it would be her that towered above the rest.

"I feel quite differently about *your* work," she said. "You know the pieces I mean. Frankly, your earlier stuff didn't do much for me, but all of a sudden, you're shooting very commercially, very intense, very exciting." She held her hands in front of her, as if she were going to grab Charlie and shake him. "You need to show here. You know nobody else can give you the publicity and exposure I can."

He nodded absently. "I'm not sure I'm ready for a show. I don't have that many of those kinds of shots."

"How many?"

He thought back over the past month. The first and best had been the plane crash. The second...

He'd dreamed of the second one for only three nights. The dream pointed him to the right place, even if the scene wasn't exact.

Broadway. A kid riding his bicycle.

Charlie still got shivers from the memory of the boy's scream being cut off as his head was severed from his neck. The taxi driver that hit him would never recover from the guilt.

Charlie had been ready, kittycornered from the

accident. The boy freewheeling down Broadway, laughing as he dodged between cars, not caring as he pedaled harder to beat the light at 23rd Street.

The taxi driver was drunk, off shift, heading home to a shitty life with a pack of miserable kids and a wife he couldn't stand. All the fuck he wanted to do was drink till he passed out. Charlie knew all this from his dream.

The taxi driver never saw the kid until blood covered his front windshield.

Charlie snapped the perfect picture. In black and white, the blood streaming out didn't seem as gory, didn't turn eyes away. Rather, people stared, almost confused, until they realized that the blood squirting out from the boy's neck really was the result of his last heartbeat. The boy's head was just beginning to tilt sideways on the way to hitting the chrome bumper that would do the chopping. His eyes were bugged out, and his mouth just started to open for his final cry.

The rear wheel of the bike was blurred, still spinning as it was raised off the ground. In contrast, the front wheel was frozen in time, crumpled by the pressure of the speeding taxi, several spokes crushed and ripped apart by the impact.

A split second earlier or later, and the photo would have been useless. Now it was art.

After that, he dreamed three nights in a row of a fire and explosion at a restaurant in Chinatown. Charlie waited patiently outside, watching as an elderly Chinese man left after his dinner. The picture that mattered was the one where the customer looked back over his shoulder, just as the door was blown off its hinges and the fireball escaped. The colors of the fire turned into wonderfully evocative contrasting grays, and you could stare at the fire for hours without thinking about the man who was about to be vaporized in the foreground.

Then was the picture of the baby falling to her death from the hotel window in the Bronx. The cruel drop contrasted with the angelic smile on her face.

The photo of the dog being sliced apart by a vicious teenaged gang member.

All in all, Charlie knew that he had a dozen of his very special dream photos in his inventory. *Death shots.* Those were what Janis wanted to show. *And,* he knew, *what everyone else wants to see.*

"Twelve," he finally replied. "There's twelve so far."

She smiled that big smile of hers again. "That's just fine. We'll aim for opening on February 14. Valentine's Day. Like it?"

"I guess. Isn't twelve a bit light for a show, though?" "We'll have a bunch of your older material in the main hall. We have two smaller rooms that we'll hang your treasures in. Six in each."

"I don't think I want to sell them."

She nodded. "I thought so. We'll sell prints. Limit them to a hundred copies. Ask five thousand each."

He didn't know what to say as he did the math. five thousand dollars times a hundred copies times twelve photographs. Six million dollars. *Ludicrous.* He laughed. "That'll never work. Nobody'll pay that for a print."

"Trust me. They will. I'll be sure to get the Japanese here. The Brazilians are very big on this kind of work as well. And of course my American regulars will eat it up. You don't need to do anything except sign the prints. I'll take care of production and framing. My commission is forty percent. Deal?"

She stood and held out her hand. He shook. "Do we need a contract or something?"

Janis shook her head. "I only work with people I trust and people who trust me." She smiled. "I'll be in touch. We'll start renovating The Gallery tomorrow. It's got to match the exhibit. Bring me the negatives of all the work by the end of the week, so I can get the images in my mind. The recent ones and the older ones. That'll all help with my planning."

She started to walk him out. "This is going to work really well, Charlie. You're going to be rich."

And then she was gone. He stared at the nearly empty walls of The Gallery, thinking about how fast his life had changed.

Chapter 7

Selina was on the east end of Long Island, in a small town called Port Simpson. It actually felt more like a village than a town to her, with less that five thousand people living there. It was far away from everything else she knew on the Island, a small patch of quiet isolation, separated from the rest of the world by an unspoken agreement among its residents to pretend they were living back before twelvehour work days, stress, and fear.

She always loved wandering the narrow streets, picking up little trinkets in the dollar stores or other small items to bring back for Becky. Even Charlie was always curious to see what she might find.

Selina might never have found the town if Jamie McKay hadn't set up his practice there.

Selina and Jamie had gone to high school together, PS 281 in Brooklyn. She always liked his outgoing manner and his politeness, and that brought them together as friends, but conversations between them had always been tame, almost boring, and she knew that meant there would never be a spark of romance between them. They dated twice, before Selina called it off, not wanting either of them to be hurt later.

Sometimes, friendship trumped romance.

After high school, they went their separate ways. Jamie to NYU and then on to the Med School. Selina didn't have the grades or the desire for university, and she ended up studying graphic arts at a college in Brookhaven, where she eventually met Charlie.

She lost touch with Jamie for four years, then found a postcard in the mail announcing he was hanging up his shingle in Port Simpson. She called immediately and became his first patient. The only hard part was when she had to strip for a physical. That never got easy. She knew there were times Jamie wondered, *What if things had worked out differently in high school?* but he never mentioned it.

Now, the town had lost its innocence. It no longer was the place Selina could escape to when things got bad. It was just the opposite. Port Simpson was where her cancer was found. By her old friend.

She stared at him across his desk, almost defying his diagnosis.

Jamie reached out for her hand. "Lina, you know we need to do the chemo. The cancer has spread too far to allow surgery to be an alternative. Same thing for radiation. This is the only choice."

"I know. But, I'm not doing it."

"That doesn't make any sense."

"It would if you saw what chemo did to my mother."

Selina thought back to those terrible days. Mom lying in her skinny little hospital cot, barely able to hold her head up. Weary, bone tired, and in so much pain Selina just wanted to take the pillow and crush the pitiful bit of remaining life from her. Before the chemo, she'd seemed so much better. Maybe it was just an illusion, but it was a powerful one. She cast her thoughts aside and said to Jamie, "Besides, I feel just fine."

Fine. Just fine. Very slight. Fine. Some days, her stomach felt like she was digesting ground glass. Pains jabbed at her from all sorts of places when she least expected it. Every place from her neck to her crotch twisted and fought her, but she had no intention of telling Jamie that. *Just fine.*

He sighed and pulled his hand back. "Have you told Charlie and Becky yet?"

"No. I'm not ready to do that yet."

"Lina, you need to be fair. You "

"What I need is to be sure I have all my ducks lined up. I need you to do me a favor."

He shook his head, not understanding. "You know I'd do anything. What?"

She pulled a brown nine by twelve envelope from her purse. "This is my will. I want you to keep it."

He took the envelope from her. "Hey, I'm not a lawyer. I shouldn't be taking this."

"Yes, you should. Let me tell you what it says."

Jamie put the envelope on his desk and leaned over, listening to Selina's last wishes. She had several items and used her fingers to count them off.

She looked into the air, not at his face, while

reciting her points. When she was done, she looked at him. "You need to fight for me, Jamie. I won't be able to fight for it myself."

He looked deep in thought. "That's so... Are you really sure?"

"I've thought long and hard."

"I'll keep this in my safe. I still think you should hire a lawyer, though."

"No. It's got to be you."

He gave her a hug as she left.

Selina walked down the main street, down to the end of town, where the houses gave way to fishing huts. From a viewpoint high above the water, she could see the huge boulders that covered the landscape for miles giving the town its nickname, Boulder City.

My last visit, she knew. There would be no reason to come back. There was no hospital in Port Simpson and when the time came, she'd likely end up in Hampstead or Brookhaven or one of the other larger towns to the south. Away from the water.

Regardless of her persistence with Jamie, she still wondered if she had done the right thing with her will.

I'll never know for sure, she knew. *Unless there is a heaven up there after all.* She looked up, the clear blue sky filled with beauty and promise.

Chapter 8

AFTER HIS MEETING with Janis Kensington, Charlie was having trouble focusing his thoughts on anything except the money.

Six million bucks. For prints, not even originals.

He thought back over and over to the conversation, still not believing he had heard it right.

The Japanese would like his stuff. Janis made it sound so offthecuff, like everybody would understand that. He couldn't figure out who these Japanese people might be. Let alone the Brazilians. That puzzled him even more.

He was sitting in The Ram's Head, a quiet bar near The Gallery. He sipped a Bud and glanced at his watch. Three o'clock was earlier than he normally would be drinking, but this was a day to celebrate. He really wanted to get back to Long Island and tell Selina, but on the spur of the moment he'd called Tom Dodd and convinced him to pop out of his ivory tower for a quick one. He needed to chat, and there was nobody else who would understand except Tom.

Six million bucks.

Fuck.

But then, Janis would keep her share. He couldn't remember what she said exactly about that, but even if he kept half that was still three mill.

He wondered how much would go to income taxes. Half? He still ended up in seven figures, no matter how you cut it.

The most he had ever made in one year was twenty-six thousand dollars. Without Selina's success doing design work, they'd never have been able to afford the great home they had now. She'd been the big breadwinner in their marriage. Now that was going to change, and he liked that idea.

"There you are!"

Charlie jumped at the booming voice behind him. He stood up, knocked the table and braced himself as Tom gave him a big bear hug, patting him on the back as he squeezed him.

"It's great to see you, Tom." Charlie waved to the seat on the other side of the table. As Tom squeezed himself in, Charlie waved across the room to the waitress and held up two fingers.

"It's been a long time, Charlie," Tom said.

"God, it sure has. What, ten years since the tests? Three or four since the last time we actually got together?"

"Five." Tom grimaced, his version of a smile. The big man almost always struck everybody with the same thought when they first met him. *Madman.* His huge size overpowered everybody who saw him, six foot six, three hundred pounds, every ounce of it muscle. When he shook hands, most people found their fingers buried in the cave he formed.

His wild beard and long hair were pitch black, and he never worried about keeping them neat. His fingers were the only comb he owned. His beady black eyes stared like demon beacons.

Madman. Charlie smiled at the usual first impression. He knew how ridiculous the thought was, with Tom being the kindest person he knew. And maybe the smartest.

The waitress dropped two more Buds on the table, and offered a glass to Tom. She didn't get very close. He smiled a crooked grin at her and waved the glass away. She couldn't move fast enough.

"Ahh, I still got the touch, right, Charlie?" He laughed a roar as the waitress lost herself in the crowd. "Can still scare 'em for no reason."

Charlie laughed in spite of himself. He knew that Tom took a perverse pleasure in how people reacted to him.

They toasted to old friends and to each having a good year to come. As they drank their beer, they got caught up on the small events that had happened in the past few years. Selina's business, the house, Becky, Tom's latest girlfriend, his practice. Nothing big, just old friends catching up. Nothing about Charlie's recent fame.

They were halfway through the second beer (Charlie's third), when the time came, and Tom asked, "So, what are we here for, Charlie? Must be something big."

"Can't we just get together for a beer?"

"'Course we can! We just never do. There's always a reason, isn't there?"

Charlie nodded. There always was. "I'm not really sure how to start."

"Well, just start talking. I'm not going anywhere."

"Remember when we first met?"

"Sure. You came to my clinic. Thought we could help you get some sleep."

Tom Dodd was the Senior Researcher at the Sleep Disorder Clinic at Manhattan College. He knew more about sleeping problems than anybody else in the state. Maybe more than anyone else in the world. Charlie'd thought it was worth a try, that maybe Tom could help him sleep.

"It's hard when you can't sleep," Charlie said. His voice was sad as he remembered all the years he stared at the ceiling. "You try, but then you wake up as soon as you drift off."

"Yeah. You're a tough case. Never did much to help you, did I?"

"Not your fault. You tried." Charlie circled around the problem, finding his own way to get to his point. Tom waited, sipping his beer more slowly now. "How come people can dream in black and white, Tom?"

"Whaddaya mean? Some do, some don't. Most people dream in color, but they don't always know it. Actually, most people don't really know whether they dream in color or not. You ask 'em and they'll say 'I think...' but most of 'em never really know."

"Yeah, yeah, but black and white as a concept

didn't even exist until photography was invented. Everything was always in color before that. So, how can we dream in black and white if it's an artificial invention?"

Tom leaned back. "What's gotten into you? You never cared about anything like this." Then he seemed to understand. "You've been dreaming! That's it, isn't it? You've had a black and white dream, and that's what you wanted to talk about."

Charlie nodded. "Many dreams. And I've been sleeping for five or six hours straight."

"Five or six hours? Fuckadoodle! I can't believe it. After all these years. When did that start?"
"A month or so back."

Tom whistled. "God damn it all to hell. I don't know how many times we hooked you up and measured every little impulse passing through that brain of yours, and we could never figure out why you couldn't sleep. You weren't like any other patient. Usually people really do sleep and really do dream, but they just don't know it. You were the only patient I ever had that never entered REM sleep, not even for a minute. I'm still amazed you aren't dead."

Charlie smiled, remembering all this from when he was Tom's patient. The *Journal of the AMA* had published Tom's account of "C.P.," bringing Tom to the forefront of sleep research.

"But now you're sleeping and dreaming. Wow. What happened?"

"I don't know. It just happened one night. Right around the time of the first picture."
"The plane? I saw that one."

"Yeah."

"Success brought you sleep. It looks like that's a clue."

"No. It was the other way around. Sleep brought the success. I had the dreams first." Charlie took a deep breath and added, "I dreamed of what to shoot. I had the same dream night after night. It told me where to go and also to shoot in black and white."

"The dream told you?" Tom's voice was lower now, professional, his psychology training taking over. *Playing back what he heard, to keep the subject talking,* Charlie knew.

"Yeah." He took a drink and waved for two more.

"Charlie, you know dreams can't tell the future."

"Actually, I know they can. They do. Mine do."

"Start over. Tell me about the dreams."

As the beer arrived, Charlie ordered a plate of chicken wings with honey and garlic sauce; he was feeling the effects of the drinks and needed food in his stomach.

He told Tom the story of his first dream, and the ones that followed, leading him to the plane crash near Harver's Cove. He added the quirky bit about waking at 4:42 each night and how that was the exact time of the crash.

Tom pulled out a pad of paper from his briefcase and scratched notes down.

Charlie munched on a wing as Tom looked back on his scribbles. "Quite a story, you know." He smacked the pad down on the table. "But, Charlie, you gotta clear your head a bit. Everything you've told me can be explained by coincidence or wishful thinking. Your dreams aren't somehow predicting the future. That just isn't happening."

"How could I know to go where that plane went down?"

Tom picked up his notes. "Let's see what you said." He turned back a couple of pages. "You dreamed of a place that you know very well, right? Your neighborhood, almost. So, you certainly can't be surprised about the sign and whatever other details you say were so clear, right?"

Charlie protested, "But the accident?"

"I'm getting to that. You dreamed about a police chase and a car going into the water, two cops drowning." He looked up. "None of that happened, right? It was just a dream. Nothing more, nothing less."

"The plane "

"The plane was not in your dream."

"Come on, Tom. What about telling me to take the shots in black and white? The pictures wouldn't have been the same in color."

"You'd know that better than me, being the photographer and all that. You asked me earlier about dreaming in black and white. Let's get back to that." He took a drink of his nowwarm Bud and made a face. Charlie took the opportunity to wave for some more beer.

"The fact is, nobody really knows the truth about dreaming. We don't know why we dream, how we dream, or what advantages it has. I mean, we don't know why we ever evolved the ability to dream. We only have a few theories."

"You told me once that it's the brain's way of

consolidating and processing the information it gathered during the day. A housekeeping exercise."

"That's one of the more popular theories. As to how we dream, that's even less well understood. We do know that we never really 'see' dreams the way you think we do. There's no movie screen in our mind. When we dream, color or black and white is a layer that we impose ourselves on a bunch of electrical impulses. The answer to your question about how we can dream in black and white is simply that it's a color scheme we now know about and can easily drape over our dreams. It's not surprising in the slightest."

"Yeah, well, why would my dreams be black and white?"

"As I said, you're a photographer. Who better to know if a twilight shot would be better in color or not. You're taking the dream and stretching it to meet an idea that you know is impossible."

"All the dreams, Tom?"

"Come on, now. Think about it. In every single dream you told me about, you never once dreamed the sequence of events that really happened. You didn't dream of a kid on a bike getting hit by a taxi. You dreamed of " He turned the page on his pad.

"Yeah, I know. A guy jumping off a roof. I get that. But the dreams always pointed me to the right place."

"New York City is full of tragedy. You've been in the right place at the right time with your eyes open, ready with your camera. There's really no mystery to it."

The right place at the right time. Charlie leaned back, knowing he wasn't going to win the argument. For the first time since his initial dream, he wasn't even able to convince himself. He tried to grasp at anything that still didn't fit. "The times! I kept waking at the same time every night." He slapped the table. "Explain that."

Tom grinned again, and Charlie slumped back, knowing that Tom had already thought of an answer.

"It didn't happen."

That puzzled Charlie. "Well, of course it did. Are you saying I'm lying?"

"No, no, my friend. I'm sure you remember it clearly. But, you were almost certainly continuing your dream for a moment after you woke. It's called a hypnopompic hallucination. You thought you were awake, but you weren't. It's very common."

Charlie took another drink. "Sure didn't seem like a dream to me," he muttered.

Chapter 9

Selina hated waiting, particularly hated when the appointment she was waiting for wasn't going to be pleasant. This was the third time this school year that she had been called in to see Becky's teacher.

She hated that Ms. Foster was a decade younger than her but still insisted on being called formally, rather than by her first name. *Who needs this crap?* she thought. She also hated that Ms. Foster overreacted to every little thing. Last year's teacher, whose name Selina couldn't quite remember, was much more tolerant. So, Becky was a bit disruptive. Wasn't that the teacher's job to sort out? They're the ones in the damned classroom when things got out of hand. Becky was always quiet at home. What did they expect Selina to do, when she never saw anything to discipline Becky about?

She just didn't need this now.

The only good news was that this would likely be

the last time she'd ever have to go through this stupidity. "The last time," she said aloud to the empty walls. The finality of everything was finally starting to settle in on her, a month after being told it was coming.

Selina still didn't feel that sick. The bone pains were a lot more frequent, and some pains in her midsection seemed to randomly attack her. Nothing she couldn't deal with.

Nothing that should be killing her.

"The last time," she repeated. "The last time."

Selina was starting to collect her own set of phrases. *The last time. Fine, just fine. Very slight.* She was sure others would come along.

Now, she remembered the first time she had come to the old brick school, Becky tagging along beside her for enrollment day. A sunny day, she remembered. Warm.

She remembered the first time she met Charlie, the first time she felt his kiss, the first time they made love. Their first anniversary. The first time she'd gotten pregnant. That hadn't been Becky, but rather an accident they had quietly taken care of.

The silence in the empty classroom seemed to swallow all her memories like quicksand. She felt them being pulled away from her, leaving in their place only vacant shells memories that she'd now never have.

The first time she should have gone to Greece. For some reason, this was high on her list of missing memories. Her sister, Louise, had gone to Greece years ago and brought back a thousand and one stories of the food and the Parthenon and the islands and... and she couldn't remember much else, but it sounded like something she just should have been able to do before dying.

Selina had always sworn that she and Charlie would one day live all those same adventures. But one day never came and now never would.

Just one missing memory among many.

She found herself taking silent inventory. Planning Becky's wedding. Their silver anniversary. Grandchildren. Other trips: England, an Alaskan cruise, San Francisco, Las Vegas, New Orleans...

So much to see, no more time.

"Stop that," she berated herself.

She stood and moved to the front of the classroom, starting to read poems that were pinned up with bright red check marks on each. Anything to take the missing memories away.

She looked for Becky's name and found a poem by her. It was no more immature than the others, she decided.

"Mrs. Parkinson, thank you for coming in."

Selina turned to see the young teacher drop a pile of papers and books onto her desk. She was just as Selina remembered her from a few weeks ago. Short, stout, couldn't be more than twenty-five or so, deep red hair spilling down her shoulders. She wore wire glasses with square lenses.

"I'm glad you called me," she lied. "You said that you had something to show me."

"Yes, yes. Becky is doing much better in class these days, so whatever you're doing at home, keep it up, because it's working!" Selina could hear the exclamation mark at the end of the sentence. Ms. Foster always seemed to carry a large supply of them to be sure to get her points across.

"I'm glad we're able to help." Selina felt silly, taking credit for something that she wasn't doing, but if it made the meeting go faster, she was all for it.

"Yes, yes. But, you see, we still have some little things to work out."

"Such as?"

"Well, the main thing is that we had this great art class last week!"

"Yes, and?"

"Well, the assignment was to draw a picture of somebody from the child's family. We were mainly interested in ensuring that the child knows how to properly symbolize body shapes, general characteristics of the head, and so forth. You understand."

"Okay."

"So, I'd like you to see Becky's picture. She actually drew you!"

Selina smiled. "She only had me or her father to choose from."

"Yes, well, of course. I have them at the back of the room."

They walked between two rows of desks to get to the back. There was a long tablelike ledge that spanned the back, about three feet wide. Along the ledge were a dozen piles that looked like different assignments. Some were collected into folders, some just stacked loosely.

"Yes, yes, here we are," said Ms. Foster. She

carefully moved the top group of pictures to the side, exposing the picture that Selina supposed must be her. She could see Becky's scrawled name at the bottom.

Selina wouldn't have recognized herself, but she suspected few parents would have. The picture showed a woman in a blue dress, red shoes, and long brown hair, much longer than Selina's real hair. She wore glasses in the picture instead of contacts, but that was understandable, as she sometimes wore reading glasses at night.

"It's not very artistic, but I'm not sure what the problem is," she said. "Surely it's not much different from the other children's work, is it?"

"Oh, the quality isn't the problem. Here, let me move it to the light, so you can see more clearly." She carried the picture to a nearby window, and then Selina could see what the concern was.

Selina should have seen it right away. It wasn't the picture of her that was the problem; it was where she was situated in the picture. Surrounding her, in a light shade of brown was a clearly drawn coffin. Selina looked at the straight lines surrounding her image and felt a chill.

"You see the problem." The teacher swirled her hand around them. "We think this indicates negative thoughts. I know I'm new here, so I asked some of the other teachers. They haven't seen anything exactly like this before, but we were all concerned."

Selina kept staring at the picture. Negative thoughts? No shit. She wasn't going to say what the coffin represented, and she sure didn't know how

Becky had come to know, but it was very clear to her that it was simply Becky's way of drawing the future.

Chapter 10

CHARLIE PULLED INTO the driveway about six o'clock and was glad to see that Selina's car was gone. She hated the times he drove after drinking. Hell, he hated it himself and knew it was stupid. Today, though, he thought he'd been safe. Just a few beers. Nothing much, but it was celebration time. It wasn't affecting him.

He could hear Selina in his mind. "Don't be ridiculous. Of course it's affected you."

Yeah, yeah.

Becky wasn't home, either. Must be with Selina.

He took a beer from the fridge and drank a bit of it, in case Selina came home and smelled alcohol on his breath. Fact is, he could use another one anyway.

Charlie went down the stairs to his makeshift darkroom. There was a section of the basement that he'd cordoned off and built flimsy walls made of tar paper and plywood. Not very sturdy, but it sure kept the light out. It was a nice size, about ten feet by twelve and was covered wall to wall with hanging negatives.

Not from his special shots; those were safely stored away. These were crappy things that had been hanging there since being developed. Some had been dangling for years.

None of that stuff mattered anymore. What mattered was the more than three million bucks he would be taking home from his death shots.

He didn't really like to use that term, but what else was there? Every one of the twelve had been taken at the instant that somebody died.

The Japanese would love them, Janis said. *And the Brazilians.*

And her American regulars. Let's not forget them.

But five thousand each for a print? He still had trouble imagining it.

He polished off the beer just as he heard noises from upstairs. He turned off all the basement lights and climbed up to see Selina and Becky in the kitchen. He made sure to bring the empty beer bottle up with him.

"Hey, kiddo!" He gave Becky a hug.

"Dad!"

After extricating himself from her, Charlie gave Selina a hug, too. He held her tightly to him, feeling how much he did love her, in spite of some of the tension that always seemed to be in the air.

Selina said, "I went to see Ms. Foster today." Charlie must have looked puzzled. "Becky's teacher," she added.

"You went to my school?" Becky was surprised.

"Yes. Ms. Foster said you're doing much better and she just wanted us to know that."

"Oh." She looked over her shoulder, toward her room.

"It's okay. You can go."

Becky raced off without another word.

Charlie said, "You look like there's more to the story."

"It's nothing."

Charlie was happy with the opportunity to shift the topic. "I met with Janis Kensington today."

Selina stared at him in disbelief. "Really?"

"She's going to arrange a showing of my stuff."

"At The Gallery?"

"Sure. Where else?"

"Oh, my God, that's unbelievable. Charlie, I'm so proud of you! Sit down, tell me all about it."

Her eyes were wide, like silver dollars, and Charlie felt her radiating pride in him.

He told her the story of his day, the meeting with Janis. Then he stopped suddenly.

"Charlie? What is it?"

"The dreams can't predict anything, right?"

"Of course not."

He wiped his eyes and moved back to hold her again. "I didn't want to tell you before, but I guess..."

She pulled back and looked into his eyes. "What?" she asked softly. She wiped the corners of his eyes and patted his beard.

He composed himself and said, "Last night. I dreamed that we were going out somewhere. I had a gun in my pocket. We got in a fight. I don't really remember what about. I got upset and mad and took out the gun and killed you."

Selina sat silently.

Charlie didn't say anything more, either.

Chapter 11

CHARLIE HAD THREE MORE beers before calling it a night. Selina was already asleep when he tiptoed into their room and quietly lay down beside her. It was past one in the morning. Much later than he'd been getting to bed lately. *Avoiding the dreams,* he knew.

He had a passing thought; he hadn't asked Selina how her day had been. Other than the brief mention of meeting Becky's teacher. The thought quickly passed.

Now that darkness covered him and silence permeated their home, doubts crept back into his mind. *I shouldn't have told Selina that I dreamed about killing her.*

Finally, he surrendered to the pull of sleep.

And he woke up, checked the time of the clock. 4:42 a.m. As he knew it would be.

Charlie went to the bathroom and splashed cold

water on his face then went back to the bedroom and looked at the clock. 4:43. He dressed and went to the kitchen, putting the coffee on.

After sitting quietly for two hours, Charlie was joined by Selina, who came into the kitchen, stretching. "Hey, sleepyhead," he said. "Good morning!" He gave her a long hug.

"Morning," Selina said as she looked at the coffee pot. Empty.

"I'll make another pot," Charlie said.

Selina nodded at him and sat at the table. "Did you dream?"

He hesitated before answering. "Yeah. A silly one."

"That's a nice change then. Tell me about it."

Charlie started the coffee brewing and sat down across the table from her. "I dreamed of your Aunt Jeannie."

"Jeannie? Haven't heard from her in " She stared up at the ceiling, as if the answer were up there. "I give up, three years?"

"I dreamed she fell and broke her ankle."

Charlie stared at Selina, watched her face as she pursed her mouth, seemingly not knowing what to say. "It's just a silly dream," he added. "Don't give it a thought."

"Yeah," she finally said. "Sure."

He got up and poured her a coffee, adding lowcalorie sweetener and skim milk. He carried it back to her. She was reading the newspaper, his dream forgotten, which was just fine with him.

Selina left to do some shopping. She told him where, but Charlie couldn't put his finger on it.

He couldn't get interested in taking any photographs. Nothing called to him. No death dreams lately.

Except Selina.

Yes, except that. Just the one time. He didn't like to think about that.

By the time the new pot of coffee was drained, the last cup was bitter and lukewarm. He scowled but drank it anyway.

The Brazilians will love your work.

For some reason, Charlie kept thinking back to this, wondering who the Brazilians might be and why they'd be the right audience in particular for his death shots. Were they a morbid society in general? Did the fact that the pictures followed dreams enchant them for some reason? Or were they just fine connoisseurs of art? He hoped for that, hoped that the people who paid five thousand bucks for a print wanted them because they would appreciate the artistic aspects of the pictures.

Or maybe Janis was just a really good sales person.

That part, he knew, was true. In his gut, he worried that maybe that's all it was, that she could sell crap just by smiling and declaring it good.

Charlie finished the last slug of the nowcold coffee just as the phone rang.

"Hi there." Charlie rarely answered the phone, preferring to let all calls go to voice mail. Nobody ever called him except telemarketers. Any real people phoning were looking for Selina or Becky, so best to let voice mail take care of it.

But, it might be Janis.

"Hello, is that Charles?"

He vaguely recognized the voice but couldn't place it. "Yes, who's this?"

"Charles! So nice to hear you. This is Selina's Aunt Jeannie."

A shiver ran up his back. He had a flash of insight, that she was going to tell him that she had fallen and broken her ankle.

The dream was true.

And that meant the other dreams... the one about him killing Selina

"Charles?"

"Sorry, Jeannie. I've been thinking of "

"That's fine." He could hear the oh so upright tone of her voice, lording over him. He remembered she had once lived in England for ten years or so with her second husband, some Earl or something. "Charles, I wonder if I might speak with Selina."

"I'm afraid she's out at the moment. Can I give her a message?"

"Perhaps. Perhaps you could ask her to phone me. I've got a new number."

"Hang on." He grabbed a pen and paper. "Okay."

"I'm still in L.A., so the area code hasn't changed. 5551980."

Charlie repeated the number and then asked. "Is everything okay, Jeannie? How are you feeling?"

There was a pause at the other end of the line, and Charlie thought that the humming of the phone stretched for hours.

"Just fine, dear. I'll look forward to her call, at her convenience."

He hung up the phone slowly and stared at the phone number.

If Selina calls, she'll find out that the dream came true, he knew.

He crumpled the note and tossed it into the garbage.

Chapter 12

It was finally Valentine's Day. Charlie woke with a thundering hangover; after a few moments, he remembered all the beer from the night before.

He dryswallowed three Extra Strength Tylenols and put a pot of coffee on.

It was a little before six a.m. *At least it's not fucking 4:42,* he thought.

Valentine's Day.

His showing.

"I'll finally get to see the Brazilians," he mumbled. He yawned and rubbed his eyes.

Selina joined him after he had downed three cups of coffee. She snuck in from behind and hugged him. "Your big day," she said. There was obvious pride in her voice. "You must be excited."

"Yeah," he agreed. "It's going to be quite a night."

"Becky wants to come."

Charlie turned around to face her. "Do you think

that's a good idea? I mean, the photos are pretty graphic."

"Just the others. The old ones. We won't let her go to the side rooms where the new pictures are."

"Sure. It'd be nice for her to be there, I guess."

Selina gave him a kiss on the cheek. "I'll be spending most of the day thinking about what to wear."

Charlie laughed. He knew that she wouldn't really think about what to wear until thirty minutes before they left for The Gallery, and whatever she grabbed from the closet would be perfect.

The day dragged on and on. Charlie kept checking the time every half hour, and each time he did so, the clock seemed to move more slowly.

Finally, it was time to head out. He wore a new pair of jeans with a denim shirt. *Can't look too successful,* he thought. *The money won't change the way I dress.*

Selina wore a glitzy light blue dress with a silver necklace. It was Charlie's favorite dress. He stared at her, feeling his love for her shining through.

They drove to The Gallery without much talking. Only Becky seemed to be in a chatty mood, asking questions about The Gallery from the back seat.

"It's going to rain," she said as they drove slowly over the Queensboro Bridge toward Manhattan. "Rain big."

Charlie didn't care about the weather, but he took a peek out his window anyway. "Yeah. Looks like it."

Becky leaned up into the front seat. "How come you

guys aren't happy?"

Selina looked over her shoulder. "Put your seatbelt on."

"We're almost there. Aren't we, Dad?"

"Almost. We're happy. It's just that we haven't done anything like this before. Nervous would be more like it."

He could hear Becky move back and click her seatbelt back on.

There was no parking lot nearby The Gallery. Charlie wasn't surprised when he pulled in to see valet parking. He left the engine running as they all climbed out of the car.

Selina squeezed his hand and smiled. "It's going to be great."

He nodded and took a long breath as they went to the elevator.

Several other people were also waiting. They were chatting about his photos. He wondered if he should introduce himself but remained quiet.

The elevator arrived and took them up three flights to the main entrance.

Selina smiled and squeezed his hand again.

"Ah, there you are!" Janis Kensington called from about twenty feet away and rushed over to them. "You must be Selina."

"Hi."

"Wonderful dress."

Janis gave Charlie a quick hug. "And this is Becky. I'm glad you're here!"

She whispered to Charlie, "Good. Family image is important to the Brazilians. Very religious folks."

Charlie looked around. There were already several dozen people looking at his photos. The back rooms with his death shots weren't open yet.

The main gallery was huge maybe fifty feet in each direction. Floor to ceiling windows adorned the north and south ends. Charlie saw several of his pictures hanging in clusters on the walls and small "trees" scattered randomly around the floor. He wasn't sure if he liked the layout, but Janis was the pro at this. He trusted her.

Across the room, a bar was set up.

"Want anything?" he asked Selina. "I think I could use something to calm my nerves."

"I'll get some wine in a bit. I'm going to walk around with Becky and look at the displays."

"Janis?"

"Not for me. You go ahead. Your work is done, but mine is just starting."

There were three men ahead of him when he reached the bar, and he had a chance to listen to them without them knowing who he was.

"Pretentious shit, if you ask me," the first one said. "Who's going to pay for these?"

"Not these, you know. The good stuff doesn't show for another hour," said the second.

"Yeah," added a sweating fat man with a tie that was swinging around his neck. "It a good thing there's an open bar."

They laughed. Charlie smiled, his heart sinking as their words burned into him.

"Sir?"

He hadn't realized he was alone now, and the

bartender was staring at him. Probably already asked him what he wanted. Shit.

"Scotch. Neat."

"Yes, sir."

Charlie looked around the room while the bartender fixed his drink. There must have been forty people in the room, mostly men, more arriving with each elevator ding. He could hear small giggles coming from one corner, where a woman was pointing at a photo and snickering along with two men.

Fuck.

"Sir, your Glenfiddich."

He looked at the glass and chugged the drink back in one gulp. "Another," he said.

"Of course, sir."

"Double."

Charlie took the second drink back with him to find Selina. She was showing a photo to Becky. It was a scene of the Statue of Liberty taken with a telephoto lens from the top of the Empire State Building. Being above the statue and far away gave Liberty a grace that he hadn't seen in many similar photos.

He remembered the wind blowing fiercely against him as he took the shot. All his photos were his children, and he remembered each of their births.

This one was special. Or so he always thought.

Now, it seemed very... ordinary. He could feel his heart beating as he looked at the picture and felt disgust, felt that all he wanted was to rip the damned thing off the wall and go hide in the bathroom. He knew his cheeks were red, and that wasn't from the Scotch, but rather from knowing he'd humiliated himself.

"It's pretty, Daddy."

He just stared at the picture. Pretentious shit.

"Charlie, are you okay?" Selina put her hand on his shoulder, and he shook himself from his reverie.

"Sure. Fine."

"What's wrong?"

"Just nerves, I guess."

Selina smiled and gave him a hug. "Becky likes this one. Can we get a print for her room?"

His first thought was that his daughter wouldn't have any shit like that on her walls, but he knew that was taking himself a little too seriously.

"Sure, of course." He patted Becky's head. "If that's the one you like, we'll get you a copy."

At eight o'clock, a small spotlight shone in the center of the room, and Charlie saw Janis standing on a small podium.

"Welcome everybody, to a very special showing!" She held her arms out and her charisma flowed. Everybody in the room clapped, and there were a few hoots.

Charlie took a sip of his fifth Scotch. He knew Selina thought it was his third, and he knew her radar was already up about him drinking too much.

How could he not drink too much tonight, though? Six fucking million bucks on the line.

He didn't hear much of Janis' introduction, which was short in any case. After a moment, the doors to the two side rooms swung open dramatically, in synchronization with a Celtic chant starting to play mystically over a couple of hidden loudspeakers.

The crowd split like the Red Sea, half moving to each room, leaving Charlie, Selina, and Becky alone with Janis. At the far end of the room stood the lonely bartender.

Janis laughed. "Do I know how to clear a room?"

Selina pretended to laugh along with her. "That's good, isn't it? They're all in a hurry to look and hopefully buy."

Janis pushed some of her white hair away from her eyes. "Well, not really. This is the official opening, of course, but none of these suckers can afford to buy a print for five thousand bucks. They're all phonies, trying to pretend to be somebodies."

"What?" Charlie stared at her, not sure what that meant. "You mean you won't be able to sell them?"

"Oh, don't worry. They'll all be sold in a week. I promise you, I've got that all under control. But tonight is all about publicity. You'll be in all the papers tomorrow. But buy? Pshh. Like I say, these people are all phonies. Wouldn't know a piece of art if it hit them over the head."

Charlie stared at her like she had just said that her customers all lived on Mars. "They won't buy?"

"No. C'mon, Charlie, think about it."

Think about it? It seemed he couldn't think straight about anything, and he had an urge to run down to the lonely looking bartender. It seemed like he had more in common with him than anybody else tonight.

Already some people were wandering out of the side rooms, talking among themselves, some shaking their heads, some just nodding or laughing.

"Do you think Bill Gates or Paul McCartney would

walk in here tonight if they wanted a print?" asked Janis.

"Paul McCartney?" said Charlie. "Well, no, there'd be security issues and everything. I'm sure you'd find some way to get a print to him without his actually coming here."

"Exactly. Now you understand."

"All the prints?"

"All sold privately. Nobody buys from me in public. That would be so uncouth."

Selina said, "Wow. So, why have The Gallery at all? Why the opening tonight?"

"Just pure publicity. All the work here is just about sold, but the publicity keeps The Gallery name out there in people's minds. My next artist wants that. Same as Charlie benefited from me keeping The Gallery name in everybody's mind from my previous showing. The buyers aren't here tonight, but they'll certainly hear about the night."

The laughter was getting louder, and Charlie felt so much better. Who cares what these clowns think? The real buyers know.

All of a sudden he was proud to have his Liberty photo going on his daughter's wall.

He looked back down to the bar. "Selina, I'm going to the bathroom. Back in a bit."

After another drink and a trip to the men's room, Charlie felt the alcohol. His head was warm and his thoughts swum around in his mind.

Paul McCartney might buy one of my prints. Of

course Janis didn't actually say that; he was just an example. But, maybe not. Maybe he'd bought a death print. Maybe more than one.

Six million bucks.

And free Glenfiddich. What more could you want?

He laughed as he tried to melt some ice in the urinal. His aim wasn't very good tonight, but it didn't matter. He balanced his glass on top and tried to focus on the chalk board in front of him. Fuck the ice.

Shit shots, someone had written. He erased it.

He walked carefully back to Selina.

"I just had a funny call on my cell," she said.

"Funny how?"

He looked around for Becky. She was a few pictures away, looking at a photo of the New York Stock Exchange. *Shit shot, surely not.* He couldn't help but smile at the inadvertent rhyme.

"From my Aunt Jeannie."

Charlie focused back to Selina. "Jeannie?"

"She said she called the other day. Did you talk to her?"

He shrugged. "Sorry, I thought I told you she called."

"Anyhow, she got my cell number from Mom."

"And how is dear old Jeannie?" He took a sip. Just a sip.

Selina's eyes caught his, deep pools. Something was wrong.

"She fell and broke her ankle."

"Fell?"

"Just like your dream."

Chapter 13

THE SHOWING CLOSED AT ten o'clock. Quick in and out, back to the real world. Charlie remembered wondering why The Gallery didn't stay open later, but now it all made sense. Nobody here was really a potential customer, so why stay open till the wee hours?

He saw Janis stifling a yawn as she helped to shepherd the lookyloos out. A quick peek down the other end of the room showed the bar to be closed up. *Okay, I probably had enough anyway. Maybe too much.*

Becky was sitting on one of the chairs huddled in one corner. The lonely chairs reminded Charlie of a group of teenage girls at a school dance, huddling together, wondering if any boys would ask them to dance.

He walked over and took Becky's hand. "Time to go, kiddo."

She nodded. "I'm pretty tired. That was fun,

Daddy."

They met Selina by the door, who also looked a bit run down. Just for a moment a thought flashed through his mind.

She looks sick.

His thought dissipated when Becky asked, "Daddy, can I sleep in the car?"

"Sure thing. We'll be home in no time."

They said their final goodbyes to Janis, and each of them gave her a cordial hug. Selina pulled the front door open. "Damn. It's raining."

The rain drizzled down, not a torrent like they sometimes got on Long Island, more like a lazy shower, as if the clouds were as tired as they were.

"I'll bring the car around."

"Charlie, are you okay to drive?"

A rush of anger welled inside him. He wanted to say, *Of course I'm fucking okay to drive. Get off my back.*

The anger quickly left him. He knew she was right to ask. He had at least six scotches tonight. Maybe one or two more, but that was all. And none for a while.

"Sure, don't worry. I didn't have that much. Just enough to take the edge off."

She didn't look convinced, but he knew he wasn't slurring his words or anything. He was fine.

Charlie waved off the valet, saying he wanted to pick up his own car and then ran down to the parking lot half a block away. He was soaked by the time he got inside. The windshield was clouded up, so he turned the defogger on full blast for a minute until he could see better.

The wet streets seemed darker than black as he pulled the car out, the headlights shining to little purpose as the beams were sucked into the tarmac, providing little illumination for him.

Selina and Becky climbed in quickly, avoiding most of the rain.

He could almost see the stream of rain swaying back and forth in a mystical dance as the lights from the marquee helped him see his way off. Pretty, he thought. He heard Selina click her seatbelt.

"I sure hope the bridge isn't too bad," she said.

"Not this time of night. Too late for the hardcore businessmen, too early for the real partiers."

"Becky, you lay down. We'll be at least an hour getting home."

No answer. It seemed like she's already followed through on her plan to sleep.

The only sound was the constant flapflap of the windshield wipers and the small whooshing sound of the defogger.

Sometimes, he knew that he and Selina could sit for a long time without needing to talk. Just being together with their own thoughts was enough. Tonight didn't seem to be one of those nights. He wanted to hear her voice. He reached over and held her hand.

"What'd you think?"

"It was good to see your work displayed so nicely," she said. "I really liked how they kept your new ones isolated."

"Yeah. I think Janis put on a nice show. I wish we had a chance to meet some of the real customers, though."

He felt her slight shrug. Felt it like longmarried people can feel every move the other makes, even if they're nowhere nearby.

"It must have cost her a lot."

"Not in the scheme of things. She's getting millions in commissions."

"Yeah, but still..."

"Damn rain."

They drove south down Second Avenue and pulled into the lane directing them to the Queensboro Bridge. At the last minute, Charlie swerved to pull back from another car who slipped in on his right. "Fuck!"

"Charlie! Becky is here."

"Damn asshole cut me off."

"I know, I know." She patted his knee. "It's okay, we'll get there. Just take it easy."

He turned to her. "What? What do you mean."

"I just mean that we're not in a big rush. It's hard to see, and you should be careful, that's all."

Suddenly, Selina lurched forward and grabbed her midsection, a small painful "Oomph" coming from her. "Selina? What is it? Are you ?" He thought back to the fleeting thought of her being sick. "Are you okay?"

"LOOK OUT!" she screamed. He turned back to the front and saw a truck pulling in front of him.

Acting on reflex alone, he pulled the wheel hard to the right. *Going too fast.*

The car bounced off a median, and he pulled back hard to the left to compensate, knowing as he did so that it was the wrong thing to do.

And then they were in midair. He knew they must have crashed through the safety barrier somehow. His scream joined Selina's.

They hit with a massive explosion, the car landing in the East River. Charlie banged his head and had trouble seeing.

Ohmygod, ohmygod, ohmygod.

All around him was black, cold, inky water. He felt a piece of shattered glass in his eye.

Water rushed inside, a torrent sinking the car faster.

He finally reacted, freeing himself from his seat belt.

Selina was unconscious beside him.

Becky. No sounds came from the back seat.

The water was getting higher, flooding the car. Only a few inches of air remained. He shook Selina but got no response. She was totally under water.

No time.

He reached behind him and pulled, surprised that Becky's body swam over the seat. *No seat belt, kiddo.*

The entire car was filled with water. He couldn't breathe. Couldn't hear.

Couldn't see Selina. Couldn't find her seatbelt clip.

My darling, he thought.

He pushed Becky out the shattered driver's window, pushed her and grabbed onto her ankle. She still wasn't moving on her own.

His lungs were bursting with pain, and it was all he could do to not swallow the river. He didn't know which way was up.

Eventually, he did swallow, and soon all he could feel was the cold, the lovely cold, and the darkness calling to him.

Chapter 14

SIX MONTHS PASSED.

The flakes of drifting snow disappeared, replaced by misty fog, spring showers, and now a summer drought. Charlie passed his forty-first birthday, unnoticed even by himself.

He woke up and stared at the ceiling, tears leaking from his eyes, thinking of Selina again.

When he'd pushed Becky through the car window, he tried to turn back and find Selina, but he couldn't save them both. It was a split second decision, and then even that decision was taken from him as the water rushed into his lungs.

Eighteen hours later, he'd woken in the hospital. He found out he'd been saved by several people jumping into the frigid water when the car crashed through the barrier.

Somehow, he fought to lift himself and Becky to the surface, and it was only once they broke into the night sky that he passed out.

Charlie couldn't remember any details. He just remembered abandoning Selina.

Her funeral was three days later.

Lots of people came. Friends, relatives, business associates. He was surprised how many he didn't recognize. They said all the things that people say at funerals.

"Let me know if there's anything I can do."

"Selina would have wanted you to save Becky instead of herself."

"She's in a better place now."

"She was so young."

"It's God's will. It's not our place to question Him."

Pats on his back. Casseroles delivered to his home. Letters. Sympathy cards.

He hated it all. What was he supposed to say in return? "Oh, yes, she's in a better fucking place. Yes, of course she would have saved Becky first; that's what parents do who love their kids. What can you do? Bring me back my wife from her grave."

But, he smiled when he had to, thanked when he was able to, and quietly stayed away from as many people as he could.

He wanted to hide from the world, but of course he couldn't. He had to take care of Becky.

Charlie yawned and stared at the ceiling. He could see a small crack in the paint. He stared at that crack every morning, as if it symbolized his life.

Cracked.

He wiped the tears away with a blanket, trying not to concentrate on Selina, even though he wasn't succeeding. Six months, and he missed her more than ever.

Missed her especially since he knew he'd killed her. His weapon of choice wasn't the gun in his dream, but the Scotch was just as deadly.

Since that night, he hadn't touched a drop of alcohol.

Why couldn't I have done that a day earlier? He asked himself the same rhetorical question he always asked, and still received silence back in reply.

He pulled himself up and felt the morning complaints from his body. Ever since the accident, his back hurt, his knees crumpled if he crouched a bit, he had non-stop headaches, and even his fingers seemed to tingle constantly, a reminder to him that he changed that night, never to go back to the way he used to be.

The doctors couldn't find anything physically wrong with him, but he felt the pain and numbness in his body all the time.

He skipped breakfast again, knew he'd likely pass on lunch, too. Since the accident, he'd lost fifteen pounds and never did eat any of the casseroles that Selina's wellmeaning friends brought him.

The car ride took fiftyseven minutes. A two-hour round trip visit that he'd made every day since the accident.

He parked in his usual space, near the middle of the row of spots lined behind the Baxter Clinic. Becky's home.

"Morning, Mr. Parkinson." The receptionist smiled at him, as she did every day.

"Good morning, Sandy." He scribbled his name on the signin sheet and looked at her. Drab gray hair dangling loosely around her chubby face. He thought she was in her sixties, but who knew? Maybe she just seemed a lot older than she really was. God knew that these days, he certainly looked older than he was.

"Nothing new," she said without him asking. It was the same ritual every day. He always felt a tiny spark of hope on the way to the hospital, that maybe today something would be different. It never was.

He nodded and walked down the quiet hallway. Becky's room was at the far end. Room 442. He finally knew why he always woke at that time. It was another message that came true.

On a whim, he stopped at the coffee machine on the way and dropped some change in, picking up a terrible imitation of a cup of coffee.

He took a sip and walked into her room. The door was propped open as always. The only sounds were the beeping of the machines surrounding Becky.

The machines keeping her alive.

Charlie sat beside her and put his coffee on the dresser.

Becky was lying on her right side, facing him. "Hey, kiddo. I'm here."

Her eyes stared at him as they always did. Well, not really at him, but in his general direction. They were Selina's eyes—warm and inviting.

"It's getting hot outside. Too hot. You wouldn't like it..." He stopped himself, knowing she'd like the hot sticky summer heat a lot better than being imprisoned here, even with air conditioning.

He picked up her hand. It was limp and didn't respond to him at all. He didn't have much to say to her today. Nothing much new ever happened to him any more. His days were wasting away, just like hers. The only difference was that he had a choice about his.

"Your Great Aunt Jeannie called last night. That was nice of her. She just wanted me to say hi to you. I told her I would."

Beep, beep, beep.

He patted Becky's hair, smoothing out the few odd strands that were falling over her eyes.

"Maybe we should get you a trim?" he asked. He smiled, wondering if she would like that.

Like that? he asked himself. *Why do I keep on doing that? She can't like anything any more.*

He thought back as he did every day to the first conversation with Becky's neurologist, Dr. Spencer. It was just after she was admitted. "Your daughter is brain dead, Mr. Parkinson." No leading up to the bad news slowly. He just blurted it out. He looked irritated, but Charlie knew that was silly. It was just a reflection of his own irritation. He knew what Spencer was going to say, knew it as surely as he knew about the plane smashing into the water eight months ago.

He knew because he had dreamed it. The night before Spencer told him, Charlie knew she'd end up in Room 442, knew he'd be sitting here holding her hand every day for the rest of his life.

Dreams don't lie. Not to him.

Even so, he had wanted hope. "Isn't there anything we can do?"

Spencer shook his head. "I'm sorry. If you look at her EEG, it's just flat. There's nothing there. Without the machines, she'd..."

Charlie nodded. "She might know I'm here. She needs me."

"You should think about... her future."

Charlie didn't know at first what he was referring to. "You want to pull the plug?"

Just for a moment, Spencer looked uncomfortable. "Of course, I can't recommend that. It would have to be your decision."

"I can't do that."

Spencer gave him some forms to sign and then left. He had broached the subject a couple of times lightly since then, but Charlie was firm. He could never kill his daughter.

He took a sip of the coffee, now cold and just as awful as he knew it would be.

"Kiddo? Can you hear me?"

Beep, beep, beep.

Charlie shrugged and pulled back the blue cover that was on top of Becky. He moved her so she was lying on her back and then lowered the side of the bed that was between them.

He took the near leg and started to exercise it. He lifted up at her knee and pushed her leg in, getting the circulation going and trying to help her muscles stay active and not atrophy, just as the nurses had instructed him.

"Mom would be proud of you. You're doing really well."

After a few minutes, he moved to her other leg, and then her arms. Every day, he did the same cycle, spending an hour moving her limbs, keeping them ready for the day they'd be used again.

Most of the time he spent with her, he was quiet, not having anything new to tell her, so he was glad that Dr. Spencer agreed to him doing a little bit of physical therapy on her. It gave him something to do with her, so the visits didn't stretch out into eternity.

After the hour of exercise, he placed her back on her side, just as he found her.

"Bye, kiddo. See you tomorrow."

Chapter 15

For probably the twentieth time since Selina had died, Jamie took her will from his fireproof safe in the back room of his office.

The will was short and to the point.

But, even after six months, he was still undecided what to do with it.

It didn't make sense. Especially now. Jamie knew Becky's condition as well as anybody, since he was her doctor as well as Selina's.

Persistent Vegetative State. She was brain dead and would never wake. Never.

Jamie had dropped by the clinic that morning. Becky was still the beautiful young girl he remembered, but there was no sense of life in her. There never would be.

She deserved better, but he couldn't provide it.

Charlie wanted her kept alive, even though Jamie had tried to explain to him that there was no point.

Jamie crossed himself. He valued his Catholic beliefs, but sometimes, his medical training told him to go against doctrine. This was one of those times.

He placed the will on the top of his desk and read it one more time.

I, Selina Maria Parkinson, am of sound mind, but perhaps not of sound body. I am dying of cancer. But, right now, I am thinking clearly. This is my final set of wishes.

First, all the assets I share with my husband, Charlie, should go to him. I have nothing but complete love for him, and I know he's always loved me, too, even if he couldn't always show that.

Second, as much as I love Charlie, I know that he is often selfabsorbed, and he thinks little of others, even those he cares about. Because of that, I want my daughter, Becky, to be cared for by a relative. My Aunt Jeannie would be best. Becky will be better off, and so will Charlie.

This is a hard decision to make, and I hope Charlie will forgive me for it, but this is what I want for my daughter.

Jamie imagined Selina writing the will, knowing it would be secret until after she died, expecting Jamie to act on it and have Becky declared a ward of the court.

"Lina, you know I can't." He folded the paper in thirds and put it back in the safe. No lawyer in the world would let that will hold up in court. It was signed but not witnessed, but more importantly, no court would take Becky from her father for no reason.

"You were further gone than I knew..."

But, even after he locked the safe, the will nagged at him. Selina never imagined Becky being kept alive by equipment that breathed for her and fed her. If he could use the will to gain control of Becky's future, even for five minutes, maybe he could give her the release she deserved.

Maybe.

Chapter 16

A MONTH PASSED.

"Becky?"

Darkness spilled around the hospital room, which was already haunted with depressing thoughts. Charlie held his daughter's hand and squeezed, knowing he'd receive no reaction back.

Tonight, her eyes were open wide. If he turned his head away from her, he *thought* her eyes might twitch a little bit, wanting to follow him.

"Just my imagination, isn't it, kiddo?"

The hospital was a lot quieter than it was during his daytime visits, but once in a while he wanted to see her at other times of day. Just in case he saw something different.

He never did.

He leaned over and kissed her cheek, felt her warm skin against his lips.

You're still alive, he thought. *I know you're in there.*

He stared at her, his eyes only a few inches from hers, silently imploring her to notice him, call his name, hug him. He thought he saw his own reflection in her large brown eyes.

He grimaced, hating himself for it. *She's not dead!*

But that wasn't Doctor Spencer's view. He'd caught Charlie as he walked to Becky's room. "Mr. Parkinson," he said in his most businesslike tone. "We need to have a chat. Catch up on Becky's progress."

Charlie knew where the conversation would be going, even before they slipped into Dr. Spencer's small office.

Spencer smiled. "It's very hard on you, I know."

Charlie concentrated on not crying. Not in front of him. "Of course it's hard," he finally said.

"We continue to do our weekly tests, but as you know, nothing ever changes. And it never will."

"It might. I can't give up on her."

"Of course not. But, you need to realize you're not doing her any favors. That's not your daughter in that bed. Becky is "

He didn't finish the sentence.

Charlie stood. "I know what you think."

"You need to release her. And yourself."

Charlie slammed his fist on Spencer's desk and leaned over. "I need to fucking take care of her."

Spencer held his hands up involuntarily to protect himself. "No need for that, Mr. Parkinson. No need at all. Of course, the final decision is up to you."

Charlie pulled himself back and took a deep breath of stale hospital air. He didn't say anything else, just slowly walked out of the office and down to Room 442.

As he looked down at her pretty little face, though, Charlie knew that Dr. Spencer's constant message was having an effect. He hated it, but when he was tired, like tonight, he could feel his hope seep out and leave him with a feeling of pure loss. In front of him was only a dead corpse, just like Selina had been. Dead and rotting.

Except for the machines that kept pushing oxygen through her lungs. Not quite rotting, but dead all the same.

"No!" He leaned over and held Becky to him, choking with tears. "I'm so sorry, kiddo. God, all I want is to take that night back."

He cried and cried, held her to him, praying for her to give him one small hug back.

It didn't happen.

After a few minutes, he collected himself and arranged her carefully back in the middle of her bed. He used a Kleenex to wipe his own tears off her cheeks.

Her eyes stared at him.

"It was hot again today," he said quietly. "I wish we had air conditioning sometimes."

An hour later, he left, and he was sure he could feel Becky's eyes following him out the door.

Chapter 17

CHARLIE'S HEAD HURT. He blinked his eyes open and stared at the ceiling of his bedroom. Something didn't look right.

His back hurt. Not as much as his head, but

"Floor," he mumbled, as he realized where he was.

He pushed himself up into a sitting position, grabbing onto the side of his bed to steady himself.

Beside him, a nearempty bottle of Scotch lay on the floor, a wet stain surrounding it.

The bottle looked like an alien, something that didn't belong in his home anymore.

Finding his way slowly to the bathroom, he fished around in the medicine cabinet and eventually found some Extra Strength Tylenol. He dryswallowed three of them.

His face in the mirror surprised him. He leaned on the sink and looked at his reflection. His face had grown several deep wrinkles that crawled across his forehead, and his eyes were spidered with red lines.

"You miserable fuck," he said to himself. "Damn good thing she isn't around to see you like this."

Charlie splashed water on his face and tossed his head back. He hadn't trimmed his long gray hair since the funeral, and now the rubber band holding it was needed to keep it from flopping around; before it was for style.

"Fuck style. Fuck the world."

He went back to the bedroom and picked up the Scotch. There was only about an inch left, but he wasn't sure how much had drained onto the floor. Somehow, he knew most of it was inside him, though. Along with a few beers that he had on the way home from the hospital.

He remembered seeing the bar on the way, just off the Long Island Expressway. It was a rundown joint, with only half of the neon sign shining:

ille B

He pulled off the road at the next exit and found his way back. Even as he was doing it, he knew it was stupid. Throwing away his success at being sober on a whim. And he knew that he'd be driving home after drinking. *Some people never seem to learn*, he knew.

But, sometimes the nights just seemed so long. So lonely.

Miller's Bar was nearly empty. The bartender was a young kid, probably working his way through college. Only a few other people were there, crowded at one end of the bar. They seemed to be playing some kind of game on paper.

He ordered a beer, felt it go down real smooth. *God,*

that's good.

The second beer arrived within five minutes. And then he stopped counting.

Charlie took a fourth Tylenol for good measure. He poured the last of the Scotch down the sink and put a pot of coffee on.

The phone rang.

Damn.

The phone was never good news any more. He had cast aside all his friends, and so the only people who called were from the hospital.

He glanced at the wall clock. Almost noon.

"Hello." He tried to sound calm.

"Charlie!"

At first he couldn't place the voice. Female, bright, and bubbly. Then it came to him.

"Janis? Is that you?"

"Of course it's me." There was an awkward pause, Charlie not knowing what to say. Finally, Janis continued. "I have your last royalty check here, for the last two hundred thousand. I was going to pop it in the mail, but I thought I should give you a call."

"That's kind of you."

"I never phoned after the accident. It was a bit awkward under the circumstances."

"Sure. You can just drop the check in the mail. That'd be fine."

"How are you doing, Charlie?"

He felt himself getting angry. How was he doing? He was fucking well doing absolutely shitty. Most days he sat around wallowing in misery and selfpity, waiting to spend an hour with his veggie daughter, and that just made things worse. And last night, well, just maybe he had tried to kill himself.

"I'm fine," he said.

"I knew it would be hard for you to get past things, but "

"But?"

"Have you done any more shots?"

The word meant nothing to him. Shots? Then, he realized she meant more of his death shots. The thought of picking up a camera hadn't occurred to him since

"No. I don't think I'll be doing that any more."

"You should think about it. The Japanese were very pleased with the first set. They'd like more."

The whole idea of photography seemed to belong to another person, not him. If it wasn't for the damned showing at The Gallery, Selina would be beside him right now.

"Ain't gonna happen."

"Well, maybe later. I'll keep in touch." Her voice was more curt, and he knew that he had offended her. "I'll get the check out right away by courier."

He hung up the phone before she could say goodbye.

Chapter 18

ANOTHER WEEK PASSED. Charlie stayed away from alcohol, but he thought about it a lot.

One Friday night, he looked through his bedroom window and saw a full moon hanging in the sky. It was a burnt orange color, which looked odd. The photographer in him wanted to grab his Nikon and shoot it, but there would be no context. The moon was too high to get a decent shot with any landscape that would highlight it.

He shrugged the thought aside. There were more important things to worry about.

Like the fact that he was standing at the window with no memory of getting out of bed.

Except for the dream.

He leaned on the sill and stared through the glass, trying to remember it.

Becky.

She was in her hospital bed, but she smiled when

he entered her room. "Dad!" Her eyes shone and her voice sounded slightly higher than it did in real life. Or was it? Was his memory fading of what she really sounded like? And was that her real smile? Slightly upturned lips, a couple of teeth poking through? He hated that the small details of her life were dissolving from his memory. What would he forget next?

"It's time, kiddo."

"Time? Time to go home?"

"Time to free you."

He replayed the dream in his mind, horrified, knowing what was going to happen. He must have gotten out of his bed, dramatizing the play in his bedroom as if she were there, her bed just snuggled up against the window.

He closed his eyes and continued his memories.

"I don't understand, Daddy. Where's Mom?"

"You'll be with her soon."

And then he remembered reaching out, grabbing her neck in his hands and squeezing the life out of her. "It's for the best," he whispered. "You have no life right now. Doctor Spencer is right. You need to be released."

She tried to scream, but nothing came out. He could feel the small bones in her neck shift and crumble beneath his viselike hands. He put every ounce of strength he had into killing his daughter.

Her eyes bulged out. She fought, trying to fend him off, but after being bedridden for so long, she had no ability to do anything. Her feeble efforts soon died.

It only took a minute. Her eyes seemed to glaze over and stare blankly up at him.

Now, he could see the horror in his face, reflected

back by the window. His heart was beating fast enough that he could feel it.

Charlie shook his head. "I could never do that. Never could do that, kiddo. You know I love you. I'll take care of you forever."

Two hours later, Charlie had finally gotten back to sleep when the door bell rang. He blinked at the clock.

4:42 a.m.

"What the hell?" He saw flashing red lights diffusing up from outside his window, and just for a moment, he knew that the lights were exactly the same as the lights in his first death dream. The lights on the police car that had barreled down into the Long Island Sound. A sense of déjà vu grabbed him and wouldn't let go.

The doorbell rang insistently, and he could hear talking outside.

Something's wrong.

He grabbed his housecoat and ran to the door.

Two cops stood there.

The one in front said, "Charles Parkinson?"

"Yes. What's going on."

"Mr. Parkinson, I'm sorry, but we have some bad news." The cop took off his hat and held it in front of him. "I'm afraid your daughter..."

"Becky? What about her?" Charlie almost screamed at the cop.

"She's dead, sir. She was murdered earlier tonight."

Charlie felt dizzy. "No. That can't be right."

"I am sorry, sir."

"How?" But, he knew.

"She was strangled. We don't really know how it happened or who was responsible. So far we have no witnesses or anything. The crime scene technicians are only now starting to work."

Charlie stumbled to the couch, not believing what he was hearing. The two cops followed him in. "We'll catch the killer, sir. That bastard will be brought to justice."

Charlie silently flexed his hands.

Chapter 19

A MONTH LATER, CHARLIE and Tom met in a small Italian restaurant in midtown, a couple of blocks west of Times Square. There were only about a dozen tables in the place, each with a red gingham tablecloth, stubby off-white candles that remained unlit, and cheap silverware.

No tourists ever went to La Boheme, because it just wasn't splashy. They would glance in the front door, turn around and walk away. That's exactly how the owner liked it.

Tom ate there three times each week, and Charlie had joined him a couple of times. Normally he loved it; the restaurant served the best pasta in midtown. Silly tourists.

Today was different, though. It was hard to face Tom, hard to be forced to deal with the dreams. Hard to talk about how he had killed both his wife and his daughter due to the dreams.

Well, at least Becky, he told himself. *Selina wasn't*

killed by a dream exactly.

Tom slurped down a large fork of Spaghetti Bolognese and wiped his napkin through his beard. "We should do more tests," he said.

"I can't believe you're saying that. What about killing my fucking daughter? Was that just my imagination?"

"Charlie, that wasn't you. The cops'll find out what happened eventually. You can't blame yourself for a dream. Maybe subconsciously, you agree she needed to be released. Everyone understands that."

"I know I didn't do anything. I just dreamed about it. And that made it true."

Tom nodded and took another bite of spaghetti. Charlie picked at his rotini but didn't really eat much. "We can tape your night this time. That way, neither of us has to rely on our own subjective experiences."

The waiter came by right then. "Another glass of wine, gentlemen?"

Charlie shook his head. Tom nodded for one more.

"Shit, Tom, I just don't know what to do."

"Your dreams can't predict the future. I still insist on reminding you of that."

Clarity came to Charlie and he looked into Tom's eyes for the first time. "I've got it," he said quietly. "The dreams don't predict the future."

"See?"

"No. They don't predict it. They *cause* the future."

"I don't grasp the difference."

"That very first death shot. The dream wasn't predicting that the plane was going to crash into the Sound. If I hadn't dreamed it, the plane would have been fine, but once I had the dream, the plane was destined to crash. My dream killed that pilot."

The waiter replaced Tom's glass of wine. "Is there anything else I can bring you gentlemen right now?"

Tom waived him away. "You're nuts."

"Is that your clinical opinion?"

"C'mon, that's even weirder than believing that your dreams can predict what's going to happen."

"It's the only thing that makes any sense. You know I'm acting out my dreams, but you didn't carry it one step further. I'm acting out my nightmares. And, they're coming true."

A half hour later, Tom and Charlie were back on Broadway, heading toward Times Square. Charlie would catch a subway north to where he parked his car, while Tom would head south, back to his university clinic.

As soon as they left the restaurant, they could hear the noise of thousands of tourists milling around. Not for the first time, Charlie was thankful he rarely had to come to this part of Manhattan.

"They all sound so happy," he said.

"They're on holiday. Of course they're happy. They're living their dreams." Tom barked a laugh at that. "Different kinds of dreams from yours."

Even Charlie smiled. Then he suddenly stopped walking and just stared for a minute. Somebody behind him cursed and quickly raced around him.

"Tom?"

Tom had moved ahead, not realizing Charlie had

stopped. He came back to him. "What is it?"

"You gave me an idea. Those tourists have *great* dreams. Why can't I have great dreams too? Real dreams, I mean. Make some good happen instead of all the horrible things that I've caused."

Tom put his hands on Charlie's shoulders and stared in his eyes. "You've really got to understand. This isn't what's happening."

Charlie didn't answer. He just blinked. "Selina. I could dream about Selina."

Then he started walking away from Tom, rushing to the subway station.

Chapter 20

Two weeks later, Charlie did dream of Selina.

Before sleeping, he searched the house for old photo albums. He wanted to see every picture of her that he ever took, and he took a lot, since she was often the foreground subject in his photographs when he wanted to show the scale of a background composition.

She never failed to give him that blazing smile in each shot. Somehow, he never appreciated it as much as he did now.

He kept himself awake until after 1:00 a.m., making sure he immersed himself in good thoughts of her. He memorized her bronze skin color, the exact length of her hair, the tiny specs of silver shining in her dark brown eyes.

Her laughter and constant smile.

Selina cozied up on the couch sleeping with that same smile, a book dangling from her fingers.

Selina standing in front of the ferry leading to Ellis Island, holding her arms out like a game show host presenting a new car to a winning contestant.

Selina hugging an orange tabby kitten at a local pet store.

Selina holding Becky when she was a baby.

Charlie frowned when he saw that one and put it away. One step at a time.

By bedtime, the living room floor was covered with small paper images of Selina, her loving smile staring up at him from all parts of the room.

As he fell asleep, he remembered how it felt to hold her in his arms, to kiss her, to make love with her. Even though almost a year had passed since her death

(her murder)

he could remember every detail of how she felt, how her hands would caress him, how much he truly missed her now.

And he did dream of her.

Pleasant dreams, exactly what he was hoping for.

He woke at 4:42 a.m.

Lingering memories of his dream held onto him, and he basked in the mental haze. He and Selina were getting married again, renewing their vows on their twenty-fifth anniversary. That would be years in the future, but he liked the thought.

They didn't have a traditional wedding this time but rather hired a minister to come to their home. The reception started in the middle of the afternoon, with fifty or so guests, and after a couple of hours of fun, they held the wedding ceremony and revowed to each other.

Selina wore a cream-colored dress with a small veil hanging gracefully from her hair. Charlie wore a tuxedo, and he smiled at that after waking, since he'd never worn one in real life. One day, this dream would come true as well. He knew it would.

His eyes snapped open and he looked at the clock. It ticked away quietly, but he saw the time just before it flipped over to 4:43.

"Selina?"

Part of him didn't expect an answer, but he knew that part of him really did. He didn't get what he wanted. The house remained silent, and the space beside him on the bed was empty.

He rubbed his eyes, feeling sorry for himself.

Coffee, he thought. *Need coffee.*

Charlie shuffled into the kitchen and pulled out the tin of Starbucks that he kept on the shelf above the sink. He was in the middle of the third scoop when he heard her.

"Charlie?"

He froze. Listened. Surely it was his imagination.

"Charlie?"

No, it was real.

He walked to the living room. He knew her voice. His heart pounded as he walked, and he had trouble catching his breath.

Selina was on the couch, just waking. She was in the same position as one photograph he looked at last night. Her hand even dangled as if she were holding a book.

"My God. Selina!"

He ran to her and held her to him. She called his name again.

This can't be real, he thought. *But it is.*

"It worked," he said as he cried into her hair. "You're back."

He could feel her nodding into his shoulder.

Charlie finally pulled back and stared at her face. Her beautiful face. Every bit of her was exactly the same. He kissed her even while crying.

Finally he pulled away and said, "I've missed you so much."

It was then that he noticed her expression. She wasn't smiling. Her eyes had a pleading look, and she said, "It hurts so much."

"What? What hurts? Where?"

She didn't answer at first, just stared at him. Tears ran down her face.

"You should have left me."

He shook his head. "No."

"How long?"

"Don't worry about that. All that matters is that you're back."

"How fucking long, Charlie?" She choked out the question.

"About a year."

She nodded. "That's why it's so much worse." She shook her head as more tears fell down her cheeks. "I had cancer. And now, it's so much worse. I don't know if I can stand the pain..."

"Cancer? How could you?"

"Where's Becky?

"Becky?" He felt numb, not knowing what to say.

"I want to see her."

Charlie shook his head. Selina tried to move from the couch, but he held her in place. "Becky's dead."

Selina looked at him and then passed out.

Chapter 21

SELINA WAS HOOKED UP to an IV and two other tubes that Charlie didn't know the purpose of. She groaned in her sleep, and in her rare lucid moments, she looked up at Charlie, and all he could read in her face was hatred. Hatred for bringing her back, but more for having killed Becky. He never had a chance to explain what happened, and he knew Selina probably figured Becky died in the car accident.

Just as well. The truth was worse.

Charlie had called 9-1-1 when Selina fainted in the house. He could see dark red and purple welts covering her body, and he had no idea what they were.

Well, that wasn't completely true. She'd told him, hadn't she? Cancer.

The doctors in the emergency room checked her out immediately, no waiting for her today. Charlie told them Selina had cancer, even though that sounded silly. How could such a slow disease be an emergency? He saw the same thoughts written on the interns' faces.

They soon believed him, and gave her a large shot of Demerol to help with the pain.

Now, the IV kept her pain at a manageable level, but it also kept her unconscious most of the time.

"Why did you bring me back to suffer like this?" she mumbled. Her voice was slurred, and he could barely understand her.

Charlie took her hand and squeezed it gently. "I didn't know," he said. "Why didn't you tell me?"

"Why didn't you notice?" she asked.

He didn't have an answer to that. Actually he did. He knew that he didn't notice because that's just the kind of person he was. Selfish. Only noticed things that directly affected him.

He didn't answer.

"It hurts so much more than drowning. So much more."

Part of him wondered why Doctor McKay didn't say anything about Selina having drowned the year before. He was the physician who declared her dead, but obviously the dream had erased all that. All he ever said was that he hadn't seen Selina in some time. It was obvious McKay knew about Selina's cancer.

He wondered what was in the coffin that was buried in Forest Hill Cemetery.

Even when Selina was asleep, tears seeped out of her eyes. "You can't know how much it hurts," she said. This was the most she had talked since being admitted.

She could barely breathe. Her lips were cracked and dry, as if her life were being sucked out one second at a time. She always cried from the agony.

He wanted to tell her about Becky, how he had saved her from drowning only to have her end up in a vegetative state that was worse than death. He couldn't find the words.

Doctor McKay told him there was nothing they could do other than palliative care, to try to minimize the pain. She might last a day or a month. Maybe longer. Selina had always been strong. There was no way to tell.

A month. Maybe more.

He leaned over and hugged his wife. "I love you," he whispered to her. "I'm so sorry."

He hoped to hear her say, "I love you, too," but all he could hear was her harsh and uneven breathing. He pulled back and saw that she was unconscious.

He folded her hands across her stomach, placing his own hand on top of hers.

"I love you," he said again, his voice choking. "All I wanted was for us to be together again."

He stayed with her for another hour, but she continued to sleep, occasional groans escaping her lips.

Chapter 22

CHARLIE HAD ALWAYS LOVED living on Long Island.

Selina, too, he knew. He loved being so close to the city and at the same time being away from it. Close to everything he wanted to photograph, but far enough away to not feel locked into skyscraper city.

He loved the house he'd shared with Selina and Becky. The view down from the back deck to the Sound. The trees below that swayed in the wind.

The sounds of Selina cooking dinner. The laughter when Becky screamed at the stupid people on those silly game shows she watched.

But now it was all an empty shell.

He pulled his Mazda into the driveway and locked it.

Selina hadn't regained consciousness while he was at the hospital, and since she rarely seemed to wake during the night time, he left to go back to their home.

The house was silent, not offering the slightest

welcoming sound to him after he locked the door.

Even the house seemed to find him guilty.

He went down to the dark room in the basement, looking for a picture he had hanging from the ceiling lines.

All of a sudden, a rage rushed through him. He could feel the anger burst from him after hiding it for the past few days, since he had brought Selina back from the dead.

"Fuck!" he screamed. "Why did it have to be like this?"

He grabbed a three-foot-long board that was balanced on top of some bricks. Together they formed a small bench that he once used to store chemicals.

He swung the board around, crashing it down on several bottles of fluids. The smashing felt good to him, and he did it again, and again.

His cameras next. He threw them with all his power into the brick walls, each falling lifeless to the floor.

"I want my fucking life back!"

He started with his fists next, smashing all his developing equipment. One by one, each of his precious items were broken, smashed, and left as so much rubbish.

He ripped all the pictures hanging on the ceiling lines in half, littering the floor with bits of crumpled memories.

All but the one picture he had located earlier.

The basement was a disaster, and finally he felt his anger dissipate. He felt empty, a worthless shell of a man.

"Selina," he said. "I just wanted to be with you."

He slowly crunched his way through the ruins to the stairs and climbed back to the main floor, not bothering to either close the door or to turn off the basement lights.

He went to the living room couch and lay down in the same place that Selina had come back. He imagined he could feel where her body had pressed down, could smell a whiff of her lingering scent.

Only a small light shone in the kitchen; where he rested was near dark. It took a moment for his eyes to adjust, and then he stared at the picture he saved.

Fifteen years had passed since their wedding day. The original, real wedding, not the retaking of their vows that would now never happen.

Selina wore a long white, beautiful dress, with a long train that hung back behind her in the picture. Her face didn't look all that much younger than it did now; she just didn't age very much.

"So beautiful," he said.

In the picture, he wore a nice dark blue suit. Not a tuxedo, but as nice a suit as he had ever worn. He was pretty sure that the suit still hung in a closet somewhere. He had never had a chance to wear it again. In the back of his mind, he had sometimes imagined wearing it at Becky's wedding.

He wore his silver hair trimmed, shorter than normal, and he could see a small stud in one ear. The hole had grown over years ago.

In the picture, he was grinning from ear to ear. This was the only picture of him he knew of where he was smiling. He just wasn't a big smiler.

For an hour, he stared at the picture, taking in

every detail, but adding bits in his own mind, bits he would need when he slept. As he closed his eyes, Becky became part of the wedding party Selina's Maid of Honor.

And finally he did doze off. The photo hung in one hand as he slept.

He dreamed of Selina and himself coming back from the exhibition at The Gallery.

He relived the drinking, the drive home, and finally the truck pulling in front of them, forcing them off the road.

This time there was no external noise, only soft choral music surrounding them. Their car and the stranger's truck spinning in synch, a metallic ballet.

Becky was sleeping in the back seat, but this time, her seat belt was strapped around her. She was as beautiful as her mother.

The crash came. Nobody screamed. The car bounced peacefully off the median and back. They were falling through thin air and then into the water. They all knew this was their chance to be together forever. Finally, peace.

Becky laughed softly in the back seat.

Selina smiled and reached for his hand as she said, "I love you, Charlie."

Burying Reena

Reena Virk was a real teenaged girl who was persecuted and eventually killed by her classmates in high school in Saanich, British Columbia. It made news headlines because of the brutality her so-called friends showed her. The murder happened in 1997, but since I lived in B.C., it was big news and I never forgot it.

In late 2010, I was invited to contribute a story to the Shocklines anthology being published by Cemetery Dance Publications. I took the opportunity to write a story vaguely based on the story of Reena Virk. The thought of how horrible teenagers can be to one another was shocking, and I knew one day I'd be writing about it.

Of course, being a horror and dark fantasy writer, I couldn't just retell the real story. My story took a twist quite different than the one in real life.

- 1 -

SUE JOHNSON WAS WATCHING from the woods with HER gang. The trees hid most of the details, but she could see Reena Sandhu standing near the edge of the parking lot. She was holding hands with Michael.

"There. There," whispered Janie. "She's there."

"Yeah, I see her. Just need that fucker to leave her alone."

Sue stepped out from behind a tree and tried to get a better look through the tall redwoods. She knew Reena couldn't see her, since the trees cast long, dark shadows everywhere.

"Come on, you dumb cunt." She shook her head and glanced at her watch. Almost six o'clock in the evening. "Let's get this show on the road."

Finally, she saw Michael lean over and kiss Reena's cheek. His laugh filtered through the trees, grating on Sue. He took a few steps backward, still saying good-bye, then finally walked away.

Reena stood looking at him for a few seconds, then started walking into the forest. When she hit the shade, she crossed her bare arms. Even though it was near the end of June, it was still a cool day without the sunshine.

Sue knew she'd be coming this way. *Creature of habit.* She could see Reena's shoulder-length black hair seem to disappear as she entered the shadows, and her dark skin turn even darker.

"Coming," Sue whispered. "Get back."

She moved back behind the tree and didn't move until she heard Reena's shuffled steps coming close. The other three members of the gang were hiding behind other trees to the sides.

Reena's footsteps crunched on the bark mulch path. Just as she was about to pass, Sue stepped out. The three others moved into the path behind Reena.

Reena jumped. "Jeez, Sue, you scared me." She put her hand over her heart and smiled. As always, Sue was surprised at the lack of an accent. Even though Reena was born in nearby San Francisco, she still looked and sometimes dressed like she belonged in Delhi or Bombay or wherever her family came from.

"Didn't anyone tell you not to wander the woods alone?"

Reena smiled. "Yeah, but it saves me ten minutes. I don't walk this way after dark, though."

Sue just stared at her.

At five foot six and a hundred and sixty pounds, Sue was almost seven inches taller and fifty pounds heavier than tiny Reena. Sue's face was plump, her lips pursed in anger, like they always seemed to be, and her eyes flashed and glanced back to the forest entrance as she talked. "That some Paki thing? That shawl?"

Reena heard a twig snap and turned to see Sue's friends standing behind her. Janie, of course, was always near her. Sue's gofer. And two guys that she'd seen around Sue, but she didn't know their names. She hesitated, looked at them all, and knew she was surrounded.

"My heritage is Indian, not Pakistani. But, no, this is just a shawl I bought at Walmart. Nothing special."

Sue shook her head. "Looks foreign to me."

Reena shrugged.

"Glad school's over?" Sue blocked the path, almost daring Reena to keep walking into her.

Reena took a step. "I've got to get going. My parents are waiting for me."

Both girls were sixteen, but that was the only thing they had in common. Sue had been arrested for stealing cars on two different occasions, joy-riding in the middle of the night, drunk. She was still on parole. She knew there were rumours about her torturing dogs, too, but she'd neither admitted nor denied them. She quite liked the stories. It scared people. Kept them in line. Reena, on the other hand, was a typical goodie two-shoes.

"Your parents? Your dad's that old guy at the 7-Eleven who can barely speak English, right? What's with the fucking turban, anyhow? Why didn't he just stay in India if he doesn't want to be an American?"

Reena glanced at the path, and Sue knew she was wondering if she should run around her. She moved a step closer. "Don't worry," she said. She gave a fake smile and put a reassuring hand on Reena's shoulder. Then she tightened her grip and nodded to the others behind Reena.

Reena just stared at Sue as her arms were wrenched behind her. "What are you doing? Tell them to stop."

Sue moved even closer. Her smile was for real this time. "Shut up, you stupid bitch." She walked behind and watched as Mackie finished tying Reena's wrists together with several loops of rough twine.

Reena dropped her purse and turned her head, trying to see behind her. "Sue, stop this right now. Let's just walk away before this goes too far."

Sue didn't answer. Instead she pulled a long blue silk scarf from her pocket and used it as a gag, snapping Reena's head back while she tied it in back.

Reena choked as the gag bit into her mouth. She tried to yell, but it was too late. The scarf muffled her voice so only a thin, panic-filled croak escaped.

Sue walked back to the front of Reena and pinched her cheek. "Poor little Paki. You don't like being called that? Well, maybe you should move back to India, cause you sure don't belong here."

Reena's eyes leaked a few tears, and she kept trying to scream. She squirmed, but Janie, Mackie, and Joel kept her from getting anywhere. They all laughed, and mumbled agreement with Sue.

"What now?" asked Janie. Her voice was almost a grunt. Sue's friends were all outcasts, like herself. Janie was her biggest partner-in-crime, and she'd do anything she was told to do.

"You know the plan."

Sue looked around in all directions. Nobody. She then kicked Reena's legs out from under her, causing her to collapse in a heap. Her head hit a branch, opening a two-inch cut on her cheek. Her muffled screams turned to cries of pain, but they still couldn't be heard more than a few feet away.

Her frail body was shaking from her crying, but she still looked up, saw she wasn't being held, and tried to scrabble away.

"Oh, no you don't."

Sue pushed Reena's head to the ground with her foot, rolling her sideways, back and forth, opening the cut on her face wider. When Reena wouldn't stop trying to escape, Sue took a step back and kicked her in the head. Reena still tried to crawl, so Sue kicked her a second time, harder.

Silence fell over the group. The gang was all watching Reena, while Reena herself lay still, unconscious.

Sue broke the silence. "Serves her right for dating a white guy." She waited for any of the others to disagree, but of course they never would. Sue was Queen to their drone. "Pick her up," she ordered.

Mackie and Joel each yanked Reena up and held her by one arm each. Both were weight-lifters, and they had no trouble holding her. Her head lolled to the left side.

Janie walked beside Sue, leading the boys through the forest to the spot they had selected earlier. The woods were dense and few people strayed off the marked paths. Sue smiled. She owned this forest. Never saw anyone else in her little section. As they walked, she and Janie pulled back branches to allow the boys an easier time carrying Reena. It was like they disappeared into a country all their own, a country where Sue ruled with an iron fist.

After ten minutes, they found the small clearing where they hung out. A lightning strike in the distant past had knocked over a few trees, creating an area almost ten feet square where not much grew. The fallen trees were perfect benches, and they'd placed a small pup tent nearby for privacy.

They dumped Reena, but she still didn't wake. Sue knelt down and felt under Reena's light blue dress, under her bra.

"Still beating," she said. Her hand lingered on Reena's breast a bit longer than necessary, but then she snapped it back.

"What're you looking at?" She stared at Mackie.

"Nothin'."

"Get the damned box."

Mackie and Joel walked a few feet behind the tent and picked up the home-made coffin. They'd spent the morning banging it together from the old packing crates that littered Joel's back yard. His father imported fine pottery from Rotterdam and resold it from their house.

The coffin was crude but strong. They placed it on the ground.

"Should we untie her?"

"Why the fuck not? Won't do her any good." Sue took a Swiss Army knife from her jeans pocket and sliced through the twine.

A quick lift from the boys, and Reena was in the coffin. "Where's her purse?" asked Sue.

"I got it," said Janie. She tossed it in the coffin, by Reena's feet.

Sue spent a few minutes nailing the lid down tightly.

All four of them were needed to carry the box to the grave and lowered her into it.

Sue expected to hear Reena banging on the lid at any time, but that didn't happen.

They filled in the hole and patted it down hard, burying Reena.

She laughed and lit a cigarette. "Fucking teach that Paki bitch good."

It was after seven o'clock. Time for dinner.

-2-

Michael Stanwick stared at his cell phone, willing it to ring. It was after 8:00 p.m. Reena was supposed to call by 7:00.

Where was she?

She was never late to call. One of the things you could count on was Reena doing things *exactly* when she said she would. If she was supposed to call at 7:00, she might be off by a minute or two either way, but no way in hell she'd be more than that. Some weird compulsion of hers made her just about the most predictable person on Earth.

So, where was her call?

He had the TV on in the background, had glanced at it a bit to check the news, but there were no stories that could possibly have delayed her. Some mid-east peace agreement was broken, there was a terrorist plot foiled in London, and predictions were out for the hurricane season.

Nothing interesting going on in San Francisco. No reported fires, major car accidents, whatever.

Nothing that would have kept Reena from calling.

Maybe her parents grounded her for something? That was really a stretch. He'd met Reena's parents, and they were the kindest, most unassuming people in the neighborhood. They'd do anything for her. He knew they didn't look kindly on her dating him, but even with that, they kept their opinions to themselves. She'd laughed about it. "You just gotta dye your skin a bit and convert to Sikhism. They'd love you then."

He'd tried Reena's cell phone, but the call went straight to her voice mail. He hesitated to call her land line. No point worrying her parents or anything.

Michael was seventeen, would be eighteen in September. He was off to college in the fall, and while part of that was exciting, part depressing, since he'd no longer be in classes with Reena. They were heading to different colleges.

That'd be okay, though. A couple more years and they'd be married.

He walked down the stairs and found his mother sitting alone on the front porch. "I'm going to check on Reena. Can't get ahold of her."

"Oh." His mother was drinking a beer and seemed a bit out of it already. "Hope she's okay."

He left without further comment. He had enough to worry about with Reena, and Mom would have to wait till another time to become a concern.

There was a cool breeze pushing him forward as he walked, almost like nature was trying to hurry him along. "Silly," he said.

Reena's house was about a mile away. He was rushing and got there in about ten minutes.

There was a police car in front of her house, with its lights flashing.

Michael stopped at the corner, staring at the car. *Is she okay? Is somebody else hurt?*

No ambulance. Just cops.

On the porch, he could see two officers talking to Reena's father. Michael hadn't seen them immediately, because they were hidden in the shade.

The radio in the police car was on, with odd squawks leaking out of the open window. One of the cops on the porch was taking notes, but the other one was looking out. Looking right at him.

Michael started walking again, feeling guilty for no reason he could figure out.

When he reached the front of the house, Reena's father noticed him and pointed. "There he is." His accent was thick, but Michael didn't have any trouble understanding him.

The officer who had been watching him walked down the front steps, his hands at his sides, as if he were a gunslinger in an old John Wayne movie. He imagined the cop calling out, "Hold it right there, pardner, or I'll fill you full of more holes than a brick of Swiss cheese."

Michael swept the image away but couldn't help but watch the cop's hands. They seemed hypnotic, his right hand flinching nearby his gun.

"Michael Stanwick?"

Michael blinked and nodded. "What's wrong? Where's Reena?"

The cop pulled out his own notepad. "When's the last time you saw her?"

"We finished rehearsal at school. Left about six o'clock, six-ten, something like that."

The cop just nodded him to continue.

"She went through the woods. It's how she always goes home." He glanced at Reena's father, who was leading the other cop inside. Reena would never want her father to know she took the shortcut through the woods, but...

"I was waiting for her to phone. At seven o'clock. She's never late. Something's wrong."

The cop shook his head. "That forest goes for miles in all directions."

"She'll be okay, won't she?"

The officer looked at him. "She probably just lost track of time."

"Not Reena."

He shrugged. "We'll see." He made another note. "You've been dating?"

"Yes. About eight months."

"Have any recent fights?"

"Fights? No! We're great together."

"Are you seeing any other girls behind her back? Maybe she found out and didn't like that?"

"What? No, of course not. We're incredibly happy together. There's nobody else."

The officer nodded and glanced back at the house. "Give me your full name and address. I'm sure she'll show up tonight, but if she's still missing tomorrow, we'll open a file."

Michael didn't understand. "Aren't you going to search the woods?"

"If she's still missing tomorrow, we'll check into it."

Michael gave his full name and address, and the cop closed his notebook. "Anything else?" he asked. He glanced back at the house again.

Michael shook his head and then blurted out, "I love her."

The cop nodded and walked back to the porch.

-3-

Reena woke.

Her back hurt and her head was throbbing. She was disoriented and confused. She kept her eyes closed as she tried to remember what day it was.

Tuesday.

She remembered the end of practice and walking through the woods. Seeing Sue and her gang.

"Oh God, where am I?"

She blinked her eyes open but saw nothing. Her first thought was that she'd been blinded. She kept blinking her eyes and she licked her dry lips.

Maybe my eyes need to adjust to the light. Something sounded wrong about that idea, though.

She'd been here for some time now, wherever here was. Her eyes shouldn't still need to adjust.

She started to cough and her head moved from the wood beneath her and struck the coffin lid above her.

What?

She reached up and felt the lid, feeling more confused than ever. Then she felt the sides of the coffin and realized she was trapped inside something.

Oh God...

"Hello?" She called out and listened for a reply but nothing came. "HELP!"

She called several times but no luck. Nobody answered. She forced herself to calm down and really listen, but she heard nothing at all.

The coffin was tight and had very little head room. Reena tried to push up but she had no leverage with her arms. In any case, the lid wasn't budging.

She did her best to feel the contours of the sides and realized that the box was in the shape of a coffin.

Small sprinkles of dirt fell between the top boards.

"Oh, no..."

I'm buried underground.

Panic struck her and she again tried to push the lid up and pound on the sides.

"HELP ME!"

Ohmygod, ohmygod, ohmygod.

She pounded and pounded but all she succeeded in doing was to allow a bit more dirt to fall between the cracks of the lid. The coffin itself didn't budge.

She struggled for what seemed like a very long time, but she hadn't checked her watch so she didn't really know how long it was.

Finally she fell silent, exhausted.

She could feel her heart pounding and she couldn't stop herself from whimpering.

"SUE! PLEASE GET ME OUT!"

No answer.

She imagined six feet of earth above her. Would they have put her that far under? Maybe. They had it all planned. She could see that now. Nobody has a spare coffin just sitting around.

Why?

She took a deep breath, wondering how much air she had. The coffin was longer than Reena was. She could shuffle down a couple of feet, but it was really narrow and low, so there couldn't be much air trapped with her.

Her back was shooting lightning bolts into her. She wondered if something was broken. It felt like blood was running from her head but she couldn't tell for sure. That hurt like hell, too, but she couldn't get her hands up to her head to feel the injury.

I'm going to die here.

Once again, she felt a well of panic rising in her and she started to cry. She wanted to stop but that wasn't possible.

Thoughts passed through her mind. The times she'd shared with Michael, hoping they'd be planning a life together soon. The promise of heading to college next year and her ambitions to go for an MBA down the road. The love she'd always felt from her parents, who'd sacrificed so much for her.

She needed to live, but her heart told her that wasn't going to happen.

She burst into a long bout of crying, beating the walls of her coffin and hitting her head on the lid, opening her cut even more deeply.

Reena fought the coffin and lost, and eventually she found herself worn out from her frantic efforts and lay there, dazed and tired.

Finally, she saw something, as dull yellow and pink ribbons of light flashed across her eyes. She wasn't even sure her eyes were open at first. She closed them and still saw the ribbons floating in front of her. She tried to reach to touch them, but her arms were still trapped.

The lights were beautiful, filled with small frilly details, like colorful little gerbera daisies. The light threads merged into a pinwheel and called to her.

"So pretty," she whispered.

She needed the lights. They called to her too strongly for her not to touch them, so she sat up and reached for them, but the lights moved up higher. A small part of Reena's mind was aware that there was no room for all this, but the bigger portion of her needed to hold her little daisies.

The pinwheels swirled around, full of hues that Reena couldn't recall seeing before. She floated up toward them and followed the lights through the dirt.

She didn't care how far she had to travel through the ground, but at some point she burst out into the night landscape. She was surrounded by dark trees and nearby were the shovels and other tools that Sue's gang had used to bury her.

The lights were gone, and Reena stood bewildered above her own grave.

She was invisible and couldn't even see her own body. When she tried to speak, no sound came out. She could make herself float high above the ground or come back to it.

Her body was below the grave, and she needed to find help from somebody to dig her up before it was too late.

-4-

Sue Johnson sat on the ground, not far from where Reena was buried. The clearing was large enough for the gang to have a small fire going as they drank a case of Budweiser. She'd stolen the beer from her father's shed where he kept half a dozen cases. Sue had cleaned out all the cases since April and if he'd noticed, he didn't have the balls to say anything to her.

Everyone knew better than to fuck with Sue. She smiled at the thought. She loved running her little section of the planet.

Mackie was sitting on her right. He was only sixteen and a grade behind Sue, but he was her best soldier. Ever since she blew him under the bleachers of the school stadium a couple months ago, he'd do anything for her. He was big and strong, a linebacker on the football team, and if he'd told her to snap Reena's neck, she knew he'd do it without hesitation.

Joel was good too, but he thought too much.

Janie treated Sue like a goddess, but she was just a girl and didn't have the muscle that kept Sue at the top of the food chain.

She checked her watch.

"She's been down there an hour."

"Good," said Mackie. "I hope the bitch is enjoying it." He'd had six beers and was totally drunk, slurring his words and barely able to sit without falling.

"Damn straight," Sue said.

She felt dizzy, so she stood and picked up one of the empty beer bottles. She stared at a tree ten feet away and threw the bottle at it. It missed by a couple of feet but shattered when it hit a rock on the ground. She threw another and had a similar result.

"Fucking aim's off tonight."

For some reason she thought that was incredibly funny and she started to laugh. She laughed harder and had to lean over when she started choking from the effort.

The others laughed with her, even though none of them really knew what was exactly funny. It didn't matter. The night had been so exhilarating, and they'd all felt the wonderful thrill when that last patch of dirt got patted down over Reena's head.

"'Kay, we need to have a pact or something."

They all looked to Sue.

Janie said, "Like you mean to keep it a secret? Nobody's stupid enough to spill."

"We need a fucken pact. A blood pact."

She took her Swiss Army knife and walked to Mackie. "You go first."

Mackie didn't hesitate. He stuck out his hand and Sue sliced a cut right through his palm. Blood sprung from it immediately.

Sue cut her own palm and pressed it to his. "Blood bond. We can't betray each other."

Mackie nodded.

Sue went to Joel and then to Janie and cut their hands too. They all clasped each other and swore secrecy.

In her knapsack, Sue had brought a roll of cotton bandages that they all used to bind their cuts.

Sue barely felt the slicing of her hand. It was just one more necessary link in the chain of events.

"You're dead, Reena," she said.

"Dead," said Mackie.

"Dead," added Janie.

"Dead," said Joel.

Sue smiled. She sat down with her back against an old oak tree and popped the cap on another beer. She closed her eyes as she sat there, just wanting to enjoy the moment.

Serves you right, bitch.

Three days earlier, Reena had betrayed her, and Sue hoped she was thinking about that as she suffocated.

The English test was horrible. Sue was failing the class. It wasn't so much that she gave a crap about that, but she just didn't want the snotty teacher, Mrs. Simms, to keep looking down her goddamn nose at her like she'd been doing. Little bitch had way too much attitude.

Sue'd been checking her answers on the BlackBerry hidden inside her desk. When stupid Simms wasn't looking, she'd click away at her keys to find the answers. How stupid was this teacher, to let her get away with that?

Reena was sitting in the row behind her and to her right. Near the end of the hour-long test, Sue watched as goodie two-shoes Reena got up and went to talk to stupid Simms.

The next day, the tests were returned. Sue's mark was a big fat zero, for cheating.

-5-

Reena floated near her grave, still not quite comprehending how her body could be buried below her. She tried to scrape the dirt away but her hands were phantoms that had no substance. She could feel them the same way that some amputees could feel their own phantom limbs, but in her case her entire body had that feeling.

She could see through her virtual eyes, but she couldn't talk, couldn't touch, and she had no need to breathe.

Am I a ghost?

She didn't think so, because she knew her body was still alive underneath the ground.

Her mind was clear about what she had to do: she needed to find a way to have somebody rescue her.

She—

—heard something. She tried to focus where the sound was coming from.

Over there.

She floated through the trees and saw Sue Johnson sleeping on the ground. There were several empty beer bottles scattered around her and the remains of a bonfire. It looked like her friends had been there earlier as well. It was a party place.

Sue had a blood-stained bandage on one hand.

Help me, Sue. I won't cause you any trouble, I promise!

Her call for help was silent, as she knew it would be, and Sue kept snoring.

Reena wondered if Michael had missed her yet. Of course he had. He was as reliable as she was and he'd know something was terribly wrong. He'd be hunting for her right now, but how could he ever find her? Even if he thought she was somewhere in the forest, there were thousands of acres, and he could walk right by her grave in the night without seeing anything unusual. By the time the morning sun showed the ground had been dug, she'd be long dead.

She'd hoped to make love with Michael sometime during the summer. They'd been dating the entire school year, and although the time hadn't been quite right yet, she knew she'd feel comfortable soon, as the days grew warmer and their relationship grew. She wanted him to be her first, and she was pretty sure she'd be his first too. It felt so nice to think of being with him that way. She tried not to think long-term, but it was hard. She hoped for so much more with Michael. Now, it was all gone. Her hopes and dreams were being killed along with her body, and Michael would never know how much he'd meant to her.

Why did you do this, Sue?

The question had puzzled her so much, but then she remembered the English test. Really? Could she have blamed Reena?

But I didn't turn you in.

Reena thought about how it might have looked when she went to talk to Mrs. Simms. She'd only felt she needed to explain to the teacher why she wasn't able to finish the last essay question. She was almost out of time and just wasn't sure of how to say much about the theme of Romeo and Juliet. It just wasn't coming to her, but she couldn't just leave it blank. She needed to just say something to Mrs. Simms, so she wouldn't think she hadn't tried.

The bell rang as they spoke.

"Don't worry about it, dear," said Mrs. Simms. "I'm sure you'll do fine."

-6-

Sue woke with a headache.

"Damn."

She stood slowly, trying not to fall over. She felt like she was still half-asleep, but she had to pee.

"Where'd you all go?" she asked when she realized Mackie, Janie, and Joel were all gone. "Pussies."

She'd expected them to stay with her all night, but she hadn't really planned on falling asleep, either. The night air was cool and she felt goose bumps on her arms. She rubbed them and realized that one small gesture was now something Reena was incapable of. The box was too narrow for her to be able to rub herself. She laughed.

"Are you dead yet, my little Paki?"

Probably not. It hadn't been long enough yet.

She pulled her jeans down and took them off. Then her panties. She squatted, holding a nearby tree for balance. It felt so good when she peed. She didn't care that drops of urine splashed her legs.

She sighed and then got herself dressed again. The camp had no more beer.

Shit.

She yawned and started to walk out of the forest. She knew the woods intimately and had no trouble navigating her way out to the suburbs of Hampton Beach, her own hated Frisco suburb. Her first thought was to head back to her own place, but she'd taken the last of her father's beer.

"Damnit, Mackie, you should have stayed with me." He'd often said he'd be happy to steal beer from his house. Well, tonight would have been a good time to prove that.

Now what?

She walked through the back alley behind the tiny business section of the town and looked into a dumpster that was loaded with garbage. The lid was heavy but she found a half-full bag of potato chips inside. She ate some of them and then saw a man walking down the alley in her direction. He looked to be about forty, wore a light jacket and nice jeans. Probably a tourist. Tourists meant hotels. Hotels meant alcohol.

He seemed to pick up his pace a bit when he got close to her and stared straight ahead, as if she was invisible.

"Hey, can you help me out?"

The guy stopped but didn't seem to know what to say at first. He looked at her and then looked to the end of the alleyway.

"Get me some beer, will you?"

"Oh, I can't do anything like that. I'm just heading to my car to—"

"Look, you can fuck me."

She took her T-shirt off so he could see her in her bra. She knew her tits would get his attention.

"I really have to go."

"You want me. I know you do, and you can have me. Just get me some beer."

He started to walk around her. "I'm sorry."

She took her Swiss Army knife from her pocket and stabbed him in his side. "Fucking shit."

"Oh God!" He stumbled away from her and pressed his hand to his side. Blood oozed between his fingers. "Oh my God."

He somehow managed to run away, toward the main street at the end of the alley.

Sue stared at him for a minute, knowing he'd call the cops. Damn. She wiped the blood on her jeans and closed the knife, putting it back in her pocket. Then she ran back to the woods.

She didn't stop until she found Reena's grave. Somehow this place felt safe to her. The police wouldn't find her here and the tourist would leave town with nothing but a reminder of her written on his skin.

There were still no sounds from the plot of ground in front of her, no surprise of a hand reaching up from the ground. It was near 2:00 a.m., and once again, Sue wondered if Reena was dead yet.

In any case, she wouldn't last much longer.

-7-

Reena had returned to her body after seeing Sue. She was still alive but she didn't know how long that would last. Part of her kept trying to panic and she'd find herself screaming and banging on the coffin, but she knew that was hopeless. Even if somehow she could break through the wood (which seemed impossible), she'd just be buried in the avalanche of dirt that would follow. She'd be just as dead. The only advantage would be that it would be faster.

Her heart sank and she tried to take a deep breath. She had no clue how much air was left but it couldn't be much.

Nobody was in the woods looking for her. The only person around was Sue, and there was no chance of her helping.

"Michael," she whispered. She wanted to hear his name one more time even if it was from her own cracked lips.

She wanted to add, "I love you," but it was going to be too hard to imagine saying that for the last time.

She felt her body tense with anger and frustration and she willed herself to relax once again.

Reena had no idea how she'd left her body behind earlier, but maybe if she could do it again, she could find some way to get help.

Closing her eyes, she tried to relax her muscles and then reach up with her mind. After a few minutes, it worked. The wonderful ribbons of daisy-shaped lights returned. Whatever happened when she smashed her head earlier had given her the ability and she sure needed it now.

Once again she traveled up through the dirt and to the surface. Sue was sitting near the grave, just staring, not saying anything. For a minute, Reena wondered if she was asleep but then she saw her eyes blink.

"Sue! Please help me!"

Sue had no reaction, even when Reena floated right in front of her and yelled.

She gave up, moving up higher and out of the woods. She started out veering around trees as she floated but she soon realized that was silly. It was just easier to go in a straight line and pass through any obstacles.

Michael. She needed him.

She found her way to the suburbs and passed her own home.

"Mom," she said. "Dad..."

She thought of going to see them, but her soul (or whatever she now was) kept carrying her to Michael's house. He lived with his mother in a small bungalow a few blocks from her. It was a bit run-down, because his parents had neglected normal maintenance. The paint was peeling, some of the wood siding had come loose, and there was a broken window in the basement.

Reena didn't care about any of that. She just cared about Michael. She floated through the walls directly to his bedroom. He was lying down but not asleep. He was curled on his left side, eyes open, lost in thought.

"MICHAEL!"

No response. She yelled again, but he didn't know she was there.

His fingers were fidgeting, drawing small circles on his sheet. Somehow, she knew those were drawings of love, for her.

She couldn't pick up a pen or find any other way to communicate with him. Once again, she felt overwhelmed by frustration.

"Michael, I love you."

He didn't notice her.

Reena wanted to hug him, to feel his body one last time. She turned sideways, even though she didn't really have any dimensions at all, and tried to pretend she was lying beside him.

They'd laid together a couple of times, but that was as far as they'd gone. Now she wished she had let him make love to her. She wanted to know what that would have felt like.

She wanted to kiss his mouth and she moved her presence closer.

And she found herself inside his body.

What?

She could see out of his eyes, feel his finger scrabbling on the sheet, breathe his air.

Michael! I'm here!

-8-

Michael bolted upright in his bed. *What the fuck?*

There was an urgency he felt. Reena needed him. He felt that, deep inside, but he had no idea how or why. All he knew was that she needed him.

Some even deeper part of him felt a wash of love spilling over him, Reena's love, and he wanted to bask in that but he knew he had no time. She needed him.

But where?

"Reena, sweetie."

He knew she wasn't nearby and couldn't hear him but he needed to try something. He needed to go somewhere and to try to find her.

Near the door were his hiking boots and he put them on. He had liked to go hiking with Reena through the woods and he felt the need to go there now.

Almost as an afterthought, he grabbed his walking stick, a six-foot long shaved stick that acted like a third leg on long hikes. He'd never really needed it but sometimes he'd taken it along with him on their longer walks, mostly in case Reena wanted it.

He hurried to the door and ignored his mother calling to him about where he was going. It was the middle of the night and that meant she was close to passing out from drinking. She wouldn't remember anything he told her, and he couldn't waste the time.

Reena needs me.

The woods were about a mile from his house. He jogged the entire way and went into the woods using the same entrance Reena had gone in earlier. It was almost pitch black and cold.

He moved slowly, trying not to trip over the roots and branches scattered everywhere. There wasn't any real path maintained by the city or anything like that, just some routes through that were easier than others. Once inside the forest, he knew it was easy to get lost. Three years ago some kid had died after going into the forest and not being able to find his way back out. His body wasn't discovered for months.

He heard insects chirping and stalled when he heard a rustling in the brush nearby. He wanted it to be Reena but knew it wasn't. It was some animal and he held his walking stick out as a weapon. The rustling moved away. He could feel his heart beating rapidly.

Then it became clear to him: Sue was responsible for Reena's disappearance. He felt it like an old memory that he'd just tripped across. She was somewhere in the woods and had done something bad to Reena.

He had to find her.

-9-

Reena felt the pull of her body and had to leave Michael. Her spirit was yanked back as if she were tethered by an elastic band. She could only leave her body for a short period before she was called back; the energy used was just too much for her to spare if she wanted to live much longer.

Just before merging back into herself, she noticed her body lying still, almost lifeless. It was a useless hulk of meat without her being.

When she climbed back into her skin, she took a deep breath. Her body had been almost on life support while she was gone, shallow breathing, only occasional heart beats. Now she was back whole. If she'd stayed away much longer, she'd have returned to find her body dead.

"Which might happen real soon anyhow," she said.

The air smelled of her sweat. She had to take long deep breaths to get much oxygen, and the effort was hard. When she rubbed her fingers together, it was like sandpaper. Her skin was dry and scratchy and she had trouble even clenching her fists. Everything seemed to take so much willpower now. All she wanted to do was rest.

She forced herself to try to move, to not give up hope. Michael was looking for her, somewhere up there.

Bringing her arms up to her chest was still possible, and she did that to get some blood flowing. She flexed her ankles as well and—

—kicked something.

What?

Her purse. She should have noticed it earlier, but she had been so panicked and had missed it scrunched down at the end of her coffin.

She tried to hook her foot around the handle but she couldn't catch it. There was no way to reach to it with her hands so she kept trying with her feet. She scooted down to the bottom of the coffin and jammed her right foot underneath the purse.

It lifted and she could flick it a little bit forward. She pressed it again against the side and flicked it farther. She could almost reach it with her arm now, but not quite. She compressed her body as much as she could, forcing herself into the very end of the casket. She stretched her fingers and could just barely touch one strap. One final push and she wrapped her baby finger around the strap and pulled the purse up.

She was covered with sweat from the work. Drops of perspiration fell into her eyes, so she shook her head to clear her vision. She blinked and reminded herself to take long, slow breaths.

Over the next few minutes, she was able to gently move her purse up onto her stomach. It was wedged between her body and the coffin lid, which gave her the ability to reach it with both hands.

The purse snapped open and she felt inside.

First was a pocket book she'd been reading: an introduction to Indian history. She pushed it aside and it fell with a thunk to the bottom of the coffin.

She found her makeup container and dropped that aside, too. Nothing in there would help her.

There was a hair brush, and she thought for a moment about using it to pound the lid, but screaming hadn't done any good, so she didn't think the small noise that would make would help, either. She dropped it to the side.

Other small things got discarded. All useless. Then she found her nail file.

She used it to try to dig between the boards of the coffin lid. Maybe she could loosen them enough to— well, she didn't really know what would happen if she could. The nail file bent quickly, being much less strong than her inch-thick prison wall. She abandoned it.

The purse was empty and so were her spirits.

Just as she was about to push the purse back to the end of the casket, she remembered the small outside pocket of her purse. She turned it around and took her cell phone out and, for the first time since Sue started to murder her, she smiled.

She flicked the phone open with a practiced hand and was momentarily shocked by the light. It actually hurt her eyes, but she didn't give a damn. That light would save her life.

For the first time, she could see where she was imprisoned. She could see how strong the wooden frame was and how futile it was to imagine escape. She used the phone as a flashlight and among her fear and terror, she now felt claustrophobia sink in. The coffin wasn't much bigger than she was, and now she could see how little room she had.

Little room meant little air.

How much longer could she last?

She blinked and looked at the phone. No bars. She couldn't phone out.

"No," she moaned. She tried anyhow, pressing 9-1-1. Nothing.

She shook the phone as if that would somehow establish a connection. Nothing.

That's when she started crying again, her last hopes for survival now gone.

-10-

Sue was starting to sober up. She'd fallen asleep again but a tree limb snapping in the wind jolted her back awake. She checked her watch: 4:42 a.m. Surely the bitch was dead by now. She felt tired as she sat staring at the dirt patch where she'd buried Reena.

It was still dark, but soon the morning light would come. She'd go home when that happened. Till then, she just wanted to enjoy her thoughts.

"Good-bye, you stuck-up bitch," she said. She held out an imaginary wine glass and toasted to Reena.

It was her own fault.

Sue thought back to that chance meeting three weeks earlier. She knew Reena, of course. They were in a couple of classes together. Everybody knew Reena. She was the one that turned the boys' heads when she walked by. She was the one that everybody wanted to be friends with. Well, everyone except Sue and her friends.

It was a Friday afternoon, and Sue had been killing time in the parking lot of the school, waiting for Janie to join her. Janie had picked up a nickel bag of weed and they were going to go smoke their brains out.

Reena wandered close by, and Sue watched her.

"Hey," said Reena. "How're you doing, Sue?"

Sue couldn't help but stare at her. Her skin was such a beautiful mocha color, it just called to her. Reena smiled and showed perfect white teeth and her eyes sparkled with life.

For the first time in her life, Sue felt speechless. She had never been attracted to girls before. What the fuck?

She felt it, though. She stared at Reena and just nodded. Her mouth was dry.

"I'm just waiting for my guy," said Reena. She laughed and moved closer to Sue. "How about you?"

"Waiting for friends."

Reena nodded and kept smiling.

Sue felt her face redden and for some godforsaken reason she blurted out, "You're beautiful." She put her hand on Reena's shoulder.

Reena closed her mouth and her smile almost evaporated.

"Thanks," she said. "I—"

She didn't finish. She turned her head and looked back to the school. She pretended to have the sun in her eye and moved a bit away from Sue, into the shade of the old corner store that had stood forever at the back of the parking lot. Sue had to move her hand from her shoulder, and she felt shame cover her like a blanket.

"Sorry. I didn't mean anything."

"It's okay. I'm just not that way."

That shocked Sue. "Well, I'm not that way, either! Jeez, I was just being friendly, for fuck's sake."

Reena nodded. "I'm sorry, but I've got to go find my boyfriend. See you around."

Stupid bitch.

Well, who's laughing now, Miss Reena? Where's your boyfriend now?

She wanted to laugh, but for a moment, she imagined herself buried beneath the ground with no chance of getting back out.

It almost made her feel guilty.

Almost.

She stood and stretched and decided it was time to head home.

-11-

Michael was lost. He had been wandering in the woods for more than an hour and the sense of purpose he'd felt earlier had left him. He'd been making random turns through the trees but he had no idea where to go. He'd never really explored the forest, not like Reena, and he had no idea where to go to find her.

Not to mention the part of him that even questioned whether she was even being held in the woods anywhere. There was a time earlier where he knew that without a doubt, but that certainty had fallen by the wayside.

He turned and tried to find his way back the way he'd come. Fortunately, there were hints of sunlight spilling through some of the trees now and he could make out some of the footprints he'd left behind as he'd entered.

He used his walking stick to move some of the branches that blocked his path.

When he figured he was halfway out, he heard something and stopped still.

To his right, he could see a shadow. He squinted and realized it was Sue.

"Hey!" he called.

She was about twenty feet from him. She looked at him and laughed. "Guess you're here for your Paki girlfriend? Good luck with that."

"Where is she, Sue?"

"Fuck you."

Sue started walking again and Michael hurried over toward her. He grabbed her shoulder.

"What have you done with her?"

"Get your fucking hands off me!"

Sue pushed his arm away and then reached into her jeans and pulled out her knife, opened it and waved it in front of her.

"Bring it on, baby. Come get me, you brave little motherfucker."

"Sue, I just need to get Reena safe."

Sue hesitated, as if she might turn to run. Michael knew that if he lost her, he'd lose the chance to save Reena. He gripped his walking stick in both hands and then swung it like a baseball bat. He smashed Sue in her mid-section and she crumpled to the ground.

"Oohh..."

"WHERE IS SHE?"

He leaned over her and held the point of the walking stick to her neck. He pushed down to the point she had trouble breathing and he could see her eyes grow wide with fear. He wanted nothing more than to push just a little bit harder, to spill her blood on the forest floor. He had visions of jabbing her body with the stick and taking revenge for the girl he loved.

He hesitated, though. He didn't want to go to jail for the rest of his life; he just wanted to find Reena.

That hesitation gave Sue enough time to get a better grip on her knife. She swept it in front of her and cut into Michael's ankle. He cried out and then she stabbed him hard with the knife.

He jumped and dropped the walking stick, reaching down to his ankle. He collapsed from the pain and crawled a few feet from Sue. She jumped up and ran away.

Michael didn't know what to do. He didn't know if he should try to pull the knife from his ankle or whether that would just cause him to bleed to death.

The pain shot into him like liquid fire and he leaned against a tree. No way he could walk.

He pulled his cell phone from his jacket pocket and dialled 9-1-1.

They told him to wait there and not remove the knife.

He sat, his back against the tree, tears running down his face. Some of the tears were from pain, but most were from his sense of loss. He'd failed Reena. He knew he'd never see her again.

-12-

Reena was taking such deep breaths, she started to choke. It was harder and harder with every breath.

Somewhere along the line she'd dropped her cell phone to the side and the light was gone, so she was surrounded by darkness. She didn't really care anymore. In some ways it felt like a blessing to not have to actually look at her prison walls.

She said her last prayers. Mostly she prayed that her body would be found soon, so that her parents wouldn't go a long time without knowing if she was dead or alive. They'd been wonderful to her and she couldn't stand the thought of them suffering any more than they had to. She tried not to think of what they would be going through in the next few days and weeks.

Her fingers and toes were totally cramped.

Just let it be over, she pleaded.

After almost totally giving up, she felt a tiny surge of energy. The daisy light ribbons were back. She used the regained energy to sit her ghost self up and then to rise back up through the dirt to the forest floor. She liked being a ghost, because she couldn't feel the pains of suffocation and the terrible fears she felt in her coffin. Her body was resting again now.

Reena knew she wasn't really a ghost, because she was still alive, buried down in her grave, but she didn't have another word for it, so she called herself a ghost. She floated above the plot of ground and the faint sunshine showed her where the ground had been patted down on top of her.

She floated higher, above the trees and could see the first arc of the sun rising above the ocean, far to the east. To the north lay San Francisco, but she couldn't see that far.

Her body was already calling her back, but she refused to go. She knew this was her last chance to escape and she lowered herself to the forest again and floated toward the exit. She had no plan other than getting away from her body.

"Please, help."

The voice was soft but she heard it clearly. *Michael.*

Reena veered to her right, flying right through all the trees in her path.

There he was. Oh Michael...

She saw the knife in his ankle immediately. He was talking on his cell phone and she knew he had called for help.

She moved to him and looked into his eyes, those beautiful eyes she loved to stare at. She looked at his lips and tried to pretend to kiss him, even though she couldn't feel his skin.

I love you, Michael.

He just leaned back and sighed. "I love you, Reena."

Oh my God, you heard me! I love you!

"I wish I'd been able to get Sue to tell me where you are. I have no idea where to find you."

He leaned over and touched his ankle and then moaned from the pain of the knife.

He hadn't heard her after all.

Reena felt the pull of her body again. It was getting stronger. She had an overwhelming desire to return, but she didn't want to.

She tried to ignore the pressure to return and she climbed inside Michael's body again.

The life force inside him felt so wonderful. She felt strength but mostly she felt his love. He was thinking of her and the love just washed over her.

Suddenly the force pulling her back to her body snapped.

Reena realized her body had just died.

She felt sad, knowing she would never again feel Michael's soft kisses, never again laugh with her Mom, never again see her Dad smile with pride at something she'd done.

Never again.

Her life was over, even though she still lived a ghostly existence inside Michael.

She felt the agony he felt. She felt the anger and frustration. Mostly she felt his amazing love. He had truly loved her, and she bathed in that love now, wanting nothing more than to just thrive inside him.

Reena pushed a thought as hard as she could: I love you, Michael.

He hesitated. She wondered if he could sense her being with him.

She pushed the thought again, even harder.

Then she relaxed, totally drained of energy.

He swallowed. "I hear you. I don't know how, but I hear you. I love you, Reena. Always and forever."

She wanted to cry with happiness. Somehow, she knew they'd work things out.

Tails

I love dogs.

I once owned two dachshunds (one of whom was a model for a story that appears later in this book), and now my family has a passive-aggressive Havanese.

One of the things that I love is there inability to hide their emotions. You always know when your pet is happy, because her tail is wagging. Sometimes that tail can seem like it's out of control.

There's times when my dog will be lying down, looking at me, and if I talk to her, her tail starts waving, even though, if I only looked at her head, she looks bored to tears. She can't fool me, though, when that tail is banging around!

Once upon a time, I was talking to somebody about this phenomenon and they said, "Wouldn't it be great if people had tails?"

Well, this story pretty much built itself in my mind immediately.

Around the same time, Kevin J. Anderson was hunting for stories for his new anthology, Blood Lite II, a collection of humorous horror stories. I'm not sure how this story might be classified as horror (and Kevin made the same comment), but he loved the story, and I was very pleased to be in the book.

Marie was late getting home from work, but she had a good reason. I could tell as soon as she climbed out of her car.

It's not that I snoop on my wife or anything, but I just happened to be looking out the big bay window in the living room when her tan Honda Civic pulled into the driveway.

She yawned briefly, then clamped her mouth shut as she slammed the door and pushed the button on her keyless remote. I could hear the car's faint beep drift through the window.

She smiled and waved at me, her long blonde hair flowing behind her in the wind. For about the millionth time, I thanked the gods that had brought us together a dozen years earlier.

Of course, smiles are deceiving, so although it was nice to see, that's not what told me she was in a good mood.

It was her tail, pointing up to the sky that gave her away. It was doing some serious wagging.

I love Marie's tail. It's a beautiful blonde color, exactly matching her hair. She keeps it immaculately groomed, even though that costs her a lunch-hour every couple of weeks when she heads to the groomer.

My tail, on the other hand, is pathetic. I can't remember the last time I had the thing trimmed, let alone a complete grooming.

When Marie came through the front door, I smiled and gave her a long hug and kiss. I reached behind her and loosely grasped the base of her tail. The feel of it swishing faster and faster was so damned erotic.

Her tail was average length, about two feet, but wonderfully thick—my fingers barely reached around it. My own tail started to sway slowly as I rubbed hers.

"What's the good news?" I asked when we finally broke apart.

She laughed and glanced behind her. "Can't much hide it, can I?"

My tail was swaying in time with hers now. I was always so happy to have my wife home. She worked in downtown Detroit, twenty miles away, making tons of money investing other people's cash, while I looked for marketing opportunities on the Internet. Most days, my wagger dragged pretty low until I got a good look at her coming through the front door.

"Let's get a glass of wine," she suggested.

I poured as we slid into a couple of old rattan kitchen chairs, carefully guiding ourselves through the wooden slots.

Thwack, thwack, thwack.

I laughed, knowing she was dying to tell me what was up. She wouldn't be able to stop swinging until she told me.

"I got a promotion!" she finally said. It looked like she wanted to leap out of the chair, but she held back at the last minute, not wanting to injure herself. "Vice President of Investment Banking!"

"That's amazing! I'm so proud of you!"

We clinked glasses while I secretly wondered what investment banking might be. I had absolutely no idea what Marie really did from nine to five, but it was easy to see she was ecstatic.

Thwack, thwack, thwack.

The wine had been sitting in the fridge for a week or more, a bottle partially drunk in front of the latest Survivor season premiere. I wondered if we had more wine in the basement. It seemed like we might want to be doing a lot of celebrating.

Thwack, thwack.

I was momentarily surprised that it was my tail banging the chair this time. Not as rapidly as Marie's, but at least she could tell I was happy for her. She smiled broadly when she heard the sound, and my heart melted as it always did, which just made my tail swing a bit faster.

We caught up on the rest of the day's news. My side was pretty boring. The letter carrier dropped off a couple of books I had ordered, I picked up a pre-cooked ham to warm up for dinner, and the cat had puked on the living room rug.

I didn't much want to concentrate on the cat mess, so I told Marie about a homeless guy who was wandering the street earlier in the day. "You wouldn't have believed how terrible he looked. Tail just hanging straight down from his tail-hole, and I could see bugs crawling all over it. I thought I was bad about getting to the groomer, but maybe it takes somebody like that to really show you how lucky we are." I sipped my wine and added, "No life in him at all. Limp as a dead snake."

Marie nodded. I knew she didn't really care about things like that.

She told me more about the meeting where she got her promotion.

"I hadn't expected anything at all like this," she said. "Robby called me in after lunch, and I'm sure he knew I was worried. I was just swaying back and forth restlessly. He must have enjoyed watching me."

Robby was the president of the investment company. I couldn't remember his last name. I'd only met him once and wasn't impressed.

"He just stretched things out, didn't tell me what we were meeting about for almost ten minutes. Yapping about this and that. He even made me stand the whole time. I'm sure he was just enjoying watching my reaction. At least I thought so, at first, but..."

I looked at her. "But?"

She shook her head. "He was just making a point."

Now I was more puzzled than ever. He sounded like an asshole to me, making her show her emotions in front of him.

"How did you do?"

"Damned tail just wouldn't stay still. Slow circles, but sometimes it tried to hide between my legs. I was worried sick, thinking maybe he was going to fire me or something. There was that series of layoffs a couple months ago. Remember I told you about that?"

My tail drooped and dragged back and forth above the linoleum as I tried to think back. Did she tell me something about that?

"Don't worry," she said, letting me off the hook. "Like I said, he was just trying to make a point."

"I still don't understand," I said.

"My new job... so much of it involves talking to *very* senior investors. Chief Financial Officers of Fortune 500 companies, mostly." She gulped down her wine and went to the fridge to pour some more.

No thwacking any more.

"What's wrong?"

"Well, it's just that the deals are so much bigger than I'm used to. If I'm talking to a prospective customer, and I know I've got him hooked, I can't have my tail lifting up and pointing up at the ceiling. The customer would know how excited I was." She shook her head. "The sale would be killed."

I was confused. "But, that's just the way the world works."

Marie reached out her hand and touched mine. "I'll have to have it amputated."

I couldn't believe what I was hearing. Her beautiful blonde tail cut off? What? How could she even think of that for one second?

"Everyone in a senior position does it these days. When's the last time you saw a press conference by any government official with a tail?"

"But, that's different. They're always lying to us, and they don't want us to know."

"Well, yes. I won't be lying to anyone, but the principle is the same. I can't do the job if my tail is always giving my thoughts away."

I never did tell her I approved, and neither did my tail, but of course she did it anyway. I tried to support her as best I could. After all, I loved her more than anything.

We had the stub of her tail cauterized. Now, when I want to see it, I just have to go to the living room; Marie's tail is mounted above the fireplace.

When she comes home now, I can't tell how she feels. She climbs out of her Civic and smiles, but I don't know if it's real or an act for my benefit.

She never mentions that my tail rarely swings for her when she comes through the front door.

I can't help it. She just doesn't look human anymore.

Ursa Major

In one way, this story has been one of my most successful.

It started with a vacation with my then-girlfriend (now wife) to a cottage in northern Ontario. Fatima had two young daughters, and I was trying to bond with them, to hopefully become a family unit.

The cottage was in a remote location (although not as isolated as the cabin in the story), and when we returned home, I started to write "Ursa Major." I wrote one chapter each day, thinking of it as a locked-room murder mystery. I wanted to ensure my characters had no obvious way to escape their fate (except for the one way they ended up using, of course).

As I wrote each chapter, I emailed it to Fatima to read. She loved it, but she also told me, "That bear better not kill that little girl!" She was joking to some extent, but she also knew the story was based on me trying to bond with her older daughter (who was about six years old). She didn't want the daughter in the story killed by the bear. Too close to home.

I sent an early draft to Roy Robbins of Bad Moon Books. Roy was my publisher at the time, and he suggested I make the ending ambiguous. I did that, and it ended up being perfect for everyone! Roy published the book and it was a finalist for the Bram Stoker Award. I was surprised and very honored.

This story was optioned by a Hollywood studio for five years. Alas, it then went where most Hollywood stories go to die.

I once started a sequel called "Ursa Minor" but other projects kept getting in the way. Maybe one day...

CHAPTER 1

THE LITTLE GIRL SAT ON a pint-sized canvas chair. She'd been staring up to the sky for what seemed like forever. Of course everything boring seems forever to a six-year-old.

"You're not my daddy."

Dan couldn't help feel a twinge in his heart. "No, I'm not, Nichole. I'm not trying to be a new daddy to you. But your mommy and I are very close friends."

Nichole didn't answer and Dan wasn't sure if she was looking in his direction or back up at the stars. It was past 1:00 a.m., and although they'd seen a few meteors, she hadn't been impressed.

"I love Daddy. I wish he was here."

"Daddy loves you, too. We all do."

"I don't like you. I want to go home."

Dan bit his lip, like he always did when he was under stress. Some ideas always seem better in the planning than in the execution, and this weekend seemed like it was going to be one of them.

"She'll love it," he'd insisted to Leah. They'd been dating almost a year and a weekend alone for him and Nickie had seemed like a brilliant idea. He'd booked seats on an Alaskan Airlines flight from Seattle to Fairbanks and rented a car. His cousin owned an honest-to-God log cabin out in the middle of nowhere, and Dan wanted to take Nichole there and have a night to watch the Perseid meteor shower. It would be great, he insisted. She'd bond with him and that would make things so much easier for he and Leah.

Nichole had other plans. She just wanted to go home.

There had been lots of meteors shooting across the sky. Maybe fifty of them in the half hour they'd been watching, but Nichole had only seen a handful. She'd looked away or blinked or rubbed her eyes. One meteor tore a blazing trail across the sky bright enough to illuminate the nearby trees, and Dan had stared at it, not believing it could be that bright.

Nickie missed it. She'd been playing with a scab on her knee. He'd pointed out the Big Dipper, Jupiter, and even the Milky Way, but nothing caught her interest.

"Can we go back now?" she asked. "I want to play with Pupply."

Dan thought of the wasted thousand dollars bringing her to Alaska. *Nothing to do about that now,* he thought.

"Sure." He started to fold up the chairs. "Did you like the stars at all?"

She shrugged. "Can we go home now?"

"We have to stay here till the day after tomorrow. Sunday morning we'll go home to Mommy."

"And Daddy."

"Yeah."

Dan wished he'd brought Leah here instead of Nichole and the dog. Leah was always so happy to do interesting things, but they never had much time to be together because of Nichole. He still wanted that life they'd talked about, with the three of them living together as one little family. Somehow, though, he had to get Nichole on board with that idea.

Leah had divorced the asshole two years earlier, but she'd been careful never to say anything negative about him to Nichole. Nothing about the drugs or the abuse or the other women. Dan understood why Nichole still loved her daddy; he was the perfect father whenever she was around.

He took her hand and they walked back toward the cabin. When they were about halfway there, Dan thought he heard a noise ahead.

"What was that?" shouted Nichole. She grabbed Dan's hand harder.

"Shhh."

"It's a monster!"

He crouched down and whispered, "It's not a monster, sweetie. Let's just be quiet and walk back to the cabin. We'll—"

There it was again. A low growl that resonated and echoed through the woods.

Nichole hugged Dan. "I'm scared."

He lifted her off the ground and left the chairs. He'd go back for them in the morning.

"It's okay. Really, it's just some animals in the woods. They won't bother us."

She buried her head in his neck and he heard her panting a bit. He rubbed her hair and kissed her forehead.

The cabin wasn't far from the clearing they'd been sitting at, maybe two hundred feet, but right then it seemed like two hundred miles. Each step seemed to take more courage than the one before. Dan was surprised at how the fear covered him. It was probably just a stupid raccoon or something.

And the growl came again.

Louder this time. Dan held tight to Nichole, knowing now that it was a bear. Brian, his cousin, had mentioned in passing that there'd been occasional bear sightings near the cabin, but he'd never had trouble with them. Grizzlies.

Shit.

He was walking slower but he couldn't help himself. Finally he could see the outline of the cabin in the darkness. His eyes were well adjusted to the darkness, but there was no moon, just starlight. He saw the bear walking around just outside the door. It looked big, but it was hard to judge in the dark. He couldn't see the color, either. It could be black or brown.

Grizzlies are brown, he knew. Then he questioned himself. Did he really know that? He wasn't completely sure.

He stood still, holding Nichole and shushing her. She hadn't seen the bear and he held her so she wouldn't get a glimpse of it.

"Why are we stopping?"

Her voice sounded like thunder in the quiet, but the bear didn't seem to hear her.

"Quiet, sweetie. We're just waiting a bit."

"Is there a monster there?"

"No. There's no monster."

The bear turned its head and seemed to be sniffing.

Double shit.

Dan looked back the way they'd come, but it was so dark, he didn't think he could run away. The path was covered with branches and stones. He'd trip for sure.

"I want Mommy."

"Shhh..."

The bear stood up and stretched its arms out and made a thundering roar that made Dan feel sick. The bear was looking right at them, but he still didn't think it could see them. The wind was blowing from the bear to them so he hoped it couldn't smell them.

The door to the cabin was about six and a half feet tall. Dan knew that, cause he was close to that height himself. When the bear was standing up, it was way taller.

Must be close to eight fucking feet tall.

Could bears really be that tall? It must weigh more than a thousand pounds...

It started to sniff the air.

Dan couldn't climb a tree carrying Nichole, and he wasn't convinced that would work anyhow. He was pretty sure he'd heard that bears can climb trees. Hell, this one might be able to just knock a tree down.

He would have to scramble back the way they came if the bear attacked.

"Sweetie, I might have to run."

"Why?"

"There's a bear at our cabin. Don't worry, though, it won't bother us. We might just want to get away from it. I read in a book that bears never want to hurt people."

"Did the bear read that book, too?"

Dan pulled her head to his neck again to quieten her.

The bear fell back down so it was on all fours, and it padded its way around the back of the cabin. He couldn't see it anymore.

He hoped that meant the bear was gone forever, but he decided to wait, to be sure. He couldn't see his watch in the dark.

One one thousand, *two* one thousand, *three* one thousand...

After two minutes of not seeing the bear, he started to walk toward the cabin.

"Don't talk, sweetie. We're going to the cabin now."

Nichole kept quiet, and Dan held her tight as he moved slowly. He didn't want to make any noise he didn't have to, so he watched the ground again, avoiding twigs whenever he could. A couple of times, he flipped back to look at the sides of the cabin. Still nothing.

Twenty feet to go.

Ten.

The bear roared and lumbered around the corner of the cabin. The animal was huge, even on all fours. The top of its head reached as high as Dan's chest.

He froze for a second. Nichole's screams kicked him into action and he ran the last few yards to the cabin. The door was made from the same heavy logs that the rest of the cabin was, and it pulled out, so he grabbed the handle and yanked. He knew the bear was running toward him; he could feel the earth shake.

The door opened and he squeezed himself and Nichole through just as the bear reached them. It roared and bit into Dan's jacket. He didn't let it slow them down and he heard the fabric rip.

Inside, he heard Pupply let out a small whimper. The dog knew something was wrong.

He swung around and pulled the door, but before he could close it, the bear stuck its head inside. Dan stared into its eyes and felt his bladder open. He didn't care. He just needed to get the fucking door closed.

The bear had other ideas. It flicked its head as if to knock away a fly, and the door went flying open. It could have been made of balsa wood instead of heavy logs.

Nichole screamed again and Dan scooped her up. He wanted to run to the bathroom but the door there was only flimsy plywood. The bear could break it down without a thought. Instinct sent him to the only other room, a storage room that had a door made of logs that matched the rest of the cabin.

"Pupply!"

The little brown dachshund was already close to the storage room, and it ran in behind them. Good thing, since Dan had no plans to go back for it.

He raced through the door and put Nichole down. He pulled the door as fast as he could to close it.

A second later he felt the cabin shudder as the bear pushed the door.

"Please, God... please hold the fucking door."

Nichole was a heap on the floor and was sobbing openly. She pulled Pupply close to her.

Dan held the door with his hands, knowing he couldn't do much to stop the bear if the monster really wanted inside.

The pressure eased. The bear seemed to have moved away from the door.

Dan could hear Nichole's cries along with his own panting. He knelt down and then sat beside her. "It's okay, sweetie. I won't let the bear hurt you. I promise."

"I want to go home!"

"I know. I want that, too. We'll go home in the morning. As soon as it's daylight, we'll drive back to the city and get the first plane home."

"The bear won't let us!"

"He'll be gone soon. He just wanted to scare us."

"I'm scared."

"I know. But soon the bear will be gone and we'll be asleep in our beds. Pupply can sleep with you."

They were talking in the dark. There were no lights other than a small window that let a hint of starshine in, but other than that, it was pitch black. Brian had added the storage room to the main cabin some number of years ago, but he never bothered adding lighting.

Dan leaned against the side of the room beside the window and held Nichole. He whispered to her that everything would be okay.

He guessed it was about two o'clock, and he wasn't about to count seconds. It seemed totally quiet in the main part of the cabin, but he wanted to wait a half hour or so before taking a look.

There were no lights out there, either. He didn't have a flashlight, having dropped it along with the chairs. He didn't smoke, so no lighter. His cell phone was in the car, because there was no service in the wilderness, so he couldn't use the light from it.

Nichole had stopped crying. She just held onto him and took long, deep breaths.

He whispered to her, "Patty cake, patty cake, baker's man. Bake me a cake as fast as you can..."

"I don't like that song."

"What songs do you like, Nicky?"

"Sing me 'Chisel Boy.'"

"I don't know that one. How about 'Three Blind Mice'?"

"No."

They didn't talk for a few minutes. Dan listened, but he couldn't hear anything in the main part of the cabin.

"I'm going to take a look to be sure the bear's gone home."

"No! He'll eat us!"

"It's okay. Really. We have to check."

"NO! It's dark!"

He stayed with her.

Chapter 2

Nichole was asleep with the dog. For a while, Dan had held her in his arms, feeling as much relief and security from her as she felt from him. Maybe more. She wasn't the one who pissed herself.

Dan had rubbed her hair, feeling the black strands slip through his fingers. He could easily imagine the concern written on her face, since he'd seen it dozens of times before. Nichole worried about everything. If she misplaced a toy, she'd start crying. If Daddy was ten minutes late picking her up for his weekly visit, she'd be despondent. She was a girl who needed everything to go exactly right, or she'd start crying.

Leah kept telling him that she'd grow out of it, and he believed her. Six was such a young age.

When he had been six, all he had to worry about was which cartoon to watch on Saturday morning. Now, at forty, he was starting to feel the first signs of age creeping into his body. He'd given up playing his weekly baseball games with the guys, struggled to stay awake past ten at night, and sometimes felt like his muscles were fighting him.

Oh, to be six again...

He carefully lay Nichole down and stood up, stretching his arms. He took his sweater off and put it under her head for a pillow.

Through the small window, he could see the stars. He didn't see any meteors.

He carefully moved to the door and turned the knob. It was a tight fit and made a popping noise when it sprung open. He wondered if it'd always been like that or if the bear had caused it.

There was still no sound.

Dan swung the door open and looked around. The room was almost as dark as the storage room, but it seemed safe. He took one step—

The roar came from the part of the cabin he couldn't see, behind the open door. He pulled the door back shut as fast as he could and then heard the bear bang its body against the wood.

"Fuck!"

He leaned against the door, knowing it was mostly useless.

Nichole woke and called, "Mommy!"

"I'm here, sweetie. Dan. Just stay where you are."

The bear stopped banging the door but it bellowed and Nichole started crying again. Dan sat and held her to him.

Several times the bear roared and then it got quiet again. Dan thought he heard it pad away from the door, but he might have been imagining that.

He was surprised the door hadn't shattered into a million splinters. There was no way the bear had put all its weight into it.

He's waiting for us.

The thought made him shudder. Shouldn't the damned thing just leave them alone? Bears didn't just wait for their prey, did they?

He tried harder to think of what Brian had said about grizzly bears and what he knew about them. They were fucking big, that much he knew.

"They're not herbivores. They eat almost anything," Brian had said. "You think of them as eating berries or maybe fish, but they'll eat animals, too. Even big mammals like moose or elk."

Swell.

Dan couldn't hear anything, but he wasn't about to check to see if the bear was gone.

What if the door closed behind the grizzly and it didn't know how to get out of the cabin?

What if he was hungry and just figured he knew there was food here waiting, so why go anywhere else?

What if he was just the meanest fucking bear in Alaska and just wanted to finish what he'd started?

Dan tried to shut down his mind. This wasn't helping.

He yawned and lay down beside Nichole. He used the sweater as a pillow for him and she had her head lying on his shoulder.

I'll protect you, Nickie.

Part of him wondered if he'd be able to keep that promise. Somehow, they both fell asleep.

Chapter 3

Dan blinked his eyes open, feeling confused. His neck and sides hurt from sleeping on the floor. Then it all came back and he stood up, staring at the door to the main part of the cabin.

Sunlight streamed into the room. He checked his watch: 7:42 a.m.

Saturday?

Yes, Saturday, he decided.

Nichole was just waking too. Pupply had been sleeping by her feet, but she was awake now too, and staring up at Dan.

"I want water."

"Yeah, I bet you do, sweetie."

He put one ear to the door but didn't hear anything.

"I have to go pee pee. I want Mommy."

Dan couldn't hear anything in the main room of the cabin, but after last night he knew that might not mean much.

The window was at eye level. It was about twelve inches square.

Outside, all he could see were bushes and trees. The sun was up and it looked like a warm day out.

If he broke the window, Nichole could get through, but there's no way he would let her go. What good would that do? He'd still be stuck there.

"I want Mommy!"

He went and picked up the little girl and smiled. "I know you do. I do too, sweetie, and I'm trying to be sure we can go see her."

"I have to go pee pee!"

"Can you wait a few minutes? I have to check to see if it's safe."

He put her down and she sat cross-legged. Pupply yawned and crawled into her lap. The dog was a miniature dachshund and would never outgrow Nichole's lap.

Dan put a finger to his lips. "Shhh."

He listened again at the door and then cracked it open.

The bear was there. It was lying down, staring right at him. When he'd opened the door, the bear growled and started to get to its feet. He shut the door immediately.

"Goddamn it."

"I *need* to go pee pee!"

One good thing: the front door to the cabin was wide open, so the bear wasn't trapped there. It could leave whenever it wanted. They just had to out-wait it.

The storage room was narrow, only about six feet wide and eight feet long. There wasn't a lot of stuff actually stored in the room, but what was there was in the far end. Dan went to take a quick inventory.

There were two large boxes filled with decorating magazines. It looked like Brian had big plans for the cabin that he never followed through on.

There was a toolbox that made Dan's eyes light up until he opened it and found only some short screws and nails and a screwdriver. Not even a hammer. There was an orange tarp that might have been used to cover stuff outside when it rained.

He found a well-stocked first-aid kit that he hoped they wouldn't need.

Extra light bulbs. A fishing pole. A lantern but nothing to light it with. Bug spray.

A small box full of baggies that seemed to contain marijuana. Dan wasn't an expert but it smelled that way to him.

The last box held bedding. He pulled that out and brought it over to Nichole. "This will be more comfortable to sit on."

"Is the monster still there?"

He nodded and tried to smile, but his mouth didn't seem to want to cooperate.

Nichole sat on a baby blue comforter. There was a small pillow in the box, too, and she put that at one end. It was a decorative pillow, like the kind Brian had left on the couch, but Nichole could use it for sleeping.

Fuck that. We're not gonna be here another night.

Behind a box was a fan—a white fan about twelve inches in diameter that stood on a base. He couldn't think of any way to turn the fan into a weapon. He looked around the room and there was no electrical outlet, but even if there had been, the bear could swipe the fan from his hands with its baby claw.

"That's it, Brian? That's all you left us?"

In frustration, Dan threw the fan against the boxes containing the decorating magazines. He wanted to hit someone.

"Fuck!"

As soon as he said it, he remembered Nichole and he took a deep breath to try to calm himself down. When he turned, she was staring at him with tears in her eyes.

"I'm sorry, sweetie. I shouldn't get mad. I just want us to go home."

She moved her hand between her legs as tears fell down her cheeks.

"Oh, God, I'm sorry, Nickie. Come here."

She stood and shuffled to him, staring down at the floor. There was a stain where she'd been sitting.

"Take your panties off and we'll get them dried."

She pulled her underwear off and handed them to Dan, who hung them from the corner of the window. It was warm there and they'd dry in a couple hours, he figured.

Then he went and ripped out some sheets from the magazines.

"This is the closest we have to toilet paper, sweetie."

She pressed the paper between her legs and then dropped it. He kicked it to one side.

Pupply walked to the door, shook her tail, and started to whimper.

Jesus, now the dog has to go out.

He got some more paper and spread them out and then lifted Pupply onto them. Maybe she'd remember how she was trained...

The dog immediately walked off the papers and over to the door. She lay down staring at the door and made a small "woof."

"Do you have breakfast?"

"No, all our food is out there, Nickie." He pointed to the door.

"But I want water. And cereal."

"Me too."

They were quiet again for awhile. Dan didn't know what to do. There was nobody around for many miles, no way to contact anybody, no weapons, no food, and no water.

He knew there was a rifle in the cabin, but there was no way to get to it. Same for the short wave radio. Brian had planned for needing help -- just not from the storage room.

Leah would be waiting at the airport tomorrow afternoon for them, and if they weren't on the plane, she'd panic and call his cell, but she wouldn't get him.

"Where is this cabin, exactly?" she'd asked.

"Outside Fairbanks."

He took her hand and led her to the computer, calling up Google Maps.

"Here's Fairbanks, just about smack in the middle of Alaska."

"Right in the middle of nowhere, you mean?"

He zoomed in.

She laughed and pointed at the monitor. "There's a place called North Pole right near there."

"Don't tell Nickie. She'll want to go there. Anyhow, see how Highway 3 goes west? We follow that road about a hundred miles until we find an old gold mine. It's been abandoned for many years, but there's a side road there that goes north. The road kind of turns into a gravel road and then dirt, but eventually there's a fork. We take the right fork and then go another twenty miles or so. The cabin isn't very far from... well, it's not showing here, but I think it's called Fools Road or something like that. Named for the gold rush."

Leah looked up at him. "I can't remember all that."

"Don't worry. I've been there a half dozen times and I know exactly where to go. Brian wanted privacy, and he sure as hell found it."

"Write it down. All the directions."

He nodded, and now he wished he'd followed through on that promise.

Nichole looked like a miniature version of Leah. She had black hair running halfway down her back. Leah's hair was the same color but shorter. Sometimes she wore it in pig tails, and that turned Dan on like crazy.

They had the same sparkly green eyes, the same smile, even the same light chuckle when they laughed.

He missed Leah.

"Sweetie, I have to go pee pee now, too. We'll use this corner over here as our bathroom."

"That's our *bathroom?*"

"Yes."

He unzipped his jeans and stood in the corner, staring at the walls. When he finished urinating, he zipped back up and was surprised to see Nichole standing near him.

He felt himself begin to blush. Maybe she'd never seen anybody go pee while standing up.

She giggled. "You look so funny!"

In spite of everything, he couldn't help chuckle himself.

He led her back to the comforter and then saw the dog again. He lifted the dog over to their corner bathroom and put her down there. She sniffed but then trotted back to lay by the door.

Dan sat beside Nichole. "At least it's light out now so we can see."

"Do you have a gun?"

"No. Not even at home." He decided not to say anything about the rifle. She'd see it if he got a chance to grab it.

"How will you kill the monster so we can go home?"

Good question, he thought.

"I think he's going to get tired of waiting and leave us."

"But what if he doesn't?"

"He will."

She stared at him and asked again, "But what if he doesn't?"

He hugged her. "I don't know yet, Nickie. But I'll think of something."

Chapter 4

Three o'fucking clock.

Dan felt like pacing but there was almost no room to do it. The storage room seemed even smaller than it had earlier. He'd never been claustrophobic, but the feeling of being trapped was getting to him.

He was hungry. And thirsty.

Pupply finally couldn't hold her bladder anymore. She crouched and let a long flow of urine go, right by the door where she'd been sitting most of the day. It trickled between the floorboards. At first Dan had a flood of anger, because he'd tried to get the dog to go in the corner a few times to no avail. She just kept moving back to her post by the door. The anger was quickly gone, though. He knew the dog was as unhappy as he was.

His mouth was dry, and he knew that Nichole's was too. He could see her lick her lips every once in a while in a losing battle.

How long could they stay there with no food or water? Dan felt an urgency he hadn't had before and once more went to look through the meagre supplies that were in the corner, checking and double checking each box. He tried to envision each item as a weapon but nothing really clicked. He could throw the lantern at the bear but the damned thing wouldn't even notice the blow.

He grabbed the fishing pole and thought about using it to somehow ensnare the bear's neck and strangle it.

When he took the rod closer to the light, though, he could see that there was no reel and no fishing line. It was just the pole, which would be of no help whatsoever. *Shit.* He threw the pole back into the corner.

Nichole watched Dan as he pored through the boxes. He glanced back at her now, and saw that she watched his frustration. A tear rolled down her cheek.

He went to sit beside her, both having their backs against the wall beneath the window.

"We'll be okay," he said. He patted her thigh and smiled at her.

"How?"

Nichole looked up at him with her big green eyes wide open. She didn't believe him.

"I don't know yet," he admitted. "All I can tell you is that I'll think of something. I promise."

She looked back down at the floor. "Mommy told you to take care of me. I heard her."

"Yes. And I'm going to."

"You shouldn't have brought me here."

"There was no reason to think a bear would be here, Nickie. But I really believe it's going to get bored soon and leave."

She didn't reply.

Dan had seen a photo of Leah when she was six years old, and it was like she and her daughter were twins. That was good news for Nichole, who would grow into a beautiful woman like her mom.

If she lives through the weekend, he thought.

He wanted to slap himself for that thought. Dan taught a class in motivational skills at the local college and knew that when people are under stress, they can start to talk themselves into giving up or making bad decisions, all based on feelings of hopelessness or despair.

Think positive.

"You're going to have quite a story to tell your friends," he said.

She didn't answer.

"Do you know how I met your mommy?"

Nichole looked up at him and shook her head.

"She came to see me, to talk about you."

"Why?"

"She was worried about you. She wanted you to be happy after Daddy left."

Dan had an urge to peek through the door, but he didn't want to see that damned bear again.

"I told her you'd be happy. And you have been. It's nice to have two houses to be able to live at."

"Are you going to marry Mommy?

He hesitated before answering. Leah wanted Nichole to see him gradually be a bigger and bigger part of their lives, rather than shock her with big steps. But now, she'd asked him...

"Yes. One day. Not for a long time, though."

She didn't reply and Dan wondered what she was thinking. Finally she said, "I guess that's okay."

There was a bump at the door.

Nichole screamed.

Dan put his arm around her shoulder. "Shhh... don't yell, sweetie. That'll just encourage him."

She tried to stop but ended up snivelling and crying, trying to be quiet. Snot ran down to her mouth.

The door creaked as the bear put its weight against it. Dan knew the door couldn't hold up forever but there wasn't anything he could do about it. There was no place to hide.

"Here," he said. "Let's go behind the boxes in the corner."

He picked up Pupply and led Nickie to the far end of the storage room, where they sat behind the boxes of magazines and drugs. If the bear broke the door down, the safety of the boxes would prove to be an illusion, but it helped Nichole feel better and she was able to stop crying. She wiped her nose on her shirt.

The bear stopped pushing.

Dan listened but didn't hear anything. He put a finger to his lips to tell Nichole to stay quiet and then moved toward the door.

Nothing.

He put his ear to the space between the door and the door jamb, and he could hear the bear making small noises, as if it were panting on the other side of the door.

Dan's heart started to race, and he had a vision of the bear listening to him on the other side of the door.

He glanced back and saw Nichole staring at him, wondering what was happening.

He closed his eyes and kept listening. The panting seemed to get quieter, and maybe he heard the bear walking away. Maybe.

There was a new type of sound now. More noise like pressing, but not against the door to the storage room. He wasn't sure but he thought it was coming from the main door to the cabin, as if the bear was pressing against the beams holding the door. The door itself wasn't closed, so it had to be the jamb.

Or maybe it was something else completely.

The noise stopped. One small slap was all that followed. There were no further noises. No pressure, no pantings, no foot steps.

He opened his eyes and once again put his finger to his lips for Nichole. The bear was gone. He could sense it.

Five minutes passed. Ten...

Dan turned the door handle as slowly as he could, wanting to make no noise at all.

As he tugged the door open a few inches, he could see the room. There was no sign of the bear.

He waited again and then opened it a few more inches, enough to allow him to easily see into the cabin.

The stench hit his nose. He could see a huge pile of bear shit not far from the door. It was a mound about a foot tall. It looked bigger than several Pupply-sized mounds. Flies crawled across it.

Dan tried to ignore the smell. There were parts of the cabin he couldn't see without opening the door wider, which he was still reluctant to do.

He stared at the door to the cabin, wondering if the bear was just outside.

That's when he saw the rifle.

It was mounted on the wall near the door, hanging vertically, easy to get to if you need it after coming into the cabin.

Wish I grabbed that before, he thought.

He opened the door a bit more, ready to slam it back shut if the bear was still in the cabin. He did it as slowly as he could, not wanting to make any sudden movements.

He felt his heart beating again as he inched out and looked around the cabin. The bear was gone. He breathed a sigh of relief and started to walk toward the main cabin door. He would close it or grab the rifle, or both.

A few more feet, and then the grizzly walked back into the cabin and roared.

For a split second, Dan and the bear stared at each other.

Even walking on all fours, it was standing as high as Dan's stomach. He couldn't believe how massive it was. Its hair was brown but much of it seemed tipped with a silvery color, making it seem like the hair would be prickly like a porcupine.

The bear stared at him and opened its mouth. The teeth were long, especially the two sharp daggers that would rip his body apart. Those incisors had to be at least four inches long.

Its mouth and snout were covered with blood. It had been feeding on something big outside.

The grizzly roared and tensed its muscles, ready to pounce.

Dan jumped backward into the storage room just as the bear leaped. Again he felt the weight of the animal pushing on the door.

It stopped suddenly, though. As if it knew it didn't have to try very hard. Now that it had satisfied its hunger with something else, there was no rush. He could outwait Dan and Nichole.

Dan slumped with his back to the door, feeling helplessness and frustration wash over him.

Chapter 5

Dan blinked his eyes open and gasped for air. He was disoriented and blind. As he blinked, he started to see tiny hints of light from the window.

He pressed the *Light* button on his watch: a little after one in the morning.

His neck and back had spasms of pain from lying on the floor. He'd used the tarp he'd found as a pillow, and it wasn't doing much good.

Nichole slept beside him and Pupply slept at her feet. He could hear both of them breathing and that was a huge relief.

In his dream, Nickie had died. He'd had to carry her limp body back to Leah. The girl had been ripped to shreds by the bear and he carried the remains of her corpse to her grave. Leah was dressed in a long black dress and veil and she stared daggers at him as he gently lay her daughter into her small hole in the ground.

Of course Leah would blame him if anything happened to Nickie. He had promised to take care of her. Worse, he'd laughed at the suggestion there was any need to take any real precautions. Nobody had expected them to be terrorized by a grizzly bear, but Leah had been very clear that she wasn't all that keen on him taking her daughter two thousand miles to the middle of nowhere.

If anything happened to Nickie, how could he ever ask Leah for her forgiveness?

Leah was the kindest, sweetest woman he'd ever known. At thirty-three, she was seven years younger then he was, scarred by a terrible marriage. When she finally had the courage to throw the bastard out, it took every bit of energy she could muster.

"I needed to protect Nickie," she'd told him. "I needed to not let her see what kind of monster her father was. One day, he'd turn on her as he did on me, and I couldn't allow that."

"You did the right thing," Dan said after hearing her story.

Just listening to Leah when she had her first session with Dan made him angry. He controlled himself because it was unprofessional to react to a client that way, but there was such a deep sweetness to Leah, an unadorned wonderfulness that permeated her and spread like an aura, that he couldn't help himself.

For the first time in eight years of practice, he stared at a client and saw a beautiful, kind woman. He didn't see what he was supposed to. He wasn't being detached and clinical. He wanted to help her in a more personal way than he'd ever thought possible.

What the hell is going on? he'd asked himself over and over.

He knew he should stop seeing her. It wasn't professional to treat a patient he could feel himself falling in love with.

At the end of each session, she smiled at him. A huge, wide smile that must have felt forced but that tugged at his emotions and turned him inside out.

After four fifty-minute sessions, he said, "Leah, I have to stop seeing you. I won't be charging you for today, and I can't let you schedule any more sessions."

"Why? What happened?"

He couldn't tell her. He couldn't find the words to say that he had lost all sense of objectivity in her case. He just stared at her and felt a tear fall to his cheek.

That's when she smiled again and he couldn't help himself. He moved to her and hugged her, and she hugged him back just as hard.

There's no way he could allow her daughter to die. It would kill Leah's soul, too. And that would ruin him. He knew he couldn't survive if that happened.

Patting Nickie's hair, he tried to lick his lips but he couldn't seem to work up enough saliva. His tongue rolled over cracks in his lips and on his gums. It felt like he was licking concrete. Nickie would be feeling the same thing.

He placed her head on the small pillow and stood up to stretch. Pupply woke and yawned and watched as Dan moved to the small window.

He'd looked at the window so often now, he was sure he knew its dimensions exactly, but he had to check one more time. He centered his head and could see there was absolutely no chance at all of him squeezing through. It looked like Nichole could get through, if the glass was gone, but that wouldn't actually do her any good. She was in the middle of nowhere. If she left the cabin on her own, she'd be just as dead after a couple days. If the bear didn't get her, she'd still die of hunger and thirst.

It was cloudy out, but Dan could see a hint of the moon behind the clouds, illuminating bits of the landscape. All he could really see were trees, though. During the day, he saw the dirt road that led back to where his rented car was parked.

He couldn't hear the bear, but that didn't mean anything. He knew bears were often nocturnal and there's no chance he could do anything against the beast in the dark. Even the moonlight failed to give him any assurances tonight.

After ten minutes of staring out the window, he went back to the tarp and tried to sleep. His back and neck complained, though, and his mind refused to shut down. He stared into the darkness for the rest of the night, thinking occasionally of the dream where he carried Nickie's dead body back to her mother.

Chapter 6

Noon. Sunday. Dan stared at his watch again as if somehow he was calculating wrong. They'd been held hostage for thirty-six hours or so.

Nickie was standing at the window on her tip-toes, trying to look out, but she couldn't quite see. Dan lifted her up so she could look out.

The window faced south and the sun was blazing down at them. Nickie squinted as she looked out.

"It's so hot."

Dan nodded and kissed her cheek. "I know."

The storage room felt like a sauna, but there was no way to cool it down.

He'd heard the bear in the other part of the cabin moving around earlier, panting with the occasional growls.

Just another day with our grizzly little friend.

"Are you looking forward to going back to school?" he asked. Nichole would be going into grade two in a few weeks.

She nodded.

"Can you break the window?"

Dan pursed his lips. He should have thought of that. He lifted her over to the side of the room and asked her to hold Pupply.

He went back to the tool box and found the screwdriver and used it to smash the glass window. It seemed harder than he expected, but after a few hits the glass shattered and fell outside.

Part of him wished the glass had fallen inside, but the pieces were really way too small to use as a weapon, so it was best it all be outside where Nickie couldn't cut herself.

He ran the screwdriver around the edges of the window, clearing away the tiny bits of glass that didn't fall out.

Suddenly, he grabbed the screwdriver like a knife and stabbed the wooden walls. Maybe he could enlarge the hole. He jabbed over and over, trying to chisel the opening. No dice. Only tiny slivers of wood fell off by the time his hand was too tired to keep going.

A cool breeze blew into the room. It felt amazing on his face. He picked Nickie up and held her back to the window so she could feel it, too.

"Mmm..."

Nichole closed her eyes and just soaked in the cool breeze. "Can you give Pupply some air, too?"

Dan lifted the little brown dachshund up to the window. The dog sniffed brightly at the fresh air and seemed to perk up.

"Daddy gave me Pupply for my birthday," said Nichole.

"I know. He's a nice dog."

"I was three and couldn't say 'Puppy' right. I called him Pupply." Nichole laughed and Dan couldn't help joining her.

"That's a nice name."

"He'd protect me."

Dan wasn't sure if Nickie meant the dog or her daddy and decided to not ask her to clarify. He wasn't sure he wanted to know.

"You said we'd go home today."

"There's nothing I want more than that, sweetie."

"Yeah."

She took Pupply and sat in the corner. Dan looked at her and thought she was losing weight. Maybe he was, too. Or maybe it was just his imagination. He looked back out the window and breathed in the fresh air. The sun beat down on his face.

And then...

He remembered watching an old episode of *Survivor* a few years back. It was one of the things that he and Leah first found they had in common. They'd tape the show and watch it after Nichole was in bed. Well, mostly they'd be making out on the couch with Survivor playing on the TV, but they managed to get the gist of the show.

One guy had started a fire with the lens of his eyeglasses.

Dan grabbed some papers from the magazines and crumpled them into a loose ball. He held his glasses up to the sun and tried to focus the heat onto the paper.

It's fucking hot enough, he thought.

He held the glasses as firmly as he could and tried not to let them move.

"What are you doing?"

"Trying to start a fire. Maybe I can burn the bear with it."

"Oh."

The light from the glasses didn't seem to focus as well as a magnifying glass would. He kept trying but after about ten minutes, he started to wonder if it was pointless. Dan remembered reading the old Ray Bradbury novel, *Fahrenheit 451,* in high school. That was the temperature that paper burned, and it made him wonder if he could possibly get that much heat. The paper was glossy, too, and maybe that made it less likely to catch fire.

He kept trying, as sweat ran down his face. His arms started to tire, and at one point, he thought he saw a tiny whiff of smoke, but it was gone before he could really focus on it.

Damn.

He pulled the eyeglasses back inside and let his arms fall to his sides.

He stared at the boxes of crap in the corner and remembered the baggies of marijuana. He'd never suspected Brian was into that shit.

He had no idea what temperature it would start to burn, but it couldn't hurt to try. He found the baggies and put some of the pot on a single sheet of paper, rolling it up like a huge cigarette. Once again he stood in the window and tried to light a fire with his glasses.

This time he saw traces of smoke much sooner. He kept at it, and after a few minutes, he could see the marijuana catch fire. Then the paper surrounding it caught as well, with the tip burning freely.

He grabbed the ball of paper he'd made earlier and used the makeshift cigarette to light that. It caught easily, and in turn he used that to light a big set of papers that he had rolled into a tube. It was like a torch he was now carrying.

"Yay!" cheered Nichole.

Dan knew he wouldn't have a long time so he steadied himself and walked to the door.

"Stay back, sweetie."

He pushed the door open and didn't hesitate. The bear was sitting in the middle of the room but it immediately raised itself to be on all fours and growled. Dan rushed to it, hoping to still catch it a bit off guard. He also knew that if he hesitated he'd lose his courage.

He walked deliberately, not running, so that he wouldn't cause the flame to go out.

The bear stood up on its hind legs and Dan was only two feet from it when he stopped. Fear overcame him as he looked at the towering animal.

He knew the burning papers would do nothing to hurt the bear unless he could stab it in the eye and cause it to be blinded. Then he could do the same thing for the other eye and maybe, just maybe, he and Nichole could escape while the bear was blinded.

But...

Now that he was here, the bear towered over him. It was easily eight feet tall, maybe even more. Its head was high and it was roaring into the air, looking up.

The animal stunk of shit and decaying flesh.

He couldn't reach its eyes with his makeshift torch.

The bear roared again and Dan found himself staring directly into its snout. Its mouth was wide open. The teeth had dried blood on them and saliva dripped from a corner of its mouth.

Ursa Major.

The Great Bear. A flash image of the big dipper zipped through his mind, and he felt the irony of loving seeing Ursa Major in the sky the other night. Now it seemed like that was a million years ago.

The image vanished as the bear roared again and took a step toward Dan.

He broke from his trance and shoved the burning papers toward the bear's face.

Faster than Dan imagined, the bear swatted the torch away like it was a mosquito. He screamed a second later as he felt the bear's claws tear through the flesh of his arm.

He was wearing a long beige shirt and the arm sleeve was shredded. Blood spilled out between the rips.

Dan's arm fell to his side, as if he had no strength left. It felt like he'd been hit with a steam roller that turned his arm into tapioca.

He turned and ran back to the storage room, pulling the door shut behind him, before the bear could get moving and attack him again.

He leaned against the door.

"Pupply!"

Dan fought the pain to look at Nichole. "What? What?"

"Pupply ran out to help you!"

Shit.

He was out of breath from fear and pain, and he hesitated, not knowing what to do. The fucking dog was out there with the grizzly.

He listened at the door and Nickie ran there too and copied him. At first he couldn't hear anything, but then he heard a small noise. He wasn't sure what it was.

A thought came to him... maybe Pupply ran out the cabin door and the bear chased him. If that happened, now was the time for their escape. Maybe that's why it was so quiet.

He moved Nickie away from the door, excited, feeling their escape was at hand.

His left arm was still aching and bleeding but he totally ignored that. He used only his right arm to open the door and peek out.

The monster was there.

It was chewing the remains of Pupply. On the floor was the last remnants of the dog's carcass. Its head was there and its hind legs, but most of the middle section was a squishy bloody mess. It wasn't recognizable at all.

The dog's face seemed to be looking back toward Dan, and he thought he could see the pain and horror in its eyes as the bear continued to munch on its body.

The bear looked at Dan and growled, like it was laughing.

Even when it was alive, the dachshund was smaller than a single paw of the bear. It wouldn't be enough to satisfy its hunger and cause it to move on.

Dan closed the door and looked at Nickie.

"Did the monster get Pupply?"

He held her to him. "Yes, sweetie," he whispered. "The monster got him."

Nickie cried into his shoulder and he forget about his ruined arm, holding her tight to him with both arms. He didn't have a clue what to say to make her feel better.

"Danny," she whispered... and for a second, he thought she'd said, "Daddy."

He hugged her and kissed her cheek and wondered if he'd ever be able to fulfill his promise to bring her home safely.

Chapter 7

Dan went to get the first aid kit and found a roll of bandages. He wrapped his arm to try to stop the bleeding.

He and Nickie were getting used to peeing in the corner of the room, but they didn't have to do it very often, since they had no water to drink. He was actually losing track of time and when he saw that it was 7:00 a.m., it took him a couple of minutes to figure out that it was Monday. Could they really have been trapped here for two and a half days?

Leah would be expecting their plane to land tonight. What would she do when she found out they never boarded?

She'd want to contact him, but there was no way to do that. She'd eventually think of calling Brian, but...

Before the trip, he'd promised to leave Brian's phone number. Somehow it had never happened. She'd only met Brian once or twice and Dan wasn't sure she knew his last name. Probably not. Who'd remember a name like Montichelloe? She might have looked for a Brian Lange, hoping he'd have the same last name that Dan did, but it'd be hopeless.

Maybe she'd think to call some other relatives to find Brian.

Or maybe she'd just hope they'd missed the plane and would be on the next one.

Even if she somehow tracked Brian down, he lived in New Jersey. Would he really want to drop everything to fly to Alaska and check to see how things were going? Wouldn't he wait another day? Two?

Nickie was looking emaciated. Her lips were as dry as parchment and had lost all their color. She looked like a corpse as she slept.

The night had been rough. She kept crying about Pupply and saying how she wouldn't be able to sleep at all without him lying with her.

"I need him," she cried.

"I know, sweetie."

"He's never left me. I always sleep with Pupply."

"He's sleeping now, baby. He's in heaven and you'll be back together with him one day."

Hopefully not today.

"Is he with God now?"

"Yes. God is taking good care of him for you."

She cried and whimpered until about three o'clock before she finally fell asleep from exhaustion.

Dan looked down at her and felt his heart break for her. She was only six years old and had so much life ahead of her.

He felt a rush of anger flood through him. *I've got to fix this.*

It was like he was ordering himself to get up and fucking *do* something.

He looked back at the storage boxes and did yet another mental inventory. As much as he tried, the only thing close to a weapon was the screwdriver.

His left arm was a mess. He checked under the bandages and his flesh was still covered in blood and parts were still seeping. He knew that attacking the bear with the screwdriver wasn't likely to end up with any better result than the fire.

But what choice do I have?

He went back to the tool box and picked up the screwdriver, looking at it. At least it was a nice long one, about eight inches, not counting the yellow plastic handle.

Dan thrust it like a sword. "Gotcha," he said to his shadow.

He convinced himself it might work.

Nichole was still asleep and might stay that way awhile. Maybe that was best. He moved to the door.

Dan had first met Nichole about a month after he'd first hugged Leah in his office. When she'd returned his hug, he knew that he'd found someone very special. He couldn't have her as a patient anymore, but that was the least of his concerns.

They started dating, but they did it quietly, not wanting anybody to know that he was dating a former patient. They went to dinner and to the theater and they soon realized they wanted to spend all their time together.

Once when they were in a coffee shop, a song played on the radio. "I Knew I Loved You," by Savage Garden. The song talked about a man who felt he had dreamed a girl into life.

"Oh my God," he said. "That's exactly how I feel about you."

She smiled, that smile, the smile that always made his heart jump.

"I love you," she said. And then she added, "It's time for you to meet Nickie."

That night, he drove to her house and Leah introduced Dan to her as a friend. Nickie was shy and tried to pretend he wasn't really in the house. It took a half dozen visits before she overcame her shyness enough to say "Hi."

Nine months later, they were cooped up in a log cabin, being terrorized by the monster she'd dreamed about.

"I'm going to save you, sweetie," he whispered. He took one last look at her to be sure she was sleeping and then slowly opened the door to face the monster.

The bear seemed to be sleeping. It didn't move when Dan swung the door open. There was nothing left of Pupply except a bloody stain on the floor near the bear's snout. Maybe the scent from the dog's blood would make it less likely to smell Dan.

He moved inch by inch, carefully closing the door behind him and being sure it was secure. He wanted to be sure Nichole didn't follow him if she woke.

The room stunk of death and decay. The only noise was the sound of the bear breathing heavily. Its eyes were half-open and Dan wasn't sure if it was really asleep or not.

He could see the rifle hanging by the door. It was hanging vertically, pointed at the ceiling. There was a single barrel and Dan was sure he'd be able to fire it quickly once he had it in his hands. He thought of trying to get around the bear to just grab the rifle, but its back end was right below the gun. He couldn't get to the rifle without the bear moving.

The beast was huge and Dan wondered if all grizzlies got this big. It must weigh at least fifteen hundred pounds, and most of that was solid muscle.

He took another step.

The bear opened its eyes wide and stared at him. He felt his stomach lurch and wanted nothing more than to turn back and go hide in the storage room again. He'd have pissed himself again if he had anything left.

Then the bear lurched up to all fours and roared and jumped at Dan. He wasn't expecting it to jump and didn't have time to aim the screwdriver. The bear hammered into him and he dropped the tool. He felt the animal's jaws bite into his cheek. The pain of his flesh being ripped off his face was horrible.

The bear chewed while it held Dan down on the floor. It roared and bit into his upper left arm, where it had scratched him earlier.

Then it clawed his face, turning the flesh into streaming pieces of bloody tissue.

Dan fought and screamed but he was pinned by the bear and was totally helpless.

He knew he was going to die.

The pain made him scream again. He felt weak and could no longer even pretend to fight back. The bear chewed on a bit of his thigh.

Dan passed out.

They'd been dating for two weeks when they first made love.

It was the most amazing sensation Dan had ever felt. He held Leah in his arms and told her to close her eyes. He kissed her face softly... every bit of it. He kissed her eyelids and her cheeks and her temples and her forehead. He treated her body like the precious gem it was.

When he entered her, it was the most wonderful feeling he'd ever had. Intimacy washed over him and made him realize for the first time what true love really felt like. He wanted that feeling forever.

He remembered that feeling now as he regained consciousness—the feeling of true love taking over his senses.

The feeling passed as the pain hit him. He groaned from the horrible pain that seemed to radiate from everywhere at once. His head, his arms, his sides, and his legs all called out to him, screaming at him to do something to help.

He could barely move. It took several minutes to get to where he could force his right eye open. It was crusted with blood, but at least it opened. The other one didn't. There was so much pain coming from that area, he wondered if he still even had an eyeball there.

"God, please help..."

He was lying down. Something was on top of him. Leaves. Branches. Mud.

He tried to sit up but it was too difficult. He could barely move his arm and press the button to see the time. 11:00 a.m.

Nickie.

He'd left her sleeping four hours ago.

That thought gave him the strength he needed to try to sit up. He blinked his working eye and realized he was buried in mud and branches.

Stored away like food in the cupboard for when it was needed.

He shuddered at the thought of being a meal-in-waiting, but he wasn't sure he could do much about it. He was in a shallow grave, about a foot deep. He tried to stand but couldn't get any leverage on his left leg. It felt like dead weight and screamed more in pain at him. He panted and felt tears rolling down his cheek, forced out by the agony.

He wanted to die. He just wanted it to be over.

Except for Nickie. He thought of her, alone in the storage room, probably terrified, not knowing where he went.

Fuck.

He pushed and managed to pull himself out of the grave. It seemed to take every bit of energy he had. There was a pine tree nearby and he used it to climb to his feet. He found a long stick to use as a crutch and started to carefully walk, almost dragging his left leg as he went. The pain stabbed through him with every step.

"God..."

He walked a few feet and started to get into the groove of taking a step and then having a breath, taking another step...

The bear hit him from behind. He screamed in pain as it dropped him to the ground and started chewing on the back of his head.

He passed out again. This time, when he woke, it was dark out. He was back in the hasty grave, buried in mud and sticks.

Pain and frustration rolled over him. He cried.

Chapter 8

Somehow, Dan fought through his depression and felt a new surge of anger rush through him. The weekend was supposed to be a way for him to bond with Nickie, and now they were both trapped and maybe going to die.

He wondered what Nickie was doing. It'd been six hours since he tried to go after the bear with the screwdriver.

Stupid idea, he knew.

He managed the strength to sit up and look around. There was no sign of the bear. He was surrounded by trees, but through them, he could see the cabin in the distance. Maybe seventy feet away.

Last time the bear had surprised him from behind, but there was no sign of the damned thing in any direction now.

Bears could run a lot faster than he could, even at the best of times. Now, with his body being so broken, he had to be careful not to attract its attention.

In the cabin, Nichole probably was terrified, not knowing what happened to him.

At least, that's what he hoped was the case. If she panicked and went looking for him... how could he ever face Leah?

He still couldn't open his right eye and he reached up to touch it. It was a mass of bloody goo. The eyelid was crusted shut. He tried not to think about it.

Pain still lightninged through his body from all parts. The worst was his head. He reached up and found blood and gore covering just about every bit of his head. He thought he could feel a crack in his skull. There was a spot in the back that felt soft, like a sponge. Part of him wondered how he could still be alive, but mostly he just wanted to get back to the cabin and get the fucking rifle.

His left leg still hung limp as he pulled himself out of the grave. His torso was shredded from the bear's teeth and claws.

He wanted to be dead quiet, but he couldn't help letting out some moans from the pain as he stood. He found another branch to use as a crutch and once more looked behind him to be sure the bear wasn't around.

So far so good.

Each step crushed the nerves in his feet. It felt like explosions and he couldn't figure out how to stop the pain. He wondered if his body could take all this agony without causing a heart attack.

"You promise, right?" Leah had held his face in her hands. "You won't let anything happen to my baby, right?"

He laughed. "It's just a quick camping trip. Nothing can happen."

She still wasn't convinced, but Dan knew nothing could go wrong. He'd gone camping dozens of times, both alone and with Brian. They'd fished and cooked weinies over a fire, but mostly the camping was an excuse to drink lots of beer and gossip about people. They'd bitch about their employers or their families, and each would have embellished stories to outdo the other.

It was silly to worry. It was just a fucking camping trip.

"We need this trip, baby. We need to find a way for Nickie to accept me, and I'm sure this will go a long way for that. Who doesn't like sitting out watching the stars and a meteor shower?"

"Well, she is only six."

He shrugged. "I know she'll love it."

Leah finally smiled. "You're trying so hard and I really appreciate it. Even if this weekend doesn't work out, I know that one day she'll learn to love you."

He couldn't let Leah and Nickie down.

Foot by foot, he moved through the trees, trying to stay as close to each one as possible, both to use them as support and to hide from the bear.

The cabin seemed impossibly far away, with each new agony hitting his resolve and making him wonder if he shouldn't just give up.

But the rifle was there.

He moved as steadily as he could and then found himself in the open. The cabin was in a small clearing and there was now twenty feet to go.

He glanced behind him. Nothing.

The branch was helping him walk but once he moved into the open space, he'd be an easy target.

Nickie.

He took a deep breath and moved forward. He tried to move a bit faster than through the trees and didn't want to look back again. It would just slow him down and not make any difference.

Ten feet.

The bear walked around from behind the cabin, as it had that first night. Dan felt a sense of déjà vu as the bear roared and started moving toward him.

Dan felt the frustration race through him, fueling his need to move faster. He did that and somehow found the resolve to move his left leg. He hopped and skipped to the cabin door and tried to pull the door shut behind him.

Fuck.

The goddamned bear had its head inside the cabin and was forcing the door open again. It flicked it away like a pretzel.

For a moment, Dan thought of going to the left side to grab the rifle, but he knew he couldn't get it down and aimed in time. He made a snap decision and shuffled to the storage room again, barely being able to get inside and pull the door shut.

The bear smashed against the door, but it held.

Nichole was lying flat on her stomach below the window, not moving.

Dan froze, praying that she was alive. Part of him wanted to not know, to go back out and let the damned bear rip him to pieces. That would be better than knowing that Nichole was dead.

He heard an echo from Leah. *Take care of my baby.*

The bear had stopped making noise and the cabin was deathly silent. He inched toward Nichole. His mouth was shut tight and he fought back tears.

There!

He saw her chest move. She was alive.

Dan didn't care about the pain stabbing his body. He rushed to her and crouched down on his knees, carefully rubbing her back.

"Nickie?"

She blinked her eyes open and stared up at him. Her expression turned to fear and he knew that the blood covering his face was scaring her. He used his T-shirt to try to scrape some of the gore off, but it stung and parts of his face were missing.

"I'm okay, sweetie. I know I look bad, but it's okay."

"Did you kill the monster?"

"No. I tried."

She sat beside him. "Your head is hurt."

"Yeah." *And everything else.*

"Mommy says there's no such thing as monsters."

Her eyes were wide open as she seemed to be studying his face. She added, "Daddy too."

"Well, we know better. Monsters are real."

She smiled and hugged him.

"Is it really just a bear? Why won't it go away?"

"This bear is special. It even has a special name." He almost told her the bear was Ursa Major, but the words slipping from his mouth were "Ursa Monster."

"Oh."

"Don't give up, Nickie. I'm going to get us out of here."

"How?"

"I still don't know. But I will. I promise."

She slumped to his chest and started to cry. "I'm hungry."

He rubbed her hair and kissed her forehead and held her to him, rocking her gently in his arms. When she was settled, he went to get more bandages from the first aid kit, using the remaining amount. He swallowed some painkillers, but the motivation to keep fighting didn't come from wrappings or Tylenol. It came from a six-year-old girl.

Chapter 9

Tuesday afternoon.

It was more than a day since Dan had returned to the storage room.

Three and a half days of being captured by the bear, the fucking animal that he could still hear in the main part of the cabin. He wanted to scream at it to just go away and leave them alone, but he knew the bear had too much invested in them. It wasn't going anywhere. It would just wander out briefly to eat some other bit of food it had stored away, but it never left long enough for Dan to get the rifle.

How long could they live?

Nichole sat underneath the window. He tried to take an inventory of the changes in her.

She was clearly emaciated. He could see it in her cheeks and the rest of her face. Her eyes were sunken and looked like they might fall back into her head, although he didn't think that could *really* happen. Not until she was dead.

Her voice was weak and thin. She had no saliva and her lips were a wreck of cracks and blisters. Her skin color was darker than normal except for her ghost-white lips.

He had felt her forehead earlier and she felt cold, like death was creeping into her, stealing her heat. Her hair was just as dead, hanging like brittle strings. She stank.

He knew he had all these symptoms, too, but on top of that, his body was ruined. He knew he had bite marks that went right through his skull and cracks in bones throughout his body. The stinking blood covering his body was turning dark and hard, and he looked like a zombie.

Somehow, as bad as he looked, he wasn't scaring Nichole. She just accepted him as he was.

They didn't talk much. That took energy and somehow even Nickie knew she might need that energy later. Every once in a while, she'd smile at him, though. That always made his pain ease just a little bit.

He wished he could write Leah a letter, to tell her how he'd tried his best to save Nickie, and to tell her that he loved her one last time. He couldn't find anything to write with other than blood, though, and he wasn't going to do that to her.

He stood and tried to stretch his arms, but they hurt too much. He stood above Nickie and looked out the window, trying to get some fresh air. The storage room just reeked.

In the distance, he saw a deer. It was young, probably only a few months old, and it was standing between the trees about twenty feet from the window. Dan thought of holding Nickie up to see it, but decided against it. Instead he thought of the deer as food.

How can I get that fucking bear to go after the deer?

Cobwebs seemed to be clouding his mind. He blinked his one good eye and tried to concentrate.

Bait.

He chastised himself for not thinking of that before. If he could get the bear to go after some other animal, it would let him get to the rifle and close the cabin door.

The deer lifted its head up and then pranced away through the trees.

"Don't go," he whispered.

"Danny?"

Once again, it sounded like Nichole was saying Daddy, but he knew that wasn't the case. It didn't matter; he wanted to believe that even if it wasn't true.

"I'm thinking, sweetie. If we can get the bear to go after something else, we can get free."

"How can you do that?"

Dan clutched the edges of the window. That was the problem. He had no idea. The deer had been perfect, but the bear didn't notice it. Who knew when another animal would come by.

He looked out, hoping to see another animal. For the next ten minutes, he didn't see anything.

He slumped down beside Nichole.

"Danny? How can you do that?"

He looked at her hopeful eyes, the eyes that needed to believe in him, and he knew the most important thing of all. He had to save her life.

He had to.

And as hard as it would be, he knew how he had to do it.

"Sweetie, I need you to do something special. It's how we'll be safe."

"What?"

He took a deep breath. *Bait.*

"I'm going to lift you out the window, so you'll be outside."

"No! The monster's out there!"

"You need to do this, Nickie. Remember, my promise?"

"You said you'd get me home."

"Pinky swear!"

He held out his little finger and she did too, and they shook.

"You know I'd never break a pinky swear."

She nodded.

"When you're outside, you need to run to the front of the cabin. Go to the car and then call my name. Then, crawl underneath the car and wait for me."

"Why?"

He hesitated. She had to have the courage to do it, but he couldn't lie to her, either.

"That will make the bear come to you."

"No!"

"But you'll hide under the car and be safe. Then I can get a rifle in the cabin. I'll come out and kill the bear."

She stared at him and crunched up her mouth.

"I don't want the monster to get me."

He put his hands on her cheeks and tried to smile.

"We're going to do this, Nickie. We're a team now, and we're going to take care of each other. I'll kill the bear with the gun."

She stared at him and then finally nodded.

Dan lifted her up and put her feet through the window and carefully let her down to the ground. It took every bit of will he had to not drop her, as the pain engulfed his body.

"Go to the car and call my name, sweetie. Call me nice and loud, over and over. Kay?"

She nodded and walked away, around the corner of the cabin.

Dan put his ear to the door of the storage room, praying to a God he wasn't sure he believed in to just this once answer his prayers.

For a couple of minutes he couldn't hear anything at all but then he heard a faint calling, "Danny! I'm at the car!"

He tried to hear if the bear moved, and he thought maybe he heard it.

"Danny!"

And a moment later, "Danny! Help!"

He shoved the door open and ran into the main cabin room without thinking. There was no sign of the bear and he knew that was because it was outside with Nichole.

The rifle hung on the wall near the door and he didn't hesitate to grab it. He wanted to rush out to see if she had made it under the car, but his mind overtook his heart and he went for the rifle.

He ran outside and saw the bear.

It had Nickie in its jaws and was swinging her around like a rag doll. Shit, she hadn't made it under the car. She didn't make any noises. His heart sank as he watched the monster slowly kill her.

"Danny..."

It was faint, but he heard it, and it shook him into action. He aimed the rifle and took a deep breath. It was about twenty feet away from him. He needed to be calm, to aim carefully. He'd only get one chance.

Click.

Fuck.

There were no bullets in the goddamn rifle.

He wanted so much to rush the bear, to grab Nickie and free her. Every instinct in his body called him to do that, but he knew that would just result in both of them being killed.

He ignored her cries and ran back to the cabin. "Where do you keep the fucking bullets, Brian?"

He saw a drawer near where the gun was hanging and yanked it open. Towels and oven mitts... and a box of bullets. He snapped the gun open and shoved a handful of bullets inside. He put the rest of the box in his pocket.

When he ran back outside, he couldn't see the bear or Nichole.

Panic set in, not allowing him to think clearly. He looked around the side of the cabin, where the bear had been hiding twice before. Nothing.

Then it came to him. It was probably burying her in the same area it'd buried him. Keeping his meal hidden for the day he needed her.

He moved into the woods and listened, but he couldn't hear anything. The bear's secret burial place was about thirty feet away and he hated crunching the leaves and branches under his feet as he walked. He kept the rifle pointed forward, wanting to be able to shoot immediately. He hated that this meant he was vulnerable to the bear swatting the gun away.

There.

The bear had put Nickie in the same grave he'd been in. She was covered in mud that it'd piled on her. Dan couldn't see her face, and couldn't see if she could breathe.

He pointed the gun and put pressure on the trigger. He knew he had to be calm. Nerves would make him miss the bear.

"Hey, you motherfucker!"

The bear turned and sniffed in his direction before howling and walking toward him.

Dan waited, letting the bear come closer. When it was ten feet away, he felt his nerves starting to hit him, and he pulled the trigger.

The bullet hit the bear in the face and it fell down. It howled and squirmed on the ground, but after a few seconds it stood up on its hind legs and got ready to charge Dan. He shot again and hit the bear directly in the chest.

The bear barely slowed down. It howled and moved closer to Dan, this time on all fours.

He shot it again. And again.

The bear fell, only three feet from Dan. It stared at him but no longer howled. It stared at him, and Dan could feel that it was only collecting its strength for one last rush.

He put two more bullets in the rifle and aimed at the bear's head. Blam. Blam.

Both bullets ripped into the animal's brain.

Its head lowered to the ground, and its heavy breathing stopped.

Dan stared at the dead bear for a few seconds and then poked it with the rifle. Nothing.

Nickie.

He ran to the makeshift grave and pulled away all the branches.

She was face down. Mud covered most of her except her head. Just like him. He knew she could have broken bones and her head had deep cuts, but he had to get her out. He pulled her body out of the mess and lifted her.

She didn't make a sound and was totally limp in his arms.

"Please, God..."

He put his ear to her mouth, and he could feel her breathing. Very shallow, but it was there. She was alive.

He walked toward his cabin, taking care to not get close to the bear. He didn't need any more surprises at this point. He kept looking back, but the bear stayed dead.

Nickie was alive. Hurt badly but alive. He knew the nearest hospital was in Fairbanks, but he could call for a medical evacuation and they'd rescue them. He carried Leah's precious girl into the main room of the cabin and fired up the short wave radio. To his immense relief, the batteries were fully charged and he was able to contact the authorities for help easily. They promised to send help and be there within an hour.

"I love you, Nickie. It's all over. Help is coming. We'll have you back with Mommy soon."

Her eyes opened and blinked. She whimpered and then said to him, "I love you too, Danny."

The pain didn't bother him when he heard those words. He just felt relief.

That's when the second bear walked into the cabin. It stared at Danny and Nichole. He was holding her close to him and she didn't see the second monster.

It was smaller than the first bear, and Danny realized it may have been a mate to the one that had terrorized them.

I guess you'd be Ursa Minor.

The bear continued to stare at them.

Danny willed it go to away. He didn't have the gun with him and they couldn't reach the safe room without the bear getting them.

Please. Just leave.

He stared at the monster, trying not to move.

"Danny, can I be the flower girl at your wedding?" asked Nickie.

He hugged her to his chest and nodded as the bear continued to stare at them.

Sarah's Story

Chris Hedges emailed me one day to ask if I'd be interested in writing a chapbook for him. It would be the first project for his new press, Alter Ego Press. I was very happy to have him choose me, and I wanted to do as good a job as I could for him.

Similar to "Ursa Major," I thought of a challenging plot, where Sarah herself could somehow enact revenge on her father when it seemed absolutely impossible for her to do so. After all, how many options would a quadriplegic actually have? I loved the challenge, and I hope I was able to do justice to the situation.

When it was published, the chapbook was amazing. Chris had done a fabulous job of designing the chapbook. Reviews were positive, but for whatever reason, sales weren't as high as we hoped. There was never (to my knowledge) a second chapbook created by Alter Ego Press. It's a shame. I would have collected them all. Unfortunately, the publishing world is difficult, with many challenges. I was (and still am) proud of what we created here. I hope you enjoy this one.

THIS IS WHAT MY DADDY TOLD ME:

Sarah, this is your story. It happened when you were a little baby. You were the cutest little thing, and we loved you so much. It was a dream come true when Mommy brought you home from the hospital.

But you were very colicky. It seemed like you cried all the time, and sometimes it was pretty darned hard to deal with. I don't blame your mom. At least I try not to. Sometimes, when I wake in the middle of the night and think of what happened, I get angry and I get up and pace around the room, and I look outside at the moonlight and just wish I could rewind time and undo everything.

But I can't.

So I stare out the window for hours. It's worse in the winter because that's when it happened.

You'd had your first birthday on January 22. It was a really great day and you hardly cried at all. You seemed to love being the center of attention when my family and Mommy's family came over for a little party. That night, everyone was gone, the dishes were clean, the gifts that you didn't really understand were put away, the balloons were still bouncing on the ceiling where they'd floated, and you were overtired. You didn't want to go to sleep, and you cried and cried, but eventually you did manage to find a way to drift off.

But only for awhile.

The guests all left about 8:00. The birthday party had turned into a bit of an adult party, with Mommy taking the opportunity to blow off some steam and have a few glasses of wine with her sisters. I almost asked her to cut it back because you never slept well and who knew what might happen.

I also knew that asking Mommy to cut back on her wine once she started was a very bad idea. She was an angry drunk and I guess part of me was scared of facing her alone that night and having her say to me, "So, you think I drink too much, do you?" I think about my fear of her a lot.

She really was a mean drunk.

Anyhow, the point is that I didn't stop her. I watched her have two glasses of wine, then three, and I really didn't care after that.

I took you for your bath and put you to bed at 8:00. Like I said, you cried because you didn't want to go to sleep. You really were dead tired, but you were determined to fight going to sleep with every ounce of your being.

You still fight that way. I love that.

Mommy's sisters left and she lay down on the couch, saying she wanted to watch some silly reality

TV show. I normally don't remember what shows she watched but I remember everything about that night. I remember how she didn't bother to move her dirty wine glass to the kitchen, how she barely acknowledged I was there, how she had the show on too loud and I was worried it would wake you. The show was called *Scavenger Hunt*. Some stupid race-around-the-world thing.

She fell asleep within minutes. Passed out would be more accurate, I guess, but whatever.

I went to my office to do a bit of paperwork. Even back then I had to work two jobs to make ends meet for us. The bills and other paperwork would pile up during the week and I'd deal with them on the weekend.

That Saturday night I was working on trying to put together some semblance of a budget. We were overdrawn at the bank by two thousand dollars and we had three credit cards that were just about maxed out.

My day job paid okay. It's the same job I have now at the factory, but my part-time evening job was just minimum wage, covering the late shift at the magazine store downtown. Some days it didn't feel like it was even worth going to work.

I was so tired on the weekends. Every fucking weekday, I'd work at the factory and then another four hours at the store after dinner. Your mother usually at least cooked dinner, so that was good. Usually.

Saturday was the only day I had off, and that was the day I'd stare at our bills, at our bank account, at the thought of daycare bills if mommy ever decided to go back to work, and of course, my biggest fear: what if we ever had a *real* health problem without any insurance?

Well, we know how that turned out.

So, that night I was staring at a spreadsheet I'd put together and I was immersed in it.

I didn't hear you cry, but you must have. Even more amazing, Mommy heard you and actually got up to get you. Weekends were my turn to take care of you when you cried at night, since she had to look after you all week.

The figures in the spreadsheet were starting to all blur together for me. It was like I was in a coma, barely able to move or even keep my eyes open.

She told me later that she'd woken from your cries and didn't even think about it being the weekend. She was confused from the wine.

You were crying loudly and she almost tripped as she climbed the stairs to go get you. I can just imagine her stumbling up the steps, almost like a film shown in reverse of her falling down the stairs.

"Shh..." she would have said. "It's me, Sarah."

She would have picked you up and cuddled you and tried to stop you from crying. As much as I hate her for so many other things, she really did treat you well when she held you. She didn't lose her temper with you.

Maybe you stopped crying. I think you must have because I would have heard you. I was in the basement, but I could always hear you anyhow. Parents do. That night, though, maybe there was a chance I'd fallen asleep or half-asleep or something, because I didn't hear you till it happened.

Mommy carried you downstairs. I can imagine her being very careful with every step, double-checking her footing, because even she knew better than to risk dropping you when she was drunk.

And drunk she was. Stinking drunk, so that when I came running upstairs a bit later, she was still slurring her words and not making any sense about the blood and what had happened, and I just wanted to slap her to get her to make some fucking sense about what had happened!

She'd been warming up a bottle of milk in the microwave. I found it there the next day.

The week earlier, she'd tried something. When she was warming up your bottle, she sat you on the kitchen counter, right beside the microwave. You perched there and cooed and laughed. You liked it there.

I was aghast when she told me she'd done that. Maybe when you were older it would be okay, but at one year? I wanted so much to tell her not to do that, but... well, I'd felt her anger too many times. I didn't say a fucking word.

She did it again that night. When I heard you scream, I was shocked awake and somehow noticed the time on the computer: 11:11.

That was supposed to be the time you make a wish if you happen to notice it. I didn't have time to make any wish. I ran up the stairs and saw your little body sprawled on the floor. You were unconscious.

Eventually your mom told me that you'd slipped. She was looking at you the whole time but wasn't close enough to stop you. You slid off the counter and the back of your head smashed into the countertop on your way down. Your head flipped forward and your face hit the floor first. She said you seemed to bounce and turned onto your back. I don't know if I believe all that because babies don't bounce, but your face *was* covered with blood and you were on your back.

Mommy was screaming and she went to pick you up, but I stopped her. There was something about the position you were in... something about the angle of your neck and your legs, and...

Well, everything was wrong. It was all fucking wrong and I just couldn't let her make it worse.

"Call 9-1-1!" It was the only time in my life I'd ever yelled at her, and I think that shocked her as much as the accident.

"I was watching her. I don't know how—"

"Call fucking 9-1-1! Don't just stand there, you stupid bitch!"

I'm not proud of saying that, but it's the truth, and this is your story, Sarah. I have to tell you everything.

I crouched down to your crumpled little body and put my ear to your face. I could feel your tiny breath and I silently thanked God for that.

The ambulance took forever. It was almost 11:30 when they arrived and Mommy cried to them about how it was an accident and they didn't care. They just wanted to fix you. That night, they were my heroes.

You see, I felt so helpless. What father wouldn't? I didn't know if I should just pick you up carefully and take you to the hospital myself or if I'd make things so much worse. If you'd died with me crouched on the floor beside you because I didn't take you myself to the hospital, I don't know what I would have done. I felt enough guilt that night for a thousand fathers, but if I'd been part of your death, I just don't know if I could have stood it.

I was sitting there with you the whole time, looking down at your beautiful face, wondering if I'd ever see you grow up into a teenager, a woman, having a life of your own independent from me. I sometimes wondered what an amazing future you would have, and my whole reason to live was to find a way to turn you into the most amazing woman ever.

And there you were, your crushed little body not moving. Her story didn't really make sense, about you bouncing onto your back. I think you landed on your face and she turned you over onto your back. Then she realized she shouldn't have done that in case your spine was hurt, but she never admitted it. Just said you'd bounced.

For once I desperately wanted to hear you cry. I pleaded with you to call out and scream in pain, just so I'd know you were still really there with us.

You didn't cry that night. I actually never heard you cry again, which seems really weird, but it's true. It was like the shock had taken the cry and flushed it away.

I also missed your smile, but that came back eventually.

It was two days before the doctors confirmed that you were paralyzed from the neck down and would be for the rest of your life.

You didn't need a machine to breathe like some

quadriplegics do. Thank God for small mercies.

My hopes of seeing you dance with a future boyfriend went flying out the window with your mother's empty wine bottle. I'd never teach you to catch a baseball or ride a bike. I'd never take you to Disneyland and watch you scream in delight at Magic Mountain. I'd almost certainly never walk you down the aisle to meet your fiancé at the front of a church, and I'd never see you care for your own babies as they grew up.

All of those futures were gone, because I hadn't heard you cry that night.

Your mommy felt bad, too, of course, and for a few days she actually stopped drinking. It didn't last.

A week after the accident, she was in a bar. She told me she was going shopping, but I was used to not always knowing the real story. She left and was hit by a car. I sometimes wonder if it really was an accident or if the guilt got to her and this was her way to escape it all.

I buried her and never really had time to grieve, because I needed to learn how to take care of you. Maybe part of me didn't *want* to grieve, which is another part of me that I wish I didn't have to tell you, but like I said, this is your story, and it has to have the truth. All of it.

I hate that I was part of this, Sarah. All I can say is that the whole rest of my life has been and will continue to be devoted to you. I love you, sweetie.

That's your story. That's why you're in that wheelchair and why you're not like everyone else that you see on the TV or the Internet.

That's what my daddy told me when I was ten years old. And sometimes I asked him to tell me it again. I've heard my story from him about once a year, and I'm sixteen now. I don't need to hear him tell it ever again. I've memorized every teensy weensy detail, every single one of his lies.

"Hey, sweetie, how was your day?"

Daddy was wearing a light blue T-shirt with dark brown slacks. I wondered if normal people thought that looked right. It's just an example of how my world never seems to fit what everyone else might experience.

I've never left my basement, never even seen the main floor of my own house. I once asked Daddy to take a video camera through the house and play it back to me, but he'd never gotten around to it. He says he doesn't want to make me miss a normal life and that we should just concentrate on what I can experience. The first time he told me that, my heart sank. I was about eleven and it made me feel like a prisoner in my own home.

I've never been to a grocery store, and I'm fascinated by the idea of walking into a place that has a million different things for sale. I'd want to grab everything off the shelves and shovel it all into my grocery cart. I'd want to buy six different flavors of ice cream instead of just vanilla. I'd want to buy a different brand of breakfast cereal every time. Right now, Daddy always buys me Fruit Loops.

I see on TV where people have birthday parties. I see them go to church and to shovel snow off their sidewalks. I see them going to work and to school and to the playground and to places to meet other people and...

"How was your day, Daddy?"

"Good. I'm tired, though. I'll cook dinner a bit later."

"I'm hungry now, though."

It was almost seven o'clock. Breakfast had been more than twelve hours earlier.

As much as anything else, though, I was hungry for his company. He didn't know I hated his guts but he knew I loved his company. For my entire life, I've lived in our basement and he's almost the only person I ever see.

"I'll be back in an hour. I just need to rest."

"Okay."

I reluctantly watched him climb back up the stairs. When I was a kid, I used to stare at him in awe when he climbed stairs. I couldn't imagine being able to stand on two legs in the first place, but then somehow balancing enough to climb a flight of stairs? It seemed like a miracle.

Before I was thirteen, my daddy was my hero. He took care of me after my mother ruined my life. He didn't abandon me or try to put me in some kind of home or anything like that. He fed me and bathed me and laughed with me and he told me my story so I'd never forget it.

As if.

Six years ago, on my tenth birthday:

"Happy birthday, sweetie!"

"Thanks, Daddy!

He gave me a hug and kissed my cheek.

"I've got a very special birthday present for you today, Sarah."

"Really? What is it? Tell me!"
"You'll see!"

He set up a folding table in front of me and brought a heavy box down from upstairs. From the box was born a television set.

I had no idea what it was. I asked him but he just fiddled with it and plugged in some wires and eventually clicked a little wallet-sized gizmo and light shone from the television.

"Oh my goodness!"

There was a person inside the box! He was small and it seemed like it was only his head but then I saw more of him and then other people and they were talking to each other and I was speechless.

"It's a TV," said Daddy.

Well, that didn't mean anything to me. He could have called it a QZ for all I knew.

It was magic.

It took an hour or two for me to get past the idea that there was some kind of sorcery at work here. Daddy told me a bit about how the box worked, but it really didn't sink in and didn't matter. All I knew was that I'd have company during the day aside from

Helen.

Helen was my occasional nurse. She came by twice a week and checked on me, giving me shots when I needed them (which I never felt), checked my heart rate, and other stuff. Daddy made sure she took good care of me, but I only saw her an hour each week, split into two equal visits.

She'd never mentioned TV to me.

Daddy also showed me another box that evening. It was a computer. He set it up beside TV and showed me how the Internet worked.

More magic.

I remember falling asleep that night thinking I was surrounded by magic and miracles. I wanted TV to be on all night but Daddy said no, that wasn't the way things should work. He'd turn it on each morning and turn it off each night.

He said I should watch PBS. I shrugged inside, not knowing what that meant. All I cared about was TV and Internet from that point on.

I needed Daddy to use Internet. He would come down and sit at the table for about a half hour each night and move the mouse to find me things I wanted.

"Can I see China, Daddy?" "Can I see an airplane, Daddy?" "Can I see something purple, Daddy?"

There was nothing purple in my basement. I loved when they'd show a woman wearing a purple dress on TV.

Daddy was very good to me. He turned TV on every day and he showed me so many stunning things on Internet. He would show me people dancing and whales leaping out of the ocean and tornados and far planets and water molecules and Mickey Mouse.

And I soaked in every new wonder like a human sponge. Every day I saw things that I honestly could never have imagined before.

I wanted to move the mouse. I wanted to find a way to see what TV would be if it wasn't PBS. I wanted these things more than you can possibly imagine.

Daddy had taught me how to read when I was eight, and sometimes Internet showed me things that had words and I could understand most of them. He would show me something called The Bible and say it was important but he never explained why.

"Don't covet thy neighbour's house," was one of the things he read from The Bible. "Let he who is without sin cast the first stone."

I tried to smile when he read things because he made them seem important. All I really wanted, though, was to grab that mouse and fish through the ocean of knowledge that Internet held. I wanted to know everything it knew.

It was so tempting. I was alone for at least twelve hours every day while Daddy was at work, except for those couple of visits by Helen. She didn't pay attention to TV and wouldn't help me with Internet.

"Your father hires me for a purpose," she said. "And that purpose doesn't include silly cartoons."

I was alone in the house at least eighty-three hours every week. TV showed me PBS. Internet was dark.

In two years, that meant I stared at that mouse for close to ten thousand hours. I tried so hard to lift my arm out to touch it. At times sweat would drop from my face as I exerted pressure to try to move my atrophied and rotten muscles.

I never believed it was a waste of time. In fact, just the opposite. Every time I tried to reach out and touch that mouse and failed, it just seemed to give me a stronger incentive to succeed next time.

Internet just sat quietly while Elmo sometimes laughed at me from TV.

Even though Daddy had told me the story of how I became a paraplegic, and he told me there was never going to be any hope of me so much as moving my little pinkie finger, I never believed that.

The resolve came from somewhere deep inside me, and sometimes after Daddy lay me down in bed to sleep at night, I'd stare in the dark and wonder if me trying to move my arm to reach the mouse was just because if I gave up and admitted I'd never manage it, what possible reason would I have to live?

So I tried every day, all day. It was always my right arm that I imagined reaching out to the mouse.

I pushed and I pulled and I fought with myself for hour after hour, day after day, and then when I was thirteen years old, a miracle happened.

The mouse moved.

Yes, I'm sixteen years old now. I weigh a hundred and four pounds. I'm four foot eleven inches tall. I have very short black hair that I wish was longer, because the girls on TV have long hair, but Daddy says it's too hard to take care of, so Nurse Helen cuts it once a month with a pair of scissors. It's ragged but what does it matter? Nobody has ever seen me except Helen and Daddy.

I have breasts and I had my first period when I was thirteen. That was a mess and a bit scary because I had no idea that was going to happen. Now, Nurse Helen takes care of that, too.

It was only later that I realized that the mouse moved that first time just before I had that first period. My body was changing, maturing, sprouting hair on my legs and under my arms and bleeding from my vagina.

But none of those changes was as significant to me as the first time that mouse inched forward.

I felt my heart pounding hard, sweat pouring down my face, and I was crunching my teeth so hard, I'm surprised I didn't crack one.

At first I wondered if it was my imagination, but after a few seconds, the screen saver disappeared and the monitor showed me my home page, www.google.com, where I always got Daddy to start my surfing.

It really moved.

I felt totally pumped but also completely shocked and surprised. I wasn't actually expecting the mouse to move; I was trying to get my arm to reach over and move the damned thing myself, but my arm was motionless. The mouse had moved on its own.

Could I do it again?

I concentrated, but this time, I focused all my energy into moving the mouse directly. This time, it happened sooner and with more assuredness. I watched the cursor on the monitor as I moved the mouse in a small circle.

Exhaustion hit me that first day, and I stopped my experiments. I believe I was already bleeding, but that didn't get discovered for a couple of hours. I closed my eyes and may have drifted off to sleep in my day bed. In any case, when Daddy came home, he was in a foul mood.

"Shitty day, sweetie. Just a shitty fucking day."

I never really heard people talk like that on TV, but I knew by then that they weren't real. Daddy had explained that they were just figments of somebody's imagination and I shouldn't trust them for how real people act.

He would always tell me how real people act, he said.

Of course I believed him. I believed everything he'd told me up to then.

"What happened today, Daddy?"

He sighed and sat down in the chair by the computer. "Stupid people."

He was drinking a beer, which he said was just a kind of juice that I wouldn't like the taste of, and he didn't offer anything to me.

I knew better than to tell him anything important when he was in a bad mood, so no matter how excited I was about being able to move the mouse on Internet, I just kept that to myself. I figured I'd tell him the next day.

"Jesus, what's that!"

I didn't know what he was referring to. I could see he was staring at my body but I couldn't turn my head.

"What a mess..."

I didn't say anything. I assumed I'd peed myself again but I wasn't sure. I just quietly thanked him for taking care of me. That's what he expected and what I believed was the right thing to do. I loved Daddy and without him... well, I wouldn't have lasted twenty-four hours. He was my personal God, my saviour, my life.

He cleaned me up and I heard him talk on telephone to Helen. He told her to come over and bring some sanitary napkins. I had no clue what he meant, but later, she explained.

He spoke nicely to her and said, "Thanks, love," when he hung up. I was so happy that he had somebody to help him.

The following day, Daddy went to work after feeding me some toast with strawberry jam and a glass of milk. I thought about telling him my news then, but part of me held back. I thought it might be a fluke and wanted to perfect what I could do before telling him.

That day, I found it much easier to move the mouse. It was like my brain had rewired itself somehow and I could just "reach" the mouse as easily as the imaginary people on TV could reach for an apple. I could click on the mouse too, just like Daddy. It took a lot of pressure at first to do that, but with more practice, I could point and click, and over the next several days, I learned how to type.

I never told Daddy. I had decided I wanted it to be my secret. I hadn't had any secrets my whole life to that point, because everything that happened to me was completely because he arranged for it to happen. I know that was just the way God wanted things — well, that's what Daddy told me, anyhow — but it left no room for secrets. When he came home every night, I'd be in exactly the same position he left me, not an inch different. The only secrets were my thoughts.

Now, I had a real secret. I liked that.

I kept practicing, clicking around on Internet like nobody's business. I found web sites I'd never seen before and I loved it when I could find stories about other paraplegics and how their lives were managed.

All the people I read about lived out in the real world. They weren't stuck in a basement like I was. That was a shock to me. I assumed I was no different from anybody else in my position, but that wasn't the case. I read about wheelchairs and field trips and visits to the park and even some people who'd gone to watch hockey games live!

But the biggest surprise was yet to come.

It took a long time for me to put the pieces of the puzzle together, because when your world turns upside down, it's hard to realize that it's really you that's standing on your head.

Here's what happened:

The computer Daddy brought to the basement for me was one he had used upstairs for years before.

That computer had emails and scanned images of things that he would never have wanted me to see.

It also had an old journal he'd written years earlier as some kind of cathartic process or something.

He never cared that all this stuff was on the computer because he knew I could never read it.

Well, he was wrong.

It took me several months to find all this and realize that when Daddy had told me my story all those times before, he'd conveniently changed a few details.

It wasn't my mother who'd been drunk that night and dropped me, causing me to be paralyzed; it was him.

My mother did die from being run over by a car, but it was from the grief and guilt she felt from not facing him when she knew he was a terribly delinquent father.

He didn't work that hard after all. He had inherited money from rich parents, not to mention a substantial life insurance policy when my mother died.

And Nurse Helen was his fuck-buddy, not a real nurse. She helped hide his dirty little secret: me.

I don't know you. I don't know if you're a kid or an adult, male or female, rich or poor, healthy or a cripple. What I do know is that you're human. You've got feelings and you understand happiness, sadness, hate, love, and joy.

I loved my daddy. I really did. He'd talked about God to me, the big guy in the sky who took care of people, but to me, my daddy was my God. He sacrificed so much for me, and I always felt unworthy of him. I was a burden, a boat anchor he was stuck with.

No more.

I know now that he made me into this boat anchor on his own. And he blamed my mother. I don't know if I can ever regain positive feelings for her after he's spent so many years poisoning her memory in my mind, but I very quickly changed how I felt about him: my unquestioning love turned into stark, naked hate.

I wanted revenge, and I knew exactly how to go about it.

The next two years of my life, I spent practicing moving things. I loved using Internet and TV, but I also found I could lift heavier items, like the chair my daddy sat in. I could lift it in the air by just pretending my arms were carrying it and twist it in the air like it was performing acrobatics. I found I could control the tiniest gestures and also lift heavy objects. The more I practiced, the easier it became.

I was still a prisoner in my own dead body, though, until a little light bulb seemed to flash inside my mind.

I typed into Google, "How do muscles work?"

The human body has more than six hundred muscles, and I started with the muscles in my right hand. I concentrated on them until I could feel their structure, feel the way they connected to each other and to bones. It took a long time to manage it, but I did eventually find out how to use my mind to contract the right combination of muscles.

My hand curled into a fist.

That was the most amazing thing that had happened to me in my entire life. I relaxed the muscles and then spread my fingers apart and then pulled them together again.

After a week, I could move my arms in a more-or-less coordinated way, and two weeks after that, I stood up.

I was very wobbly, so I used some of my powers (what else can I call them?) to hold myself up, the way I could hold chairs in the air. I walked slowly, shuffling like a zombie in a George Romero movie, but I walked.

I moved around the basement and saw things from a completely different point of view. My eyes were higher than in my chair and I could stand on the far side of the room looking back to the pathetic prison that chair had become over the past few months.

When Daddy arrived home each night, I was back in exactly the same position. He never knew anything was odd.

It was almost a month later that I forced my body to climb the stairs and I saw the rest of the house I lived in. It was beautiful. I'd seen enough TV now to know a nice house when I saw it. The kitchen had granite countertops and the cabinets were made of cherry wood. I checked and that's much nicer than most people have. The furniture was dark, elegant wood and his bedroom was huge.

I stepped outside and the wind hit me. The sun blazed down and hurt my eyes until I got used to it. The noise of cars driving by was much louder than I expected, and I got scared. I went back inside and hurried down to my chair.

Even a prison provides comfort from the unknown.

My planning took eight more months.

"Hi, sweetie."

"Hi, Daddy."

"We'll have beans and wieners for dinner in a bit. I

just want to rest for now."

"That's okay."

I'd already helped myself to some chocolate chip cookies an hour earlier, so I wasn't that hungry.

As he was about to head back upstairs, I called him. "Daddy?"

He let out a heavy sigh. Until recently, I never knew that was a sign of irritation.

"Yes?"

"Can you come here?"

"What is it? I really need to rest. I had a hard day at the office."

"Do you ever think about how hard my days are?"

He turned to stare at me. "Of course I do, Sarah. Every day of my life."

"I don't believe you. Can you come here?"

He walked back to me and I realized then that my plan absolutely had to work. I wouldn't get a second chance.

"You've told me my story many times."

He nodded.

"But you changed some things. It was really you who dropped me, not Mommy."

"Baby, of course I didn't drop you. Where did you get that kind of idea?"

"There." I lifted my arm and pointed at the computer monitor.

For at least a full minute, Daddy didn't say anything. He just stared at my arm, not comprehending that I could move it.

"Sarah?"

"Look at the fucking monitor!"

He did and he saw the notes he'd written about my accident. He knew then that I knew the truth.

"Oh God..."

"All these years, you lied to me."

He turned and shook his head slowly, but he didn't say anything. Not even when I stood up to face him. He seemed to be mute.

Finally he blurted out, "You can stand..."

"I can do a lot more than stand."

"How? I mean, that's wonderful, but how?"

"You lied to me all these years."

I took a step closer to him. He turned and looked toward the stairs. I couldn't let him run away, so I used invisible tentacles to hold him in place.

"What?"

"Sit down, Daddy."

I moved his body for him, one step at a time, swivelling him, and plunking him down in the chair that had been my seat for the past fifteen years.

I kept his mouth locked shut, not wanting to hear a damned thing he had to say.

Then I went to work.

My imaginary limbs can be turned into any shape I want. I reached inside Daddy's neck. I felt his muscles and the air flowing down his esophagus, and I maneuvered my touch to his larynx. I sliced his vocal cords. He tried to jump and he moaned, but I kept him seated with his mouth shut.

Then I reached through his legs and his arms and sliced the appropriate muscles. It was quite a few that I need to sever to be sure he'd never move again. I wanted him to truly understand what my life had been like – the life he had given to me I now gave back to him.

After a while, he passed out from pain, but that didn't stop me from completing my work. The pain would go away. The paralysis wouldn't.

It felt good to perform each tiny snip, to feel each muscle snap back. His body jerked as I did my work.

When I was done, I emailed Helen from Daddy's Yahoo address and told her: "Dear Helen. I've found somebody else and I want you out of my life. Do not call or email me. You were always only useful for sex, and only marginally good even at that. I never want to see you again."

I figured that was cruel enough that she'd never want to talk to him again.

Another year has come and gone, and Daddy is still nicely stuck in his chair. I sometimes tell him my real story, to remind him of why he's in this predicament, but mostly I just treat him like a stuffed animal or a doll. He's like part of the furniture. Just like me.

The Gray Zone

When I first started publishing stories on a frequent basis, many of them dealt with some aspect of time. My first three books were The Memory Tree, Placeholders, and Miranda, all of which had unusual ways to deal with time. I didn't want to just do a typical time travel book that was the same as all the others that came before it. I wanted to explore new and different ways to think about time.

I guess you could say I was obsessed with time. I still am. (The novel I just finished writing in 2018 is yet another addition to my thoughts on time.)

Back then, though, I wanted to write the "final word" on time twisting stories. I tried to imagine the biggest, most awe-inspiring concept I could, and I thought of the quote in the book from Stephen Hawking who asked (paraphrased) why we remember the past but not the future.

I think of that question a lot, but this was the only time I used it in a story.

This one is set in three locations, Montreal, Vancouver, and Aswan. I've lived in the first two and have visited Aswan several times. They are three of my favorite places on the globe.

This was the first book purchased by Roy Robbins at Bad Moon Books, but the second one he published. I was very grateful to Roy for publishing eight books of mine over the years. My success as a writer can certainly be attributed in large part to Roy.

Chapter 1—Aswan (1984)

It's PEACEFUL HERE. Has been all summer.

I didn't plan on staying in Egypt this long, but when I hopped onto the cruise ship going down the Nile in July, the idea of leaving seemed to fall away. Even though Cassie's waiting for me back in Montreal, the thrill of the ancient land asked me to stay

(just a little bit longer)

until now. The Egyptians have been so kind to me for the past three months, it's hard to imagine going back to the western world.

My home in Aswan is the back of a mud house. It was built by my landlord, Mohammed, who is only forty or fifty years old but looks seventy. He has a long gray beard and pencilthin arms. He's weak, and his eyes are runny and constantly leak.

Mohammed invited me to stay at the back of his home in exchange for teaching his son, Achmed, a bit of English. The deal was very onesided, since Achmed already knows the language pretty well. Mostly we talk about how he likes Egypt and how it's different from

Canada. He has trouble imagining so many things. Achmed is only thirteen years old, lively, always running around playing soccer in the streets with his friends, laughing and dancing as if the world is at his fingertips.

He's out in the street now, hopping to some internal rhythm, daring the neighbor boys to sneak a goal past him.

Achmed will almost certainly follow in his father's footsteps and grow old before his time. He's never seen a television set, could never imagine sitting in a comfortable easy chair watching *Dallas* or *MASH* or Johnny Carson. I'm not even sure there's a single TV set anywhere in the city. Maybe in the hotels.

Sometimes I hear music drifting out of houses or storefronts. Radios, tape recordings, maybe even some kids singing in a back room. The Egyptians love their music as much as we love *All in the Family*.

Achmed kicks his left leg out and makes an improbable stop. He's really on his game today.

"Great save!" I call to him.

He turns his head and takes a deep bow in mock appreciation. The other boys mutter and walk back toward their end of the makeshift soccer field. The ball is held together with brown tape, and it doesn't roll right, so it takes Achmed even more than a normal amount of concentration to shepherd it back down the street.

Back in Anjou, when I was his age, we played street hockey every winter. I always pretended to be Henri Richard, *The Pocket Rocket*, my favorite player from the Montreal Canadians. Anjou is a suburb of Montreal, and everybody there is hockey crazy. Sometimes even the adults played street hockey with us.

I shared the same name as my hero. Well, almost. Henry, not Henri, since my parents were English. I always hated that "y" at the end of my name. When my mom wasn't around, I always pronounced my name Henri, with a flamboyant French accent. *AhnRHEE!*

Here in Aswan, everyone plays soccer instead of hockey, but I can live inside Achmed's mind and understand the intensity he plays the game with. He kicks and has his shot blocked by his friends. The ball bounces over and hits a small dustcovered car. I've never asked Achmed who his favorite player is. I'll have to do that. Not that the name will mean anything to me all the games are broadcast only in Arabic.

"He good."

I turn and smile at Mohammed, who's watching his son hop backward down the dirt road that passes for the main street here.

I nod. "He's having fun, don't you think? The freedom of the young, right?"

I'm not sure if Mohammed understands every word I say. Likely not. He's glancing sideways at me as if he's unsure whether I've really asked him a question or not. He finally nods his head slightly.

"Felucca ride to south islands. Tomorrow. You come?"

I hesitate, wanting to be sure I heard him right through his thick accent.

I've never been invited onto Mohammed's felucca before. I think it's an honor thing. Something about only family and close friends being allowed in the boat.

Hell, I don't really know what the deal is, but I know it's a big thing to him that he asked me to join.

"Sure. I'd love to. What time?" I point to my watch. Mohammed's always been fascinated by my Timex, especially the silvercolored chain. I see his eyes arrow right onto the watch face, squinting to look at the hands. When I leave Aswan next week, I'm going to give it to him as a farewell gift. I'm not sure what he'll do when the battery runs out, but it should last him a while.

"Sunrise. Bring water."

Mohammed and his family will just scoop water to drink from the Nile, but I can't do that without getting sick.

"Achmed steer felucca. First time."

I bow my head to Mohammed. "Very kind of you to invite me."

Without saying anything else, he shuffles back inside his house. There's no door and the only windows are empty holes between the mud bricks. The walls are stronger than they look. I've seen Achmed bounce his soccer ball off the walls for an hour without the slightest dent showing.

Achmed has the ball again and is trying to keep it in the air with his feet. It looks like an overgrown hackysack. He's been like a son to me. Well, maybe not *exactly* like a son. I mean, I'm only twenty-two myself, and he's thirteen, so maybe he's more like a little brother. Whatever, he basically adopted me when I first landed in Aswan. My first stop of course was the High Dam. It's one of the biggest tourist attractions in the city, so of course I went there.

Big mother of a dam, let me tell you.

And standing in the middle, near the concession stand, was Achmed. He ran from one side of the dam to the other, looking out at the huge expanse of Lake Nasser on one side, running fifty feet to the other side to see the comparatively small trickle of water that eventually flowed to Cairo and beyond.

"Baksheesh!" he'd shout to every tourist.

At first I waved him off. All kids in Egypt call for baksheesh to every tourist they see. They know we almost never give any money, but they figure what have they got to lose by asking?

Achmed was different from the others. He came right up to me, beamed a smile with his entire face, and just grabbed my attention like no other kid ever had before. He wore an offwhite galabea, the same as all the other boys. I could see it was a size or two too small, but that didn't seem to bother him. Once I stared into his eyes, it was impossible not to give him a few piastres.

"Thank you, sir," he said with a formal bow.

I laughed at the scene, feeling like I was an actor in a Shakespearean comedy.

"You speak English."

"Some. Not good like you, sir."

And he bowed again, laughed, and pocketed the change as he turned to look for other tourists.

"Hey, do you know the city good enough to be a tour guide?"

Achmed was caught a bit off guard. I doubt he'd been asked that before.

"Some. I can take to big market and quarry. Big

obelisk there." He paused to think. "Maybe Papa take to Elephantine Island. Maybe Philea. Cleopatra's bathtub there. Bring rubber duck for picture."

So began our three months together.

It's hard to think about leaving. I've told Mohammed it's time for me to go home, and I'm pretty sure that's why he arranged for me to go with the family on their felucca tomorrow. I'm also convinced it's why it's going to be Achmed's first time to steer. To say goodbye to me.

I haven't told Achmed I'm leaving yet. After the ride. I've still got to figure out how to get back to Cairo and arrange a flight home. Maybe Cassie can arrange the trip. Probably easier for her than me. The phones in Aswan are very unreliable, and finding a travel agent who can actually book a flight from Cairo to Canada would be a challenge.

Achmed's game is breaking up. The ball belongs to one of the other players who's carrying it off. I'll buy a new ball for Achmed as a farewell gift.

It's late afternoon. Time for a nap. I yawn and tussle Achmed's curly black hair as we walk into his home.

The house is really just one big room, with a few large cubbyholes for bedrooms. The walls are made of uneven dry mud, covered with brightlycolored portraits to disguise the roughness of the surfaces. The pictures are caricatures of longdead relatives. I think the two largest are Mohammed's mother and father. They look even older then he does, but of course who knows? Everyone looks old here. The heat, the hard work, the lack of food... it all combines together to rip the years off the local citizens.

Achmed sits in a corner on a small mat. Soon, he'll lay down and sleep there.

The main part of the house only has a small table with benches on each side. A stone oven is built into one wall. Two gray pigeons sit on a small ledge, quietly looking around the room. They don't know that one day they'll end up inside the oven.

On the other side of the room is a small terrarium, with wire mesh reaching up about six inches on all sides. I pick up one of the baby crocodiles and hold it in my hand. The other two crocs ignore me. It still seems weird to have crocodiles as pets. The one I'm holding sits and looks at me without fear; it's smaller than my index finger. I put it back alongside the others, near the water inside the cage.

I walk through the center of the house and out the far side. There's no back yard or anything, just a small area of debris. I've got a small pile of hay I sleep on. Beggars can't be choosers, and the one thing I wanted to do on my trip was to see what real Egyptians live like. I'm not sure everyone lives like this, but this is certainly one way. I lie down and close my eyes, thinking of Cassie.

I wake just as the sun is starting to lighten the sky. My neck is sometimes sore after sleeping on the hay, but today, it's not too bad. It's near the end of August, and it's already eighty degrees out. A good day to spend on the water.

Achmed is near the door, not far from me. He's

kneeling on his small rug, facing south. I just watch and keep quiet. After a few moments of prayer, he rolls up his mat and walks into the house. Only after he places his rug back in storage does he come back out and smile at me.

"We ride Nile today."

I nod. "And you'll be steering. Are you nervous?"

Achmed lowers his head a bit, but I can see he's dying to shout to all his friends about the big day. "Papa has big felucca. Nobody steers but him before."

"Achmed!"

The yell comes from inside the house. It's his mother. Instantly, Achmed jumps to attention and walks inside.

I barely know Shani. She's never spoken to me, and I have no idea if she knows a word of English. She wears dark purple or green robes that cover her head, but unlike the most devout women in the city, she lets her face show. Her eyes are brown and sad.

Mohammed's other two wives are nowhere in sight.

Achmed is almost as tall as Shani, so she faces him and whispers a long set of instructions to her son. She's staring him right in the eyes, imploring him to listen, to be careful. I know she's likely telling him to be strong, be a warrior, don't disgrace your father.

In my mind, though, she's saying, "Hold on tight and don't let your feet slip. You know how easy it is to fall. Are your feet strong enough? You don't have to do this yet, you know. We can call it off. Maybe you're too young."

Just like a Canadian mother.

Achmed answers in reassuring tones and tells her

he's going to be very careful, that his feet are agile and strong, and that he'll be back home before she even knows he's gone.

Or maybe she's telling him to get out and feed the chickens, and he's answering he'll do it when he gets home.

Just like a Canadian teenager.

Whatever the actual words, Shani sneaks a look over at me. She looks like she blames me for making her child grow up too fast. Then, she gives Achmed a quick hug. She walks out the front door and off to do whatever she has planned for the day.

"Where's your father?" I ask.

"To the dock. We go meet him."

Achmed's house is hidden in a small clump behind the Mena Hotel, about a ten minute walk from the Nile. The scattered houses look like they were built at random locations, sometimes only a few feet apart. I'd walked down there many times before, because in all of Egypt, the world revolves around the river. Without the Nile, there would be no Egypt. It's just as true now as in Biblical times.

More than two hundred thousand people live in Aswan, but it still manages to have the charm of a small town, where everybody knows everybody else.

I sometimes imagine Mohammed walking into a bar and having everyone yell out, "Norm!"

Except of course, there's no bars in Aswan. Or if there are, they're well hidden, and I've never seen them. I've heard that rich Saudi sheiks know where to go to drink, gamble, and do other things they can't do at home, but those places are secreted from me.

Mohammed has the felucca all set. The sail is already raised, towering thirty feet above the hull. We walk on a wobbly narrow plank leading us onto the boat. Mohammed talks to Achmed in Arabic, and I again imagine a last minute chance to change his mind.

Achmed laughs and moves to the far end of the sailboat.

Mohammed pulls the plank in and unties the felucca, pushing us in a small arc onto the river.

Achmed climbs up and soon I can only see his feet. I know that hidden from view, he's using his hands to do something to control the sails. A halfinch thick rope hangs down, which I think is somehow connected to what he's doing above. His bare feet control the rudder, gently moving the control lever back and forth. I recognize some of the movements from when he was playing hackysack with the soccer ball.

"You're doing great, Achmed!" I call up to him. He doesn't answer, but I know he'll be beaming that huge smile of his.

We're sailing quite fast, and the wind feels good in my face. Mohammed sits and stares at Achmed's feet, while I sightsee.

I'd taken a felucca ride earlier in the summer. It's one of the mustdo activities for tourists, and there's never a problem finding somebody to zip you around in their boat for a few Egyptian pounds.

Not Mohammed's, though. As near as I can tell, he inherited the boat from his father, and maybe it was passed down from earlier generations, too. To Mohammed, it's sacred.

My eyes close of their own volition. Cool breezes glance off my face, and all I can feel is happiness. I wish Cassie was with me, but I'll be home soon, and one day, I'll bring her back to show her where I spent my magical summer. Aswan just might be the best city in the world.

Ninetythree days I've been here. And I think every one of those days, a different stranger was kind to me. It's just the way of Egypt. What's not to love?

"We go Philea."

I blink my eyes open to see Mohammed looking at me.

"Cleopatra's bathtub?"

A tear leaks from his left eye. Even so, he smiles and nods. "Island moved when high dam built. Otherwise would drown."

"Like Abu Simbel?"

"Statues cut in pieces and put back together."

There are still a million things about Aswan I don't know. Sadness rushes over me as I realize I'm running out of time to discover everything. A renegade thought trips through my mind: Why do I have to go back to Canada?

And then the everpresent image of Cassie appears and answers that.

"Help!"

Mohammed and I both turn to the back of the felucca. I wonder why Achmed called out in English, but that thought is swallowed easily as I see no scrawny boy using his feet to steer. Only the dangling rope hanging down. The boat is spinning in lazy circles now, and I grab onto the side. I also have to duck as the boom of the sails swing by.

"Achmed!" Mohammed is on his feet, years of practice allowing him to dance easily to the other end of the boat, where his son should be.

He calls out again, but there's no answer. I pull myself along the side of the swinging boat, looking out to the water.

There!

Behind us, already about forty feet away, I see Achmed's small head bouncing around. There's a red smear being washed away from his brow, but it reappears, and I know he's cut badly. He must have hit his head when he slipped. He isn't moving, just being bounced around by the waves.

Mohammed groans and covers his mouth. "Achmed!" He grabs the rudder, to turn the boat, but there's no way he can get there in time.

There's no time to think instinct takes over, and I dive from the side of the boat. It's easier than trying to climb all the way to the back of the boat while it's rocking. The water is warm and clear. I swim as far as I can underwater and finally surface, taking in a huge breath.

Part of me remembers not to swallow the water, but mostly I just swim as fast as I can.

Achmed isn't there anymore.

I turn around and see the felucca well behind me. Mohammed is holding his arm straight out, pointing to my right. I follow his direction and swim farther, taking another look back.

How long has he been under water?

Mohammed points downward.

I dive; the water gets dark as soon as I'm under a few feet. I can't see anything, but I wave my arms around, hoping to hit Achmed by accident.

Nothing.

I keep going deeper and deeper, feeling the pressure build up in my lungs, but I don't care. I can't leave him. Down farther.

That first day we met, Achmed told me, "Nile brings life to all of us."

(And takes it, too.)

No. Not today.

My lungs are burning, and I know I'll have no choice but to swim back to the surface soon. I start to panic, wondering if I can actually make it back or if I'll be drowning along with my little friend.

And then I hit something. It didn't really feel like a body, but I grab onto it and change direction, pulling myself and the thing I'm holding back up to the surface. Bubbles of air escape my mouth, and just for a second I lose my hold. Instinctively I grab the thing again and double my efforts. *I'm not going to make it.* I'm going to die and Cassie will never know what happened to me.

Suddenly, the water color lightens and then I'm above the surface. I gulp the wonderful air into my lungs, and at the same time, I pull the dead thing up.

It's a foot. I twist Achmed around and get his head above the water while I paddle. His eyes are closed. I breathe into his mouth and hit his chest, not really knowing what I'm doing, just that I have to try *something.*

And somehow I hit the right combination. He spits

out water and gulps a deep breath, coughing and spitting, his eyes bulging in terror.

The blood starts to flow again on his forehead, but that's the least of our worries.

Mohammed has turned the felucca around and pulls up near us. I push Achmed's arm up and Mohammed grabs onto it, pulling him into the boat. I didn't think he had the strength to do that, but he does it without hesitation. Once he sees that Achmed is breathing okay, he helps me over the side, too.

I collapse and try to catch my breath.

Mohammed goes to a bench and lifts the seat, pulling out a first aid kit, or at least a reasonable facsimile. He's talking quietly to Achmed, but I don't understand anything he says. I don't think he's berating him. It looks like he's telling him how brave he was. Maybe that's just what I want to believe.

Achmed ends up with a cotton bandage around the top of his head. I hope he gets to see a doctor, but I know that's not very likely. He'll carry a bad scar on his forehead for the rest of his life.

I'm holding the stick that controls the rudder so we go more or less straight. There's not much of a wind right now, so the sail doesn't move. We're almost stationary while Mohammed takes care of Achmed. I feel like an outsider, a peeping Tom watching as the father kisses the son on the cheek and hugs him. He whispers and smiles, and Achmed eventually smiles back at him.

One day, I'd like a son.

With the excitement dying down, I free myself to think again of Cassie. She's waiting back in the McGill ghetto for me to come home, probably wondering why in God's name I could possibly want to stay so long in Egypt. I can hear her saying, "How many pyramids could you possibly look at?"

I smiled at the thought. She'd never really think that. Cassie's happy when I'm happy. I know that. When I tell her about my summer, I know the first words out of her mouth will be, "You've got to take me there."

Mohammed leans back and smiles at Achmed. In English, and in a loud voice, he says, "Good first steer."

Achmed actually laughs, and I smile. Mohammed looks at me and raises his eyebrows.

"Terrific job!" I say. "You've really got a story to tell your friends now."

Mohammed comes over and sits beside me, unconsciously taking control of the rudder device.

"You save him." He puts his hand on my shoulder. "I thank you kind."

The look in his eyes tells me everything. He wouldn't have been able to swim out to save his son.

"I have gift."

"Oh, no," I say. "You don't need "

"Yes. Please to steer."

I take the wooden arm from him as he prances catlike to the front of the felucca. He moves some pieces of wood around and opens a small drawer hidden behind. When he comes back to me, he's carrying a small, purple velvet pouch.

"Ramesses the Great was king of time," he says. He's looking into my eyes, as if daring me to contradict him. I know about Ramses II, of course. He was the greatest of the ancient pharaohs. I had no idea what Mohammed means about the king of time, though. I assume it's an error in his English.

He pulls the drawstring on the pouch, and I see there are two small yellow vials inside.

"From my father. From his father." Mohammed seems to want to say more, back to more generations, but he doesn't have the words for that.

"Stole long ago from Ramesses tomb." He uses the Egyptian name when he speaks, a softer version compared to the English *Ramses*.

"Really?" I must look like an idiot. The only tomb in recent history that was found with anything inside was King Tutankhamen. Either this is nonsense, or those vials are very, very old.

"Ramesses the king of time," he says again. "I save for Achmed. You take one."

He hands a vial to me and motions for me to open it. I twist the cap off and hear the snap of air rushing in. Inside is a dusting of white powder. Following Mohammed's pantomimes, I pour the powder into my left hand.

"Eat."

He reaches into the Nile and scoops some water into the palm of his hand. "Take water."

I don't know how to argue, how to tell him the Nile is full of microorganisms that will likely make me sick if I drink it. He swallows the water in his palm.

What the hell. I'm going home. Who cares if I'm sick for awhile on the plane? And I can't insult my friend.

Besides, I know I already swallowed some water

when I was searching for Achmed.

I follow his lead and scoop some water into my empty hand.

When I hesitate, he again says, "Eat." He points at the powder. "Time..." Again, he seems to want to say more, to explain, but the words fail him.

After three months of living with Mohammed, there's no question of trust. I swallow the gritty stuff. It immediately dissolves into a bitter liquid that sticks to my tongue. I almost choke, but Mohammed moves my hand to my mouth, and I swallow the clear Nile water. It's cool and tastes wonderful.

I scoop another handful of water, to wash away the last of the bitter taste.

"Time. You go to time now."

I nod, without any understanding at all.

Achmed is smiling at me. I wonder if he knows what the heck this is all about.

"Move now. I steer us home."

"I guess I'll never get to see the bathtub, eh?"

Mohammed smiles, showing his few remaining teeth. "Big hole. Doesn't look like bathtub."

"But it was Cleopatra's, right?"

He climbs up, and I move to sit by Achmed. Mohammed's feet take control of the steering mechanism as he controls the sails above. He grabs the dangling rope Achmed must have tripped on between two toes and moves it aside.

I put an arm around Achmed, and he leans in to me. I know Cassie would have some wise and kind words to say to him, to tell him how good he did, that next time he'd be way better. That it's not his fault, that steering a felucca is a hard trade, that he should be really proud.

I say none of those things. In truth, I don't know how hard it is to steer a felucca. I stay quiet, just hold Achmed to me, thinking more of Cassie than of him.

Cassie is amazing. Smart, pretty, and sexy. I think of the first time I saw her...

Chapter 2—Montreal (1982)

...huh?

Mohammed is... gone. Achmed, too.

My feet aren't lifting up and down of their own volition to counter the action of the Nile waves.

I'm looking out through my own eyes, but nothing makes any sense. My breathing is ragged and hard, and I find myself leaning over a bit, lightheaded and

(scared)

confused. The things I'm seeing are coming from a place that can't be. Instead of the desert sun beating down on me with the cool breeze brushing my cheeks, the sky is now overcast, and a threat of a storm hangs in the air.

Gone are the other feluccas, the grimy sea scent, my own light blue galabea I always wear so I mix in with the Egyptians. Now, I'm wearing jeans and a T-shirt. I recognize the upsidedown words on my chest, *Rolling Stones Tour*. It's from 1978.

I shake my head and take a deep breath. There's a lamp post beside me I use to steady myself.

I must be going crazy. Or dreaming. A nightmare, more like it. But, I feel real. I know it's not a dream.

Hundreds of people are lined down the street, all

staring at the passing parade. Far to my left, multicolored floats grind their way down St. Catherine Street, and they stretch forever to my right as well.

St. Catherine?

Yes. I recognize it immediately, with the many stores huddled side by side with French signs advertising new records, books, souvenirs, and clothing.

I'm in Montreal.

And I also know when I am. It's the day I met Cassie.

There's a bagel store behind me, and the fresh smell of the dough drifts all around me. It's a scent I'll never forget. I lived in and around Montreal for twenty years, and the city etched itself into me like fingerprints.

"Salut!" A hockey player is sitting on the trunk of a convertible, his feet dangling into the back seat. He's waving and calling out. If I wasn't so confused, I'd know who he is, but right now, it's all an impossible blur running through my mind like rerunning an old eight millimeter movie my father took of us when we played street hockey.

It's June 24th. *La Fete Nationale.* Quebec's national holiday. Up on the mountain, celebrations would be going on all day long. It's the first holiday of summertime, and the one all families look forward to. I can imagine little kids wading out into Beaver Lake, while their parents sit around the edges, talking and laughing with the strangers beside them.

I met Cassie at this parade. I followed her and

Oh, my God. There she is.

The float is stopped right in front of me. Maybe farther down St. Cathy's, an earlier float had to slow down or stop due to some small hitch.

The Eniskillen Marching Accordion Band is right here. Twelve accordion players with two bass drummers at the rear, marching in place while playing "When Irish Eyes Are Smiling."

Some of the accordionists are off key, but they smile and laugh, and the crowd cheers them on. There's a little girl dancing an Irish jig near me.

Most of the musicians are about forty years old. The one in the middle of the last row is Cassie's father. He's fat and balding and is sweating, even though it's not a hot day.

My eyes leap to the front of the float. Two baton twirlers do their thing, tossing their rods into the air and making unlikely catches before they hit the ground. Although they're synchronized with each other, they aren't really in step with the accordions. Not that it matters.

The girl on the far side has long red hair, bright fire hair. She wears a perpetual smile I know isn't at all related to being on show. It's just the way she always is.

My heart is pounding, and again I feel a bit faint, clutching again at the lamp post for support. I must be
(dreaming)
dreaming. But, no. It's too real. I feel alive, living through this weird déjà vu thing exactly like it happened the first time.

Cassie has more people's attention than any of the accordion players. She's tall and thin and when she tosses her baton, it's with utmost confidence that it will come back to her fingers. She even glances at the audience at times while twirling behind her back.

She looks right at me.

I feel an amazing electric shock as we lock eyes. I'm sure her smile grew even larger when she saw me, but now she turns to look at the other side of the street.

She doesn't recognize me.

"Alors!" shouts the hockey player in the car ahead of the band, as they all start inching down St. Cathy's again.

I still don't understand. Just a few minutes ago, I was with Mohammed and Achmed. How'd I get to Montreal two years ago?

Part of me doesn't really care, and as I think about Achmed, I can no longer quite picture his face. I know he's got thick black curly hair and a big smile, but those are just words right now rather than real memories. The missing image of my little friend overpowers seeing Cassie just for a moment. I try to focus on Mohammed, with his scraggly gray beard and the mask of wrinkles he wears, but I can't quite get a clear image. I know I'll meet him in my future, and that memory is out there, but it's fading, the same as normal memories fade after not being used for a time.

Shit.

The marching band is far enough down the street that I can only hear the occasional bar of their music. Another band is coming closer and drowning out the accordions.

Cassie.

I can't see her.

A few drops of rain start to splash down as I maneuver my way through the crowd. Some people raise umbrellas, making it even harder to get through. Finally, I duck onto the road, beside a truck pulling a giant blue telephone from Bell Canada. It's covered in bright pink flowers and is flanked with a sign advertising their services. There's a man in a tuxedo on the float waving at the crowd. We all ignore him, since nobody knows who he is.

I walk briskly, and after about five minutes I catch up with the Eniskillen marching band. Cassie is still there, flinging her baton into the air, but the drizzle is making it harder for her to see. Doesn't matter; she never misses.

The parade turns north on Crescent Street and into the party district. We pass *The Wrong Number,* my favorite place to drink, along with *Thursdays* and all the other nightclubs and bars. Tonight, the street will be blocked off to traffic while thousands of people zip around, checking out all the pickup spots.

The parade ends near the bottom of Mount Royal. There's a large parking lot behind the hospital, and here, all the attractions disband and pack up for the day. Most of the floats are folded in on themselves, and the place looks like a giant's playspace, where he's scattered a bunch of toys around in all directions.

The rain's stopped, at least temporarily, but Cassie's bright blue dress has darker circles spotting it. The pattern almost looks deliberate.

"You're awfully good with that baton," I say. I smile, but I'm nervous and can't quite seem to make it work.

"Thanks!" She pats the side of her outfit. "I'm a bit

of a mess, though."

For a few seconds, I don't know what to say. Cassie looks at me expectantly.

"I'm Henry." Weird, I just introduced myself to the woman I've loved for the past two years. I did it without thinking, as if we've never met.

"Cassie. Cassie McDougall." She nods and then looks around. "That's my dad. He's driving me back home. Nice to meet you." She starts to walk off.

"Wait!"

She looks back at me. "Yes?"

And that smile hits me. Not her *normal* brilliant smile, but the special one. The one I sometimes think she reserves just for me. She leans slightly forward, staring deep into my eyes. I can see her tongue slightly lifting in her mouth, as if she's reaching out to kiss me.

And then the sun comes out, shining through the clouds, as if ordered by God himself to show this girl in the best possible light.

We both glance up and for some reason it seems extraordinarily funny. Both of us snicker. This is the moment I fall in love. My heart seems to skip a beat, and my throat tightens. I can't seem to breathe. All I can do is stare at her.

"Are you free? I mean for, like, dinner?" I finally ask.

"It's not even lunch time yet."

Stupid moron, I chide myself. "Well, lunch. That's what I meant."

"I don't go for meals with boys I've just met."

For a second, I'm not sure how to answer that. Of

course she wouldn't go out with strangers. "You can invite your dad."

Oh, shit, just what I'd like. First date with her father tagging along.

She brushes her red hair back past her shoulders and seems to consider. "Maybe just to someplace nearby. I'll tell Dad I'll meet him at home. Wait here."

Before she leaves, she leans in to me and asks, "You're not some kind of weirdo, are you?"

Before I can answer, she laughs and looks behind her.

As she talks to her father, the weirdness hits me again. It didn't strike me as odd when I talked to her except for that one thing about introducing myself; it was just like we were meeting for the first time. In fact, we spoke word for word exactly what I remember us saying two years ago.

Or just now.

What happens next? I wonder. Vague future memories swirl around my mind. We'll walk south, looking for a place to eat and will start talking. We'll both be surprised to see we end up all the way in Old Montreal. We pop in for pancakes. No, crepes.

The memories aren't clear; it's like trying to remember what I had for a specific meal a long time ago. But these are memories of my future.

While Cassie talks to her father, I wonder again what happened to Achmed. I wish I knew...

Chapter 3—Aswan (1984)

Achmed is patting his head, holding the towel in place as Mohammed steers the felucca back into his tiny dock.

What?

Now, I'm even more confused. I was just with Cassie. Wasn't I? She's talking to her father. I sit quietly on the boat, wondering if I'm going crazy. I can feel the gaze of her eyes on me, much stronger than all the memories of her I brought to Egypt. It was just a moment ago.

"I know," says Achmed, responding to something I must have said. "But maybe Papa stop letting me steer again."

Words come out of my mouth, even though I'm still fighting for context. "I'm sure you'll be back in the saddle again very soon. Probably as soon as your head heals."

"Stupid rope."

I'm kicking myself for not saying something about the rope when it dangled down onto the back end of the boat. Now I can see that Mohammed doesn't let it near his feet. I should have noticed the difference.

"You'll never make that mistake again."

Achmed looks out to the water and scoops up a drink. He knows I'm just saying platitudes, and that's not helping.

Soon, the boat nudges the dock, and we all climb out while Mohammed loops a rope around the tethering pole.

Achmed is light on his feet and easily hops out, walks right off toward the city. He wants to be alone.

The older man is slower, tying the sails down, checking that various locks are set, then allows me to help him to the dock. He doesn't need the hand, of course, but it's a gesture of friendship.

"Achmed's not happy," I say.

Mohammed nods. "Better tomorrow."

"Will you let him steer again?"

Mohammed looks me in the eyes like I was an idiot, and I know there's some other Egyptian tradition I'm not aware of.

"He master of felucca now. I help."

The summer heat is intense and debilitating. I hadn't noticed it much on the water, but now we're back, it's like we're baking inside his small stone oven at full heat. I feel my energy draining with every step.

"Tea."

I nod as Mohammed leads the way through a maze of streets to a small shop. There's only three tables in the place. No front door. Hell, no *front* at all. Same as most of the shops here. There's just the tables, sitting on the sidewalk with the owner working a bit farther back. Fortunately, there's a roof with a ceiling fan, so it's much cooler.

Mohammed chats with the owner for a few minutes,

talking as much with his hands as with his mouth. I smile and nod when he looks or points toward me. I'm sure he's talking about the trip and how I rescued Achmed. I wish he'd hold the chatter till after the tea arrives.

Eventually, a young girl comes out with our tea on a plate. The owner yells at her. She nods and goes back to bring out a hookah pipe. It's a nice shiny one with apple +-chips mixed in to add a fruity flavor to the smoke. It goes great with the tea. Mohammed and I pass the pipe back and forth.

"That powder you gave me. You said something about time."

He nods.

I feel a bit silly now. The memory of Cassie has faded, and I'm no longer sure it's different from any other memory. Just a tad more real, though, and I know only a few minutes ago, it felt very different.

"Did I just go back in time?"

Mohammed stares at me and then just takes another toke of the pipe.

What a lunatic he must think I am. Go back in time? How about using one of the rugs from the carpet schools to fly to Luxor? How about finding a genie in a bottle and having three wishes granted?

I drink my tea, hoping for once that Mohammed didn't understand me. I can't help but stare at him, and I imagine my own face with a pleading look.

He smiles again, not ashamed of his few yellowed teeth. "You go to time? Now?"

Out on the street, there's a clatter of noise as a tour bus pulls up on the other side of the street. Japanese this time. They all pile out and look around in wonder. Tourists only ever stop in this part of town if they have extra time after visiting the quarry and the dam, so they must be a bit ahead of schedule. The tour guides tell them about the surprise shopping trip, and the visitors all thank her and traipse off to various stalls. None will come here, since they're afraid of any place that looks like it sells food or drink. They're hunting for cheap cotton clothes and miniature sphinxes made of fake alabaster.

"Yes. I mean it sounds silly, I know, but I think I was back with my girlfriend."

I rub my hands down my cheeks and close my eyes. *Fuck, what a mess.*

"You see girl?"

"I mean, it was like I was back two years ago. I left your felucca and was back in 1982."

He nods and again takes another sip of his tea.

"You travel your life in order. Why?"

"Why?" I didn't understand and just shook my head.

"Why remember past but not future?"

His question sounded silly. Of course people could remember the past and not the future, because the future hasn't happened yet.

"Past and future same. Like string with bead on it. You move bead from one end to other. Powder is gift of time. Now, you move own bead where you want."

"What? That makes no sense."

"Sorry. English bad."

"No, no. I understood you just fine, but how can somebody move their 'bead' to a place they haven't lived yet?"

"You try. You see."

Hard to argue with that, but neither was I willing to try to jump into a future time. I couldn't figure out how that might work, even theoretically, let alone for real.

I drank the rest of my tea in silence and took one last drag of the pipe before wandering back home and leaving Mohammed to chat with the owner again.

Chapter 4—Anjou (1975)

I'm at home with Mom and Dad. I'm thirteen.

I got here by thinking about Mom. Today is May 29, her birthday. I was with Achmed when I just happened to think about her. I guess it was because he was talking to Shani again. It's been a few days since the accident on the boat, and he doesn't need the bandages any more. Shani was washing him off.

He's the same age I am now.

Shani frowned and for some reason that made me think of my own mother, and here I am.

At first I felt really small and skinny, but that passed soon. Now I just feel like me.

"Henry!"

Mom's voice is sharp, and I jump up and run into the house. "Mom?"

I can't help staring at her. She's old. Almost forty. The wrinkles on her face seem to scream her age all around. I wonder where Dad is. He's not in the condo, unless he's sleeping, but that wouldn't be like him.

"I need you to clean up your room."

I nod and start up the stairs.

That's not enough. She calls out, "Why do I have to do everything around here? You'd think I could have one damned day off."

Her voice stops me on my climb, but I don't turn around to look at her. There's no point. I know I'd see anger and bitterness, directed at me because I'm the only person in sight. If Suzie were here, she could just as easily be the one getting blasted. Suzie moved out when she turned eighteen, a few months ago. Lucky her.

I don't have much of an answer for Mom, so I start climbing up the steps again and close the door behind me after I enter my room.

The bed is unmade and there's a glass of water, halfempty on the bedside table. My blue pajamas are on the chair at my desk. I take care of these things, but I don't see anything else. I look critically around the room. All my games are piled neatly on a shelf, my plastic vampire models all in their place, no other dirty clothes scattered anywhere. I'm not sure Mom actually looked in my room to see if it was messy, just assumed it was.

I leave the door closed. Let her think I'm doing lots of cleanup before going downstairs again.

Sitting at my desk, I pick up my OPeeChee hockey cards. The check lists are sitting square in the middle of my desk. Three players are unchecked, and it's driving me crazy. Of course, one of the three is Henri Richard. He's retiring this year, so I really need his card.

I hear a crash from downstairs. And another. Some kind of glass thing. Happy Birthday, Mom.

I'm quiet, hoping I don't get dragged into whatever is happening down there. Maybe Dad's back. I can't hear him, but Mom is yelling at someone. Or something. Even though I know she can't hear me, I barely move, not wanting to alert her I'm still here.

After about ten minutes, it gets quiet again. It's 11:00 in the morning.

Another fifteen minutes go by, and I think it's safe to leave.

I climb down the stairs, being careful to stay on the left side of each step. The right side squeaks sometimes. I can hear snores from the living room, which is good. I breathe a bit easier as I reach the bottom of the stairs.

Bits of something blue are on the floor. Farther over, I see a tiny china head. Larger pieces of the figurine are scattered on the floor, into the living room. It's the Virgin Mary statue I'd given Mom earlier today for her birthday. I thought she'd like it. Guess not.

Part of me wonders if I can glue it back together, but that's just silly.

I run out the front door. Never did see Dad.

Chapter 5—Vancouver (2002)

I wake to hear Cassie crying. I roll over immediately and see her clutching the side of our bed in pain.

"Cass, what is it? Bad dream?"

I lean up on one elbow and reach out to hold her. She cries out in pain when I touch her. Fuck. Something's really wrong. I jump out of the bed and flip on the light. In the far side of the room, Jumbles lifts his head and meows.

"Where's it hurt?"

I don't know what to do. She's covered in sweat and tears.

"Cassie, *where's* it hurt?"

"Dad? What's *wrong?*"

Alaine's standing in the doorway. "Go back to bed, son. I need to help Mom right now."

"What's wrong?" He walks in and clutches Cassie's leg, as if he can stop her pain by hugging her ankle. He's now gulping air, feeling her fear.

She glances down at Alaine and tries to calm down, but she can't. Some kind of pain keeps ripping into her.

"I'm calling an ambulance." There's a phone on our bedside table, and I call 9-1-1. After yelling at the operator to get me help, I drop the phone and go back to my wife.

"It's okay. Help is coming."

She whispers, "My neck. My arm." Just those four words take an enormous amount of energy.

I reposition the pillow beneath her head.

"Try to relax, sweetie."

Alaine is trying not to cry. "Watch out the window for me, Bud. Tell me when the ambulance shows up."

He moves to the window, not wanting to take his eyes off his mother.

"So much pain," Cassie says.

"They're almost here. They'll take care of you."

I hold onto her hand with one hand and carefully move her hair out of her eyes with the other. In all the years we've been together, I've never seen her cry until tonight. Not even when she gave birth to Alaine.

Cassie closes her eyes and grits her teeth. She has no strength in her arms. What could it be?

Herniated disk in her neck, of course.

I remember now. The hospital will diagnose it easily tonight.

She opens her eyes, her beautiful, terrified eyes. "Only a little while longer. They'll give you Demerol at the hospital, and the pain will go away."

Cassie blinks, maybe hoping I'm right, but knowing I should be as in the dark about what's happening to her as she is.

"I promise." I hold her cheeks and stare into her eyes. "The pain will go away."

"There it is!" yells Alaine. He runs down the hall to the front door, and I can hear him open it. After a moment, he yells again, "This way. My Mom is hurt."

Two paramedics look at her and ask me what's wrong. "I think it's a herniated disk. In her neck. She's in a lot of pain."

"When did this start?" asks one of them.

"I just woke up about fifteen minutes ago, and she was like this."

I want to scream at him to start working on Cassie; it seems like forever before they do anything. Eventually, they gently lift her onto a stretcher. She cries out again in pain. She can no longer even whisper to me, her body shaking as if she were walking naked in the Arctic. I've chewed the inside of my mouth to shreds, feeling so helpless.

They let me and Alaine both ride in the back of the ambulance. Both of us are dressed in pajamas, and neither of us cares. We just want Cassie to get some relief from the awful pain she's in.

The hospital is only ten minutes away. Feels like ten hours. The siren is whirling away, and I know we're going as fast as we can, but I just want to get her there faster. Faster. Faster.

And then I'm in the waiting room with Alaine. I gasp at the newest time jump. A nurse is leading Cassie over to us in a wheelchair. We both run over to meet her.

Cassie tries to smile, but her face muscles aren't working very well. Her eyes bob around, not focusing on us, but she knows we're there.

The nurse says, "She's okay. Just a little woozy. We've given her some Demerol for the pain, and here's a prescription for Tylenol 3. Follow the dosage instructions, and the pain should be manageable. You'll need to get her to a neurosurgeon as soon as possible."

"How do I find one?"

"Your family doctor will do the referral."

Cassie tries to stand and falls into me. "Home," she says.

I feel a wave of relief, since it's the first painless word she's said to me all night.

There's a taxi stand outside the hospital and we catch the one in front. It seems weird now to be dressed in pajamas, now that the crisis has passed.

Alaine demands to sit beside Cassie, so I help her into the middle of the back seat with us on either side, and we drive home in silence. There's a calmness in the air, as if we're sailing down the Nile...

Memories of Achmed and Mohammed flood through me. They've left solid memories, and I'm looking forward to meeting them for the first time whenever I go back to 1984.

I'm no longer bothered by having memories of my future, of living my life in unconnected bits and pieces. That's just the way my life works. The farther in the future, the vaguer the memories are, but that's the same as the memories from the past. I don't remember things that happened when I was ten as well as I do those of last year.

Cassie whispers to Alaine. I tense, wondering if she's in pain, but when he giggles at whatever she says, I'm able to relax.

The taxi pulls up to our home on 43rd Avenue. I

brought my wallet with me to the hospital, but I have no cash, so I pay the driver with a credit card, adding a five dollar tip. He doesn't offer any thanks.

"I'll help," says Alaine.

We both guide Cassie into the house and up to the bedroom. She falls back asleep shortly after we tuck her in.

Alaine and I sit beside her on the bed. I move some stray hairs from Cassie's face.

"Is Mom gonna die?"

The question shocks me, and I realize Alaine doesn't know what happened. I hug him tightly to me. "Of course not. She's going to have a very sore neck for a couple of months, but she'll be fine." I smile to reassure him.

Alaine is crying silently. His small body is shaking and I feel terrible. I should have told him what was going on sooner.
"It's okay, Bud. Everything's going to be just fine."

He keeps right on crying. Eventually I lift him up and carry him to his own room. I lay down beside him, cradle him, stroke his head, and kiss his cheek while he falls asleep.

Chapter 6—Vancouver (2012)

I'm fifty years old now, and I feel every sore muscle and extra pound I'm carrying. I don't like myself this way. At least that's what I think now, but it's clear I've never done anything to be in better shape, even though I'll know my future state when I go through the earlier days of my life.

It was hard to get here. I'm near the Gray Zone.

Thinking of my future now, even this close, my memories are clear enough for the next year or so, but after that, it's like they fall into a fog. Every time I try to pierce the haze I get a headache and no answers.

I have a feeling I die then.

This is as close as I've ever gotten, and it was a chore to push myself to 2012. It's easier living any earlier portion of my life, easiest by far to live as a child or young adult. Each year closer to the Gray Zone is slightly harder to reach.

Maybe I shouldn't even try, but there's a part of me that demands to know. *What happens?*

"Henry?"

I must look like an idiot, just staring blankly into space.

"Yeah, I'm going."

"You okay?" Joey blinks and rearranges his thick eyeglasses.

I glance at my watch. Two minutes late already. "Shit. I lost track of time."

The lecture room is just down the hall from my office, so it doesn't take me long. There's thirtythree students in theory, but in practice only about two dozen attend my lectures. Most of the rest dropped off when we started covering quantum mechanics.

"Sorry I'm late, everyone." It's a second year astronomy course, but all the students still look like little kids to me. None of them used the time waiting for me to study. Instead, they've been chatting each other up, sending text messages, or God knows what else with their little thumb pads.

"Today, we'll be continuing our discussion on the nuclear reactions inside a supernova, from a quantum perspective."

Most of the students' eyes migrate to look at me while I write out a couple of basic formulae on the white board.

But after I scribble the first equation, I find I don't much care about the topic. It's all so damned esoteric and specialized. Who cares

(about the Gray Zone)

what the exact sequence of neutrino transformation is? Why worry about the polarization states of gluons? Other people have already wasted years working this stuff out, and if any of my students care, they can just google the answers.

I turn back to the kids. They sit and stare at me like sheep. "Why did God create us?" I ask.

Silence and confusion fills the room for a moment. Finally, Shelby calls out from the back of the room. "Are you mixing up your classes, Professor?"
A few students chuckle, but they see I'm not laughing.

"No, I'm asking from a scientific perspective, not a theological one. We've talked about all the equations before." I wave at the halffinished ones behind me. "We know they work, but why *should* they? Why would God decide e should be equal to mc^2? Why not mc^3? Why not something totally different altogether?"

Nobody seemed interested in replying.

"Why should the force of gravity be 9.8 meters per second squared?"

I hesitate but then ask, "Why should we be able to remember the past but not the future? All our scientific equations work in either direction. mc^2 = e is just as valid as e = mc^2. There's no reason for time to flow forward."

I see Joey sneak in to the back of the class. Even though he's a grad student, he tries to attend as many of my lectures as possible, since he teaches my labs.

Lynda finally answers. "If we could remember the future, we'd be breaking causality, which is a basic feature of our universe." She folds her hands together, unsure if she's right.

"No, that's not it." I turn to my left and Steven adds, "There's no law against causality. It's just never been seen to be broken."

"Quantum computers break it," I say.

"Only by reaching into parallel universes."

"And so, why can't we do the same?"

Steven shrugged and looks at his watch. "Are we

going to be getting back to an actual science lecture today? Finals are in three weeks."

Fucker.

He looks at me in defiance, the smartest kid in the class, but he's only interested in the numbers. Equations, variables, reactions, solid answers to clear questions. I could see him working at Mount Palomar one day, but not Cambridge.

I glance around the room and see nobody else is interested in time's arrow, either. I turn and reluctantly finish scribbling the equations I'd started.

God, I feel old.

After finishing the lecture, I cancel the afternoon session. Mornings I teach astronomy, afternoons I teach theology. Day in, day out.

I just can't get the interest up today. Somehow, lecturing on the origin of the universe is more interesting in a science setting, but the students don't give a shit. In theology, the students listen, but only seem to be interested in a single answer.

None of them care about time's arrow.

I leave the UBC campus and drive to our home in Kerrisdale. The nice neighborhood seems like window dressing draped over my psyche.

"Hey, you're home early."

Cassie gives me a welcome hug. I don't want to let her go like I'd slump to the floor in this saggy old body if she didn't support me. I pull her head to my shoulder and wish I'd taken her to Egypt all those years ago. She kept saying she wanted to go, to see if we could track down Achmed and maybe even Mohammed, see what happened to them, but...

"You okay?"

"Yeah. It's just..."

"Henry?"

I shuffle into the living room and sit on the couch. "I always wanted to be called Henri."

"Henri?"

"Like The Pocket Rocket."

She stares at me without understanding. Who can blame her? I must look and sound like an idiot. She clutches at my hand.

"Can I get you a beer? Something?"

I close my eyes and shake my head. "Just tired."

I can feel her fingers rubbing my hand. Nobody ever was as lucky as me in marriage. "I wish I knew what happened to Achmed."

"Alaine's over at a friend's house. Why don't we go out for a nice dinner at the Keg?"

I take a deep breath and blink my eyes open. She has a tissue ready, and I use it to wipe my face. I nod. "That'd be nice."

"Maybe you should have a quick shower first."

I blow my nose into the tissue and walk up the stairs. Old creaks through my knees. I wish I was young.

Chapter 7—Anjou (1975)

And then I am.

As I walk up the front walk to my house, a weird feeling flushes through me. I shake it off. I've long since realized there's no point in trying to concentrate on what's about to happen; even if I can locate the memory, it doesn't change anything.

I'm thirteen, and I feel about a jillion times better than I did just a few moments ago. The heavy weight is gone, the sadness evaporated. Instead, summer sunshine hugs me like a duvet, and I know I'm grinning from ear to ear.

Ten minutes ago, we left school. *We*, as in me and Amy. I walked her home, and before she ducked inside her basement apartment, she giggled, looked around, and kissed me. On the lips!

That's the memory I want right now, not some weird thing that happens way in the future when I'll be a thousand years old or whatever.

Amy Sterling kissed me!

"Suzie!" I couldn't wait to tell my sister; her car was in the driveway. She's always teasing me about how much I like Amy.

Threethirty on a Wednesday afternoon. That's about

the only time it's safe to yell in the house. Mom works Monday, Wednesday, and Friday afternoons down at Place Ville Marie, helping sell clothes or something.

"Suzie!"

I run to the back of the house, but nothing. Cigarette smoke hangs in the air, as always, and there's two empty cans of beer on the sink. Dad must have come home for lunch.

The TV is on, tuned to *The Match Game.* After clicking it off, I call out one more time. Finally I hear

(something terrible)

a sound from upstairs. I'm not sure what it is. For another few moments, the house is silent again, but I can feel my heart pounding.

I climb the stairs, not worrying about the creaks. When I'm halfway up, Suzie's cries become more clear, and I run the rest of the way up. I want to hurry, but at the same time I don't want to go to her at all. It's not good. I'm sweating and biting my lip. Forcing my feet forward like I'm walking through quicksand, the bathroom door calls to me like a siren.

This time I'm whispering. "Suzie?"

She continues crying. I can see her legs on the bathroom floor, the door hiding the rest of her. She's wearing the long white socks that are her trademark.

"Mom..." she cries.

I finally reach the bathroom and push the door open with a shaking hand. The door bangs against the tub.

I'm frozen with fear. Mom is covered with blood, dried and sticky. I think there must have been water in the tub earlier, but it's all gone now, and a pink wash covers the porcelain. Her hair is matted, and long cuts cover her arms from her elbows to her wrists.

I've never seen her naked before.

Her head slumps to the side, as if she's licking the tub.

Part of me refuses to believe what I see. I reach down and shake her, then gasp at the sticky blood covering my own hand.

I realize my pants are wet. I've peed myself.

"Mom?"

I finally break off and look at Suzie, who's head is down. She's still sobbing but no longer making any noise. Her hair covers her face, but I push it all back and hold her to me. *Somehow, I have to be strong,* I know. I have to help my sister.

But I have no idea how.

She looks up, and her face is all red. I almost don't recognize her.

"We have to call for help," I say. "Maybe they can save her."

Suzie starts laughing. "Help her? Are you stupid? She's fucking dead!"

"But..."

I stare back at Mom, watch the blood congeal between her legs, see her sagging breasts with their awful gray color.

And I know Suzie's right, of course. There's nothing anyone can do.

I start to cry.

Chapter 8—Montreal (1982)

Cassie and I met a month ago. That's a month ago as the calendar turns, not a month ago in my own memory. My heart knows I'm falling madly in love with her for the first time.

"Where to now?" she asks.

When I wrap my arms around her and pull her close to kiss her, I'm lost. Cassie is my whole universe, and all I want to do is hold her.

Eventually, we separate and I lick my lips. This is the happiest time of my life.

A nagging *something* pokes at me, reminding me of just having left Mom's body, but in my new time reference, that happened a long time ago. Seven years ago, not the seven minutes ago I know it really was.

"Back down?"

Cassie nods. We've spent the afternoon at Beaver Lake, on the top of Mount Royal. We grab a couple cans of Coke at the chalet overlooking Montreal and start walking down the makeshift steps and pathways that lead us eventually to downtown.

We don't really need to talk about where we'll go from there. I just take the lead, and we head to my apartment in the McGill student ghetto.

Our first time.

She knows where we're going, since I've told her where I live, but she smiles and laughs and we both know it's right.

Since the parade, we've grown closer and closer. When my eyes shut each night, I visualize her lying beside me, my fingers running through her long red hair, her blue eyes staring into mine. I can see her perfect body in my mind anytime I want. It's like a photograph of her is tattooed on my retina.

And I know she feels the same about me. She shows it in every move, every kiss, every caress.

We get to my apartment after about an hour's walk down the mountain and through the city. The ghetto is full of cheap, unspectacular housing for McGill students, as well as lowincome people who just can't afford anything better. It's not a place most people are proud of living in, but it's mine.

I lead Cassie up the three flights of stairs to my room. Clean and neat. Has been since I met her; I knew one day she'd be seeing it.

Cassie's home is in Westmount, where all the rich English people live. Her dad's a lawyer when he's not banging the drum for the marching accordion band.

"Nice."

I smile, knowing she's being kind. "Not quite what you're used to."

"It's *nice*," she says again. "Show me around."

I can't help but laugh. "It's pretty much what you see here. That's where I do my homework." I point to a small desk piled with astronomy and religious texts. "That's where I cook. The bathroom is right there, and my bedroom is over here."

She walks over to the small kitchenette and then flips through the textbooks.

"No TV?"

I shake my head. "I have a radio."

She clicks the radio on. I normally listen to a local rock station, and *Bohemian Rhapsody* by Queen drifts out from the tiny speakers.

"Show me the bedroom."

My mouth suddenly goes dry. I nod and take her hand, as I open the bedroom door. There's only a small single bed and a dresser in the corner. Thank God I'd remembered to hide all my dirty laundry before I left this morning.

Cassie kisses me and after a moment, we lie down in the bed. In a few moments, all my dreams come true.

Chapter 9—Vancouver (2014)

There's somebody in the house.

I've snapped awake and am lying quietly beside Cassie. She hasn't awoken. I don't move, not wanting the swish of the sheets to drown out the sound.

I know I heard something. It wasn't a dream.

But now the house is silent. The only sound I can hear is the almost nonexistent traffic noise filtering in from the other side of the house. There's no creaks, no whispers from downstairs, but I know I heard something.

They must have cut the alarm system.

I think of waking Cassie, but I'm not sure she'd believe me.

There's a baseball bat leaning against my side table. I grip it tightly, careful not to pull it too fast and bang it against the table. The bat's never been used; it's been waiting for

(the Gray Zone)

for today.

I look around and try my hardest to remember what's about to happen. Nothing. No memory at all. It's true: I'm in the Gray Zone. I have no sense at all about what's going to happen. For the longest time,

I've had an internal safety net, but not now.

My breathing is rushed, and I have trouble convincing my feet to move forward. I glance behind me to be sure Cassie is still asleep. It's not too late to change my mind and wake her...

I inch out to the hallway. I still haven't heard anything, but I can *feel* someone downstairs. I'm holding the bat in both hands over my shoulder. I take a deep breath and remember the plan for intruders. Don't strangle the bat. Hold it firm but not too tight. I'm the only person I know who keeps a weapon ready. I knew I'd need it one day.

As I creep down the stairs, I question myself. Should I turn the lights on? Doing that would warn the burglar. If he's armed, I'd be a sitting duck.

Alaine is visiting my sister in Montreal. I'm glad he's not here for this, but I wish I wasn't the only one creeping down the stairs.

And then, I hear it again. A shuffling sound, like someone pushing furniture or sliding some of our belongings off shelves.

My head is spinning, and my knees almost give out. Panic sets in. I take a deep breath and move to the kitchen, where the sound is coming from.

I silently offer a prayer to a God I'm not sure I believe in.

The kitchen is pitch black. The windows face Montgomery Park, and there's no light at all from there.

I'm holding the bat close to my side, aimed straight ahead.

Shush.

The scraping sound is too much for me, and I lose control of myself. The shape is coming toward me, and I smash the bat down over and over. There's a deep thud at first, followed by the sound of bone cracking. My hands are wet but I keep hitting and hitting. A groan. More hits and more blood.

And then sweet quietness.

"Oh my God," I cry. I stumble backward, banging into the door jamb.

Cassie calls out from our bedroom. "Henry! What happened?"

I'm too scared to yell at her to call the police.

She rushes down the stairs, carrying a candle, which hurts my eyes.

"My God, Henry, what...?"

We both stare at the prone body. At first the head is just a bloody pulp, raw hamburger. Through the mess, though, I begin to recognize Alaine's motionless body.

It's been three days since we buried our son, and I still feel like I'm walking through a fog all the time. I force myself every day to climb out of bed, push myself to face the world. Most particularly, to face Cassie.

She sleeps in Alaine's bed each night. That first day, after the police left, I tried to hold her, but she just stood stiff as a board.

"I need to digest everything," she said as she slipped out of my grasp.

I know she's trying to figure out how everything could have happened. How was it Alaine decided to come home early and surprise us? How could the power fail the same damned night he arrived home? How could I have panicked and...

Over and over, I replay that night in my mind. I've seen it a thousand times now. The shadow moving toward me in the darkness, my fear overtaking me, my hand gripping the handle.

My son dead.

This morning, I've spent hours on the couch, doing nothing but stare into space and remember Alaine. I remember the first time we went salmon fishing, and when I first took him skiing at Whistler. The cheering when we sat in row six at the men's hockey final at the 2010 Olympics. And the times when he was small, when he would sit and fall asleep on my lap while I whispered bedtime stories in his ear.

I wish I knew what memories Cassie was reliving, but she avoids me. Since the cremation, she hasn't talked to me at all. She sometimes leaves the house for hours at a time, but I don't know where she goes.

The grandfather clock strikes noon. I can't believe it's that late already. I'm sure I only sat down a while ago, but it's been almost six hours.

Cassie hasn't come down for breakfast yet. I walk to Alaine's room, wondering if I should wake her. I silently open the door, but she's not there.

I can hear the small shower in Alaine's ensuite bathroom.

The room is full of memories, and I haven't come in here since his death. There's a stack of old CDs sitting beside his portable stereo, a few paperback books in a clumsy pile, and clothes scattered on the chair. Cassie hasn't touched them.

A trickle of water runs out from under the bathroom door. At first I don't understand and stare at it from the fog of my deadened mind.

(Karma Chameleon...)

"Cassie?" No answer. I yell again, "Cassie!" as I push open the door. Water rushes out and I see her slumped in the corner of the shower stall, redfaced and covered in running blood. The razor blades are still in her limp fingers.

Her eyes gaze out to me, but they see nothing. I don't know how long she's been here, but it's too late for me to do anything.

"No!" I cry. "Cassie, no!"

I try to focus. Turn off the water. Check to see if she's breathing or has a pulse. I pull her up and carry her to Alaine's bed, rubbing all the blood off with the blankets and sheets.

She stares up at the ceiling.

Her limbs are stiff, and one arm points to the ceiling from the elbow up.

I jump in time for a second and see the dead face of my mother accusing me. Then I'm back with Cassie.

"My love," I whisper. "I'm so sorry."

I crawl into the bed beside her and cry. I can barely breathe with the wracking of my body. I've killed her just as surely as I killed Alaine, and I'm overwhelmed with grief and guilt.

I kiss her cold cheek and pull her to me. I can't leave her. She and Alaine are everything to me. How can they both be gone?

The pain is too much. I reach out in my mind to find another time to be. Any other time.

Chapter 10—Vancouver (2010)

I'm sitting with Cassie, each of us holding a glass of Merlot, watching an old movie on TV. The love seat we share is perfect for us; I can feel her hip on mine, and I'm sure that half the time we watch the movie, my hand is resting on her thigh.

Weird. I don't know when I came from. I almost always know when I've just been. I yawn, trying to stay awake.

Alaine is sleeping on the floor, a small pillow the only hint of comfort he was interested in. He always likes watching a movie with us on Friday nights, but I know that won't always be true. For now, I'm blessed.

"Pretty boring, isn't it?" Cassie yawns and plops her head on my shoulder. "I'm not surprised he didn't make it till the end."

"Can't win them all."

I pour a bit more wine for both of us as the closing credits roll.

"Want to watch the news?"
She shrugs. "Suppose."

I flip the channel, and we wait for the commercials to end.

And then the lights go out.

Cassie snaps her head off my shoulder. "Damn, not again."

I carefully walk over to the mantel and light a candle. "It's okay. We're prepared this time."

She looks beautiful in the glow of the candle. Rather than go flip the circuit breaker, I sit back on the couch and kiss her.

She holds me close and sighs.

"You're beautiful."

Cassie smiles. "Go fix the power, please."

"Don't you think this is romantic?"

She laughs. "We're too old for romance. I'm happy with getting to sleep by ten o'clock these days."

I light a second candle and leave it on the coffee table for her while I walk to the stairs leading to the basement.

"I really think we should get an electrician in," she calls over the railing. I wince, knowing I've promised to get the wiring redone for years. Somehow it never seems important. It's only a quick trip down to the basement to flip the breaker back on. What harm can a few seconds of darkness do?

So much for romance.

Right now, I just feel rejected. When the lights are back, I blow out the candle. Upstairs, I hear Cassie waking Alaine and sending him to bed. She clicks the TV off.

Sometimes, I wish she'd enjoy the occasional blackout. It really does put her in a wonderful light.

As much as I wish they didn't, her words hurt. *I'm happy with getting to sleep by ten o'clock these days.* I know she didn't mean to slap at me, but it's hard to avoid the inference. Fortyeight years old. It's not like we're ancient or anything. Alaine's only fourteen. Cassie and I have a long time to grow old together, but I dread the day Alaine moves out. We probably only have him living with us another six or eight years. Then our little family unit will be very different.

For once, I try hard to look into my future memories. I know we'll have many wonderful times to come, but then I hit the wall. That Gray Zone in 2014, only four years from now. I see nothing after it starts. Just a fog enveloping my life.

I sometimes wonder if I can avoid ever going into there, but it seems unlikely. I'm going to live that long, I know, so surely I have to experience whatever it is that happens then. Don't I?

Meanwhile, I grab onto the memory of taking Alaine to Jericho Beach next month. He'll love that trip. We'll walk out into English Bay, feel the cool water splash up on us both, cook hot dogs in a sand pit, and watch the sun set over the water. Boy's day. I can't wait for that.

Chapter 11—Anjou (1975)

"Shit. She hitting the bottle again?"

"Yeah."

"Happy fucking birthday, Mom."

Suzie stands aside and lets me into her apartment. I wish I could give her a hug, but it's a bit awkward now that she's already started dissing Mom.

"You want a Coke?"

I shrug. "Sure."

I've only been to Suzie's place a couple of other times and never really clued in till now that I only go to visit when Mom's had a hard day.

The apartment is awful. It's so small it feels like the walls are going to fall in on me. It stinks of cigarettes. Suzie lights one and then hunts through the small fridge to find a pop.

"Guess I don't have any. I got beer." She laughs but opens a can anyhow.

"S'okay. I'm not really thirsty."

She takes a long drink of the beer, looks like half the can. Like mother like daughter, I guess.

There's a long silence in the room. With Suzie being five years older than me, it's a big gulf. Sometimes it seems like she's more an aunt than a sister, but then I remember when I was little, she'd play cards with me. She taught me Go Fish and War. I know in the future we grow closer as the age difference becomes less important. Her second husband will be a close friend of mine.

"Wanna watch TV? I think there's some " She hunts for the TV Guide, but I don't really care what she thinks is on.

"I think we should do something," I say. "About Mom, I mean."

The idea seems to bounce off her and fall flat on the floor. She doesn't say anything for a minute, just blows a smoke ring and takes another drink of her beer.

"What do you mean?" she finally asks.

I know I could focus on the memory if I want, but it's too big, too scary. I close my mind off to any specifics.

"Something's gonna happen to her."

Suzie shakes her head. "Nothing's going to *happen*. Jesus. She's just going to grow into a miserable old cow, like she's been doing. What happened today?"

I remember the figurine I'd gotten Mom and how it lay shattered on the floor. For some reason I'm ashamed to tell Suzie about it. Afraid she'll think I'm an idiot or something for even buying Mom a gift.

"Just a lot of yelling."

"Yeah." She sits in the wooden chair beside me. "It's okay. You can stay here as long as you want."

"But she's "

A quick flash shows me Mom's body in the bathtub, swimming in red. Now it's gone, as if it were never really there.

"Henry? What's wrong?"

In my mind, I hear Boy George and Culture Club singing "Karma Chameleon." Is that song even out yet? I don't know.

"Henry?"

I shake my head. "I... I don't know. Something."

And a horrible thought. What if it's a better future without Mom?

I close my eyes and push the thought away. It's not too late. I can help Mom. Stop her from...

Karma's a bitch.

Was that part of the song? I can't remember.

Suzie stands. "You want a beer? Mom'd kill me but maybe it'd be good for you."

Without waiting for an answer, she grabs two cans from the fridge, pops the top on them both and puts one in front of me. She's right Mom would *definitely* kill her for that. I can almost hear the seconds ticking away as I stare at the beer. Finally I grab it. It tastes awful.

"Happy birthday," I whisper.

Chapter 12—Vancouver (2014)

There's somebody in the house.

What the hell? I'm careful not to wake Cassie as I move to the bedroom doorway. Almost as an afterthought, I pick the baseball bat from beside the bedside table.

Downstairs is silent now, but I know I heard something. *Someone.*

My mouth is dry, and my chest is heaving from fear. I take long, deep breaths, gathering the courage to act. I glance back; I haven't woken Cassie. I almost wonder if part of me wants her to wake, so I don't have to face the intruder alone.

Of course not.

The stairs are quiet beneath my feet. I think of turning the lights on, but that would just give the intruder an advantage.

I'm more frightened than I've ever been. I *know* somebody is down there, and he's not going to be

Jesus.

it's just hit me. I'm in the Gray Zone.

I've never been in the Gray Zone before. I stop at the landing halfway down the stairs. Does this mean I'm going to die here?

My hand is like a vice on the baseball bat, and I loosen my grip a bit. I need to think straight, not panic.

There's still no noise, but I know what I heard, and I know there's someone down there.

I maneuver to the kitchen and slowly push the door open.

At first, nothing. But, then, a shadow moves and is coming toward me. He's attacking. Fuck! I hit without thinking, the force of the crunch pushing my arm back. "Oh, my God," I cry.

Hit, hit, hit.

The man falls to the floor, and for a moment, all I can see is a slightly darker shadow.

"Henry! What happened?"

I can't answer Cassie. My words are gone.

She rushes down beside me and flicks the light switch. Nothing.

"Stay back. I don't know if "

"What happened?"

"I think... I think he's dead."

"Oh, my God."

Cassie moves to the mantel and lights a candle. She walks slowly back toward me. I keep the bat aimed at the body.

And then the light shows my son, and my world falls apart.

In the days that follow, I walk around in a daze, and only barely stop myself from drinking all day and all night. There are arrangements to make, and the police are investigating the death.

Cassie shuns me, and I understand. She needs time to get over it. She needs time to forgive me. I need time to forgive myself. She's sleeping in Alaine's room.

Today, I woke and couldn't find her. I walk up to check on her and find the bed empty, the shower running. For a moment, I relax, but then I notice the water running out from under the shower stall.

Chapter 13—Vancouver (2014)

Oh my God, I think I'm in the Gray Zone.

I've never been here before. My whole life has been an open book to me until now. I have no memory of anything that happens in the Gray Zone and have always been afraid of it. Somehow I'm here.

A rush of déjà vu runs though me, and then it's gone.

Shit. I don't want to be here.

I can't even wish my way out, back to my "normal" life.

It's dark. And silent.

Cassie's asleep, but my senses come to attention. *Oh, my God, there's somebody downstairs.*

I'm holding my breath, listening...

"...Fuck, fuck, fuck! No. Cassie!"

But I know it's too late. Her eyes are glazed over, and there's no life left in her.

She's covered in dried blood, but I can't help myself. I climb into the tub and pull her to me. "Cassie, my love. Don't leave me."

She doesn't answer. My tears wash some of the

blood off one cheek, but she doesn't move or answer me. I know she can't, but I want her to anyway.

I collapse into her and cry for what seems like forever.

Chapter 14—Aswan (1984)

I climb off the cruise ship after it docks at Aswan and stare at the city. It's beautiful. Somehow there's an immediate sense of peace and goodwill. I'm not sure how to explain it. The feeling just permeates everything.

The air is clean and smells of seafood. I have no plan of where to go. I vaguely remember I'll be spending several months here, so I know I'll like it.

Even after all these

(decades)

years, it's still a bit weird to know I can remember my future any time I want. Well, except for the Gray Zone I've never been there. One day...

Local men shout out to the tourists walking off the ship, offering to take them to the best markets or the quarry or help them find a felucca. Of course, most of the tourists are in groups, and the tour guides ignore all the locals, leading the visitors down the edge of the river to wherever they're going.

My time here is less planned. I just hopped onto the boat from Luxor. I'm not good as part of a group. Would rather explore on my own.

A cab driver is waving and smiling at me.

"American?" It's always the first question.

"Canadian."

"Ah, Canada Dry!" He laughs at the same joke I've heard a hundred times since arriving in Cairo two weeks ago.

What the heck.

"Can you take me to the Aswan Dam?"

"Ah. Of course, sir. Only five hundred Egyptian Pounds."

"No. One hundred."

"Sir, is a long way. A very long way."

We eventually agree on two hundred pounds, and I climb into the back of the tiny cab. It stinks of cigarettes.

The ride is pleasant, and I take mental notes of some parts of town I want to come back to. The drive takes about a half hour, and I pay the driver, who immediately starts looking for someone to take back to town. "Allah bless you, sir," he says. I wave goodbye.

The dam is huge. Standing at one end, I can barely see the other end.

"Baksheesh?"

I turn to see a young boy standing beside me. He can't be more than twelve years old, but ages are hard to determine in Egypt.

"No."

I almost walk away, when he says "Thank you, sir." When he bows, I feel a rush of recognition from long ago.

"You speak English."

"Some. No good like you, sir."

His curly black hair shines in the sunlight, but it's

his smile that really captures me. Hypnotizing.
"My name Achmed, sir."
One day I'd like to have a son.

Language Barrier

My beautiful wife, Fatima, has a mother who is kind, family-oriented, hard-working, and has many other very positive attributes.

She also does not speak English. She's Portuguese. I don't speak Portuguese, but I often end up driving her between her home and ours. Those car rides are sometimes very quiet. At other times, she will speak to me in Portuguese, telling me about her day (maybe) or the deals she found at the supermarket (probably not), or asking about how things are going with me (fairly likely). I understand none of these conversations, but it breaks up the monotony of the quiet, so it's nice.

Similarly, if I tell her something, she may get the occasional word, but anything complex would be impossible for her to understand.

What better situation to have somebody confess to a crime?

James Beach was the founding publisher and editor of Dark Discoveries magazine. He'd published a few of my stories and contacted me one day to ask if I could write a very short story that he could include in the newsletter he emailed to all his customers. His request came right when I was mulling over the idea for story, and I was happy to oblige. The newsletter was published only four days after James' original request, which must be some kind of record. It certainly is a record for me.

THE SUN WAS SHINING when I stopped in the parking lot to pick up Maria. She was standing in the doorway, clutching her small purse in both hands as if it was an anchor that she was afraid would fall if she let go.

When she saw me get out of the car, she smiled. It seemed incongruous, given the reason I was picking her up.

She walked slowly to the car, almost shuffling. She was seventy years old now, having had a birthday a month earlier. I didn't call, because the telephone is too hard. Hell, it's hard enough in person.

"Thank you, Johnny," she said.

"You're welcome."

I helped her get into the car and we pulled out of the parking lot. I didn't know what to say, so there was only silence for the first couple of miles.

"Car nice."

I glanced over at her and mumbled thanks. Her silvery hair was almost touching the roof. It wasn't really a nice car, but she was doing her best to be polite.

It wasn't always this hard. Once, it seemed comfortable to be with her and Carla. Carla was my age, half that of Maria, and she could translate anything that Maria said in Portuguese. It felt like I could talk to Maria about anything. She'd tell me about life in the Azores and how she and Carla's father Jose had immigrated to Long Island when Carla was two years old. They wanted a better life for their daughter. Who wouldn't? Carla was Maria's voice.

Maria rarely left her home. She watched the Portuguese channel on TV and read the weekly papers from Lisbon. She was happy as long as Carla was happy.

So was I.

Maria took out a tissue and blew her nose. The sound shook me from driving on autopilot.

"Hard to believe it's a year already," I said.

She looked at me, trying to see if there were any words she understood, but she didn't reply, so I'm sure she didn't have a clue what I'd said.

"I miss her."

That she understood. "Me too."

I clicked the radio on. It was tuned to an oldies channel, the channel Carla had always listened to. Once she was gone, I never touched the station. I never touched the TV channel. I never touched her clothes. I never touched her shoes. Her makeup. Her toothbrush.

God, I miss her.

"I never realized how much it would hurt," I said. "She was always the only one for me and I should never have taken her for granted." I turned to face Maria. "There was never anybody like her in my life."

Maria looked at me with her lips pursed and her glasses perched on the end of her nose like a sparrow. "Okay," she said.

Then she started talking in Portuguese. She spoke for about five minutes, barely taking a breath. She'd dab the tissue at her eyes and sometimes I could hear a hitch in her voice as she talked about her only daughter, her only reason to live.

I listened and even though I didn't understand a single word, I glanced at her and nodded and when she was done talking I put a reassuring hand on her shoulder.

That's when she started crying for real. Huge long sobs, tears streaming down her face, such terrible emotions spilling out of her.

I felt tears running down my face too. She handed me one of her tissues.

Soon we reached the cemetery. I knew the twists and turns of the road through the grounds so well I could likely drive to Carla's headstone with blinders on.

The headstone was as elaborate as I could afford, which wasn't all that much. It reached out of the ground about two feet, rose-colored granite. On the stone was written:

HERE LIES CARLA MONTEIRO SANTOS
BELOVED DAUGHTER AND FRIEND
1975 – 2012

It always bothered me that I couldn't have written "Beloved WIFE and Daughter," but although the plans for our marriage were in the works, she was killed months before the ceremony was planned.

I lay half a dozen yellow gerbera daisies at the base of Carla's stone and then touched the stone like I had touched Maria's shoulder earlier.

"Your favorite flowers, baby."

I stood back and looked at the tombstone, remembering all the wonderful days with my girl.

Maria placed a bouquet of flowers for Carla, too. She spoke more in Portuguese and then stood back a couple feet and prayed.

I'm not sure how long we stayed there. Maybe thirty minutes. Maybe an hour. It just seemed to go by in the blink of an eye and then we were back in the car.

It felt like the calendar was lying to me. Could it really have been a year? The pain I felt was still fresh.

"I miss her," I said again.

This time, Maria didn't answer.

"I remember that day so clearly. We woke up and kissed and showered together and got dressed."

Maria stayed silent, not having a clue what I was talking about.

"I wanted to be with her forever. I really did."

We pulled out on the highway, heading back the way we'd come.

"But I'd always had that streak of temper. I couldn't help it. I never could tell when I was going to blow. Had no clue it was going to be that day."

I glanced at Maria. She was staring straight ahead and dabbing at her eyes again.

"It was middle of the morning when we started arguing. Stupid. It was just about dinner. She wanted pork chops and I wanted to order Chinese. How the hell could something so trivial end up with her being dead?"

I remembered slashing at her with a steak knife. It wasn't a conscious thing, just happened.

"There was blood everywhere, and I stabbed her again as she begged me to stop. I had to take her body out to the car and drive her to the woods. I liked hunting and I knew a place near the northern shore that nobody would ever find her at."

Maria said something I didn't understand.

"But I still miss her terribly."

"I miss her too."

We arrived back at her place and I helped her out of the car and walked her to her side door.

When Maria unlocked the door, she turned and gave me a hug. "Thank you, Johnny. Carla love you."

I tried to hold back the tears. "You're welcome."

The Halloween
Phantoms

Fatima and I had a new home built for us, and we moved in at the end of June, 2011. Four months later, we prepared for our first Halloween together, and she mentioned an odd idea that she had heard from one of her cousins. The idea was the concept of leaving small items for neighbors from the "Halloween Phantom," exactly as it was done in the story. It was fun, and that first year our entire neighborhood was infested with packages from the phantom.

Merged in with this, though, was something very odd. On the evening before Halloween, we had three spooky visitors show up at our home, dressed as ghastly demons. They stood silently at the end of our front yard, and they did a very good job of spooking us.

If we move forward to the following autumn, I was asked if I'd like to write a story for Cemetery Dance. They wanted to publish a whole series of Halloween stories as part of a series of e-books.

It didn't take me long to piece together the parts of the story that actually had occurred and then just twist them a bit to add the horror elements I needed.

The story was also published in Italian a couple of years later, also as a standalone e-book.

OCTOBER 15

ELLEN WESTON WAS DREAMING of a Caribbean cruise, full of laughter, exotic drinks, and Davey doting on her, as he always did. Mostly, though, she was just enjoying sitting on the deck of the ship with the sun beaming down on her. The feeling of having free time was heavenly.

It all evaporated when the bell's ringing turned out not to be from the cruise ship but rather the doorbell in her home.

"Damn."

She glanced at her watch. 9:35. *Who the hell is here this late?*

Maybe if she just ignored it, the person would go away. But, maybe it was important.

Shit.

Ellen got up from the couch and blinked her eyes to clear her vision. She couldn't see anyone at the door, but it was dark out. Dark, rainy, dreary.

I hate October.

The wind was blowing hard outside, accompanied by freakish whistling and howling.

Once again she wished for the comfort of her home in California. Autumn in Minnesota wasn't nice.

She walked to the door, yawning and stretching her arms. She cupped her hands to the narrow window beside the door, but she could only see her own ghostly reflection staring back. Her short blonde hair hung lifeless, just like she felt.

Her eight-year-old daughter, Julie, was sleeping upstairs and Ellen wanted nothing more than to be able to go join her. The damned alarm would be going off at 5:00, calling her to another day at work. Even though she was only thirty-six, Ellen felt like she was sixty. Davey's death still weighed on her like a pair of anchors crowded on her shoulders.

She still didn't see anybody out the window.

Fuck it.

She unlocked the door and pulled it open. The wind pushed harder, causing the door to almost swing open and crash to the side wall. Ellen caught it just before it hit.

Nobody there.

Figures. Stupid kids.

She was about to close the door when she saw the bag hanging on the doorknob. It was a black sack, made of some kind of light material, almost feathery to the touch. A few drops of rain beaded up and rolled down the fabric as it would off a bird. There was a jack-o'-lantern picture in the middle of the bag, bright orange, and almost lifelike. It creeped her out, but she couldn't help touching it. The image was silky and caused her fingers to tingle.

"Hello?" she called. "Is anybody here?"

She was shivering from the frigid wind, so she grabbed the weird bag and closed the door, being sure to lock it again.

"Mommy?"

Ellen stared at Julie as the little girl came down the stairs to the living room. It took forever to get her to go to bed each night, and now another hour of her own sleep would be lost.

"It's okay, sweetie. Just somebody leaving some Halloween stuff for us."

"Really? Who? Can I see it?"

Ellen knew it was pointless to resist, so they went to the kitchen.

"It's pretty!"

Ellen had to agree. She'd never felt material like this before, and the laughing eyes of the jack-o'-lantern seemed to warm the room up.

"Open it, Mommy!"

Ellen dumped the bag onto the table. There were a few candies, some chocolate bars, and a small toy that seemed to be a puzzle of some kind.

Julie grabbed a Mars bar and looked up at Ellen. She lifted her eyebrows and used those puppy-dog eyes that Ellen could rarely resist.

"Not tonight. I don't need you filled with sugar before bed. What's the toy?"

Julie picked it up, watching it glow with some type of internal lighting system. The toy was about four inches square and had a grid of numbers all mixed up on a screen. Julie seemed to instinctively know to use her finger to move the numbers around.

"I think I have to put them in order, Mommy."

"Okay."

"Who gave us this stuff?"

Good question.

Ellen looked back in the bag and saw a piece of paper still inside. She unfolded it and read:

Greetings! We are the Halloween Phantoms, and you have just been BOO'd!!!

You now have until Halloween to fill three bags with candy, small toys, stickers... whatever you like, and distribute them in secret to three neighborhood homes. You'll ring the doorbell and run away so they only have the bag and a copy of this note. If you don't do this, you'll suffer the wrath of the Phantom Curse!

Now that you've received your bag from the Halloween Phantoms, you must affix a note to your front door saying, "We've been BOO'd!!!" This way, nobody else can BOO you again.

Hurry with your bags! As time goes on, it'll be harder and harder to find homes that haven't already been BOO'd!

Be sure to leave a copy of this note with each bag you deliver.

Happy Halloween from the Halloween Phantoms!

Ellen just stared at the note and realized it meant more work for her. Figure out some stuff to buy, head to the dollar store or wherever to pick them up, find some bags (and where would she find something as nice as this one?), pack them all up, deliver the stuff to some random neighbors that she barely knew...

It was the kind of thing Davey was so good with but she sucked at. He was outgoing and friendly and knew all the neighbors. Some of them came to his funeral, but she didn't really even know more than a few of their names.

Now she was supposed to be a part of some neighborhood game or something.

Davey, I miss you.

It'd been six months since his death, but it seemed like six years. He'd had no life insurance, so to make ends meet, Ellen had to work a second job. The only other choice was to sell the house. Julie's home. The girl had gone through too much for that.

"Bedtime, sweetie."

"Awww..."

"Now."

As usual, "now" turned into forty minutes before Julie was actually in her bed. Sleep didn't come easily and when Ellen woke the next morning, she felt like shit.

APRIL 9 (SIX MONTHS EARLIER)

Ellen was watching a game show but barely paying attention. It was something where you had to guess the price of things, but she was never very good at it and her mind was wandering.

There was a storm outside that rattled her nerves every time thunder shook the small home she, Davey, and Julie shared. Every shake of the thin walls made her miss California anew.

She hated Minnesota. Sometimes she hated Davey for bringing them there. She hardly knew anybody, and for that matter, neither did he. He seemed to want to move just to recapture some childhood fantasy. Men and lost youths seemed to be a common problem with her friends, but none of them had been dragged a thousand miles to live out their husbands' fantasies.

The phone rang and shocked her from her thoughts. Probably Davey saying he'd be late. She thought he was out working in the field, but maybe he'd decided to get out of the storm.

Who wouldn't?

"Hello?"

"Mrs. Weston?"

She didn't recognize the voice, and a new blast of thunder gave her an earful of static.

"...to the hospital."

Hospital?

"What did you say? Who is this?"

She looked over her shoulder at the staircase, but of course Julie was at school, not in her room. Wasn't she?

"Please hurry. He may not last long."

He? Davey?

"What happened?"

Static filled her ear again, and then she had a dial tone.

"Davey?"

She hit speed dial #1 to call Davey's cell phone. It rang a few times before clicking over to his voice mail.

Two minutes later she was in her ten-year-old Toyota Camry racing to the hospital.

"He was hit by lightning."

"Are you serious?"

The doctor was a woman, about forty, and the expression on her face seemed to say, "Don't fuck with me." Even so, it was too hard to imagine somebody actually being hit by lightning.

"More than four hundred people are killed by lightning every year in the U.S., Mrs. Weston. We usually get a few people admitted at this very hospital due to lightning strikes."

"He's going to be okay, right?"

She hesitated. "We're doing our best."

An hour later, at 3:28 p.m., the same doctor told her that her husband was dead. Ellen never had a chance to talk to him, to tell him she loved him, to say good-bye. All of a sudden, her complaints about the move to Minnesota seemed incredibly petty.

OCTOBER 25

Ellen was tired. Dead tired. Her legs left like jelly. Today was her thirty-seventh birthday and she could feel forty looming ahead of her. She'd woken up with a new determination to get back into shape and had just finished jogging around the neighborhood. It was a little after seven-thirty and she'd left Julie to read at home, figuring she'd only be gone a half hour.

Ellen had only lasted fifteen minutes before she had to stop and walk home. She felt sweaty and greasy from the run and just wanted to head back for a nice hot shower.

"Ellen!"

The clutch of women were a bit hard to see, since they were standing in the shadows. She squinted and saw three of them: the ABC Club. Annie, Bonnie, and Charlie were three girls who always hung out together. They rarely spoke to Ellen.

"Hi," she called. She wanted to fit in to the neighborhood, she truly did (she told herself), but somehow time and life seemed to intrude. None of the three had gone to Davey's funeral.

Ellen walked over and saw that they were all holding wine glasses, mostly empty.

"Did you get boo'd yet?" asked Bonnie.

"Boo'd?"

"Yes, you get a Halloween package and you pay it forward. Kind of a tradition around here." The way she said it, Ellen heard, *If you don't do it, you'll always be an outsider.*

She thought back to the bag that had arrived ten days earlier. She was supposed to hand out three bags of her own, but she'd forgotten about it as soon as she'd put the bag away.

"Did you all get one?"

Annie laughed. "You haven't looked around much, have you?" She pointed to her own house next door, and Ellen could see a white sign on the front door: WE'VE BEEN BOO'D!

She glanced at Bonnie's place (where they were standing) and a similar sign hung on her door, too. And Charlie's... and just about every other house she could see.

"I'll have to get onto it," she said without conviction.

Charlie leaned over to her, and Ellen could smell the red wine on her lips. Charlie put a hand on her neck and whispered to her, almost like a lover would. Her touch felt too familiar, and Ellen felt a longing for closeness and didn't pull back.

She tried to think of Charlie's hand being Davey's, but the words she whispered interfered with her daydream.

"You need to do it, sweetie." Charlie's breath warmed Ellen's ear. Ellen imagined kissing Davey, and how wonderful that always felt. "You need to. Don't skip it, because you'll always regret it. The first person to ignore the Halloween Phantoms always regrets it. They don't fuck around." Then in an even quieter voice she added, "But I do."

Charlie kissed Ellen's cheek and smiled. Ellen felt her face turn red and was grateful for the darkness provided by the twilight.

"I'll get onto it tomorrow," she said. She just wanted to escape from the ABC Club now, and she took a step backward.

She was going to say good night but surprised herself by asking, "Who started this thing, anyhow? Did one of you put the bag on my door?"

Bonnie took off her glasses and snorted. "Jesus, girl, don't you get it? This isn't a joke. Just do whatever the damned phantoms ask and you'll be fine."

"Oh. Well, okay then. I have to get back to Julie." She stared at the three women and saw no twinkle of an inside joke. Annie and Bonnie stared as if she had just grown an extra head. Charlie... well, Charlie always looked at her with a bit of extra attention. "Good night," she said as she turned and walked back to her home.

The rest of the neighborhood was dark and quiet.

And every house she passed had a sign on the door saying they'd been boo'd.

April 14

Davey's funeral was held five days after he died. The coroner didn't do an autopsy, because the cause of death was obvious. Lightning didn't leave many doubts.

Davey had been six years older than Ellen, but even so, they never really talked about his final wishes. She hadn't known if he wanted to be buried or cremated, or any other things he may have wanted. The day before, she'd walked out to his "office," which was a corner of the barn.

When they moved to Minnesota, Davey somehow found a property in a small town that backed onto a large field. The bank had repossessed it from the previous owner, and Davey bought it for way less than they ever thought possible.

"Every guy needs a place to work on things," he'd once said. "This is my space."

The barn was empty except for that one corner he called his office. Davey had talked about one day raising cows but they'd only been living on the farm for a few months. The first year they were going to stick to growing a few hundred acres of corn. That sounded like a big enough challenge, and she pushed aside the occasional musing about whether he could actually pull it off on his own or not. Fortunately, Ellen had a job as a waitress and so could help with the finances while they got the farm up and running.

What would happen to the farm now? she wondered. She decided that was a problem for another day.

The office had a makeshift wooden table, built from old pieces of particle board and two-by-fours. The only nice part was a swivelling brown leather chair that was actually quite comfortable. She sat in it and imagined her husband sitting beside her, planning their little farm.

There were some papers on the table, but of course nothing that would give her any hint of his final wishes. It was mostly lists of things he planned to do, items to purchase, important dates for the harvest, that type of thing.

Ellen closed her eyes and thought of Davey, missing him terribly, wondering how he'd been so unlucky. If only they hadn't moved to Minnesota, if only he'd stayed inside when the storm struck, if only the lightning found a juicier target somewhere close by... if only.

She tried to pull herself from the fruitless thoughts and looked around the office more. There wasn't much more to see, other than a green plastic glass that he'd used for a drink of water on the day he died. There were two cardboard boxes below the table. She opened the top one and found only paper, pens, tape, and scissors.

The bottom box was more sinister. She had forgotten about the gun.

Davey bought it shortly after they moved to Roseville, worried about moving to an unknown rural town with no way to protect his family. He'd taken Ellen out to the far end of the field one day and taught her to shoot it. She remembered him smiling as she held her arms out to steady herself before shooting. "You'll never have to use it, baby."

She'd enjoyed the target practice, more than she could possibly have imagined.

Ellen picked up the gun now and held it out, as if to shoot an invisible intruder. Davey's lesson came back easily to her. She remembered the feel of his hand on hers as he helped to steady her aim.

Finally, she put the gun back, shedding more memories of their lives together.

OCTOBER 26

Ellen believed not a whit about Halloween Phantoms, but part of her still did want to fit into the neighborhood and it bugged her a bit that she wasn't participating in the game. She found the note and re-read the instructions:

Now that you've received your bag from the Halloween Phantoms, you must affix a note to your front door saying "We've been BOO'd!!!" This way, nobody else can BOO you again.

Hurry with your bags! As time goes on, it'll be harder and harder to find homes that haven't already been BOO'd!

Be sure to leave a copy of this note with each bag you deliver.

Jesus, she hated crap like this. After dinner, she got into her car and drove through the neighborhood, looking at everyone's door.

There were no houses left that hadn't been boo'd.

"That's impossible," she said.

She drove back around the winding streets. Roseville only had about a thousand people, but surely not *every* single home had already been visited.

But after an hour, she gave up. She didn't see one solitary house she could boo, and frankly, she'd lost interest in trying.

"Fuck it," she said as she slammed her hand into her steering wheel. She drove home and threw the notice in the garbage.

OCTOBER 29

The doorbell rang again at 9:35, exactly as it did when the stupid Halloween junk was left on Ellen's door. She closed her eyes and shook her head, knowing that once again, Julie would be leaping out of her bed to come down and see what was going on.

Ellen was in the kitchen, just finishing the dinner dishes. She walked to the front door and as she expected, Julie joined her shortly.

"Maybe it's more treats, Mommy!"

I'll be so glad when Halloween is over this year.

"Maybe."

Ellen looked out the window again as she had the earlier night but again couldn't see anybody. She pulled the door open, expecting to see a bag on the door handle but there was nothing there.

Instead, there were three figures standing at the foot of her front yard, close to the street.

"Mommy, who are they?"

Julie moved a little, so she was behind Ellen.

Ellen tried to make out the figures. Her house was smack in the middle section between street lights and she'd always hated that. She'd complained to Davey when they first moved in, but there was nothing either of them could do about it.

The three figures stood side by side, facing her. They were about thirty feet from her door, which Ellen was grateful for.

They wore costumes—dark costumes with robes and hoods. The middle one wore chestnut brown while the two on either side of him were black. They just stared at her.

She couldn't make out their faces exactly, but she could see bumps and maybe fur below their hoods. The costumes were good, and she didn't like them at all.

"Can I help you?" she shouted.

Ellen was wearing a night gown and suddenly she felt very exposed. None of her neighbors were outside. She pushed Julie behind her and held onto the door, ready to close and lock it.

The three figures didn't answer her call.

"Hello?" she tried.

They didn't make a sound.

The middle one held a long stick in his hand that reached to the ground. As her eyes adjusted, Ellen could see that it was actually a piece of metal pipe, not wood. The other two didn't carry anything but they had belts and there were items inside the belts. She didn't know what they were. Rocks? Guns?

"Can I *help* you?" she tried again.

Then the middle figure started to walk toward her. He (She? It?) walked slowly and reached halfway to her, so that he was now standing in the middle of her lawn.

Ohmygod.

Ellen could feel her heart racing. Where were all the neighbors? Who could she get help from?

The figure just stood there and didn't say a word.

"Please. Who are you?"

She knew she sounded pathetic, but she couldn't help it. She'd never felt the need to protect herself before.

Julie pressed into her. "Mommy, I'm scared."

The ghoul (or whatever he was) lifted the metal pipe off the ground and then thumped it down. Again and again he pounded the pipe onto her lawn and she imagined him doing that to her dead body.

Okay, that's enough.

She leaned over and told Julie to run to the kitchen to get her cell phone.

When she looked back, the middle ghoul was walking back to join the other two, and they shuffled away toward the ABC Club and beyond. Ellen watched as they kept walking, and eventually she lost sight of them.

Julie brought her phone, but Ellen no longer felt the urgency to call the police.

"Mommy, who were they?"

"Just some teenagers out to scare us. Don't worry about it, baby."

"I don't like them."

"Me, neither."

"One of them looked like Daddy."

Ellen stared at Julie. "What did you say?"

"The one back there." She pointed to where one of the figures was standing. "The way he walked. It reminded me of Daddy."

"It wasn't Daddy. They were too small. They were teenagers. Likely some bored boys."

"Maybe girls."

"I doubt it, but I suppose it could have been."

Ellen closed the door, but neither of them got a good night's sleep.

OCTOBER 31

Halloween continued to provide the blustery autumn weather that Ellen had grown to hate. The sky was overcast all day.

When she got home from work, it was already after 7:00, and Julie was champing at the bit to go out trick-or-treating. Too late, Ellen realized she couldn't be in two places at once, so she just left a bucket of chocolate bars on her front porch for the kids to grab when they came to her home, and she walked Julie around the neighborhood for an hour. Julie was dressed up as Minnie Mouse, and even Ellen thought she looked really cute. Soon Julie wouldn't want to do things like that, so Ellen took lots of photos.

When they got back home, the box of chocolate bars looked untouched.

"No kids?" she asked.

Julie just shrugged, and Ellen knew she realized there'd be more treats for her as a result.

Bedtime wasn't until 10:00. Julie took her time getting changed, and Ellen wanted to go through all the candy to be sure it was safe.

By the time Julie finally settled down and crawled into bed, Ellen was just grateful Halloween was finally over. It was the worst ever, only punctuated with bits of Julie's laughter as she walked around town collecting candy.

Ellen had a nice long bath and almost fell asleep in the water. She shook herself awake and was about to go to her own bed when the doorbell rang.

"Oh for Christ's sake!"

This time, she wasn't just irritated, she was full-force pissed off. She stomped down the stairs and pulled the door open.

This time there were only two of the ghouls standing at the end of her lawn. The one with the metal pipe was missing.

"Where's your leader, boys? Get too cold for him?"

They didn't move.

"Time to go home, boys. Halloween is over and now you can go back to church or whatever you do when you're not bullying people."

She thought of storming out and grabbing the little monsters, but then she heard Julie.

"MOM! HELP!"

The bone-chilling scream echoed through the house. Ellen turned and ran upstairs, not even bothering to close the front door.

She pushed Julie's bedroom door open, but the room was dark.

"Julie? Are you okay?"

Then she saw the shadow leaning over her daughter and she froze. Can't be. The missing Halloween phantom was on top of Julie. She could see the figure that was just a bit different shade from the darkness of the room.

It only took a few seconds for Ellen to get her wits back, and she hit the light switch.

There was no ghoul. Only Julie.

The first conflicting thoughts were gratitude that the monster wasn't there and fear about the same thing.

"Baby?"

She moved closer and saw the blood splattered on the white sheets. And the broken face. And the arms and legs twisted in ways they were never meant to twist.

Ellen collapsed.

NOVEMBER 4

The ABC Club attended Julie's funeral, as did most of the parents and children that lived close to Ellen. They all looked at her and told her how sorry they were, but sometimes Ellen saw another side to them: written on some of the guests' faces was an expression that said, "Thank God it was you and not me."

She ignored the neighbors and just mourned her little girl.

When she returned home, the place felt empty. It was like all the joy and happiness had been sucked out of her family home and all that remained was a rotted mausoleum of bad memories.

Ellen sat on Julie's bed for a while, wondering how her life could have been shattered so badly.

She closed the bedroom door and walked out to the barn, taking the opportunity to once again wander through old memories of her, Julie, and Davey.

"I miss you both so much," she said softly.

She was chilly even with a wool sweater. The sun was starting to go down, but she wasn't interested in heading back to the house. She wasn't interested in much of anything anymore.

The gun was still in the lower box.

Ellen hefted it in her hands, wondering what it would be like to pull the trigger. Of course, she knew that when she did it, she wouldn't actually know what it felt like. She wouldn't be around anymore.

The gun was polished steel, and it reminded her of the metal pipe the phantom carried.

She put the muzzle of the gun in her mouth and clamped her lips around it. There was a part of her that wanted her to stop, but she didn't pay much attention to it.

In her mind, she prayed to her Lord and said one last farewell to her little lost family.

Loyd and Caitlin
and the Ghosts

Brett McBean is a terrific horror writer who published a trilogy some years ago. The last book in the series was Suburban Jungle. In each of the books, Brett asked a couple of authors to write short stories inspired by his books. Since I was a big fan, I was thrilled when he asked me to write a story for his final novel.

Brett has a no-holds barred approach to plotting. Anything goes. It's a wild ride reading his work, which is why I look forward to each new book.

To keep in that frame of reference, I wanted my own contribution to be wilder than my normal work, and so Loyd and Caitlin were hatched.

The first time I typed Loyd, of course I meant to type Lloyd. I hesitated before fixing it, though, and mostly just thought, "Screw it." I liked the typo.

IT WAS THE GHOSTS WHO first told Loyd that somebody was nearby. This time they'd come to him in a dream. He was sleeping peacefully, dreaming the colourful dreams of the young.

Loyd didn't really know for sure how old he was, because the world changed when he was ten years old, and he wasn't sure how long ago that was. He could probably ask the ghosts, but somehow time didn't much matter in the world anymore. Each day was pretty much the same as the one before, and the only thing that changed was how hot and clammy the summer days were compared to the cooler days of winter.

The trees took away all notion of time. Loyd had vague memories of clocks that ticked away each second of people's lives, while his parents sat in front of the television each night watching the news and drinking beer and getting older every day.

Was he fourteen? Fifteen? It didn't matter. All that mattered was that he was still alive somehow.

His dream had been an amalgam of reality and wishful thinking. Stephen, his older brother took him fishing. Loyd was ten years old again, and Stephen was thirteen. Somehow in the dream, Stephen looked a lot older than Loyd himself did now. They floated out on Lake Gawashi on a boat they'd somehow gotten hold of, and every time they cast a line, they pulled in a perfect catfish or a beautiful rainbow trout.

The dream evaporated and the ghosts showed up, all four of them, shadowy and hazy, as if he were seeing them through a thick fog. He never saw them clearly, even when they showed up to keep him company when he was wide awake.

There's somebody coming. Wake up, Loyd!

He did, instantly. Loyd never questioned the ghosts. If they told him to jump off a cliff, he'd run off the edge without a moment's hesitation, not because he was stupid, but because he trusted them with his life.

He opened his eyes but didn't move a muscle. He knew he could easily rustle the leaves he was sleeping on or roll over and snap a twig. Intruders were rare in Loyd's forest, and he hadn't lived this long by being careless. The ghosts had taught him well.

He listened and heard the footsteps. They were light and free, careless and open. There was only one set.

It's a girl, he thought.

He relaxed a bit but still listened intently. The steps were uneven, and he almost laughed at her innocence; she was skipping.

A random memory called to him. He remembered skipping in school before the world changed. *All* the kids were skipping. He remembered Miss White, his kindergarten teacher. She had long red hair, and he always thought her name was silly. She should have been Miss Rose or something.

The girl was humming. He knew the song:

> Sing a song of sixpence
> A pocket full of rye
> Four and twenty blackbirds
> Baked in a pie...

Her humming sounded really nice, but it made him a bit sad. There were no songs in his world anymore. Convinced he was safe, Loyd stood and walked around the trees, toward her voice. He still watched his step, not wanting her to see him before he saw her.

> When the pie was opened
> The birds began to sing
> Wasn't that a dainty dish
> To set before the king?

She was dressed in tattered blue jeans. Maybe she'd worn them since the world changed? On top she wore a red checkered shirt that was plastered with thick splotches of dried mud. Or maybe some of it was blood. It wasn't a girl's shirt, though. Her dad's?

He held up his hand as he walked into a more open area.

"Hi," he said.

She stopped skipping and froze.

"It's okay. I'm not going to hurt you. I just heard you humming and I thought it was nice. I haven't heard anything like that for..."

His voice trailed off, since he didn't know how to finish the sentence. Five years? Four? Damn, he hated thinking about time, because it just got so fucking frustrating.

"Who are you?" she asked. She looked paralyzed with fear.

"Loyd. My name is Loyd. L-O-Y-D. I used to have two L's in my name but with everyone gone, I didn't have anybody to ask why. So I just spell it with one L. What's your name?"

"Where'd you come from?"

"Just now, I was sleeping in a little patch over there." He pointed. "Kind of a little camp or something, I guess."

She had long brown hair. It looked full of knots and tangles. Part of it fell across her face, and between that and the twenty feet that separated them, he couldn't see much more of her.

"I haven't seen anybody else," she said. "Not since it all happened."

"Come on," he said softly. "What's your name? Can't hurt to tell me that, can it?"

"I'm Caitlin. My mom called me Cait, but nobody else."

"Well, hi, Caitlin. I'm glad to meet you."

"Anybody else here with you?"

"Nope. I've seen some men pass by a few times, but they always seemed to travel in packs of four or five.

The ghosts told me to stay away. The men might hurt me. So, I never let them see me."

"Ghosts?"

He shrugged. "Yeah. I'll tell you about them some other time."

They looked at each other for another minute before Caitlin took some tentative steps toward Loyd. He took a couple of short steps toward her as well.

"Need water?" he asked.

"Yes. I'd be very grateful."

"This way." He led her through the trees, following a path he'd walked hundreds of times before but that had no trace of his steps. The land sloped down and they ended up at a narrow river. The water bubbled and gurgled as it flushed over stones on their way to some faraway ocean.

Loyd had sometimes fantasized about following the water down to wherever it might take him. Maybe there'd be some fragment of civilization at the end, like a big port or something.

No, the ghosts warned. *Don't go that way. That way is death.*

He believed them. Of course he believed them. They'd kept him alive in so many ways. He knew he owed his life to them.

Since he'd woken, the ghosts hadn't spoken to him, so he assumed it was safe to take Caitlin to the water. They would have told him if there was danger.

They both scooped some water from the river and drank. Afterward, Loyd sat with his back to one of the massive trees that changed the world. Caitlin sat beside him.

"I'm glad I found you," she said. "I haven't talked to a single other person since the trees grew."

"How old are you?"

"Sixteen. I think. I was twelve when the trees came and killed everyone. I'm pretty sure that was just over four years ago. Does that sound right?"

He shrugged. "I was ten. So that would make me fourteen now."

"Your hair is short," she said. She reached out and touched it. "How?"

"I cut it. I'll show you later. We can cut yours. It looks awful."

She laughed. "Trying to flatter me by telling me how good I look?"

He stared at her, not understanding what she meant. "It's all tangled and stuff."

She nodded. "It's okay. What happened to your family?"

"You mean when the world changed?"

"Yeah."

"We were camping. We lived in Tampa, but I really don't know where we were camping. Dad just came home early one night and said the fucking asshole at the plant was driving him fucking nuts and he told him to fuck off and we needed a fucking vacation. So he'd gotten a trailer and hooked it to the car and we went off to camp."

"Who went?"

"Me, Mom, Stephen, that's my brother, and Janine, my sister."

"So you were camping when the trees came?"

"Yeah. I was picking some berries in a bush and all the trees started coming up from the ground."

He hesitated, thinking back to the moment when the trees spiked up from the ground, thrusting up like spears thrown by the devil. They were all around him, and one scratched his arm as it shot up, but otherwise he wasn't harmed. He started crying and fell down, hurting his knee, but he didn't really want to tell Caitlin about the crying. It felt babyish.

"I was okay, but I called to Mom and Dad. I wasn't sure where they were, cause I got turned around. It took me a long time to find them. Couple days. They were dead, of course, and so were Stephen and Janine. It rained a bit so I had water but I was starving. The trailer was ripped apart by trees but I found the fridge. There were wieners still in there, and I ate them."

"Wow. You found your parents dead."

He nodded. Mom had a tree lift her up and skewer her. She was up high in the branches. Dad was crushed by the trailer. So was Janine. I didn't actually find Stephen at all, but I was scared and I didn't really look all that hard. I just wanted to get help."

Caitlin smiled, trying to show some sympathy. "Sounds awful."

"Later that day, the ghosts showed up for the first time. They showed me how to survive. You know, what mushrooms and berries and plants I could eat and what not to go near. I would have starved without them."

"What are you talking about?"

"The ghosts. Don't you have them?"

She shook her head. "What are they?"

"Ghosts. You know, dead people's spirits? There's four of them."

"Four?"

"Yeah. Mom, Dad, Stephen, and Janine. That's how I know Stephen was dead even though I never saw his body. He's one of the ghosts."

They talked for hours, until the sun died after twilight and the night birds began their songs. Loyd led Caitlin back to his camp and they both lay down in the clearing for the night. The ghosts did not interrupt his sleep, and he didn't wake until Caitlin was up and walking around in the morning.

"Hi again," he said.

She smiled and stretched her arms. "How deep is the river?"

"Not deep. In the middle, it's only up to my belly."

"Good. Let's go for a bath."

Loyd shrugged. He had done the same thing from time to time, but he actually couldn't remember the last time he'd cleaned himself. *A month ago?* he asked himself.

Closer to six weeks, answered the ghosts.

They chose not to accompany the teenagers to the river, but Loyd didn't miss them. He wanted to spend more time with Caitlin alone anyhow.

As they walked, he realized he'd been the one providing all the answers yesterday. He hadn't asked her much about herself other than her age.

"Where were you when the trees came? What happened to your family?"

Caitlin walked alongside him, not saying anything. For a moment, he wondered if he'd actually asked the question out loud. He was used to just thinking his questions to the ghosts.

After a couple of minutes of silence, she stopped and looked right at him.

"I've never told anybody," she said. "Never really wanted to think about it."

"Okay. You don't have to tell me."

She looked lost in thought, and Loyd realized the story must be very painful. Maybe she had parents who really cared about her and maybe she saw them die, or maybe one of them died trying to save her life, or maybe they lived but died from starvation or thirst or the million other dangers that the trees brought to humanity.

Finally, she shook her head. "I'm not ready yet."

They walked in silence to the river. When they got there, Caitlin didn't hesitate in kicking off her shoes and pulling off her jeans. She was standing there just in the baggy old shirt when she leaned over and felt the running water.

"Shit, that's cold."

"It's still awfully early."

She undid the buttons on the shirt and let it fall to the ground.

Loyd had never seen a naked girl before and he couldn't help but stare.

She was very slim, much more than he had realized in her oversized clothes. And she had breasts.

He took his own clothes off and walked over to stand beside her. She took his hand and they walked into the water, til they were knee-deep.

"Wait here while I get used to the water," she said. She turned to face him, and he stared at her body almost in disbelief.

She was smiling, and he wanted to look at her face, but everything was new to him and he couldn't help it. Every few seconds, he'd glance back to her face, worried she'd be mad.

"Don't worry," she said, "I understand."

That gave him the courage to stare openly at her breasts and at the furry area between her legs. He wondered what it'd be like to touch her...

Then he felt something stir in his own body. He realized his cock was getting hard.

He felt ashamed and turned around so she couldn't see what was happening. It just got harder, as if it had a mind of its own. He kept thinking about touching her body and that just made things worse.

"Turn around, Loyd," she said. "There's nothing to be ashamed of."

He did turn around and saw her smile again.

"Just don't think you're getting any," she said.

"Getting any what?"

She laughed and he loved the sound more than anything he could remember.

Caitlin took his hand and they walked out deeper, and eventually the water did reach to Loyd's stomach, as he'd said. She dunked herself in the water and tried to stay under. He did the same, watching her with open eyes. His erection was gone, and he was thankful for that.

They had no soap, so the bath was really nothing more than a rinse, but both of them felt better when they left the water.

"What do you miss most about before it all happened?" she asked.

"Umm, well, my mom."

"Not people. What thing do you miss? Television? Books? Your bicycle? A trampoline?"

He thought back to his life back home, when he had lived with every possible modern convenience. He had everything, and now he had nothing.

"I think I miss my bed the most. I still hate sleeping on the ground."

She nodded.

"What about you," he asked.

"Easy. I miss meat. I miss hamburgers and barbequed spare ribs and steaks and pork chops and steamed fish."

Loyd felt hungry all of a sudden. "Maybe we should get out and look for food."

She laughed but they both walked out of the water and lay on the ground, letting the morning sun dry their skin.

"How can you cut hair?" she asked.

He reached over and clasped her hand, feeling totally serene and happy for the first time in four years.

"When the trees came, we were camping. I told you that, right? Well, the campground had this small store. They sold things the campers might need. Lots of ice cream bars, candy, boxes of cereal, milk, bread, stuff like that. They also had shovels and shampoo and cups and postcards and—I don't know, all kinds of crap."

"Yeah, I know what you mean. My parents took me camping sometimes, too."

"So, anyhow, I didn't know what to do. Everyone was dead. When the ghosts came that first time, they told me to go find the store. Maybe somebody would be there, but if not, at least there might be some food.

"Well, there were only dead people there. And most of the food was gone. I think somebody else got there before me. I did find a couple of chocolate bars that I ate really quickly, and I took some things I found. I don't know why I grabbed scissors, but I did, along with a post card, a loaf of stale bread that was half gone, and a compass. I never did know how to use the compass and I lost the post card. The only thing I kept was the scissors."

"That's pretty funny."

"Maybe 'cause my mom was a hairdresser. I guess it was a way to remember her."

"Yeah, that makes sense."

She sat up, and so he did too. They were facing each other. She had brown eyes and a nice pretty face, especially when she smiled.

I want to stay with you forever, he said to himself.

It was the ghosts that answered, though. *Stay with her, then. You don't need us anymore.*

He felt a hole in his soul as the ghosts disappeared, one by one.

"Mom?"

"What?"

"The ghosts are leaving."

"You must know there's no such thing as ghosts, right?"

Loyd didn't want to hear that. Part of him may have believed her, but a much bigger part wanted his precious ghosts to be real.

She took his right hand and placed it on her left breast. "*This* is real, Loyd. Not ghosts."

In spite of himself, he forgot about the ghosts immediately, and he had to shift his sitting position as his cock started to rise again.

She leaned over and kissed him on the mouth. He felt faint and started to wonder if he was dreaming. It didn't feel like a dream, though.

"That's enough for now," she said. "Let's get dressed. I want you to show me your scissors. You were right about my hair. It's like a rat's nest. I haven't had a way to take care of it."

They walked the mile back to Loyd's camp and he found the small bag hidden behind a tree. He pulled out his scissors and handed them over.

He knew he'd do anything for her, and he truly didn't care if he ever got his scissors back. She could keep them forever and he wouldn't give a damn.

"Nice," she said.

"Want me to cut your hair? Might be easier."

"Umm, no. No offence, but I somehow doubt you have much talent doing women's hair."

He laughed and agreed that he had no experience.

"How short do you think I should cut?" asked Caitlin.

Loyd didn't know what to say. Her hair was a mess, so if it was him, he'd want it cut short. But, did girls think the same way? He shrugged.

She laughed at his indecision. "I'll have to think about it." She put the scissors in the pocket of her jeans.

"Want to go on an adventure?"

Loyd felt a rush of fear running through him. He wished the ghost were here to tell him what to do. "I... I've always stayed pretty close to here. It feels safe."

She smiled and moved closer to him. "Well, I want to go on an adventure." She took his hand and slid it under her shirt so he could feel her breast again. As she did that she kissed him again. He could feel his cock starting to harden. He felt her tongue in his mouth. It shocked him a bit but he realized he liked it. He used his own tongue to touch hers, and he moved his hand on her breast, feeling her nipple.

She broke the kiss. "There's more where that came from. But, I'm going. Are you coming with me?"

He couldn't do anything but nod.

Loyd, don't go with her.

The ghosts were back.

Don't go. This is your safe place.

But he liked the way he felt when she let him touch her. And he wanted her tongue in his mouth again. He ignored the ghosts.

Caitlin held his hand as they walked, weaving through the trees. It wasn't long before he was hopelessly lost and would never be able to find his way back again.

That didn't matter. All that mattered was being with her.

"Can you tell me about your family?" he asked. His feet were getting tired after walking for such a long time and he hoped that if she told him a nice long story, it would take his mind off his feet.

"Oh, nothing special," she said. "Mom and Dad are pretty good as far as parents go. I have three older brothers and one sister. And some of my uncles and aunts live with us, too."

"Live with you?" He was confused. "They live with you now?"

"Yes. We're almost there. Just over the hill."

His feet hurt even more climbing up the steep hill. This was one time all the trees were actually a help, as he used them to pull himself up the incline.

"How many people are there where you live?"

"About twenty."

He stopped walking. "Twenty?" It didn't make any sense to him. That was like a village. How could that be? He didn't think there were any groups of people that big left anywhere in the world.

Turn around, Loyd! This can't be good!

The ghosts were powerful and Loyd hesitated. Caitlin came to him and held his hand. She put it on her cheek and smiled. "You know everything will be fine as long as we're together, right?"

Loyd wanted to be with her so badly. His eyes closed as his fingers caressed the sweet skin of her face, touching the corner of her lips.

"I have to listen to the ghosts," he whispered.

"You know they aren't really ghosts, don't you? It's just you. Your thoughts or memories or something. Just trust me, instead."

Still with his eyes closed, Loyd couldn't decide. He wanted to feel more of Caitlin, wanted to kiss her, wanted other things that he couldn't even articulate... but he'd never disobeyed the ghosts before.

"I'm sorry. I have to go."

"I'm sorry, too."

He was about to open his eyes when the pain hit him. His chest felt like it was exploding and he crashed backward to the ground. "Oh God, what happened!"

He couldn't move. Everything hurt like he was drowning in liquid fire. It was hard to breath.

He cracked his eyes open and could see the scissors buried in his chest. It didn't make any sense, though. Why would they be there?

He tried to look up but he couldn't see Caitlin. The pain continued to shoot through him. He tried to move an arm to pull the scissors out but when he did move them even a tiny amount, it just made the pain so much worse. He couldn't stand it.

You should have listened to us.

Blood covered his chest and some portion of his mind realized he'd pissed his pants.

"Caitlin?"

His voice was weak, the tiniest whisper. He still couldn't see her.

He tried to roll over onto his side, but he couldn't. He closed his eyes because it seemed easier and less painful. Sleep called to him.

"Loyd, I'm sorry."

He wondered briefly if the voice was just a dream, but he opened his eyes to see Caitlin crouching beside him. Strange people stood around near her. Mostly men. *Her family and the others in their little village*, he knew.

"Help," he tried so say, but he wasn't sure if any sound actually came from his mouth.

She moved her head to his mouth and kissed him.

"I really am sorry." She touched his cheek as he'd touched hers a million years earlier. "But I told you what I missed the most about before. Meat."

He didn't understand until he looked closer at the two men closest to her. They both carried long, sharp knives. Loyd called in his mind to the ghosts for help, but he heard nothing back. ❧

- 382 -

John R Little

Miranda

Miranda is my best-known work. It won the Bram Stoker Award in 2009 as well as the Black Quill Award. I get great pleasure in knowing that regardless of anything else I might write, I will always have this one to think back on. I still receive emails complimenting me on this story, and every one feels precious.

The story was a bitch to write. I started with a short story (only 3,000 words) as a practice round, then took the leap to write the 20,000-word version. When I did, I found many mistakes. Everything had to make sense both forward and backward in time, and some things didn't, so I fixed them.

Then I re-read the story and found something else that didn't work. And again. And again.

This kept on and on, and I thought I'd never get the story working the way I needed it to. Eventually, though, I got it as good as I could. Although there was still one "cheat," I thought it was subtle enough that nobody would notice. (And to date only one person has ever pointed it out.)

This was the second novella I sent to Roy Robbins at Bad Moon Books. As soon as he read it, he emailed me with the excitement jumping off his words. "This book will win awards, John!" I laughed at him, but of course he was right. Roy published a signed paperback edition and a hardcover "lettered" edition of only 26 copies. That edition also has a "lost" story of Miranda.

Miranda is my only story published in Croatian, in a beautiful hardcover book. It's a fine addition to my library.

Chapter 15

I WAS SIXTY-FIVE WHEN I DIED. Well, undied would be more accurate, wouldn't it?

I remember the heart attack shocking me to life. Then the pain disappeared, and I was *here*. I remember screaming, surrounded by doctors who were trying desperately to resuscitate me. Three of them, I think. All old men, older than me. I couldn't talk to them, since I didn't know the language. They pounded on my chest, urgently at first and then less so. The paddles shocked me with an awful jolt, but then that pain fell away as fast as the paddles themselves.

"!gnitserra s'eH" one of the doctors shouted. Then he swiveled to face the other doctors. A sharp metallic smell hung in the air.

They pulled back and ignored me. I blinked, and my mouth opened. I didn't know a word of English and only lonely syllables emerged.

I had no idea what or where I was. I existed for the first time.

The world was scary. Fucking terrifying.

Time inched backward, the clock reclaiming each second.

The pain trickled away, and I lay down in my narrow little hospital bed. I remember being very frightened.

Tiny ticks sounded from the equipment by my bed.

Bright light surrounded me, but I didn't squint. I yawned and closed my eyes, as if I hadn't a care in the world. After all, the heart attack hadn't happened yet.

I held feebly onto the bars of my bed and started to nod off.

The doctors and everybody else marched forward in time and would see me die soon. They all thought I was just like them, moving into a collective future. Nothing I did ever removed that notion. But, my consciousness moved backward; I grew younger over time, not older.

The scary parts of my life were in my past, unknown because I hadn't experienced those events yet. Right after I sprang to life, I could relax because the pain of my death was over and wasn't going to come back.

It felt good to be alive.

Of course, I had no reference point, no memory of anything at all beyond my death a few minutes later. All in all, though, it was good. Breathing was easy, and now that I could take the time to appreciate it, the air felt wonderful filling up my lungs.

Beeps and other random noises bounced around me. At first, I didn't know what those sounds were, but over the course of my halfyear in the hospital, things sorted themselves out. I knew those sounds weren't speech (at least I was pretty sure of that), since I had heard the doctors talking their strange language after they brought me to life.

I soon grasped the concepts of gravity, thirst, and hunger. Somehow I just knew what "human" meant, as opposed to inanimate objects. I didn't see any animals while in the hospital, except on the occasional TV show, but when I later saw dogs and cats, there was no confusion. I was a baby in an old man's skin, learning much faster than the most bright newborn.

My eyes closed and I slept.

".nosnhoJ retsiM, tser doog a evaH"

I woke up and stared at the nurse. I didn't know what she was saying. She'd walked backward into my room and swiveled around to face me, smiling a big grin before speaking.

She must've thought I was an idiot. Hell, I didn't blame her. Like everybody else, she was moving forward in time, from birth to death, and I was traveling in the exact opposite direction.

Now, don't get me wrong. I didn't know that at the time. This is a bit of Monday morning quarterbacking going on. If I only wrote what I knew at the time, this would be a pretty damned confusing story. All I knew then was that the nurse was speaking gobbledygook to me. I had no idea what she was saying, and it was pretty frustrating. Probably as much for her as it was for me.

It was only later I realized she was speaking forward, but I was listening backward.

She had a big toothy grin, and I couldn't stop staring at it. Her hair was chestnut brown and pulled back into a tight ponytail. When she'd backed into the room, her hair swung behind her shoulders like a squirrel attached to her neck. It was fascinating. Again, this is mundane to you, having seen it your whole life, but for me, every tiny new detail was a revelation.

I tried to talk, but I didn't know how to control my mouth.

The nurse rolled up my sleeve and attached me to one of those devices that measures blood pressure. I can never remember its name.

".emit tsal sa emas ytenin revo ytriht enO"

She pumped the little ball at the end of the tube and listened through her stethoscope.

I felt the pressure on my arm grow and then subside as she started measuring my blood pressure, taking the bandage back off.

She pursed her lips. ".yadot gniod si erusserp doolb dlo eht woh ees s'teL"

I stared at her again. The grin was gone, replaced by a frown. I wondered if I had done something wrong. She moved her hand above the small trash can, and a Kleenex jumped up into her hand. She unfolded it a bit and wiped the snot from it into my nose.

I felt what I would eventually know as embarrassment. She unfolded the tissue a bit more and painted some drool on my chin.

"?ew llahs, pu denaelc uoy teg s'teL"

She unscrunched the tissue and pushed it back into the box beside my bed.

".nosnhoJ retsiM, gninrom dooG"

The nurse (Nurse Tamblin, I now read from her nametag), stepped backward, giving me one last smile as she swiveled out of my room.

I was alone again with the beeps and snot.

Chapter 14

I was in the hospital for six months. Don't worry, I won't tell you all the details of every burp and fart. You all know how miserable it is to be in a hospital, especially when you're dealing with an endoflife situation. Nobody knew mine was actually a beginningoflife situation not even me, since I had nothing to compare it to.

I was scared. All the time.

It took about three months for me to lose the constant confusion I felt. I was able to figure out I was at St. Joseph's Hospital in a place called Oakland. The name meant nothing to me. Since I was bedridden and a newborn, I didn't know anything about Oakland other than the name.

I had a television, but for a long time it was useless. I didn't even know how to turn it on for the first two months. Then, without understanding English, it was all nonsense but was something to do other than eat, sleep, and watch the four walls.

Eventually, TV turned into my teacher. I studied game shows every day and began to pick up words, one at a time. Pat Sajak and Vanna White taught me English, while soap operas showed me how people lived. I wanted to be a good student.

The room I was in was big enough for three other patients, and usually the beds beside me were occupied. During my hospitalization, there were four times a dead man was rolled into the room and deposited on a bed. It was fascinating to watch them groan back to life after a few minutes or hours, and I could see how my own life had begun.

Sometimes the strangers beside me stayed in the room for a few days, but never very long. They also seemed instantly able to interact with the world, joking with the nurses, standing up and moving around. A couple of them tried to talk to me, but I had no way to answer.

I started to get frustrated. Why couldn't I understand anything? I knew I wasn't stupid.

Was I?

It was a sunny summer day when the "aha" moment hit me. It was the first epiphany in my life. All the doctors and nurses who visited me spoke backward. The other patients understood them because they spoke backward, too.

I was stunned. Why didn't I think of that before? Who said words should be spoken front to back?

Some gutter instinct told me something was very odd, but I finally started to understand my TV shows a little bit.

From that point on, I picked up English much faster. It felt weird to reverse my speech, but after a couple of months of practice, it became second nature to me. I learned to say words, then sentences.

Talking was hard, but it was harder to listen to

other people speaking to me. They were almost certain to use words not in my vocabulary, and I had to pick those out in addition to changing everything back to front.

I remember my first coherent discussion with a doctor, where I finally understood every word and could carry on a very short conversation.

"I'll be back tomorrow." This was one of the doctors who'd been there for my undeath. Dr. MacKay. Long gray hair, squareframed eyeglasses perched on a long nose. Fake smile.

He didn't like me. Not that he ever said anything like that, but I could tell. That's okay, because I didn't like him, either.

He'd just backed into my room one morning, glanced around at the other patients, swiveled around to face me, and erased some notes on my chart.

I nodded. My blood pressure was always fine.

"There. One twenty over eighty. Perfectly normal."

Pause.

"I'll just take your blood pressure."

"Fine, thank you."

"How are you feeling today, Mr. Johnson?" Then his smile disappeared, and he backed away from me, out of my hospital room.

Jerk.

I never had any visitors in the hospital. I wondered if I had any family. Kids. A wife. Presumably not, since they never came to see me. No friends. Nobody who I might have worked with.

Just doctors and nurses. And orderlies to bring my urine in bedpans.

The other patients who sometimes shared my room would all have visitors. They'd laugh and kiss and hug and talk.

Sometimes I could smell the visitors. They were just so different from all the old, nearlydead patients.

I often wondered what it would be like to have visitors who smiled and chatted about the weather. Maybe kids who would talk about baseball or school.

Hey, how about those Giants?

Most times, though, I just looked forward to my soaps, and I felt myself growing stronger with every passing day.

When I was a newborn, my muscles were as dead as the rest of me, and I struggled just to roll over onto my side. Every day brought more confidence and less bed sores.

It was a cool spring day the first time I felt strong enough to swing my legs off the bed and stand up. I steadied myself and backed over to the window. Then I swung around to see a patch of daffodils and tulips growing below. It was beautiful.

They were bursts of color so different from the blasé pastels of my room. I stared for several minutes at the flowers and the bright green lawn surrounding them. I knew I was grinning as much as Nurse Tamblin always did.

Could life get any better than this?

After about ten minutes, I felt even stronger and backed over to the door of my room, looked down the hallway to the nursing station, and waved at the onduty nurse. She nodded and smiled at me before ignoring me. The hospital stretched for a long way past her.

I slowly shuffled backward to my bed and climbed back in.

Dinner was about an hour after that. A male orderly brought me an empty tray and put it across my lap. He didn't smile didn't even look at me. I think he thought I was dying. Little did he know.

I began to wonder how they found such personalitystricken people to work there. It was very different from the energetic and outgoing people who populated the hospitals in the soaps.

I picked up the dirty plastic spoon and sucked on it. I regurgitated some vanilla pudding and spooned it out of my mouth into the little plastic container on my tray. It tasted quite good. I like vanilla better than chocolate.

After dessert, I unswallowed some mashed potatoes and roast beef, which didn't taste nearly as good as the pudding. I bit the pieces of the beef all back together again and used the plastic knife to reassemble it on the plate. I spit up a glass of apple juice, too. They weren't very creative with drinks at dinner. I only ever had water, apple juice, or orange juice. No coffee, not even decaf. I didn't miss the coffee, but when I was younger, I became addicted to it.

Eventually my tray was full, and I was feeling very hungry.

The same orderly came back, still without a smile, picked up the full tray and placed it into a cart I could see outside my room. Not a word from him.

I liked to eat, but I sure hated the hunger I felt afterward.

The days passed, and with every new one, I felt stronger and more clearheaded. My vocabulary increased, and I was able to keep up simple conversations. Even so, it was still difficult with all the new words I was learning.

"Dementia" was a word I heard a lot. And "Alzheimer's."

These were nonsense words to me. I thought they described why I was in the hospital, but they didn't mean anything more to me than random syllables strung together. For a few days, I actually began to wonder if my name was Johnson Alzheimer, since they kept talking about that disease, and I knew my name was Johnson.

Eventually, I found that Johnson was my last name.

My first name was Michael. I was five months undead when I first heard myself called that by Nurse Tamblin. Another penny dropped, and I learned more about myself.

When you're in the hospital with no visitors, very little English, and no entertainment, it's easy to count the days.

Exactly six months after my death, I was unadmitted from the hospital.

"Your condition is just going to get worse." That's what the doctor told me the day I arrived. He didn't pull any punches, describing how I was going to lose most of my faculties, my abilities to speak and understand English, and my memory would get more and more faulty as time went on.

I wanted to say, "Well, of course my memory will get worse. We've already been through that, right?" But, of course, they hadn't been through it at all. They were looking in the wrong direction.

I smiled when I was released from the hospital. I unadmitted myself and left to see the world. Even though I was still very confused, I knew it was actually me that was timechallenged, after watching television and talking to doctors and nurses for the past halfyear.

Wow... it was me going backward, not everybody else. Of course, Occam's Razor was at work, and it was obvious once I realized it, but even so, it seemed hard to accept.

I tried to talk to a doctor about it once during my hospital stay. He was a shrink. Tall, almost bald, smiled all the time.

He fakesmiled when I was with him. It wasn't hard to tell. "Don't worry. We'll take good care of you."

"I just sprung to life a few months ago. Yes, but I'm different."

"It happens to everyone eventually. You're just aging. What do you mean?"

"Doctor, this probably sounds crazy, but I'm living my life in reverse."

He never believed me. All he could see from his temporal orientation was me getting worse and worse, losing control of my body and my mind; in reality, I was actually gaining control of both, but I couldn't tell anybody that.

They'd think I was nuts. I'm a quick learner.

Chapter 13

When I left the hospital and backed out onto Cleveland Street, I had my first taste of unfiltered air. It felt great, and as the hospital receded in front of me, I took several large gulps, drinking in the freshness. Several people stared at me and drifted away. I must have looked like I was going to the mental hospital.

I laughed at the bright sunshine raining down on me.

God, it felt so amazing!

The television was a very poor substitute for what the outside world was really like. I loved it.

The colors were bright and so varied; I just stared at each new hue as I saw it. The olive green of park benches sitting among the darker green of the grass, the blue and orange stripes on the city buses... I even tried to glimpse the yellow of the sun, but I only got sore eyes for the effort. I laughed and cried as I wandered the city streets.

The colors in the park... I stopped there and crawled on the grass, feeling the tiny spikes graze my hands. I wanted more and plopped onto the ground to feel the tiny prickles across my cheeks.

It felt so good to be alive! And free!

The grass smelled so new. Everything smells like something, but I didn't always have words for the scent. Even the diesel exhaust from the buses was a wonder.

I really cared not a whit that I looked like a freak. I knew my senility was drifting behind me, not ahead. Nobody watching me in the wrong direction had a clue. It was very liberating.

"Free," I whispered. "Free to do whatever I want."

I laughed again and patted my cheeks where the grass had kissed me.

I backwalked to the bank and pulled a small piece of crumpled paper out of my pocket, unscrunching it into a nice smooth receipt.

I read the details. A deposit for two hundred dollars. Not a bad start.

I pushed the receipt into the tiny slot in the machine and fed my bank card inside. After a moment, an envelope sprung out with my money. I punched my PIN into the machine and put my card back in my wallet along with the cash.

The receipt I fed into the machine said I had 186,467 dollars in the bank.

"That'll last me a long time," I said. It felt good to say things out loud, to get used to talking in my "natural" direction without nurses or orderlies looking at me weird.

"Freedom."

I loved that word. Loved the feel of it as it slipped through my lips, loved the concept of being able to do anything I wanted without the damned hospital scheduling my every move.

Backwalking farther, I passed an old woman sitting on the side of the road, her legs tapping the curb. A skinny orange cat sat sleeping beside her. I stared in fascination at the cat. It ignored me.

I jumped a bit just before the old woman scowled at me and shouted, "That all?"

She handed me a five dollar bill. The cat blinked its eyes as I moved away. The woman, too, receded into the distance in front of me and slipped away from my consciousness.

After a few blocks, I backed around a corner onto Merritt Avenue, a short side street littered with empty Coke cans and cigarette butts. I was ready for a quiet part of town after being on one of Oakland's major streets for the past couple of hours.

I turned one more corner and reached my home. I recognized the address, 67B Kingston Avenue, from my driver's license. It was a small basement apartment, not far from Lake Merritt, where I would spend many hours in my past, watching ducks and children swim.

I lived alone.

There were no photographs of anybody else. No letters or documents indicating a love interest or even any relatives.

None.

Hmm. I guess I should have known that.

For the first time since I undied, I felt pangs of loneliness. I hadn't ever really been alone in the hospital, at least not for long. There was almost always at least one other patient in the same room, sometimes several, and nurses would often come running in to see me, whereupon I'd always be sure to press the call button.

Now, I was alone in my little apartment. That first time I shut the front door behind me, it felt like I was closing myself from the whole world, and it was much more difficult to bear than I expected.

I backed over to a worn brown easy chair and plopped down into it, then surveyed my apartment. It seemed cozy enough, with most of the furniture being made of a dark wood. Oak? I knew it was fake, a veneer of some kind, but it was well cared for. Cheap, but nice.

I backed into the kitchen to find a dirty glass and an empty beer bottle on the counter. There was almost a dozen other empty bottles of Miller Genuine Draft in a box on the floor of the kitchen, near the pantry. I brought the glass and bottle back to the living room and sat again.

I savored the taste of the beer as I regurgitated it, then spit it into the glass. The strong taste really hit me at first. I wasn't sure if it was something I liked, but all the empties told me I'd get used to it.

People were always drinking beer or wine in my favorite shows, and it made me feel like a real person to be doing that, too.

I clicked the television on for background noise. There was a western movie playing. Clint Eastwood rode backward on his horse, and the bad guys followed in front of him. I didn't really pay much attention to it.

After I filled the glass, I poured the beer up into the

empty bottle. When it was full, I snapped the cap on and put the bottle into the fridge. I took the time to see what else was there. Not much. I was sure I'd fill it up at dinnertime.

I picked up another empty MGD bottle.

After a few more beers, I had a nap, lying on the couch. All I could think about was how lonely I felt.

It was noon when I awoke. The sun's filtered light shone through the flimsy curtains covering the kitchen window.

I went into the bathroom and washed my hands. Then, I yawned and took a leak, the piss splashing up from the tank and arcing into my penis, filling me until I felt very uncomfortable. It took several minutes before I could stop thinking about that, as my body reabsorbed the urine.

I went to the door and opened it to find a woman standing there. I didn't recognize her. She had a round face with a painted smile that reminded me of a clown. Her hair was frizzled, bits flying out at odd angles.

"Have a nice walk," she said. "Thank you, Mr. Johnson!"

"I'll take care of it."

"I just wanted to remind you the rent is due tomorrow. I won't keep you."

"I was just thinking of going out for a walk. Yes, it's a great day."

"Spring in California is like nothing else, isn't it? The sun shining and everything. Isn't it a great day out? Mr. Johnson, how are you doing today?"

Her smile disappeared, and I closed the door in her face. She rang the doorbell, as I went back into my living room.

I knew I wouldn't be going for that walk, having just woken from the nap instead, but I was glad I'd gotten rid of the landlord.

Later, I found my checkbook and bank statements. I appeared to be an organized person and had a small box of cancelled checks neatly filed.

Lucinda Caldwell.

Tomorrow, I wouldn't be writing any checks to Mrs. Caldwell, since I'd be admitting myself into the hospital, but I'd need to do it in earlier months.

I found a computer in the corner, near the desk where I kept those checks. At first it was a bit intimidating, but I got the hang of it.

The Internet was wonderful. I'd have pages pop up on my monitor every time I sat down, and they were always topics I had been wondering about. Genetic mutations, left-handed molecules, and quantum abnormalities glued me to the screen, hoping for hints about why I was living my life backward.

After reading each article, I'd end up back at the Google main page and type in a couple of keywords to summarize what I'd just read.

Of all the options, some kind of genetic mutation seemed to hold the most promise, but even that wasn't really helping me understand. Why me?

I couldn't find any hint of another person living my kind of life.

Chapter 12

The next five years were relatively uneventful, and I won't go into *too* much detail about them. Just a few of the highlights.

At first, time seemed to stretch on for a very long time. I found no friends, no relatives.

In fact, I met few people at all, preferring to stay inside my little apartment most of the time. The TV was my best friend. Every once in a while, I would walk down to the bank and deal with the ATM, but rarely spoke to a teller. There were still a few in the branch, but I guess it just seemed easier to talk to a machine.

My letter carrier was a stout woman. I rarely had anything for her. I watched her from my kitchen window, picking up mail daily from Mrs. Caldwell, but only occasionally did she stop at my door. A few monthly bills and bank statements were about all I had to give her.

I did get to recognize some familiar faces at the grocery store and the nearby deli, whenever I returned my food. They would scan all my purchases before I placed them back on the shelves. One cashier always smiled at me, even if I wasn't in her line. But, then she pretty much smiled at everybody. I liked her, but she was so much younger than me, it was futile to even hope.

The only person I had any kind of regular conversation with was Mrs. Caldwell. She turned out to be a nice woman, kind of cranky at times, but I just avoided her when she was like that.

One time, she caught me off guard. She handed me the rent check as she stormed to the door and said, "Not just watch that brain rot! Or at least read some of the classics or something."

"I—"

"Anyhow, you should be volunteering in the community or something, not wasting away."

"I—"

"How can they get away with that? They just use those hidden cameras to disgrace people. It's disgusting."

"It's fun," I mumbled.

I shrugged and looked back over my shoulder at the TV, which was showing a new reality show called "Those Little Cameras!" It was trash, but at the time, I wasn't very discriminating.

"Shouldn't you do something with your life beside just sit and watch the boob tube?"
She unsquinted and smiled. It was rent day.

I closed the door and backed over to my chair to watch the beginning of the show.

She got me thinking. Maybe I was wasting my time watching television all the time.

I was like a hermit in my little apartment, and her rant had made me realize I was afraid of leaving.

Afraid to meet people and try to interact with them, even though I had mastered backtalking.

Why was I afraid?

Time passed and I spit up a couple of beers while thinking about this. What good was freedom if I was just going to be a hermit and not benefit from it? I was already sixty, five years of my life gone, never to be reclaimed.

As the afternoon hit, the sun rose up and was very bright. I opened the door and watched the sunshine pour in. It was invigorating and helped instill confidence in me. Not only was it time to get outside again, it was time to join society. I was well-versed in everything I needed from reading three daily newspapers and watching twelve hours of television every day.

Shopping was one thing. Going to deliberately meet people was quite another thing altogether.

Well, let's be honest. It was a woman I wanted to meet. Everyone on TV had a lover, and I wanted one, too... but, I'd settle for a friend. I really was lonely.

Oakland is a beautiful city, and I think spring is my favorite time of year. We don't have dramatic shifts in seasons, but even so there are some changes. The summer heat fades into nice cool breezes, and the leaves on the trees pull back into tight little buds. It's our last gasp before the cold winter winds come racing down San Francisco Bay.

I could feel the wind kiss me as I wandered down Laney Avenue in the hip part of town. There was a lot of laughter coming from the various bars, as everyone seemed in a mood to celebrate. It was Friday night party night.

I backed into a small jazz club and found an empty table in the corner.

The lights were dim, and I could smell a hint of marijuana in the air.

On stage, a black trumpeter with chipmunk cheeks bounced his horn up and down in the air in time to the music. Behind him were a saxophone player and a guy with a trombone. From where I sat, it looked like the trombone was skewering the guy in front.

I picked up the tip lying on the table and pocketed it. Five bucks.

A waiter brought me two empty glasses. I listened to the music for a few minutes and then choked up some beer into the first glass. It tasted great.

The music sang, and I recognized Springsteen. Jazzstyle? Why not?

I looked around the club; there were a couple dozen other patrons. One obnoxious drunk was waving his arms around at the other side of the room. A group of twentysomethings were huddled near the back, passing a joint back and forth.

There were about three or four women who looked alone.

I had no idea what to do. As it turned out, I didn't have to do anything.

After drinking a half glass of my beer, a woman sat down at my table and snapped, "Shouldn't you be at home with your grandkids or something? You picked the wrong girl. Jesus, you're almost twice my age."

She had a big head of blonde hair and a bright red mouth. I couldn't stop staring at her, not knowing what to say.

"Well," she added. "That's fucking classy."

"I'll pay," I said without thinking.

"Yeah," she laughed. "I just bet you do."

"I just the thing is, I really want to get to know you."

"I've had my fill today, and it looks like you've had plenty."

"Can I buy you a beer?" I asked with a smile.

The woman backed away from me, trying to get a better view of the band. And then, she slipped back towards the other end of the bar.

I spit up the rest of a beer and part of the second.

That was awful.

I thought about the woman, and I realized I would never have a chance for a relationship with anybody. When I met her, it was new for me, but it was the end of the encounter for her.

It would work that way for anybody. As I grew to know them, they would forget me until I just slipped away from their minds.

What kind of freedom was that?

Loneliness washed over me. I was a stranger in a strange land.

The other people in the bar laughed during the break between sets, sneaking kisses and holding hands. Even two blond men kissed at the bar, clearly happy with each other.

At that moment, all I wanted was five minutes maybe even five seconds just one small hug from somebody who knew me.

That somebody would never exist, though.

I choked up four more beers.

I was more alone than anybody else had ever been, and I didn't like it one little bit.

After topping up my last beer and sending them back with the waiter, I backed out of the jazz club. The band was setting up to play their first set as I closed the door and wound my way back home.

Chapter 11

The days stretched into weeks, months, and then years. I learned how to cope in a world where time ran backward, where I remembered my future but not my past.

In time, I learned a lot about the world. All about wars in the name of religion, religion that looked more like politics, politics that looked more like organized crime, and organized crime that turned into war.

Television and the Internet were my lifelines to the world. I was generally happy and didn't even notice a decade disappearing.

I didn't go to any more jazz clubs. Or anywhere else for that matter. I was back to my old hermit self. That was safer.

I aged down to fifty-five.

Freedom at Fifty-Five. Sounded like a TV commercial jingle for an insurance company. I didn't need life insurance; I knew exactly how long I'd be alive.

When I finally clued in, my life was almost twenty percent over. Wasted, just like Mrs. Caldwell told me. It was time to make something of myself.

After ten years of living alone, I entered the work

force. I was really glad when this happened. I was fiftyfive and felt stronger than ever, ready to take on the world. I was also really lonely and looked forward to the company of other people.

On my last day on the job, I found out I worked as a carpenter, for a company called *The Great Oakland Woodmakers*. We specialized in construction projects across the Bay Bridge in San Francisco, mostly in the tourist areas around The Embarcadero, especially Fisherman's Wharf. Lots of condos as well as commercial work. I had a big advantage over everybody else, since I'd arrive at the project when it was already finished, and I just had to carefully help take it all apart and stack the planks up in neat piles, ready to be tied up and sent back to the lumber yard.

I also got used to driving my car. It came naturally to me, of course, as everything did. I'd be taking my driving lessons decades earlier.

That first day, after spending a quiet evening alone, my tenyearold Nissan drove me backward through the traffic, and I just had to be careful the cars in front didn't back into me. It was very exhilarating to drive, especially that very first time, since I knew I was going to work but had no idea where that was. My car would surprise me.

The first job I worked on was a townhouse complex. The homes were all fabulous, even though the paint had already been brushed off and dropped back into the cans. Whoever would end up living here would have a great view of the Bay, and I was a little jealous. I knew I had a lot of money in the bank and wondered if I would ever own a house like these.

Maybe I sold the place I lived and that's where all my money came from?

It was nice to think something like that might await me. I imagined myself living on a cliff overlooking the Bay, a twentyfoot balcony hanging around the second floor, facing the Golden Gate in the distance.

Maybe. One day.

When I arrived, my coworkers welcomed me, wishing me a happy retirement. They patted my back and shook my hand, and they were just the most friendly group of guys you could imagine. It felt great to be with them. I must have grinned all day.

The thwack of my hammer felt solid and strong in my hand. I immediately got to work pulling out my first nail. I hit it hard twice and it popped right out. I held it carefully for the last few small taps and put the nail away.

"Last one," I said.

I hesitated a bit, just wanting to appreciate being at work, doing something useful with people who seemed to like me.

Then I shook my head and worked my way down the cedar planks, pulling out nails one after the other and placing them away, side by side.

We stopped for lunch, and I gathered with the other four guys (Tom, Jamie, Mark, and Dom) sitting on a pile of lumber. My lunchbox was empty, but I unchewed a tuna salad sandwich with lettuce. I found an old apple core in the garbage and slowly chewed bits onto it, turning it into a nice fresh beauty.

After finishing my lunch, I felt hungry.

"Sure," said Dom. "I've heard that before."

I shrugged. They were all looking at me now. "I'm sure I'll find something. I've always wanted to read more." That was weird, and I almost regretted saying it. I knew my retirement years were going to be frustrating and lonely. Why not admit it?

"What're you going to do with your spare time?" Tom talked with a nasal twang, sniffing as he spoke. It wasn't very pleasant, but he was nice enough to me.

"We all gotta get there one day," I said. "I'm as ready as I'll ever be."

"You really all set to retire?" asked Dom. He had an Italian accent and spoke as much with his hands as with his mouth.

Jamie and Mark hadn't said much over lunch. They might've been twins, both blondhaired, tall, and skinny. I had to keep reminding myself that Jamie had the moustache. He seemed bored and kept looking at his watch.

We went back to work for the morning shift. The sun was nice and warm, but it started to cool a bit as it lowered in the morning sky.

By 8:30, there was a big pile of wood sitting beside the last of the townhouses. We had gotten a lot done, and the house had gaping sections where we could see the tarpaper and pink insulation sticking out.

When I had arrived at the work site at quitting time, my muscles were really sore and I'd wondered how I would get through the day. Now that my workday was finished, I felt much stronger, my muscles completely refreshed.

I could do this.

I smiled and said good morning to everyone as I climbed back into my car and headed home for a fast shower. I read the newspaper and had two cups of coffee before climbing into bed.

As I fell asleep, I remember mumbling, "Life is good."

Chapter 10

I hate to admit it, but a lot of years went by in my life where nothing happened. I'd wake up at night and watch the late news, eat dinner, go to work for my eight hour shift, come home and crawl back into bed. I was definitely in a rut, but somehow I just didn't seem to care.

I wasted *twenty-five years,* and it all just evaporated into nothing. Here I was, now only thirtynine years old, and what did I have to show for myself? Not much. I was just as lonely every day, and my bank account was smaller than ever. I only had about sixty thousand left, with interest having chipped away at my money.

Was this all there was? It's not the way the soaps taught me.

Yes, I was free, I kept telling myself, but freedom doesn't automatically bring happiness.

In fact, with every passing day, I felt a sorrow grow in my heart. It started one December with a general feeling of loss, and every day I woke up feeling worse. "What the hell is wrong with me?" I asked.

Every day became a pit of sorrow, and I didn't know why. After a week of this, I started to cry myself awake at night.

I was completely miserable and needed to find some way to stop that. I felt just devastated.

Finally, one Saturday afternoon, I drove down to a nearby animal hospital. Tears were streaming up my face like a spring shower. I absolutely needed to get to the vet. The sign above the door read *Oakland Animal Critical Care Hospital.*

I slowly backed inside, and worked my way around the receptionist, directly into the back part of the building. I joined two veterinarians dressed in whites, each standing beside a table covered with a soft blue cloth.

A dead dog was lying on the table.

It was a small dog, not more than a foot and a half long. A dachshund. *Weiner dog.* He was on his side. I moved over to pat him. His body was warm.

His hair was mostly brown but his little face was stark white. He was a very old guy.

A tag on his front paw listed his name as "Johnson, Doof."

My dog.

I petted him, trying to wish him to life.

One of the doctors said, "We'll take care of him."

I nodded.

She added, "I'm sorry. He's gone."

She slowly put her stethoscope on Doof's chest, and then removed it.

He had a thin breathing tube glued to his forehead and running down his black snout and into one nostril. Pure oxygen that would help him breathe when he came alive. I could hear the hiss of the air flowing through it.

There!

I saw a small shiver as he took his last gulp of air. He opened his eyes a fraction of an inch and looked at me. My breath caught, and I leaned over and kissed his cheek. I couldn't stop crying.

Doof started to pant, not able to get enough oxygen. I tried to reassure him, since I knew he would only get stronger from there.

"It's okay, boy. You'll be fine, now."

The doctors backed away from us, and I called to them when they were looking at some other animals.

Doof's little white face stared up from his blanket, and I could see how frightened he was. He gasped, trying desperately to breathe. His pink tongue hung from his mouth, dry and cracked. He didn't know why he couldn't get enough air, why he didn't have any strength to move. He just lay there like dead meat.

I knew he was scared, knew exactly how he felt.

There wasn't enough strength for him to even whimper. His eyes were glassy and only occasionally would focus on me, asking me to help him.

My whole day was spent with my little dog, and he struggled the whole time. And the Friday before that. I didn't go to work that day.

Just before I left the hospital that morning, the lady vet, Dr. Burns, stopped by to talk to me.

She rubbed Doof's back. "The prognosis isn't good. All we can do is make him more comfortable."

"What do you mean had?"

"He's eighteen, which is very old for a dachshund. He's had a good run." She nodded. "It's not uncommon. Oh, yes."

"A stroke? I didn't know dogs had them."

"It looks like he had a stroke, Mr. Johnson."

That morning, I took Doof home at just about seven a.m. He was still in terrible condition from his stroke, but it was time to go. He'd gained a small bit of strength from his time at the vet.

I held him in my arms for hours. We cried together, him with pain, me with love. He tried to lick my face, but he couldn't. He yelped whenever I moved him.

Doof's eyes were shaped like tiny almonds and had thin black outlines. I stared into those eyes for hours, trying to reassure him. He didn't understand me when I said, "Everything will be all right," but I'm sure my patting him and holding him and kissing him gave him the message. We'd make it through this together.

I rubbed his small velvet ears and just held him.

At about two o'clock in the morning, I carefully put him down in the small dog bed resting beside my own. He cried out in great pain, and I hopped under the blanket and fell asleep.

A few hours earlier, Doof was perfectly healthy. He woke up when I did and followed me into the living room. We watched CNN together, him blinking and yawning quietly beside me.

I knew I had the friend of a lifetime. Finally.

Doof and I spent many wonderful years together. I'm sure I confused him, speaking forward sometimes and backward at other times. It didn't matter which way I spoke to him, since he didn't ever really understand anything I said.

I'm sure he was retarded, but that only added to his personality.

For his whole life, he seemed to be like a puppy. Even just before his stroke, he would bounce around and want to play, just like a three-month-old pup. It didn't take long to realize Doof was short for Doofus, a loving name that fit him perfectly.

As the years moved on, Doof's white hair shaded back to brown, and he became more and more energetic.

I couldn't imagine life without him.

Chapter 9

The next year, I aged back to thirty-eight. Two major events happened, and with them the world seemed to be rebuilding like the Phoenix.

In September, the World Trade Center grew out of a mountain of ash and dust, morphing into America's tallest towers.

I was glued to CNN when they rose, and I watched in amazement. They were so *big*. It was incredible. I knew there were taller buildings in Malaysia or somewhere in the mideast, but these were American, our own miracles, springing up from their graves.

The news stations had been following the cleanup for days prior to the resurrection of the twin towers, so I knew exactly when they were going to grow. It still seemed like a miracle.

Doof sat with me that whole week. I loved how he would squat for hours on my lap as we watched the tube together. Sometimes, he'd roll on his back, sleeping with his tiny paws dangling upward.

Even better news happened in March. The Nasdaq stock market soared, taking my measly stocks and multiplying their value fivefold in just a few weeks. It was astonishing, and I found myself checking my stock portfolio online every few days, not believing how much they were worth.

Following the uncrash, the stocks slowly lost value over the next few years, though. I was occasionally tempted to sell my shares, but somehow never managed to do that until they were back down to a piddling level a few years down the road. Live and learn.

Then came 1998.

August 13, 1998, to be exact. The dog days of summer brought happiness to me in a split moment.

Over the years, I'd managed to get myself into terrible habits. My worst one was drinking too much. Wine or beer it didn't matter; I was an equal opportunity drinker.

Many nights, I'd wake up and find myself completely drunk. I'd weave out into the cab that would be waiting at the curb outside my home and take money from the driver. He'd cart me down to one of the bars across the bridge, down by Pier 39. I'd shout to him as I left the cab and backed into one of the local bars. The guys I worked with would be there. I'd backtalk to them and choke up a bunch of beers until I felt more clearheaded. Sometimes, I'd unswallow some shrimp or other seafood, chew it back into one piece and arrange it carefully onto the plate for the server to take away.

More often than I'd like to admit, I'd end up eating cheese and bacon burgers, full of grease. No wonder I died so young.

There were three guys I hung out with. Dom, Jamie, and Mark. Tom never joined in, which was fine with me. I heard enough of his nasal voice at work every day.

Dom always had the most to say, arms swinging with every sentence. It was on one of these nights out with them that I met Miranda.

I'd learned over the years not to even try to meet women. I couldn't. If you think about it in the opposite way, the way most people move through time, you meet somebody and get to know them, then you fall in love, and you do whatever lovers do.

This was the biggest disappointment with my living backward. If I met a woman for the first time, it meant it was the *last* time from her perspective. She knew me as well as she ever would, but she was a stranger to me. As I got to know her better, it was my turn to become the stranger in her eyes.

Hard to form a meaningful relationship.

The only people I actually knew were people I worked with, and only because they initially assumed I remembered them. I gradually picked up details about their lives and could fake my way through superficial conversations. We weren't close enough for them to realize I didn't really know them at all.

There were no women at my job site, so I had no way to meet them.

But then came Miranda.

She had jetblack hair, long and silky, shining even in the dim light of the bar. I pulled out a piece of crab from my mouth and put it on the platter as my eye caught her at the next table.

Looking at me.

Eyes locked onto mine.

Something about her eyes. Clear and sharp. A slight Oriental look merged with her smooth, golden skin to entrance me.

I felt my heart catch with excitement, a feeling I'd never experienced before. My first thought was that this must be somebody I knew, and maybe I was wrong, that I did have a girlfriend. She was looking at me with an upturned smile, tilting her head up as if asking me a question.

She looked to be about my age, midthirties. I just stared at her.

Something about her. She was different.

Then she shocked me completely. She got up, walked to me and said, "My name is Miranda."

She spoke in my temporal direction, not reversed like everyone else.

Before I could stop myself, I blurted out, "I'm Michael. Michael Johnson."

I should have spoken in the same direction she did, but old habits die hard and all that. I spoke like a normal person, then immediately repeated myself, reversed.

"Glad to meet you, Michael."

I didn't know what to say, even when she reached out her hand. I grabbed it and then couldn't stop myself as I pulled her to me and hugged her. I heard her laugh.

"Is it true?" I asked.

"Yes." She pulled back and stared. "I didn't think I'd ever find another person like me," she said. "I thought I was the only one. But, I was watching you eat, and I could tell you have the same hitches I do. I knew you were going backward, just like me."

"I've got to talk to you," I said. "Can we find a place to sit without " I waved at her table of friends and the one with my coworkers. " without them?"

Her name was Miranda Carlson.

She had undied when she'd been eighty and had similar experiences to me, having to learn how to deal with everybody while they all thought she had Alzheimer's. She hadn't met another backtracker before me. In more than forty years, I was her first and she was mine. Both of us thought we must be dreaming.

I couldn't help but gawk at her when she told me her story. I felt like pinching myself, not truly believing there really was another person out there just like me.

And I'd *found* her.

I gave her a summary of how I'd come to life and found myself at St. Joseph's. She had a similar story, but hers was harder than mine.

When Miranda undied and later left her hospital in Philadelphia, she became a bag lady. She was still very sick when she was unadmitted, because she had little money, and the hospital had refused to take her for a long time. She was lucky she hadn't frozen to death instead of dying in the psych ward.

After she learned how to speak, she moved to northern California from Pennsylvania, to enjoy the warmer climate. She didn't know that, of course, just found herself backing up the steps of a Greyhound bus that drove in reverse across the country. She found herself taking money from the ticket office when she got off the bus in San Francisco and was glad she was there.

Over the years, she climbed her way out of being a bag lady, and by the time she was fiftytwo, she took a parttime sales job at a local coffee bar. She liked giving tips to customers and following up with the kind of service they earned, separating their lattes into steamed milk and espresso, before coming back to ask what they wanted to drink.

We talked for hours that first day, sitting alone while the rest of the world was made totally irrelevant to us.

Miranda's black hair hung to below her shoulders and curled up slightly at the bottom. She had a small dimple on her right cheek that popped out whenever she smiled, which was a lot. She loved being with me as much as I loved being with her, and it showed.

After spitting up one beer together in the bar, I took her hand and we walked out into the afternoon light. We both squinted a bit at the shock of the sunshine after being inside for so long.

"I've never held a woman's hand," I said to her as we walked. "Never thought I could."

She rubbed my arm and squeezed my hand. "It feels wonderful."

"Did you ever find a way to...?"

She looked puzzled. "To what?"

"You know. Meet guys. Have a boyfriend. Whatever."

I wasn't sure I really wanted to hear it, but she was

like my twin, and I needed to know everything.

"I've been in a couple of relationships," she said. "Neither one worked out at all. I met them at the end of our time together. They would be strangers to me, but they knew me inside and out. It was so hard. I barely knew them, but they'd kiss me and..." She shrugged. "And then by the time I got to know *them*, they wandered off, not caring about me at all, and I never saw them again."

"That must have been awful."

"The hard part was not being able to chase after them, but of course that didn't happen. Both times, I was only with them for a couple of weeks. Our kind doesn't mix well with theirs."

I stopped walking, turned to her and gave her a long hug. I could smell her perfume as I ran my hand through her hair.

That day we met, we made love. We went to her place because it was closer, and we backed up into her bedroom, slowly taking our damp clothes off. Miranda went to wash some semen onto herself before we both jumped into bed and almost immediately had simultaneous orgasms. It felt amazing to be with her. We moved together quickly, me pushing inside her over and over until we slowed down and I pulled out of her, my erection as hard as I could ever remember. I kissed her body and sucked on her breasts, and that was almost as amazing as coming inside her. I moved up to kiss her lips and we continued our foreplay for a long time, not wanting it to end.

Finally, we tentatively crawled out of bed and cautiously put our clothes on, almost embarrassed at seeing each other naked. We then kissed gently and backed out of the bedroom.

While we made love, we had several candles burning, growing taller with every passing moment. It was the best day of my life.

Within three of our backward days, Miranda moved in with me.

Chapter 8

Miranda became the only true friend I ever had. (Well, Doof was certainly up there, but no matter how wonderful, he wasn't Miranda.) We understood each other like nobody else ever could.

We spent every spare minute together, choking up wine and uncooking wonderful dinners. We loved each other more and more.

Some people might say we jumped the gun, moving in together so soon after meeting, but we knew we were meant to be together. The passing days and weeks confirmed that for both of us.

She stood five foot eight, just exactly as tall as me. Her hair was sweet and black. And she had that dimpled smile. Nobody else ever smiled at me like her. I'm sure part of that was a subconscious thing; she smiled in the right temporal direction, which just gave me shivers.

I watched her every minute I was with her. I was addicted to her. And so happy.

We'd been together for a little over a year. One day, after we finished dinner and were getting ready to go to work, Miranda gave me a big hug and a long passionate kiss. She pulled back and smiled. "Let's go on a vacation."

A vacation? My mind sprung full of great places I'd thought of visiting. New York? Las Vegas? New Orleans?

That was something I'd never done. Here I was, only thirtyfour and never had a holiday. I jumped right in. "Where?"

"Egypt."

I shrugged. "Why Egypt?"

"Why not?"

Why not indeed?

We left two months later.

It was the most amazing time. We started in Cairo, wandering back through the old streets of the Khan al Khalili bazaar. It covered many square miles and looked like a scene out of an old Indiana Jones movie, with donkeys and camels moving side by side with people and cars through the narrow streets. Vendors yelled all over the place, trying to sell their food and souvenirs.

Miranda smoked a hookah pipe; apparently it tasted like smoky apples. We watched a snake charmer lower a cobra into a small bamboo bucket.

We toured the Egyptian Museum, which housed all of King Tut's gold.

And the pyramids and the Sphinx. We crawled backward through one of the largest pyramids, seeing the sparse walls of the huge tomb, and feeling the power the ancient pharaohs held over their people.

"Can't you feel the strength?" asked Miranda when we were alone in the center.

I nodded. I could sense a million tons of rock above our heads.

As we left the central area, I took a small pebble from my pocket and placed it on the ground as a souvenir.

"Just amazing." I grabbed her hand, and we reluctantly walked back to the surface.

We stopped at a nearby KFC. The Sphinx stared at us while we unate our chicken breasts and fries and slurped our Coke back through the straws into paper cups.

Miranda looked at me, with a serious look on her face. She was quiet, which was unlike her after such an amazing afternoon of sightseeing.

"What's up?" I asked.

She hesitated at first. "You always talk about freedom," she said. She twisted her straw. "Do you really think you're free?"

"Of course. Why in the world would you doubt that?"

She added some meat to a drumstick before replying. "Well, our whole lives are predetermined. We don't really have any choice in anything. We're not like the others."

"The others?" I looked around us. The small restaurant was filled mostly with American tourists taking a break from the hot sun outside. "Normal people, you mean? Not backtrackers?"

"They have choices. We can't. Everything we do has

already been done, since it's in the past. We don't know what we've done, but everyone around us does. Dom and Jamie and the others remember you working on houses you haven't even started on yet. Those jobs are already done. You'll go work on them exactly like everybody remembers you doing."

I was totally confused. This wasn't the Miranda I knew.

"Where's this coming from? You've never talked like this before."

"Maybe it was from being inside that Pyramid. Seeing the power history holds. History is the past. The past is written in those huge boulders. We can't change it."

I reached out and held her hand, but she pulled away from me and shook her head. Her face held an ugly frown that cast a shadow over our table.

"Look around us," I said. "We're in Egypt, for God's sake! That was our choice. If that doesn't show we have free will, what could?"

"Nothing could, because it isn't true. Everything we do has already been written in the history books or carved into granite stones. We came to Egypt because we had already gone to Egypt, long before we planned it."

"You suggested Egypt."

"Yeah. I guess I was supposed to."

I didn't know what to say. Miranda was like a different person. Not just what she was saying and that dark frown, but everything about her seemed changed. Her eyes were sharp and focused, and even her hair seemed to cast a wicked tint.

I didn't like this side of her.

"We should go," I said quietly. "We have to get ready to fly to Luxor."

She nodded and as we gathered our fresh meals onto the tray and took them up to the counter, I heard her whisper a few words. I didn't know if I heard her right. "What did you say?"

"Nothing important."

I was sure she said, *My sister never made it to Luxor.*

The bus drove us backward to the center of Cairo, back to the Marriott we were staying at. It was only an hour's ride from the antiquity of the pyramids to the huge, modern capital of Egypt. We both had a quick rest and packed our bags. We had an early flight to Luxor and wanted to be sure we were on time.

The rest did her good. Miranda was back. *My Miranda.* All smiles and laughs with her beautiful dimple. I held her so tightly and promised to love her till the day I was born.

An aging Egypt Air 737 flew us south to Luxor, to the Valley of the Kings, the Temple of Karnak, and all the other amazing ancient temples and tombs of the pharaohs.

The two days we spent in the Luxor area were unbelievable. I had no idea of the treasures waiting for us.

Some of the tombs in the Valley of the Kings were

long, colorful tunnels stretching under the mountains. The walls were painted with intricate details of the life story of the dead kings and the Egyptian Book of the Dead to help the pharaohs find their way to the afterlife. Miranda and I just held hands as we walked through the tombs, pointing out small details to each other.

"Doesn't this strike you as odd?" she asked the next day. "Where is everybody?"

I'd been wondering myself. We had our pick of where to go, could even wander right into King Tut's tomb with no lineup. There were few tourists anywhere. The only people we really saw were the tour guides who would escort us into the tombs for a few Egyptian pounds. Peanuts.

"Very odd," I said. "I thought this would be a busy place. Cairo was packed."

"I'm not sure I like it," she said.

"C'mon. Let's hit Hatshepsut's Temple and call it a day."

Queen Hatshepsut was the only female pharaoh. We had both wanted to see her tomb, which was a short bus ride away, just on the other side of the mountains surrounding the Valley.

The bus was packed with other tourists, which made us feel better.

Until we saw everybody huddled in small groups, whispering and

Miranda said it first. "They're crying."

I just stared and shook my head, wondering what had happened. What we were about to experience.

My arm pulled Miranda to me protectively.

The bus stopped, and its doors swished open.

We ran off the bus and everybody started to scream, including us.

Fuck, it was awful. I was frozen in fear, wanting to do nothing more than protect Miranda, but I couldn't even seem to do that. I didn't know why I was afraid.

Miranda also looked terrified, and I knew it was fear of the unknown. For everybody else, it was the fear of what they had already seen.

We sprinted backward to the large central area in front of the tomb.

Dozens of tourists lay dead on the ground around us.

Gunshots rang out. Lots of them all at once. Machine guns or other kinds of automatics.

Terrorists. Like September 11, but in some ways worse, because we were *there*, not just watching on TV.

"Help me!" somebody called.

"Oh God, the pain," a woman screamed and yelled. Another round of shots flew from her body, and she stopped midscream, looking around in panic.

The slaughter continued. Dozens of men and women sprung up from the ground and grabbed their bodies as the bullets shot toward the killers.

There were blood stains everywhere, shrinking back toward their owners. Tourist police waved their guns in futility, not knowing how to react. Fear was etched into their youthful faces.

Bodies popped up all around us, screaming as they rose.

Then the shots stopped, and everybody looked

around casually, pointing at the temple and the nearby mountains. They laughed as they saw the terrorists climbing up the hills and mounting the top, back to the Valley of the Kings. Nobody knew they were terrorists, of course. Only Miranda and I did. They just looked like a group of bizarre mountainclimbers.

The few tourist police watched, bored to tears. "Same thing every day," I could just imagine them saying. "Nothing ever happens here."

Miranda was shaking. I held her for a long time and we backed over to the bus that would take us to the airport and our flight to Cairo.

It was time to go home.

Chapter 7

Back in Oakland, we spent many wonderful nights talking about the sights of Egypt. We never mentioned the terrorist attack. I don't know why. Maybe because ugly things in our future should be clouded in mystery, like it was for normal people.

Of course, we didn't have any pictures of our trip, because they hadn't existed before we went. Since we didn't have any beforehand, that meant we couldn't take any photos while we were there.

If you follow.

That thought was somewhat unsettling, because it reinforced Miranda's notion we didn't have the kind of free will other people had.

Were we really just programmed to follow a particular course exactly? A path from death to birth, laid out ahead of time in a circuitous but unchanging track?

How would we ever know? I thought we had made the decision to go to Egypt, but was that just a predetermined step? Predetermined since we had already been there?

Hmm.

I didn't talk to Miranda about it.

We went back to our normal lives. Me back at the Great Oakland Woodmakers, and Miranda back working as a purchaser at a book store just the other side of the Bay Bridge. She hated going over the bridge twice a day, and I can't say I blamed her. Time lost can never be regained.

Three years later, we took another holiday. I'd found a photo album showing us having a wonderful time in Venice, and as much as I wanted to say "Fuck it" to following that path, the photos looked so entrancing, we couldn't pass it up.

Venice in October was beautiful.

We went for a gondola ride through the Grand Canal at sunset, and it was the most romantic night I'd ever spent. We made love for a long time before that.

Our hotel was creaky and small, but it held an oldworld charm. It worked.

The next night, we were sitting at an outdoor café, right on the edge of the canal. Tourists walked by enjoying the warm autumn night just as much as we were. We spit up cold Nastro Azzuro beer into our frosted glasses and just gazed out at the water.

Something about Venice drills into you captures the love you feel and magnifies it a hundred fold. I felt totally at ease and in love with my woman.

"Hey," I said.

She looked over at me. "Hey right back at you."

"Amazing, isn't it?"

"It's going to be hard to go home."

I paused and finally asked the question that had been hiding in my mind for the past several years. "You never told me about your sister."

I held tightly to her hand, even though I could feel her want to pull away. She spit up some more beer and filled up her empty bottle from her glass.

"I don't know much," she finally said.

"Tell me about her. What was her name? How old was she?"

"Her name was Ricki. She was blonde, a bit overweight, old when I met her. Seemed very nice."

"Was she like us?"

She shook her head. "That's what made it so hard. I only met her the one time. When we were both in the hospital just after I undied. She came to see me. Said she hadn't seen me in fiftyfive years."

Miranda pulled her hand away and rubbed her cheeks. "I was senile, of course, and I was just starting to learn English. Just enough to get by on, I guess. She spent hours with me, but only that one day. Told me everything she had done since we last met.

"I didn't remember her. And back then, I didn't know why. It was just so terrifying. This old woman talking about playing together when we were young. Then she laughed as she told me more details of her life. Her husband, her kids."

I nodded and kept quiet, hoping she would keep talking. I never knew she had a sister.

"What are their names?" I finally asked.

She looked out to the calm water and watched another gondola drift by. "I don't remember. Isn't that awful?"

"No."

"She told me she went to Cairo once and saw the pyramids. I remember that."

Miranda paused, trying to think back to that long ago meeting. "I'm sure she told me what the occasion for her trip there was birthday, anniversary, whatever. But, I can't remember it. That was so far in our future."

"I know what you mean. Time goes so fast."

"I suppose that's why I wanted to go to Egypt. To see what she saw and have some kind of small connection to her."

"You said she never saw Luxor."

She stared at me and frowned. "Sorry. I shouldn't have kept all of this such a secret. She only got to Cairo, nowhere else. Loved it."

"Do you know when you'll meet her again?"

In the distance, I could hear "O Solo Mio" drifting through the city.

"She said the last time we saw each other was fifty-five years earlier. That would make me twenty-five. I have no idea how she ever found me in the hospital."

I took another drink, savored the taste of the beer in my mouth before spitting it in the glass. "Sounds like you have a nice surprise waiting for you down the line."

"Yeah. If you believe we don't have any free will."

"Is that where you got that?"

"How can we have any choice in our lives if we know it's been determined more than a halfcentury ahead of time that I'll meet my sister? I'll be twenty-five in only six years, and I know she'll be there."

I didn't have an answer for that.

Chapter 6

Sometimes it seemed like the natural state of the world included war. It was so normal, I never thought of it. Dying was a part of living, so why wouldn't war be a part of peace? There was war almost all the time from my first memory after learning English.

TV loved war. I remember seeing a dumb primetime game show that only lasted one season. It was called Invasion, where teams had to decide which country to bomb. The show itself was the ultimate bomb, only lasting six episodes.

Central America. Before that, North Korea. Before that, several other quickies in the middle east. Then Iraq 2 followed a decade earlier by Iraq 1. They didn't call it that, of course. It was just the Gulf War then.

I never understood any war. I'd see the devastation of the country that lost, followed by the live telecasts of thousands of soldiers trying to kill other soldiers, bombs flying back up into their bays on their planes or to faraway ships. Diplomacy would begin, and then the shouting would really start. Eventually the two countries complained about each other sporadically and went their own ways. I never understood why they didn't just choose that course without going through all the wars.

Shortly after the Gulf War ended, the smart bombs were flying all over.

I found myself walking back down the street to St. Joseph's Hospital, where I had died.

The whole building was very familiar, of course, and I didn't have any trouble finding her room.

Her.

Mom.

I was feeling very anxious when I backed into the room. Sadness, but also relief. The smell of death hung in the air like cigarette smoke.

She was the only patient, although the room could have held another. The doctors knew her time was up and wanted to give her some dignity and peace in her last days.

Her face was covered with a white sheet. I pulled it back and stared at the unfamiliar face of my mother.

White hair, all crinkly, like it hadn't been washed in weeks. There were bits of dandruff sprinkled around her.

I pushed her eyes open. Lifeless, but I knew that would change soon.

Her hands were warm. Hard and unyielding, but warm. They were mapped with coarse veins looking like they might pop any second. She was ancient. Looked a hundred, but I knew she couldn't be. A hard life had destroyed her.

I gained comfort from remembering Doof springing to life. Mom was close.

Her face reminded me of my own. I probably should've anticipated that, but I didn't. She was ridiculously older than me, but I remembered having my own sunken cheekbones and darkened eyes in this very same hospital. Her lips were pale and thin, just like mine.

We were like a set of deformed twins. Something clearly the same but so different.

Mom's snowy hair had only a few streaks that might have been black in her youth. For a moment, I wondered if she had ever been pretty. *One day I'll find out*, I knew.

In the background, I could hear Bernard Shaw talking in a fast and loud voice about the bombing in Baghdad.

She breathed.

"Goodbye, Son." I could barely hear her. I replayed the sound over in my mind to be sure I'd heard her right.

She started to wheeze and took big gulps of air.

I reached down and held her. "I wish I'd known."

"I wish I had protected you more." Mom tried to squeeze my hand. "After he put me in the hospital one last time. I left him five years ago. He beat me once too often," she said.

"Whatever happened to him?" I held her hand with both of mine.

She coughed. "Me, too."

Her breathing was so shallow and harsh, I could feel her pain as I listened to her.

I hesitated. I didn't want to lie to her, but I'd never have another chance to talk to her. "Sometimes, I wish things worked out better all around, but I'm here now."

"I wish you had come back to me," she said.

"Seven years, I think."

"I'm glad you came. It's been so long."

She blinked her eyes and fell asleep, peacefully.

I stayed with Mom for awhile, then left when it was clear she wasn't going to wake up any time soon. I talked briefly with her doctor.

I'm glad Mom's last years were free from that jerk, but I wouldn't be able to go back to see her when she left the hospital. Too much water under the bridge. I was as angry at her for what had happened as I was at him.

The most frustrating part was that I didn't even know what it exactly was that happened. Just that I felt hatred to my core for my father.

Part of me wanted to go hunt him down, to fucking well bury him for the grief he had caused my mother.

But I knew that wasn't going to happen.

I briefly spoke to Mom's doctor before leaving the hospital. He wasn't very hopeful at all. He shook his head a lot and frowned.

A day later, I found out Mom was very, very sick, and might not live another day.

Chapter 5

I left Mom at the hospital, knowing it would be a long time before I would have the balls to go visit her. It just made me angry knowing what was waiting for me in my childhood. And it wasn't like she was innocent; she was there in the house.

For awhile, I almost believed in telepathy. Could feel his fists hitting me, but of course that was just a fantasy.

I was twenty-three. How long could I be independent anyway? I'd cool down and go see her, I knew, but it wasn't going to be soon. She was back alive now and would be a big part of the rest of my life; no use rushing it.

I went back to our apartment, back to my wonderful Miranda.

It was about 9:00 in the morning, and I hugged her as we sat down to spit up some coffee together. I knew I was being quiet.

"It'll be another seven years?" she asked.

"What will?"

"Before you see your mom again. Isn't that what she said? Seven years?"

I shook my head and smiled. The same old

argument. "We have free will. I could go visit her tomorrow if I wanted to."

"Great. Why don't we go together?"

I looked at her and saw that amazing smile of hers. Her eyes locked onto mine and held. Every time she looked at me like that, my heart seemed to jump. God, I'm so lucky, I thought to myself.

"There's more to the story than you know," I finally said. "I'm just not ready to see her again."

Miranda had been browsing through the Sports section of the newspaper. She folded the paper neatly and quietly took it outside and placed it on our front porch.

"I told you about my sister. Tell me about your mother."

I squirmed, knowing how my answer would sound. "My father beat her. She told me that."

"Oh. I'm sorry. That must have been awful for her."

I nodded. "Yeah. But, he must have done more than that. Something to me, I think. Of course, I don't know what that might be. I think maybe he hit me, too."

"You could go ask her."

"No. You know the funny looks we get when we ask things we should already know. She'd think something was really wrong if I asked what happened to me." I shook my head and squeezed her hand tightly. "I'll find out soon enough."

She stood up and hugged me from behind. "I wish we could prove it. Prove we can do whatever we want."

"Well, let's go do something we would never normally do. Bowling. Mountain climbing. Go watch an artsy movie. What would prove it to you?"

She laughed. "None of those. Maybe we're *supposed* to go mountain climbing today because we've already done it."

I took my steaming coffee over to the Mr. Coffee machine and had it suck the coffee back up into the pot. The hot coffee started to drip up to the machine while I put my mug back in the cupboard.

This whole free will thing was really bugging Miranda, and I didn't understand why. As far as I was concerned, I could do whatever I wanted. I just didn't feel any different from the rest of the people around me. How do they know they have free will?

"You know how I view things?" I asked. "I think of time as a railroad track."

"Yeah? How's that?"

"Think of a train going in one direction on the track. On the track right beside it is another train speeding in the opposite direction. One going east, one west."

"Okay. So?"

"The trains pass each other. But, the eastwest axis is now time. One going forward in time, one going backward. From the outside, we can't tell which is which. They look identical, just going in opposite directions."

Miranda thought about that for a few seconds.

The coffee had separated into the grounds and the water. I scooped the grounds back into the Starbucks tin and let the water flow up into the tap.

I didn't know if my analogy was clicking. Miranda was thinking about it but not saying anything.

I added, "You think we have problems because we

can't see our past, but everybody else has the exact same problem   they can't see their future. "But we can."

"Yes."

"We know exactly where your sister will be fortyodd years from now. We know when most of the people around us get married, have children. Die. They have no more free will than we do."

I took her hand and walked into the bedroom with her. "We're the same as everyone else," I said. "Just different."

That morning we fell asleep with a thud as soon as the alarm went off. When we woke up the night before, we were in each other's arms.

We made love that night with a passion that seemed new to us. It was wonderful. Absolutely astonishing. I couldn't imagine my life without her.

Chapter 4

Two more years passed.

I'd been with Miranda for nine years.

She was the only true friend I ever had. We understood each other like nobody else ever could.

We spent every spare minute together, choking up wine and uncooking wonderful dinners. We loved each other more and more.

Then, it all came crashing down.

We had been living in a house in Oakland, both of us having given up our own apartments long ago. Our new place was bigger. Two bedrooms, and we each had a spare room to use however we wanted. I had mine set up with a TV and easy chair so I could watch reality shows with Doof beside me. Miranda liked to spend time in her den, reading.

Our home wasn't the glorious mansion overlooking the Bay I had dreamed about, but it was really nice. It was a bungalow in the eastern part of the city, near a small park that was overrun with squirrels. We loved to take empty bags to the park on Sundays. The squirrels would run around collecting peanuts and bring them back to us.

The day of the crash, I was home before Miranda,

watching the news.

The Berlin Wall was about to be torn upwards and communism looked to rise into a serious political force.

Ronald Reagan was leading the fight but was starting to back off, giving the Soviet states a chance to amalgamate into a Superpower.

As soon as Miranda closed the door behind her, I could tell there was trouble. Her face was hard, teeth gritted, eyes glaring. This was the Miranda I had trouble with, the Miranda who I first met in Cairo, singleminded, love scattered in ashes at the back of her mind. I'd seen this side of her several times now, and every time, it resulted in arguments.

I didn't like this Miranda.

But I still loved her.

"We need to talk," she said as she backed into the house. There was no question something was wrong.

"What is it?"

She went to the kitchen and grabbed a dirty glass, quickly spitting out a halfglass of wine in one gulp. It wasn't like her to drink so early in the morning.

"Miranda, what is it?

"It was horrible."

"What?"

"I found myself at a clinic today." She turned around and glared at me. "I had an abortion."

I could feel my mouth drop in disbelief. "That's not possible. You're on the pill." We had talked about this that first day we made love. She had been using birth control pills since she was fortyfive. She'd had early menopause then and didn't need them afterwards.

"Yes, yes, I'm on the pill. Goddamn it."

"Then, how?" I know I should have gone to hug her, to help her, but I was too shocked. How could she have an abortion? That wasn't her decision to make alone.

Of course, the rational side of me knew she had no choice. She would have backed into the clinic, found herself on a table where they would have shoved a dead fetus inside her. I cringed when I thought of that.

"You're pregnant right now," I said.

"Yes."

"But "

"It was fucking awful! You can't imagine what they did to me." She filled the rest of her wine glass and spilled some as she poured it into the bottle. "I must have only started on the pill because of the abortion. I probably will find I don't take them any more. No point, since I'm pregnant. Goddamn stupid bitch."

I took my own empty glass from the sink and spit up some wine. I needed it.

"Pregnant," I said.

"We must do it last week, or," Miranda shook her head. "Sometime in the last while. Couple weeks maybe." She added some wine to her glass. "I'm not doing it."

"What?"

"This is ridiculous. I want to lead a normal fucking life like everybody else."

I snorted at her, getting angry in spite of myself. "Yeah, well, join the club. We don't have a choice."

"Yes, I do."

I stared at her as she finished another glass of wine, pouring it forcefully back in the bottle, not spilling a drop this time. I had no idea what she was talking about.

"We've had a long time together," she said. "It's time for me to move on."

"What? No! You can't be thinking of leaving me..." I shook my head in dismay. "We need to be together."

"No, we need to be apart. Fucking *apart*, Michael. I am not doing this any more. I'm going back to be with the normal world."

The normal world, I knew, meant the people moving forward in time, not like us. "You can't be like them," I said quietly. "You know that."

"I know. But I can fake it. I always did before I met you."

I moved to her, tried to pull her to me, but Miranda pushed me back and shook her head. "I can't do this any more. We've had good years, but after forty-five years of living like them before meeting you, I can't really be happy with anything else. I'm one of them."

"But, you're not."

She just shrugged.

Miranda left me alone an hour earlier. It was torture to see her leave, so hard to see her back out the front door of our shared place. She recently had her twentysixth birthday, and we celebrated it, not knowing she had recently had that abortion.

I should have stopped her, but I was pissed off at her attitude. Maybe we did need some time apart.

It wasn't until the prior night that a thought came to my mind.

Once she had her abortion, Miranda left me. We didn't make love again. It was that sense of loss I was mourning, missing the feel of her body against mine when the realization hit me.

It couldn't have been me who made her pregnant.

She would be having sex with somebody else. Soon.

When she left me, she must have gone back to another lover. Maybe somebody she had just broken up with, maybe somebody she had just finished a longterm relationship with. Of course, she didn't remember it because he was in her past, not her future.

I cried as I realized I had lost her for good, and that she was going to find somebody in the real world that loved her as much as I did.

I knew it would take me a long time until I was young enough to get over her.

Chapter 3

At first I was just mad, figuring that Miranda and I could both use the time away from each other and that in a few days, we'd be able to talk more clearly about the abortion, free will, and all the other things that seemed to come between us from time to time.

I was *so* mad, I didn't ask where she was going. I'm not completely sure she knew when she slammed the door behind her.

There were only about six empty beer bottles by the door of the kitchen, but I filled them all. It didn't help, but it made me more clearheaded.

It was almost dawn, the sun starting to set.

"Miranda?" I whispered her name, almost waiting for her to answer.

"Miranda?" I said it louder, could almost hear a hollow echo bounce off the kitchen walls.

That first day was hard, but not as hard as the next couple of weeks would be. She didn't come back. Didn't phone to tell me where she was. Didn't even seem to care about all her stuff. Her clothes still hung in the closet, her favorite shoes lay quietly by the front door. The few books she liked to read over and over again. Her Nietzsche and Ayn Rand books were in tatters from being reread so often.

Even her current notebook lay open on the table in her den. She always said her notebooks entertained her. She had a dozen or so left, all neatly piled up on a chair. They were filled with doodles, little diagrams and sketches, that kind of thing. No big deal, but it helped her to relax. When she wanted a break, she'd take out her pen and undraw the latest entry in the book. She'd finished at least a dozen books while we'd been together. She almost seemed to be in a trance when erasing her work, a satisfied smile on her face.

I didn't move anything of hers. Left the notebook on the table and the others still stacked up.

Left all her makeup in the medicine cabinet.

Left her sneakers by the front door, even though I had to step around them whenever I wanted to leave our home.

I couldn't touch any of her stuff. It was like that would mean she couldn't do it herself.

Part of me also knew that as long as her notebooks and other stuff was here, she had to return to me. Otherwise, where would I have gotten all her things?

Unless, she really did have a choice about returning.

What was better? Having Miranda but no free will? Or prove we have choice, and she chose to leave me forever?

After three days, I started looking for her. I went to *The Red Claw*, the seafood restaurant where we had first met, at the same time of day.

No luck, but I didn't really think it would be that easy.

I wandered around Pier 39, always coming back to the place where a few times we had watched the hundreds of sea lions frolicking on the nearby rafts.

Then I went to her work. *Book Smarts,* a small shop just under the Bay Bridge. I recognized her coworkers although I'd never spoken to them. One of them was named Wendy. Miranda and her had gone out together for drinks, so I knew they were close.

She surprised me with her emphatic answer. "We have a Martha in the back. Are you sure you're not thinking of Martha? I'm sorry, but I don't know anyone named Miranda." She pursed her lips together tightly.

"Has she been here? You know. She works here." I knew if Wendy said she'd been there a day or two ago, that would be great news, because I'd just wait for her.

"Who's she? Don't recognize that name." She scrunched up her face. "Miranda?"

"I'm looking for Miranda. Is she here?"

She looked at me with a puzzled look on her face and then smiled. "What can I do for you?"

"Wendy? Can you help me?"

I left Wendy and backed over to my car. Miranda didn't work there yet.

I was in real trouble now. I had no way at all to find the only person who understood me, the only person who I could really talk to.

The only person I could ever truly love.

That summer turned into spring and then winter. The cold winds blew off the Bay and chilled me to the bone when I was working on some repairs to a warehouse near the water.

During the daytime, the work kept me busy and my mind occupied. It was easier; it was the nights that were tough.

I'd wake up alone. More often than not, I'd be totally drunk. A few times it was so bad I went to the bathroom and sucked up a terrible pile of vomit from the toilet. I hated the taste in my mouth but choked it all down.

Beer cases crowded much of the kitchen floor, even after taking back a couple of full cases each day. I knew I had a long time ahead of me before I would feel better.

I sat in the living room almost every night with my beer. Sometimes I would have CNN on or watch some silly sitcom or reality show, but I didn't really care much about what was happening. The TV was mostly for background noise.

This went on for almost two years. Two long and terrible years. I slowly (very slowly) got my act together and stopped drinking as much. But I never did get around to moving her notebooks or shoes. She was still a part of my life, and I couldn't let her go.

Then came another cool autumn Saturday afternoon. The sun was shining brightly, foretelling the nice summer weather that would soon follow.

I hadn't played tourist in San Francisco for years. Sometimes, time just slipped away and fun things were the first to go. I decided to spend the day hitting the main spots, just for a change. I rode a cable car and looked out at Alcatraz. Walked around Chinatown and Japantown. I hoped by getting out of the house, I could get through a day without moping around, pissing my life away.

I was twenty-four years old.

Twenty-four divided by my deathage of sixty-five meant my life was almost two-thirds over. It wasn't a difficult calculation. And part of my remaining time, I would be a little kid.

Then what? I dreaded the thought of losing my mental faculties, but there was no way around it. My brain would undevelop and I'd lose everything.

It was time to enjoy things while I still could. At least for one day.

As I was walking through the piers, I saw her.

She was alone, leaning over the railing, looking out to the sea lions, just as she had a few times earlier with me. I knew she loved them, but I had given up on finding her there.

"Miranda," I said quietly as I moved closer to her.

I wanted to add, *Oh, my love, where have you been? My life has been so worthless without you.* But all I could manage was her name. I was shaking.

I could see her shoulders tense, and she clenched the guard rail tighter. She turned to face me, and I could see tears spring to her eyes.

"Oh, Michael." She cried and put her hands over her eyes.

I grabbed her and held her tightly to me, feeling her sob into my chest. I rubbed her hair and just never wanted to let her go.

Eventually, she stopped crying. She looked up to me and said, "How did you find me?"

I smiled, trying to reassure her. "Persistence." I

couldn't tell her the truth that I had actually given up on ever seeing her again.

She smiled back, and I felt happy for the first time since she had left.

I didn't press her for details right away. She just stared into my face. The tears were all gone, pulled back into her eyes.

She looked just as beautiful as ever. Her hair was shorter, but otherwise, she was the same girl I had fallen in love with all those years ago.

"I didn't plan on leaving you like that," she said finally.

"What happened? I couldn't find you anywhere."

"When I left, I just stormed off, wanting to be alone. I was so mad, but more than that, I was just damned frustrated. Everything seemed so pointless to me, and I couldn't figure out why you didn't understand."

Miranda hesitated and gave me a quick hug, adding, "I'm just telling you what I felt at the time. Not what I feel now."

I nodded. "I understand. Go on."

"Well, I didn't have any place to go. That first night I slept on a park bench. The second night was easier to do the same thing. Then I quit my job. I couldn't keep going to work when I wasn't thinking straight. It was summer time, and it wasn't hard to make money in the park. Remember, I grew up as a bag lady, so I knew how to scrounge."

"It can't have been as easy as you're making it sound."

We started to walk along the shore line, the waves of the Bay crashing in nearby. Tourists stared past us out to the water. We were invisible.

"I thought then of a way to show that I had free will."

"What?"

She stared into my eyes. "By never coming back."

I didn't know what to say. Finally, I asked, "What do you mean? How would that prove anything?"

"If I wasn't with you, I wouldn't get pregnant. It would be like an immaculate conception. Since that sounded totally weird, I wondered what would happen. It sounds silly now, but I wasn't really in a good space, and it somehow made sense. I think I just needed some time apart."

"Maybe we both needed that," I said.

"Yeah. But I was surprised again. I was alone for most of that summer, living in the park, regurgitating only the last bits of somebody's chicken or picnic sandwich, begging people to take money from me, when "

She hesitated.

I gave her a long hug and kissed her. "It's okay, Miranda. We're back together now."

She rubbed my hair and smiled. "Well, one night, I was in the park when I noticed I had a terrible set of bruises on my face. As the hours passed, it got worse and worse, big welts and my eye started to close. I couldn't help but cry from the pain. It was dark and nobody was around to hear me. I think I sat under a tree and cried in pain much of the night.

"Then maybe about midnight "

"It's okay. Take your time."

"I didn't see anybody. But then, I pulled my dress

up and fell to the ground."

She stopped for a minute, and I rubbed her fingers.

"A big guy ran to me, then swiveled and I could see he was covered with sweat and filth. His teeth were rotten, and he stank. By then my face was terribly sore, and I knew he was going to beat the shit out of me. But then, even worse, I pulled him on top of me and he raped me."

I didn't know what to say. "Oh, Miranda..."

"It hurt so much. I didn't know what was happening at first. He just kept pushing and pounding and then he just pulled me up and ran away into the bushes. He hit me, hard, unbroke my nose and took away all the bruises on the rest of my face."

She stared out to San Francisco Bay, seeming to focus on a tanker in the distance, as if she didn't have a care in the world. After a few seconds, she squeezed my hand and said, "There are no words to describe it. That was how I got pregnant and why I had that abortion ten weeks later."

I felt ashamed. For two years, I had assumed she had found a previous lover.

"Why didn't you come back to me?" I asked her.

"I couldn't. I was so terribly hurt and angry at everything. The rapist, you, the whole fucking world. The rape just made me realize so clearly what I have believed for so long."

"The free will thing?"

"Yeah. Anyhow, I was totally fucked up and all I wanted to do was to be alone. I wished I could have washed my memories away of that day. My soul was hurt, and I couldn't find a way to go back to you to tell you what had happened. I needed to be alone."

"But, two years?"

"After a while, it became harder to imagine coming back. I don't know why. I lived on the streets for a while, and maybe I was just too ashamed to see you."

"But, we found each other again. That says something, doesn't it?"

And then she flashed that amazing smile at me. "Yes. Yes, it does."

Chapter 2

All her life, Miranda had been haunted, wondering whether she was actually able to make any choices at all or just following a path already determined for her.

I never understood why it mattered so much to her. From a practical perspective, it made no difference. She never did have an answer to my train analogy. We were the same as everybody else, just on a different track. She thought there had to be a logic error embedded in my comments, but she couldn't find it. That just seemed to make things worse.

There was one time when she thought she could prove things to herself. A time when she could absolutely without a doubt make a decision on her own that clearly went against her destiny.

It happened during the time we were apart. That was the year she turned twenty-five the year she was supposed to see her sister for the last time until she was on her deathbed.

She told me about it after we went back home that first night.

"Oh, my God, you left everything. My shoes are still in the way." She laughed and moved her sneakers to the side.

She jumped into my arms and gave me a long hard kiss before looking back through our home again. The two years apart melted away.

Just then, Doof came running in and went crazy, barking at Miranda, running around her, and then lifting his short front paws up to her ankles.

"Oh, my little boy!" She squealed like a teenager and picked him up. He made small sounds like "burf" and sniffed her face, squirming in her arms like a colicky baby. After a few minutes, he calmed down. Miranda put him on the floor. He went to find a dog bed and licked himself.

"The notebooks..." She caressed the open one on the table in her room.

All I had done in the past two years was to dust them a couple of times. "I never peeked," I said. "Just the page that was already open. Tempted, but I thought as long as the pages were unread, you'd have to come back one day and erase them."

The open page showed a sketch of a girl, a teenager, with dark hair and eyes that were large and round. "That's my sister, Ricki," she said as she looked at the sketch. "It doesn't do her justice."

"How do you know?" I asked.

"Let's have a glass of wine. It's so great to see this place." She gave me another hug. "I really did miss you, Michael."

I felt another tug at my heart and smiled weakly. "I have an empty bottle under the kitchen sink." The pronoun "I" had slipped out without thinking. It was time to get back to "we."

The wine was made nearby. As I read the label, I

vaguely recognized the name and thought maybe we should drive down to the winery soon to take back a bottle.

There were two dirty glasses in the sink, and I took them to the table, where we each spit up a small amount and clinked glasses.

"My sister." She took a deep breath. "Last summer, I went east to Modesto. I'm not really sure why Modesto. There was a news story set there and I thought, 'What the hell?' I just wanted to go someplace new."

I'd never been there, so I didn't have much to add.

"Hitchhiked," she said. "I took a couple rides but it's not that far, so it was pretty easy."

I nodded. I knew it wasn't far. Maybe two hours. "What happened?"

"It was a warm day, and I was eating an ice cream cone. Vanilla with little almond chips sprinkled on top."

"Sounds like you."

"She saw me. I was just standing on the street corner, licking my ice cream. She came up to me and started laughing and crying. She had the same kind of ice cream cone, almond chips and all."

I didn't say anything. She was staring into the distance, remembering her sister.

"Her eyes were so big and round. Hypnotizing. But, right away, I had no question about who she was. I felt a deep love for her, which was so weird, cause I had only met her that one time before, so long ago."

"Maybe somehow family " I hesitated, not sure of the right words, " somehow they transcend our differences."

"Well, anyhow, something happened. We were like old friends who saw each other every day. She was just great, even going the wrong direction. She was saying goodbye to me, of course. It was our last time together until you know. She was going to travel in Europe and maybe stay there. We made all the right kind of promises to keep in touch, but somehow those fifty-five years ended up passing before she found me again."

"Why didn't she keep in touch?"

"I don't know. I couldn't call her because I didn't know her. My guess is she had no way to find me. After we parted, I went back to Oakland and it wasn't long after that the rape happened and then I met you."

"So, she didn't know where to find you?"

"And I didn't know I should have told her where I lived."

"Wow. At least now, you'll see her again. It sounds like you were pretty close."

She nodded. "All of that's good."

"But?

"But I met her exactly when I was supposed to. It pretty much proved I had no choice in the matter. Even though I had consciously tried to avoid finding her, it didn't matter a bit."

Three months passed.

Doof and Miranda cuddled at every opportunity. Miranda and I cuddled at every opportunity, too. Having her back home was the best thing that could've happened to me.

But, still, Miranda was restless. I could feel it in her touch, the way she stared into nothingness once in a while, even the way her smile sometimes seemed fake, as if her mind was busy thinking, but she knew she had to pretend to be there for me.

Most of the time, she was there for me. But not always. Sometimes, I could see she was totally preoccupied when I walked into the kitchen unexpected. Her empty coffee cup sitting there would never be filled. Doof slept at her feet. An unnatural quiet filled the room with suspense.

At other times she'd wake in the middle of the night and go sit in the bathroom for thirty or forty minutes. I wanted to ask what was wrong, but I knew it would be the same old thing. She wanted freedom. *True* freedom, and she didn't know how to get it.

It was the thing that seemed to matter most to her in her whole life. She wanted a choice in something. *Anything.* One single decision that would be all her own.

And finally she thought of one thing that would conclusively prove she had free will. I'm sure she thought about it for most of those three months. Maybe she had the idea earlier, but it couldn't work without me as a witness, and so finding me again gave her the impetus to dust off her thoughts and consider her options.

It was 1987. I remember reading news accounts of the World Exposition that had been held in Vancouver the year before and talking to her about us taking a vacation there the previous year. She acted enthused, but in retrospect it was clear she never planned to do that with me.

July 5. The date I'll never forget. We'd gone to sleep in the morning, snoozed comfortably, and made love when we woke up in the late night. As always, it was wonderful.

She held me tightly after, holding onto me for almost an hour, silent. She might have been crying. I'm not sure.

Our last time. Of course I didn't know that then.

I was feeling slightly woozy, so I knew we'd be getting out of bed to have a few beers or some wine together. Hopefully there'd be a few laughs to go with it, and not the difficult times with the "other" Miranda, the girl who snapped and turned morose way too often.

This time, though, it was a middleground Miranda who shared the drinks with me.

She wanted to reminisce. The wonderful holiday in Egypt before the terrorists, our romantic gondola ride in Venice. All the times we had gone over the bridge to San Francisco to find a small café or a restaurant to spend a great evening together.

She reached for my hand. "I love you, Michael."

"And I love you, too, Miranda. I always will."

She nodded, choked up a bit of beer, and then she left to go to the bathroom.

I was still thinking back to our time in Venice. Now that she had me thinking about that, I really wanted to convince her to come on another holiday with me. Vancouver. Expo '86 would be the start of a whole series of new adventures for us.

That's when I heard her groan and then a crash

followed from the bathroom.

For a moment, I froze, then I jumped up and ran to her.

"Miranda?" The door was locked. "*Miranda!*" I heard her groan again. That was enough. The flimsy lock burst easily as I smashed into the door.

My Miranda.

She lay on the floor surrounded by a pool of bright red blood. She gasped and stared up at me, but I could tell right away that she was losing the fight raging inside her.

She was on her back, legs spread apart, slowly moving, and right in the middle of her chest, a long sharp knife was skewering her.

There was a second red spot just below the knife, where she had stabbed herself the first time. I had an insane admiration for her having the strength of conviction to stab herself, pull the knife out, and then do it again.

That thought fluttered away instantly.

"Miranda!" I kneeled beside her, not knowing what to do. Should I pull the knife out, or was it better to leave it in and go for help?

"No," I heard her whisper. "Let it alone." Her voice was almost nonexistent. "You know nobody can help."

I grabbed the knife and felt her holding the handle. I knocked her hand aside and yanked the knife out. I could feel it grinding against her ribs as I pulled.

Then, I pushed down carefully on the wound with a white bathroom towel.

"It's okay. We'll get you fixed up."

Even as I said those words, I knew it was hopeless.

I could see the life drifting out of her eyes and felt her last heart beat as I pressed the towel on her.

"No!" I didn't know what to do, so I shook her, tried to force her back to life. "Miranda, don't leave me!"

One last sigh. She was dead.

I held her and cried and cried and cried.

Her suicide note was sitting on the counter.

> Dear Michael:
> If you're reading this, it looks like you were right. We have free will after all. This proves it. If I can kill myself, obviously my past is ended, and I'll never meet Ricki again, never meet my parents, and never be born. All those events will be wiped out. Everything I was expected to do will all be undone. I will have done the only act in my lifetime that I know for sure was not predetermined. Don't cry for me. This is what I needed.
> I love you, Miranda.

When I finished reading the note, I looked down at Miranda again. Her body was gone.

Chapter 1

Doof and I were alone.

Even the blood splattered on the bathroom cabinets was gone. Every bit of Miranda was taken from me.

I think I was in shock. All I wanted was to know where she was. Wanted her to come back for me so I could call 9-1-1. That wouldn't have worked, since the ambulance would already have arrived before she killed herself, but crazy thoughts sprinkled my mind.

I thought I was going nuts. Maybe there never really was a Miranda maybe she was just a wonderful dream.

But, of course, her wine glass was still there. Her books. Her sketches. I could even still smell her perfume hanging beside me.

Sometimes I wonder what would have happened if she hadn't disappeared. Would her body continue to move back in time with me? How long could that last? How would the police deal with a body that sprung back to life just after she stabbed herself?

Amid all the confusion that would arise, I realized it was just as well her body had disappeared and hadn't left all the challenges that would have precipitated otherwise.

This time, she'd left me for good.

Not only me. Her parents would never hold Miranda as a baby. Ricki would be an only child. Somehow the world carried on as if she had never existed. But I knew.

So did Doof. He came into the bathroom while I was sitting on the floor with my back leaning against the toilet. He sniffed the area where Miranda had lain and then looked up at me with questioning eyes.

"Hey, boy, c'mere." I held him and patted him, both of us staring at the empty floor.

I think Miranda thought she was safe, that she couldn't possibly succeed at killing herself. Instead, she proved she was wrong. She did have free will after all. I wonder if she had a split second of satisfaction before she died.

We all have free will, I think. Some of us just choose to take the path of least resistance.

The months passed, and I didn't cry for Miranda. I wanted to, but all my tears had been used up when she left me after her abortion.

The house seemed so empty, though. I watched too much television, drank too much beer, and went to work with too many gutwrenching hangovers.

I went to the sea lions several times over the summer and watched them playing together, remembering the times Miranda and I stared at them, entranced.

Every few days, I'd see Doof walking around the house, just wandering, peeking into each room. I knew he was looking for her, instinctively wanting his mistress, whom he had yet to meet for the first time.

One day, though, his pining for Miranda hit me. *He hasn't met her yet.*

"Doof?"

I held him to me, staring into his big, woeful eyes. "How could you be looking for her, boy?"

His eyes darted around the room, and I knew then that he was trapped in the same backward world I was. He did know her, because he was just like me.

All his life, he had likely been lonely, confused, and scared half to death, not understanding so much of what was happening to him.

I told myself all this, maybe just to believe we had more in common than we truly did.

Soon enough, though, he stopped looking for her. He just stayed with me when I was at home.

Doof was growing very young. His coat was a smooth, deep brown, no trace of the white that would cover his face in his later years.

I put Miranda's books and clothes into banker's boxes and piled them into a corner of the den. I couldn't stand the thought of giving them away. She still had all those unerased notebooks.

Summer turned to spring, then to winter, and before I knew what was happening, three more years were gone, and I was down to twentyone years old. I had almost no money in the bank, since I hadn't been in the work force very long. I wondered what would happen when I completely ran out of cash.

Doof was just a pup, less than eight inches long

One day, I looked at him in his little cardboard box. I had spread newspapers around him, because he was losing control of where to pee. He always seemed to know he did something wrong, but he couldn't help himself.

"Hey, boy." I picked him up and he eagerly licked my face, all full of energy.

I carefully took him out to the car with tears blurring my vision.

We drove down to *The Pet Store On The Bay*. I gave him one last long hug before taking him inside and trading him for three hundred dollars.

The clerk in the store put him in a large cage, with several other pups. They were his siblings. He was the runt of the litter. He plopped down in a corner and watched the others suspiciously.

From there...

In another six weeks, he'd be with his mother. He'd crawl up into her womb and then disappear.

When I got home I was truly alone, and I cried again. I felt little more than a boy, and I knew my time as an independent man was coming to an end.

I missed my mother and looked up her number in the phone book.

Prologue

MY NAME IS MIKEY JOHNSON.

I AM 4. I LIVE WITH MOMMY AND DADDY IN MODESTO CALFORNA.

I NO I WAS OLD ONE TIME. I WORKED LIKE DADDY AND I HAD BEER

MOMMY SEZ I SHUD RITE IN MY BOOK BUT I DONT NO WHAT TO SAY. SOMETIME SHE SEZ WORDS I DONT NO.

I WISH MOMMY WAS MIRANDA CAUSE SHE LIKES ME. IM AFRAID OF MOMMY SOMETIME. AND I WISH DADDY DIDN'T HIT ME.

I MISS DOOF. HE WENT INSIDE HIS MOMMY. I NO THAT'S WHAT I WILL DO TOO. I WANT MIRANDA.

I WISH MIRANDA NEVER LEFT ME.

Schrodinger's Clock

White Noise Press produces the finest chapbooks in the field, so when Keith Minnion (the publisher and designer) asked me to write a novella for his line, I jumped at the chance.

I had no idea what to write, but I was itching to write another story about time. Fortunately, Keith gave me several months to think about the story. I wanted it to be a worthy addition to his chapbook line.

Quantum mechanics has always been an interest of mine, and one day I was thinking about the famous experiment called Schrodinger's Cat, when the title of my story came to me. Then I "just" had to figure a story to go with it.

Eventually the pieces fell into place. The main character is somewhat modelled after myself. I sometimes will rattle off stuff to Fatima, who patiently listens to me, even if she doesn't follow much of what I'm talking about. So far, I haven't popped into the future.

The chapbook itself was stunning what it was published in 2016, easily the most visually amazing design I've ever been fortunate enough to be part of.

This is the last story in this volume. I really hope you enjoyed it, and I look forward to having you pick up the next three volumes of my work. Thank you for being here!

When I first moved in with Jeremy, I was bursting with love, energy, pride, and a million other emotions that all coalesced around planning to spend the rest of my life with the man I loved.

At first when he suggested living together, I almost thought he was kidding. We'd been dating for two years, and although our feelings for each other had continued to grow and mature for that whole time, I secretly wondered if he'd ever be able to commit to a shared life.

He'd often get that drift in his eyes, and I knew he was thinking back on what he called his weirdities. I suppose most people would call them oddities, but of course Jeremy was unlike any other person.

He was a genius, and sometimes it seemed like every thinking minute he was focused on only one thing: understanding the nature of time.

Even when he was with me, and even when he was whispering to me, "Katherine, I love you..."

Yes, even then, I knew that only a small part of his brain was talking to me. The other part—the bigger part by far—was thinking about time.

Time was my rival, and there wasn't anything I could do to win. I just had to accept he would always have a mistress, even if she was amorphous and misty.

His obsession with time might have most of his thinking mind, but I knew I had his soul.

Jeremy was twenty-six when we moved in, and I was twenty-four. He had longish black hair that he pulled back into a short pony tail. I liked that, because it matched my own blonde pony, so it was one thing we had in common.

The house we bought had two bedrooms. It was small, but that's all we needed. I picked the place, because I wanted it to be our home, not just his.

We pretended the second bedroom was for storage and a makeshift office. I for one, was convinced we'd soon have a baby living there, but I never actually said that out loud to Jeremy. I'm not sure things would have turned out any different if I had, but that's one of the things about time—you can't go backward, and we'll never know what might have been if I'd done things differently.

Today I imagine a lot of different things. I'm now eighty-one years old, and I look back to those days when Jeremy and I had so much life left to live that it seemed to stretch infinitely far in front of us.

It's a cliché to say time flies, especially when the guy you live with is a time nut... but, what other phrase really captures things? I remember my youth so vividly. I remember the first time we made love, the tender touches of his fingers on my body, the shivers he sent through me, and the amazing feeling that for a short time I was the center of Jeremy's mind, able to push his research aside.

All that just happened, except it was more than a half century ago. Like everybody else my age, I want that time back. I want to be young and healthy and full of energy, but of course that can't happen. We all make the best choices we can during our lives, and we hope we create a nest of happy memories.

Jeremy and I were partly successful in all that, so I have no complaints.

Moving day was easier for us than most couples. I didn't have a lot of possessions, and Jeremy had even less. That was okay, though. Between us, we had a sofa, a television, a computer, a couple of chairs and a kitchen table, and of course, a nice comfy bed. That was the only piece of furniture I insisted we buy new.

Jeremy also brought tons of note books where he scribbled lots of weird equations.

"I want to tell you about my research," he insisted several times.

Really?

More likely, he just wanted a sounding board, because it helped him to work through his theories and thoughts. I was totally okay with that, even though I rarely understood what he was talking about.

That first week we lived together, he told me about how time and speed are connected. Well, at least I think that's it. Apparently the faster something travels, the slower time goes.

"I don't understand," I said. "Time is time. It's the same everywhere."

Jeremy rubbed his hands, as if he expected me to say that.

"Nope," he said. And then he drew the first of many equations he would share with me.

$$T = \frac{T_0}{\sqrt{1 - \frac{v^2}{c^2}}},$$

I stared at it and wondered if he was just writing nonsense.

But, not really.

"Imagine an astronaut traveling at a super-fast speed, close to the speed of light. In the equation, v is the astronaut's speed and c is the speed of light."

I shrugged. "Okay."

"Good. He travels to a faraway star and then comes back. He has a twin brother who stayed on Earth. When the astronaut comes back, he'll find that only a few years has passed by for him, but his twin brother has aged a lot... maybe fifty years."

"But that doesn't make any sense."

"I know, but that doesn't make it any less true."

Eventually he told me all about Einstein's special theory of relativity and how the equation fit into it. I'm not sure I ever really had much of a clue, but I learned how integrated time was into his mind.

Jeremy lived for stuff like this. He wanted to understand it more than any other person ever did.

Now, of course, I know that he was doing more than just trying to understand it, but back then it seemed like an obsession that was somewhat fruitful. He was a physicist, after all, and he wrote lots of jargon-filled papers that other scientists read and liked. I never had a clue what they said, but somebody did. When he talked to me, he at least tried to speak in English, not the gobbledygook of his papers.

The truth was odder than that, but the truth was hidden for the time being.

I should be careful not to give you the wrong impression. Regardless of Jeremy's very clear fascination with time, I know he loved me completely, more than he'd ever loved any person before. He may have been obsessed with the nature of time, but he continued to sleep with me every night, and I never worried about our relationship, odd as it was.

I loved him, then, and I still do. I just wish we'd had more, well, time, together.

"I love you," I always whispered to him every morning. I never missed a day.

"I love you, too," he always replied. I believed him each time.

Every day, our greeting felt new and meaningful and honest.

We went our separate ways to work, he to the university and me to the head office of the Jersey Insurance Corporation, where I paid invoices from hundreds of different suppliers. My job was orderly and transactional. I knew when I was done with each invoice, and I felt a sense of satisfaction at the end of every day.

Jeremy taught second year physics classes, mostly related to quantum mechanics and relativity. Until we started dating, I couldn't have even hazarded a guess as to what those two things were, but eventually I learned bits and pieces. His job always felt vague and uncertain to me. I never saw him plan a lecture or outline what he was going to do next in his research. That lack of assurance would have driven me nuts.

"Do you think time is the same everywhere?" he asked me one night.

I knew by then that when something moved faster, it caused time to slow down, so I answered without hesitation, "No, the Lorenz Contraction means that time moves slower for objects as they near the speed of light."

I felt very proud of myself.

"No," he said. "I mean just normal objects moving at subluminal velocities. Does a minute on Earth mean the same as sixty seconds in the Andromeda galaxy?"

My knowledge was long exhausted. "I don't know. Why wouldn't it be?"

"But why *would* it be?"

I wanted to answer, as if it were a test that I needed to pass.

"Because everything is the same everywhere in the universe." I paused. "Didn't you tell me that once?"

"Yes, I did, but I wonder if it's actually true. How would we know if it wasn't...?"

Well then. If he didn't know, I certainly didn't. It was the kind of question he'd throw out at me frequently, and I soon recognized it was simply him organizing his own thoughts.

I never did get an answer to that one.

Earlier, I told you I was twenty-four when we moved in. It was a busy summer for me, because I wanted our home to be perfect. I wanted it to have nice touches like a wall that was painted with chalkboard paint, so Jeremy could scribble his equations whenever he wanted. I bought some planters to put alongside the driveway and filled them up with bright colorful Gerbera daisies. I organized all our belongings, merging everything we had separately brought to make it a single household.

And I stared a lot at the empty bedroom, hoping to have a use for it.

I turned twenty-five and then twenty-six, and before I knew it, I was celebrating my thirtieth birthday. It seemed to happen in the blink of an eye. I loved our life together, and I'm pretty sure Jeremy did, too.

The empty bedroom continued to be used for storage and his studies.

I had hoped he would throw me a surprise birthday party, but instead, a different kind of surprise happened.

Jeremy didn't come home after work.

At first I wasn't too worried, since he'd lost track of time occasionally, working through some godawful long equations that meant nothing to me, and I knew he was likely lost in his own personal time loop. Knowing that didn't make me any happier. It was a pretty big birthday after all.

About 7:00 p.m., I texted him, but he didn't reply. Even that wasn't completely unheard of, so although I was starting to get pretty pissed at him, I knew he'd find his way home soon.

I stared out our sliding glass door out at the patio, the thought of a nice birthday celebration slipping away.

I texted him again at 8:00 and finally phoned his office and then his cell phone, but... nothing. He wasn't answering.

Midnight came and went, and terrible thoughts crossed my mind. What if he wasn't as happy living with me as I thought he was? What if he found somebody else he wanted to be with more?

What if he'd had an accident and was lying on the side of the road, dead?

I sat in our living room staring into the darkness. I was worried and mad and feeling sorry for myself, and I just wanted to know he was safe.

He stumbled in at 4:42 a.m. Our front door flew open, and he rushed in all excited and ran to me in the darkness, without the slightest hint of an apology.

"You won't believe it!" he shouted.

I thought he was drunk, but he didn't smell of beer or anything, and he wasn't slurring his words.

The darkness surrounded us. I'm not quite sure how he even knew I was there, but he raced right to me and hugged me.

"Where were you?" I clenched my teeth and didn't hug him back. "And why didn't you call me?"

Jeremy paused and stared at me. "Don't be upset. I couldn't phone you. I wasn't here!"

He had this enormous grin on his face, but his words meant little. I *knew* he wasn't there. That's why I was so pissed.

I pulled away from him and crossed my arms. I hated looking so defensive, but I couldn't help myself.

"Where were you?"

All of a sudden I could see his face change. The happiness he'd been showing fell away.

"I don't think I can tell you."

"You've been gone all fucking night and that's all you have to say?"

He tried to put a small smile on his face. "Happy birthday."

Well then.

I shook my head and left him standing there while I walked to our bedroom, shut the door behind me, and lay down. I wasn't going to be able to sleep, but I just needed to be apart.

Surprisingly, I did end up sleeping, though, and didn't open my eyes until after 10:00 the next morning. I stretched and blinked and saw the sunshine streaming through the window. It was the first time I'd ever slept in our bed without Jeremy beside me.

I thought again of all the things that could have kept him away from me, but then I tried to push them all out of my mind. It was Saturday, and we had planned a quiet day together. I didn't want to lose that.

After a shower, I dried my hair and tied it back into its pony. I looked in the mirror and tried not to think that maybe Jeremy didn't find me as attractive as he once did.

Just stop that, I thought. *You know he loves you.*

Didn't I?

As I walked to the kitchen, I smelled bacon frying, and my mouth started to water.

Jeremy ran to me when he saw me and hugged me tightly, before leaning down to kiss me.

"I'm sorry, babe," he whispered. "Today we'll celebrate your birthday."

He gave me that wonderful smile that had always entranced me, and we went on to have a beautiful day. I didn't mention his missing time again.

I tried to be happy about our relationship again, because I was a glass-half-full kind of person. I'd known Jeremy was different from other men since I first met him, and that's one of the things that I was attracted to.

"Isn't it an astonishing coincidence that we're both here?" he asked one day.

"What do you mean?"

"The universe formed 13.8 billion years ago. Billion with a B. And it's likely to stretch for many billions of years in the future."

"Yeah. It's old?"

"Think of that entire time span as a line, stretching from the beginning to the end. And along that line, a little dot moves forward. That's time. Time moves in a single direction at the same speed, always. And each person's lifetime is such a teensy bit of that string. George Washington's life is behind the dot and so are all the dinosaurs. Countless people are ahead of the dot."

"And we're right on the dot."

"Exactly! Right now that dot covers our lives and before we know it, it'll be gone. If we looked at the string at a random time, we'd never be lucky enough to look at it while the dot covered us. It's such an inconsequential bit of time. But... here we are."

I didn't really know what to say.

"What are the chances the dot is in exactly the right place *right now?*"

He stared at me as if I should have something intelligent to say, but I really didn't. And that's okay, because he was used to it. This was just Jeremy being Jeremy. Over our time together, he tried to explain dozens of things about time to me. Or, like I said earlier, he really just wanted a sounding board, so it was totally fine that I didn't always have a lot to add.

He was so focused on understanding everything about time, and the more he talked, the less I seemed to understand myself. He loved to ask why we remember the past but not the future. "As far as we can tell," he said, "time shouldn't have a preferred direction. So why does it always go from past to future like a river flowing by? Would we even know if it didn't?"

Honestly, sometimes the things he said sounded ridiculous, but I knew they couldn't be or he wouldn't wonder about them.

"What if time is just an illusion?" was another favorite. "Lots of physicists think there's no such thing."

I never understood that one.

It was three months before he stayed out all night again.

This time, it really was all night. It was similar to the first time... no warning, no explanation. It was just longer. The last I heard from him was around noon on a Wednesday. I was warmed up some leftover lasagne and was digging into the first bit when I texted him to ask how his day was going. We always connected at lunch. Just a thing we had together.

Good, he answered. *How about you?*

I said it'd been a good morning and then put my phone aside and pulled up Google to browse the movies playing. It'd been a while since we had a date night, and I was thinking ahead to Saturday.

I also knew it might be a day of celebration, because that morning I'd taken a home pregnancy test and a little plus sign had showed up. I had been too frightened to say anything just yet, but I planned to try a different brand later and see if I got the same result.

The Saturday date night could be magical if it went the way I hoped.

But, that noon text was the last I heard of Jeremy for more than twenty-four hours.

We'd planned on putting together some home-made pizzas for dinner, so I stopped at our local grocery store for some naan bread, grated mozzarella cheese, pepperoni, and a green pepper. We already had some tomato sauce at home.

On the spur of the moment, I also picked up a bottle of red wine. I would only have a tiny bit, and even if Jeremy didn't know yet what the celebration was all about, *I'd* know.

He didn't show up for dinner, and like the first time, he didn't answer my texts or phone calls.

As the hours slipped by, I lost my appetite, and I left the pizza fixings on the counter. This time I went to bed at 11:00 and tried not to wonder where he was or who he might be with.

I expected to be woken when he came home in the middle of the night, but that didn't happen. My clock radio started playing music at 6:00, and I climbed out of bed to see if Jeremy was home. He wasn't.

Still no texts or e-mail or voice message.

I felt sick.

I splashed water on my face and tried again to contact him, but no luck. I sat in our living room, thinking about my discarded plans from the night before, and a tear rolled down my face.

Should I call the police?

Instead, I e-mailed my boss to tell her I wasn't feeling well and would not be at work today. I almost never called in sick, even when I really was, so I didn't feel guilty.

I waited. I told myself it was too early to phone the cops. Beside they'd ask if Jeremy had ever gone missing before, and I'd have to say he had, but that this was longer. I didn't want the look of pity that would surely cover their faces.

So, I just sat there.

He walked into the house at 4:33 that afternoon. This time he wasn't quite smiling, but I could see that neither was he feeling guilty or bad. I just sat there and stared coldly at him.

"I'm sorry, babe. I wish I could have told you I was going to be gone for a bit."

"*Where have you been?*" I knew my voice was harsh and accusatory, but... tough.

He tried to hug me, but I wasn't having any of that. I pushed him away. "WHERE HAVE YOU BEEN?" I asked again, louder.

"It's okay," he said softly. "I understand why you're mad."

I clenched my mouth. I couldn't even look at him.

Now, I look back at those faraway years and wonder what that young girl was thinking. Yes, I consider thirty to be young, but that's what happens when time overwhelms you like a tsunami. You blink and all of a sudden you're an old woman with only your misty memories to hold onto.

Jeremy was everything to me. And I know now (and really, I knew then) that I was everything to him. Everything except for that unquenchable thirst of his to understand the nature of time. He was never sated, and never would be.

When he didn't come home those first couple of times, I now see that it was insignificant in the scheme of things. I should have been more willing to accept the part of his life that was separate from me. Maybe then he would have told me the truth sooner. For some secrets are far bigger than what I was imagining.

That day, Jeremy left me to stew in my own thoughts. He went to the kitchen and threw out the stale pizza toppings, and then he went to the wall we'd painted with chalkboard paint. He wrote this:

$$t_P = \sqrt{\hbar G/c^5} \approx 5.4 \times 10^{-44}$$

Then he left the room and went up to bed.

In spite of my anger, after a few minutes I went to look at the equation. It made no sense at all to me. I didn't remember seeing anything like that before, and I had no idea what it meant, but I felt in my gut that this was some kind of explanation for where Jeremy had been.

I wasn't sure if it helped or hurt. Hell, for all I knew, it was just a pile of nonsense.

After a while, I went for a drive. There was nowhere I really had to go, because I should have been working, but that didn't matter. I just drove out of the city and into wilderness, trying to drive out some of the anger that was covering me.

It worked, after a while. I realized Jeremy was going to continue to stay away, for some reason he wasn't willing to share. I had to make him trust me enough to change that.

If there was another woman, I needed to know. If he was just avoiding me, I *really* needed to know. Bottom line, I needed my best friend back.

When I got home, Jeremy was in bed, just lying there staring at the ceiling. I took off my clothes and crawled in beside him. I didn't let anything into my mind except to think of how much I loved him and how we were now starting a family together. We made love, slowly but passionately, and I knew I needed to be sure not to let anything interfere with our lives. I needed to be patient with whatever was happening with him until he could tell me.

The next morning, the weird equation was gone from the chalkboard. In its place was a cartoonish kind of diagram. It was a cat sitting in something that looked like an empty show box. A smaller vial of something sat beside the cat in the box. There was a big question mark above the diagram and a scientist seeming to ponder things.

"This is Schrodinger's Cat," Jeremy said.

"He doesn't look very happy," I said. "He's frowning."

"He's an odd fellow, and it's hard to blame him for being unhappy."

Jeremy then explained one of the strangest things I've ever heard of. He pointed to the small vial beside the cat.

"The guy watching can't see inside the box. That's poison gas inside a quantum device controlled by a single uranium atom. There's a fifty-fifty chance the atom will decay into other elements. If it does, a detector releases poison gas and kills the cat. If there's no change in the uranium, the cat lives."

"Okay, let's hope for the best."

"The thing with something like this is that according to quantum mechanics, both events actually happen simultaneously. So the cat dies and it also lives."

"That's not possible."

"It's not only possible, but it's true. The cat is both dead and alive in something called quantum superposition. However, at some point, somebody opens the box to see what's inside and the cat will end up either completely dead or completely alive. The superposition collapses and a choice happens when somebody observes the cat."

Jeremy had told me lots of weird stuff over the years, but this one seemed to be a little weirder than most. More odd to me is that I couldn't figure out why he was telling me this, since it had nothing to do with time.

"Has anybody ever tried this to see what happens?"

"No. It's just a thought experiment. If somebody actually tried it, they'd just end up with finding the cat in one state or the other. There's no way to know that it was both dead and alive before looking at it."

"Put a camera inside and record it."

"That's an observation. It'd make the situation collapse to one or the other."

I didn't really know what to say. It made no sense to me, and after we talked, I secretly went to Google "Schrodinger's Cat." Sure enough, science seemed to say that Jeremy was right. No surprise there. The act of observing something made it go one way or the other. Before that, both states were happening at the same time.

Jeremy continued to write stuff on the board, but it was a lot of equations that meant nothing to me. I think he forgot I was there, and so I went to make us some breakfast.

A few days later, I told him I was pregnant.

I admit I was very nervous. I still wasn't completely sure if he wanted a baby with me or if he'd just pretended to. Maybe he felt both, like his mind had his own quantum cat running around inside, both wanting a baby and not wanting one.

"Ohmygod!" he called when I told him. "That's wonderful news!"

Relief flooded through me when I heard his spontaneous reaction. He stared at me and then ran his fingers through my hair while he kissed me. The kiss went on for a long time, and then we just held each other closely for even longer.

I was happier than I'd ever been before. Nagging doubts still crept into my mind, but for that single moment, joy rained over me, and nothing could have changed that.

"When?" he finally asked.

"I think in about seven months," I said. "Next August."

He nodded and seemed to think about that, trying to schedule the birth into his schedule.

Life was good.

That was more than a half century ago, which I honestly find completely mind-boggling. I still remember that kiss when I told him, and the strong hug we shared.

Today I'm a frail old woman. I'm still slim, but my bones are weak. I walk very slowly and each step hurts. I try to hold my head up and not walk hunched over, but that takes concentration and patience.

When I woke this morning, I put my hair into a pony tail for the first time in years. Jeremy always loved my pony tail. My hair is white instead of yellow, but I keep it the same length I've always had it.

I live in that same house we bought together and first moved into. I don't go to the basement very often because the stairs are hard on my knees, but I've always loved our home. I keep it the way it was back then. His last set of equations are still on the chalkboard wall. They're faint, but I can still read them.

At the top of one wall is a heart with an inscription scribbled beside it:

JT and KS, June 27, 2011

I wrote that and added the heart as soon as I'd painted the wall. It was the date we moved in together.

The nursery still has the furnishings I'd put together: the crib, the dresser, and some stuffed animals. I'd never been able to part with any of my memories.

Right now, I'm sitting in our living room, remembering.

The third time Jeremy didn't come home was the worst of all.

I was four months pregnant with Billy. We agreed on the name easily for some reason. I knew other parents who took forever, but for us it was a natural choice. It was the name of both my father and Jeremy's father. We never considered a name for a girl, since both of us were convinced we were going to have a boy.

That night, when he didn't come home at the normal time, I felt myself start to panic. I stared at the clock, wishing it not to be one of those odd disappearances he'd had.

The hour hand crept along, though, and by midnight, I knew he had left me again. I went to bed and quietly cried myself to sleep. I'd really hoped that with the baby coming, Jeremy wouldn't be doing this anymore. He still hadn't told me why he seemed to need time away from me.

He didn't come home the next day or the one after that. I stewed in our home, worried sick, scared, and mad as hell.

The following morning he still hadn't come home, nor had he answered my texts or voice mails.

I phoned the police, and when an officer came to take my statement, I had to admit he'd left a couple of other times, but this was different because it was much longer.

The cop nodded sympathetically, but I knew he was thinking Jeremy had just gotten sick of me. Maybe the added stress of a new baby was just too much for him.

I knew that wasn't true. He wanted this baby, and he wanted our life together.

Didn't he?

Jeremy finally came home after five days away. He burst into our home but instead of a big grin on his face he looked frantic and afraid. He ran over to hold me.

I was having none of that. I was just so fucking angry at him.

"Tell me right now where the hell you've been," I demanded.

"Katherine, you need to calm down. It's complicated."

"I'm not calming down! You left me and I want to know why."

The worry he had on his face earlier dropped away and all I saw was some kind of disappointment, or maybe regret.

"I can't. You're not ready."

"I'm not ready?"

I lost it. I grabbed a coffee mug and threw it at him and then ran to try to get outside, away from the man I loved.

That's when I crashed through the plate glass sliding door. I was so mad, I didn't see it was closed.

I fell with a hundred shards of glass falling with me. A thousand stabs and a million cuts burned into my body. I knew glass had burst open my mid-section, and there was blood spurting out everywhere.

Somebody was screaming, and it took a moment to realize it was me. I knew my face and body were badly injured, and I couldn't move. That's when I passed out.

I was in the hospital for three days and then had to recover at home for several weeks after that.

Our Billy was gone.

Losing a child is the worst thing that can happen to a woman. It doesn't matter that Billy hadn't been born yet. He was my son, and I knew him already. He was part of my life, my family, my destiny.

Each day I'd wake and unconsciously rub my belly, my way to connect to him. That habit carried on for months.

Eventually, as with all things, the pain started to lessen, and I found a way to carry on. I knew there was a chance I would have another baby, but somewhere deep in my mind, I didn't believe it. That's exactly how it turned out. Billy was my one and only.

Jeremy struggled, perhaps not as much as me, but it was clear he was heart-broken as well.

Both of us blamed our own self, and I'm sure that's why Jeremy finally decided to tell me where he had been disappearing to.

He started by writing the same equation that he had once written but never explained:

$$t_{\mathrm{P}} = \sqrt{\hbar G/c^5} \approx 5.4 \times 10^{-44}$$

I stared at it, but of course it still meant nothing.

"This is the equation for Planck Time," he said. I felt an element of awe in his voice. "It's the smallest unit of time that has any meaning at all. There's really no such thing as a shorter period of time. It's incredibly tiny. So small, no person could ever actually imagine it."

I nodded, not sure why this meant anything, but if this somehow connected to his disappearances, I needed to understand.

"There is no shorter time. Time hops along in tiny bounces, not a continuous line. This equation is beautiful. It connects relativity to quantum mechanics in a totally unexpected way. It shows that time behaves like everything else in quantum mechanics."

Jeremy stared at the equation and then slowly turned to me.

"Remember Schrodinger's Cat?"

"Yes," I answered. "It's both alive and dead."

"Until someone observes it."

I nodded.

"Time works the same way. This is what I've been working on, how to show that time itself at the most minute level only exists if someone observes it."

"How do we observe time?" I asked.

"We do it all the time without thinking. The harder choice is to deliberately not observe it. I've spent the past year creating a kind of meditation that focuses my thoughts on the Planck Time within my own brain, trying to deliberately not observe time passing."

The more Jeremy was talking, the more confused I was getting. He knew. He could always tell if I was understanding his lectures or if he'd lost me.

"It's okay," he said. "What it means is that I found a way to stop time."

"You're kidding, right?"

He shook his head and smiled. "Those times I've disappeared? I re-programmed my own mind to ignore time. And so, time went on, but I skipped it. I skipped to sometime later without living through the parts I missed."

"You made a time machine?"

"Not a machine, more like a process."

"It's kind of hard to believe that."

"You will. I'm going to disappear in about five minutes."

Well, there wasn't much to say to that. We both went to sit on the couch, and he continued talking. He told me that the process was now programmed deep in his brain, and he didn't even have a way to stop it. It was time for him to skip and land at some point in the future.

Three months in the future, he explained.

Each skip was longer than the one before, and it was exponential.

The skip after that would be... well, he pulled out a letter and left it on the coffee table, just before he vanished into thin air.

I'm sitting in that same ancient chair right now, my bones creaking, a cup of cold coffee sitting beside me. I still remember the astonishment I felt when Jeremy disappeared right in front of my eyes. I was sure I'd blinked and he was performing some kind of magic trick, but really, I knew that wasn't like him at all. If he said he was skipping to a future point in time, that's exactly what was happening.

My fingers had trembled when I opened the letter he'd left me.

Inside were several pages of notes, equations, and a USB drive that contained his research, just in case something went wrong and he didn't return.

It was only the last page of the letter I was really interested in. It was a spreadsheet that showed the crazy exponential aspect of his skips. It showed the first one that lasted four hours, the next lasting twenty-four hours, the third was five days, and the fourth (this one) lasting three months.

The spreadsheet also showed the time diminishing between jumps. Once he returned, he would only be with me for three days before skipping to the future again.

When that happened, he wouldn't return again until I was eighty-one years old.

That time, though, he did return exactly as predicted by his formula after three months. I was waiting on the same couch, in the same position from when he left, and even though I was totally convinced, it still shocked the hell out of me when he popped into existence from nothing.

"See?" he said. He was still grinning, as I knew he would be.

I jumped into his arms and kissed him. "I've missed you so much!"

He held me tightly and rubbed my hair.

"We don't have long together," he said.

"Please make it stop. I need you to be with me."

His grin died away. "I've tried. I haven't found a way."

"I love you."

"And I love you, too." He held me again. "If I could stop it, I would."

If that was all the surprises Jeremy had for me, it would have been more than enough for a lifetime.

However, he had one more trick up his sleeve, and this one was even more unbelievable.

Unbelievable, but I knew it would be true.

We made love within minutes of his return. After three months apart, I knew all about patience, but I also knew about passion and the incredible longing in my heart to have my husband back.

It didn't matter that it was mid-afternoon. We just revelled in each other's bodies, not caring a bit about anything else.

When we were done, Jeremy rolled onto one side and said, "There's somewhere else."

"What?"

"As the times I'm gone gets longer, I've started to realize that I'm somewhere else. It's like a different dimension or something... a place outside of time."

"How is that possible?"

"I don't know. It's like someone apart from our universe observes me and collapses me into their existence."

There was that word again. Observe. I knew he was back talking about quantum mechanics again. Schrodinger's Cat was wagging its tail.

"It's a place very different. I don't have any senses there at all, but I know what's going on just the same."

I was no longer surprised by anything Jeremy told me. If he said he was taken to a place where time didn't exist, I believed him with all my heart. I just wanted to share it with him, which didn't seem possible.

He kissed me gently again and then stared into my eyes.

"There are other people there," he said.

I didn't catch the significance, and I told him that.

Jeremy took a long time to continue. "Billy is there."

No, I thought. *That's not possible. Our son is dead.*

But I stared at Jeremy and knew it was possible. Even as I was shaking my head, my body knew my son still existed in some form, somewhere.

That meant one day I might meet him.

I cried and collapsed onto our bed. Jeremy lay with me and kept his arm around my neck.

My Billy was out there, somewhere, and when I died, I might be able to find him.

Might.

Was death a place outside of time?

Jeremy couldn't tell me anything more, and our three days passed in a blur. We were holding each other tightly when he skipped into the future, and I lost the love of my life for the last time.

He'll appear in minutes. I know that.

Is he expecting to find an old woman waiting for him? Even though I have the pony-tail he loves, and maybe the obvious love I feel for him will still shine to him, will he be shocked and disgusted by the sight of me? Or will he hug me as only he ever has and kiss me passionately?

We will only have eighteen minutes together before he skips again. It's the last bit of time we'll share, and then he'll be gone, to return to normal time in three thousand years. With only a brief stop back here, he'll be gone into the even more distant future.

My own time is coming close. My body won't hold out much longer, and then I believe I'll be rejoining my family.

I only pray that's what Jeremy wants.

ABOUT THE AUTHOR

John R. Little is a Canadian writer of dark fantasy and horror. He's been publishing his unique brand of fiction since 1982. John won the Bram Stoker Award for his novella, "Miranda," and has been nominated three other times.

John loves to hear from his readers, so feel free to drop him an email to john@johnrlittle.com and let him know what you thought of this book. He is married and lives in the village of Ayr in southern Ontario.

The Collected Works of
John R Little:

Vol 1: Little by Little

Vol 2: Little Things

Vol 3: A Little Bit More

Vol 4: Lost Little Tales

Fully Illustrated Trade Paperback and Full-Color Hardcover Editions

Available at Barnes & Noble, Amazon and LycanValley.com

www.ingramcontent.com/pod-product-compliance
Lightning Source LLC
Chambersburg PA
CBHW031958120726
47898CB00004BA/1181